REQUIEM

REQUIEM

NEW COLLECTED WORKS
BY ROBERT A. HEINLEIN
AND TRIBUTES TO THE GRAND MASTER

EDITED BY YOJI KONDO

A TOM DOHERTY ASSOCIATES BOOK
NEW YORK

REQUIEM

This book was printed on acid-free paper.

A Tor Book
Published by Tom Doherty Associates, Inc.
175 Fifth Avenue
New York, N.Y. 10010

TOR® is a registered trademark of Tom Doherty Associates, Inc.

Library of Congress Cataloging-in-Publication Data

Heinlein, Robert A. (Robert Anson)
    Requiem : new collected works by Robert A. Heinlein and tributes
to the grand master / Robert A. Heinlein : edited by Yoji Kondo.
      p.   cm.
    ISBN 0-312-85168-5
    1. Science fiction, American.   I. Kondo, Yoji.   II. Title.
PS3515.E288R4   1992
813'.54—dc20   91-38909
                                               CIP

First edition: February 1992

Printed in the United States of America

0 9 8 7 6 5 4 3 2 1

To the Memory of Robert A. Heinlein
and
To All Heinlein Fans—Past, Present and Future

CONTENTS

Part III—Tributes to Robert A. Heinlein

REQUIEM

PREFACE

The year was 1910. In Kansas City a ten-year-old youngster took his three-year-old brother into the backyard to see Halley's Comet. Unlike the disappointing reappearance a few years ago, the comet made a brilliant sight, with its tail flaring across the entire sky. The sight made a lasting impression on the younger boy, one that lasted all his life.

It was his introduction to what would become a lifelong interest in astronomy, an interest expressed in a number of ways. The child would always long to go to the stars. Of course, in 1910 such a trip was unthinkable, but he longed to go in that direction. Perhaps some day . . .

By the time he was in his early teens, Robert Heinlein had read all the books in the Kansas City Public Library on the subject of astronomy. He was in some small demand as a lecturer on the subject. He had built himself a small telescope, and observed the moon and stars from the roof of his parents' home.

But the demand for astronomers has never been very great. A few aficionados can find work teaching, and with some luck, they will share time on the large observatory installations. Otherwise the would-be astronomer must remain an amateur.

Perhaps attracted by the Michelson experiment which measured the speed of light, done at the United States Naval Academy, and also by the example of his next elder brother, Robert decided that that was the place for him. The Navy also had an Observatory in Washington, D.C., and it might be that he could find satisfactory work there—someday.

Robert began reading science fiction early—the Kansas City

Library stocked books by Verne and Wells, as well as the Tom Swift books. He read everything he could find in this field; eventually he found a magazine on the stands—Hugo Gernsback's *Electrical Experimenter*. He hungrily read each issue, and even went so far as to purchase the latest issue to read on the train when he returned from Colorado, where he had gone on a mountain climbing trip, instead of getting food for the journey.

He became one of the earliest members of the Rocket Society at a time when it consisted only of dreamers.

Navy life did not allow much time for dreaming—at sea watches were four hours on, eight hours off, study time for promotion examinations took up some hours daily, and logs of various sorts must be kept. Still his interest in astronomy continued, and he bought all the books on that subject that were published.

Floundering around after an early retirement from the Navy, Robert tried various ways to earn a living. Attracted by a magazine advertisement for a contest for stories by someone who had not been previously published, he bought some paper for his typewriter and wrote "Life-Line." When it was finished he read it again, then decided that it was too good for the magazine it had been written for, so he sent it off to the leader in the field—*Astounding Science Fiction*. During those Depression days, with a mortgage to be paid off, the closest Robert could come to his dreams of becoming a space scientist or astronomer was to write about it. So he wrote out his dreams, selling them for money to pay the mortgage.

He had, finally, found a way to earn a living without ruining his health again. And it could involve his beloved astronomy. John W. Campbell, Jr. was also interested in the same subjects and encouraged speculation about them. He stimulated Robert into looking into other fields of science, writing stories about those. Robert's interests were wide, including sociology, psychology, sex and politics—anything which included interaction between people, or people and their governments.

So writing just suited him—it allowed time to study—time to write speculating about various fields, all couched in terms of fiction. There was a market there, albeit small, consisting of the few readers of the science fiction magazines. Paperback publishing did not then exist at that time in the United States.

Robert's stories blazed across the infant field of science fiction like Halley's Comet. He fast became the leading writer in the field. Any subject that attracted him became story material. He collected small curious items from magazines and newspapers, and investigated such varied fields as magic, which had been another interest of his since boyhood.

Many of his stories showed his engineering background; he did studies for many of those stories. He would calculate orbits for his spaceships, drawing charts to show time and distance coordinates. He sketched machinery used in stories. Everything he wrote was as accurate as possible within the time frame of the date on which it was written.

Science fiction ages badly. Today's engineering and science may be superseded tomorrow. If a science fiction story is to be readable for any length of time, the story itself, not the science, must engage and hold the readers' attention. The story is the real reason why some of those stories last. People continue to read outdated stories because of their interest in the characters or their actions—not to learn something about the science of that day. To overcome this difficulty the author can go so far into the future that no one living today will ever know that the science is incorrect, or he can go back into the far past and attempt to reconstruct something that happened then. Any time frame between the two runs the chance of becoming outdated—perhaps before it sees print.

Robert's stories about a first trip to the moon have been outdated for more than twenty years, yet they are still read. *Rocket Ship Galileo* is a story about an alternate trip to the moon which was possible in its day, but the first trip to the moon did not happen that way; *Destination Moon* was based loosely on that story. The novelette, "Destination Moon," was written because an editor asked for it.

We worried about the problem of outdating until we finally came to the conclusion that it would be impossible always to update old stories—let them stand as story alone—write new stories and let the old ones stand or fall as might happen.

An interesting facet of Robert's writing is his versatility. He was always trying new techniques, new genres, and new fields of inquiry. He wrote in many genres—detective stories, horror, sword and sorcery, fantasy, as well as what he is best known for—science fiction. There were also a number of stories he wrote for younger readers, including several in this book.

But of all these story types, he liked best writing science fiction.

Also included in this book are some of Robert's speeches. These have been mildly edited for smoother reading.

The juvenile editor at Scribner's laughed when Robert told her that he would do a girls' book for her. She did not believe that he could possibly do anything acceptable; he took this as a challenge, and sold several stories to teen-age magazines for girls. Two of those stories are here—"The Bulletin Board" and "Poor Daddy."

"Tenderfoot in Space" was written for *Boys' Life* at the request of the editor. It has not been reprinted until now. One of the projects which Robert had in mind for a long time was to complete a book of stories for much younger readers than those for whom he wrote his juvenile books. This project never came to fruition.

"Shooting 'Destination Moon'" was commissioned by John W. Campbell, Jr. in 1950, detailing of some of the difficulties in making the motion picture as accurate as possible. Gregg Press reprinted this article and the "Destination Moon" novelette in 1979, together with some stills from the motion picture and some of the publicity stories about it.

While Robert's speeches at World Conventions have had some circulation through tapes made at those conventions, little is known of his speech given at the French Embassy Theater in Rio de Janeiro in 1969. This speech has never seen print before. The occasion was a film festival to which a number of science fiction writers were invited as guests of the Brazilian government.

This talk was given as an introduction to a screening of the motion picture *Destination Moon*. It is Robert's tribute to Irving Pichel, who made great efforts to keep the motion picture as honest as possible despite the usual pressures of Hollywood. *Destination Moon* began the long cycle of science fiction pictures as they are shown in films today.

Robert's deep interest in astronomy and space travel continued throughout his life. He visited White Sands to see the last of the German V-2 rockets go up, travelled to Flagstaff to Percival Lowell's observatory; he went to Cape Canaveral, the Downey installation of Rockwell International, the Michoud plant outside New Orleans—anything to do with rockets; he went to JPL to see the pictures sent back by various explorer shots to Venus, Mars and the "Grand Tour."

There was an endless flow of periodicals and books which were ordered, and arrived, in his study. Books and magazines on every branch of science known to man came in, were read, and joined his almost encyclopedic knowledge. At one time he had five different sets of the *Encyclopaedia Britannica,* a facsimile of the first edition, the vaunted eleventh edition, two different sets of the fourteenth edition, and *EBIII.* In order to keep up with the flood of advancing knowledge following World War II, Robert read continuously in the fields of science, and got to know many of the advanced thinkers of his day. Papers came in, too, until finally, it became impossible to keep up with all that was being done in the various fields of the sciences.

During the 1970s, he devoted two full years to widespread reading in the fields of biological sciences and the hard sciences, physics, chemistry, astronomy, earth sciences and so on. The time was devoted to reading in depth about those fields, and during that time, he wrote only two short articles—"Dirac, Anti-Matter and You" and "Are You a Rare Blood?" Thereafter, he returned to his writing of science fiction.

In this volume, the reader can catch glimpses of Robert's personality in his fiction and more in his speeches. But more insights may be obtained by reading about what his friends and colleagues thought about his writing and his life.

Virginia Heinlein
Atlantic Beach, Florida

EDITOR'S FOREWORD

Robert Anson Heinlein departed from this world on the eighth of May 1988. This volume grew out of the special event, "Heinlein Retrospective," which was held on the sixth of October 1988 at the National Air and Space Museum in conjunction with the posthumous award of the NASA Medal for Distinguished Public Service, the highest civilian honor accorded by the National Aeronautics and Space Administration in recognition of an individual's contribution to the space program.

The title of this book has been taken from Heinlein's beautifully touching novella "Requiem."

Part I contains the works of Heinlein that are unavailable now in print (with the exception of "Requiem"), although the overwhelming majority of his writings are currently in print, reflecting the public's insatiable desire to read Heinlein. One of the short stories, "The Bulletin Board" has never been published elsewhere.

Part II consists of the proceedings of "Heinlein Retrospective" at the Air and Space Museum, including the speeches made by the panelists and special guests, all but one (an astronaut) of whom are prominent authors. Part III comprises the appreciations written by Robert Heinlein's friends, most of whom are again celebrated science fiction writers of our time.

I hope you will enjoy reading this book as much as I had pleasure in putting it together with the gracious help of Mrs. Robert A. Heinlein.

Yoji Kondo

PART I
Works of
Robert A. Heinlein

REQUIEM

On a high hill in Samoa there is a grave. Inscribed on the marker are these words—

> *"Under the wide and starry sky*
> *Dig the grave and let me lie.*
> *Glad did I live and gladly die*
>   *And I laid me down with a will!*
>
> *"This be the verse you grave for me—*
> *Here he lies where he longed to be,*
> *Home is the sailor, home from sea,*
>   *And the hunter home from the hill.'"*

These lines appear in another place—scrawled on a shipping tag torn from a compressed-air container, and pinned to the ground with a knife.

It wasn't much of a fair, as fairs go. The trottin' races didn't promise much excitement, even though several entries claimed the blood of the immortal Dan Patch. The tents and concession booths barely covered the circus grounds, and the pitchmen seemed discouraged.

D. D. Harriman's chauffeur could not see any reason for stopping. They were due in Kansas City for a directors' meeting— that is to say, Harriman was. The chauffeur had private reasons for promptness, reasons involving darktown society on Eighteenth Street. But the Boss not only stopped but hung around.

Bunting and a canvas arch made the entrance to a large enclosure beyond the race track. Red and gold letters announced:

This way to the
MOON ROCKET!!!!
See it in actual flight!
Public Demonstration Flights
Twice Daily
This is the ACTUAL TYPE used by the
First Man to Reach the MOON!!!
YOU can ride in it!!–$.50

A boy, nine or ten years old, hung around the entrance and stared at the posters.

"Like to see the ship, son?"

The kid's eyes shone. "Gee, mister. I sure would."

"So would I. Come on." Harriman paid out fifty cents for two pink tickets which entitled them to enter the enclosure and examine the rocketship. The kid took his and ran on ahead with the single-mindedness of youth. Harriman looked over the stubby curved lines of the ovoid body. He noted with a professional eye that she was a single-jet type with fractional controls around her midriff. He squinted through his glasses at the name painted in gold on the carnival red of the body, *Care Free*. He paid another quarter to enter the control cabin.

When his eyes had adjusted to the gloom caused by the strong ray filters of the ports, he let them rest lovingly on the keys of the console and the semicircle of dials above. Each beloved gadget was in its proper place. He knew them—graven in his heart.

While he mused over the instrument board, with the warm liquid of content soaking through his body, the pilot entered and touched his arm.

"Sorry, sir. We've got to cast loose for the flight."

"Eh?" Harriman started, then looked at the speaker. Handsome devil, with a good skull and strong shoulders—reckless eyes and a self-indulgent mouth, but a firm chin. "Oh, excuse me, Captain."

"Quite all right."

"Oh, I say, Captain, er, uh—"

"McIntyre."

"Captain McIntyre, could you take a passenger this trip?" The old man leaned eagerly towards him.

"Why, yes, if you wish. Come along with me." He ushered Harriman into a shed marked OFFICE which stood near the gate. "Passenger for a check over, doc."

Harriman looked startled, but permitted the medico to run a stethoscope over his thin chest and to strap a rubber bandage around his arm. Presently he unstrapped it, glanced at McIntyre, and shook his head.

"No go, doc?"

"That's right, Captain."

Harriman looked from face to face. "My heart's all right— that's just a flutter."

The physician's brows shot up. "Is it? But it's not just your heart; at your age your bones are brittle, too brittle to risk a takeoff."

"Sorry, sir," added the pilot, "but the Bates County Fair Association pays the doctor here to see to it that I don't take anyone up who might be hurt by the acceleration."

The old man's shoulders drooped miserably. "I rather expected it."

"Sorry, sir." McIntyre turned to go, but Harriman followed him out.

"Excuse me, Captain—"

"Yes?"

"Could you and your, uh, engineer have dinner with me after your flight?"

The pilot looked at him quizzically. "I don't see why not. Thanks."

"Captain McIntyre, it is difficult for me to see why anyone would quit the Earth-Moon run." Fried chicken and hot biscuits in a private dining room of the best hotel the little town of Butler afforded, three-star Hennessy and Corona-Coronas had produced a friendly atmosphere in which three men could talk freely.

"Well, I didn't like it."

"Aw, don't give him that, Mac—you know damn well it was Rule G that got you." McIntyre's mechanic poured himself another brandy as he spoke.

McIntyre looked sullen. "Well, what if I did take a couple o' drinks? Anyhow, I could have squared that—it was the damn pernickety regulations that got me fed up. Who are you to talk?—Smuggler!''

"Sure I smuggled! Who wouldn't with all those beautiful rocks just aching to be taken back to Earth. I had a diamond once as big as . . . But if I hadn't been caught I'd be in Luna City tonight. And so would you, you drunken blaster . . . with the boys buying us drinks, and the girls smiling and making suggestions. . . .'' He put his face down and began to weep quietly.

McIntyre shook him. "He's drunk."

"Never mind." Harriman interposed a hand. "Tell me, are you really satisfied not to be on the run any more?"

McIntyre chewed his lip. "No—he's right, of course. This barn-storming isn't what it's all cracked up to be. We've been hopping junk at every pumpkin doin's up and down the Mississippi valley—sleeping in tourist camps, and eating at grease-burners. Half the time the sheriff has an attachment on the ship, the other half the Society for the Prevention of Something or Other gets an injunction to keep us on the ground. It's no sort of a life for a rocket man."

"Would it help any for you to get to the Moon?"

"Well . . . Yes. I couldn't get back on the Earth-Moon run, but if I was in Luna City I could get a job hopping ore for the Company—they're always short of rocket pilots for that, and they wouldn't mind my record. If I kept my nose clean they might even put me back on the run, in time."

Harriman fiddled with a spoon, then looked up. "Would you young gentlemen be open to a business proposition?"

"Perhaps. What is it?"

"You own the *Care Free?*"

"Yeah. That is, Charlie and I do—barring a couple of liens against her. What about it?"

"I want to charter her . . . for you and Charlie to take me to the Moon!"

Charlie sat up with a jerk.

"D'joo hear what he said, Mac? He wants us to fly that old heap to the Moon!"

McIntyre shook his head. "Can't do it, Mr. Harriman. The old boat's worn out. You couldn't convert to escape fuel. We don't even use standard juice in her—just gasoline and liquid air. Charlie spends all of his time tinkering with her at that. She's going to blow up some day."

"Say, Mr. Harriman," put in Charlie, "what's the matter with getting an excursion permit and going in a Company ship?"

"No, son," the old man replied, "I can't do that. You know the conditions under which the UN granted the Company a monopoly on lunar exploitation—no one to enter space who was not physically qualified to stand up under it. Company to take full responsibility for the safety and health of all citizens beyond the stratosphere. The official reason for granting the franchise was to avoid unnecessary loss of life during the first few years of space travel."

"And you can't pass the physical exam?"

Harriman shook his head.

"Well, what the hell—if you can afford to hire us, why don't you just bribe yourself a brace of Company docs? It's been done before."

Harriman smiled ruefully. "I know it has, Charlie, but it won't work for me. You see, I'm a little too prominent. My full name is Delos D. Harriman."

"What? *You* are old D. D.? But hell's bells, you own a big slice of the Company yourself—you practically *are* the Company; you ought to be able to do anything you like, rules or no rules."

"This is a not unusual opinion, son, but it is incorrect. Rich men aren't more free than other men; they are less free, a good deal less free. I tried to do what you suggest, but the other directors would not permit me. They are afraid of losing their franchise. It costs them a good deal in—uh—political contact expenses to retain it, as it is."

"Well, I'll be a— Can you tie that, Mac? A guy with lots of dough, and he can't spend it the way he wants to."

McIntyre did not answer, but waited for Harriman to continue.

"Captain McIntyre, if you had a ship, would you take me?"

McIntyre rubbed his chin. "It's against the law."

"I'd make it worth your while."

"Sure he would, Mr. Harriman. Of course you would, Mac. Luna City! Oh, baby!"

"Why do you want to go to the Moon so badly, Mr. Harriman?"

"Captain, it's the one thing I've really wanted to do all my life—ever since I was a young boy. I don't know whether I can explain it to you or not. You young fellows have grown up to rocket travel the way I grew up to aviation. I'm a great deal older than you are, at least fifty years older. When I was a kid practically nobody believed that men would ever reach the Moon. You've seen rockets all your lives, and the first to reach the Moon got there before you were a young boy. When I was a boy they laughed at the idea.

"But I believed—I believed. I read Verne, and Wells, and Smith, and I believed that we could do it—that we *would* do it. I set my heart on being one of the men to walk the surface of the Moon, to see her other side, and to look back on the face of the Earth, hanging in the sky.

"I used to go without my lunches to pay my dues in the American Rocket Society, because I wanted to believe that I was helping to bring the day nearer when we would reach the Moon. I was already an old man when that day arrived. I've lived longer than I should, but I would not let myself die . . . I will not!—until I have set foot on the Moon."

McIntyre stood up and put out his hand. "You find a ship, Mr. Harriman. I'll drive 'er."

"Atta' boy, Mac! I told you he would, Mr. Harriman."

Harriman mused and dozed during the half-hour run to the north into Kansas City, dozed in the light, troubled sleep of old age. Incidents out of a long life ran through his mind in vagrant dreams. There was that time . . . oh, yes, 1910 . . . A little boy on a warm spring night; "What's that, Daddy?"—"That's Halley's comet, Sonny."—"Where did it come from?"—"I don't know, Son. From way out in the sky somewhere."—"It's *beyooootiful,* Daddy. I want to touch it."—"'Fraid not, Son."

"Delos, do you mean to stand there and tell me you put the money we had saved for the house into that crazy rocket company?"—"Now, Charlotte, please! It's not crazy; it's a sound business investment. Someday soon rockets will fill the sky. Ships and trains will be obsolete. Look what happened to the men that had the foresight to invest in Henry Ford."—"We've been all over this before."—"Charlotte, the day will come when men will rise up off the Earth and visit the Moon, even the planets. This is the beginning."—"Must you shout?"—"I'm sorry, but—"—"I feel a headache coming on. Please try to be a little quiet when you come to bed."

He hadn't gone to bed. He had sat out on the veranda all night long, watching the full Moon move across the sky. There would be the devil to pay in the morning, the devil and a thin-lipped silence. But he'd stick to his guns. He'd given in on most things, but not on this. But the night was his. Tonight he'd be alone with his old friend. He searched her face. Where was Mare Crisium? Funny, he couldn't make it out. He used to be able to see it plainly when he was a boy. Probably needed new glasses—this constant office work wasn't good for his eyes.

But he didn't need to see, he knew where they all were: Crisium, Mare Fecunditatis, Mare Tranquilitatis—that one had a satisfying roll!—the Apennines, the Carpathians, old Tycho with its mysterious rays.

Two hundred and forty thousand miles—ten times around the Earth. Surely men could bridge a little gap like that. Why, he could almost reach out and touch it, nodding there behind the elm trees.

Not that he could help. He hadn't the education.

"Son, I want to have a little serious talk with you."—"Yes, Mother."—"I know you had hoped to go to college next year—" (Hoped! He had lived for it. The University of Chicago to study under Moulton, then on to the Yerkes Observatory to work under the eye of Dr. Frost himself)—"and I had hoped so too. But with your father gone, and the girls growing up, it's harder to make ends meet. You've been a good boy, and worked hard to help out. I know you'll understand."—"Yes, Mother."

"Extra! Extra! STRATOSPHERE ROCKET REACHES PARIS. Read aaaaallllll about 't." The thin little man in the bifocals snatched at the paper and hurried back to the office.—"Look at this, George." —"Huh? Hmm, interesting, but what of it?"—"Can't you see? The next stage is the Moon!"—"God, but you're a sucker, Delos. The trouble with you is, you read too many of those trashy magazines. Now, I caught my boy reading one of 'em last week, *Stunning Stories,* or some such title, and dressed him down proper. Your folks should have done you the same favor."— Harriman squared his narrow, middle-aged shoulders. "They will so reach the Moon!"—His partner laughed. "Have it your own way. If baby wants the Moon, papa brings it for him. But you stick to your discounts and commissions; that's where the money is."

The big car droned down the Paseo, and turned off on Armour Boulevard. Old Harriman stirred uneasily in his sleep and muttered to himself.

"But, Mr. Harriman—" The young man with the notebook was plainly perturbed. The old man grunted.

"You heard me. Sell 'em. I want every share I own realized in cash as rapidly as possible: Spaceways, Spaceways Provisioning

Company, Artemis Mines, Luna City Recreations, the whole lot of them."

"It will depress the market. You won't realize the full value of your holdings."

"Don't you think I know that? I can afford it."

"What about the shares you had earmarked for Richardson Observatory and for the Harriman Scholarships?"

"Oh, yes. Don't sell those. Set up a trust. Should have done it long ago. Tell young Kamens to draw up the papers. He knows what I want."

The interoffice visor flashed into life. "The gentlemen are here, Mr. Harriman."

"Send 'em in. That's all, Ashley. Get busy." Ashley went out as McIntyre and Charlie entered. Harriman got up and trotted forward to greet them.

"Come in, boys, come in. I'm so glad to see you. Sit down. Sit down. Have a cigar."

"Mighty pleased to see you, Mr. Harriman," acknowledged Charlie. "In fact, you might say we need to see you."

"Some trouble, gentlemen?" Harriman glanced from face to face. McIntyre answered him.

"You still mean that about a job for us, Mr. Harriman?"

"Mean it? Certainly, I do. You're not backing out on me?"

"Not at all. We need that job now. You see, the *Care Free* is lying in the middle of the Osage River, with her jet split clear back to the injector."

"Dear me! You weren't hurt?"

"No, aside from sprains and bruises. We jumped."

Charlie chortled. "I caught a catfish with my bare teeth."

In short order they got down to business. "You two will have to buy a ship for me. I can't do it openly; my colleagues would figure out what I mean to do and stop me. I'll supply you with all the cash you need. You go out and find some sort of a ship that can be refitted for the trip. Work up some good story about how you are buying it for some playboy as a stratosphere yacht, or that you plan to establish an Arctic-Antarctic tourist route. Anything as long as no one suspects that she is being outfitted for space flight.

"Then, after the Department of Transport licenses her for strato flight, you move out to a piece of desert out west—I'll find a likely parcel of land and buy it—and then I'll join you. Then we'll install the escape-fuel tanks, change the injectors, and timers, and so forth, to fit her for the hop. How about it?"

McIntyre looked dubious. "It'll take a lot of doing. Charlie, do you think you can accomplish that changeover without a dockyard and shops?"

"Me? Sure I can—with your thick-fingered help. Just give me the tools and materials I want, and don't hurry me too much. Of course, it won't be fancy—"

"Nobody wants it to be fancy. I just want a ship that won't blow when I start slapping the keys. Isotope fuel is no joke."

"It won't blow, Mac."

"That's what you thought about the *Care Free.*"

"That ain't fair, Mac. I ask you, Mr. Harriman— That heap was junk, and we knew it. This'll be different. We're going to spend some dough and do it right. Ain't we, Mr. Harriman?"

Harriman patted him on the shoulder. "Certainly we are, Charlie. You can have all the money you want. That's the least of our worries. Now do the salaries and bonuses I mentioned suit you? I don't want you to be short."

"—as you know, my clients are his nearest relatives and have his interests at heart. We contend that Mr. Harriman's conduct for the past several weeks, as shown by the evidence here adduced, gives clear indication that a mind, once brilliant in the world of finance, has become senile. It is therefore with the deepest regret that we pray this honorable court, if it pleases, to declare Mr. Harriman incompetent and to assign a conservator to protect his financial interests and those of his future heirs and assigns." The attorney sat down, pleased with himself.

Mr. Kamens took the floor. "May it please the court, if my esteemed friend is *quite* through, may I suggest that in his last few words he gave away his entire thesis. '—the financial interests of future heirs and assigns.' It is evident that the petitioners believe that my client should conduct his affairs in such a fashion as to ensure that his nieces and nephews, and their issue, will be supported in unearned luxury for the rest of their lives. My client's wife has passed on, he has no children. It is admitted that he has provided generously for his sisters and their children in times past, and that he has established annuities for such near kin as are without means of support.

"But now like vultures, worse than vultures, for they are not content to let him die in peace, they would prevent my client from enjoying his wealth in whatever manner best suits him for the few remaining years of his life. It is true that he has sold his holdings; is

it strange that an elderly man should wish to retire? It is true that
he suffered some paper losses in liquidation. 'The value of a thing
is what that thing will bring.' He was retiring and demanded cash.
Is there anything strange about that?

"It is admitted that he refused to discuss his actions with his
so-loving kinfolk. What law or principle requires a man to consult
with his nephews on anything?

"Therefore we pray that this court will confirm my client in his
right to do what he likes with his own, deny this petition, and send
these meddlers about their business."

The judge took off his spectacles and polished them thoughtfully.

"Mr. Kamens, this court has as high a regard for individual
liberty as you have, and you may rest assured that any action taken
will be solely in the interests of your client. Nevertheless, men do
grow old, men do become senile, and in such cases must be
protected.

"I shall take this matter under advisement until tomorrow.
Court is adjourned."

From the *Kansas City Star*—
   "ECCENTRIC MILLIONAIRE DISAPPEARS"
   "—failed to appear for the adjourned hearing. The bailiffs
returned from a search of places usually frequented by Harriman
with the report that he had not been seen since the previous day.
A bench warrant under contempt proceedings has been issued
and—"

A desert sunset is a better stimulant for the appetite than a hot
dance orchestra. Charlie testified to this by polishing the last of the
ham gravy with a piece of bread. Harriman handed each of the
young men cigars and took one himself.

"My doctor claims that these weeds are bad for my heart
condition," he remarked as he lighted it, "but I've felt so much
better since I joined you boys here on the ranch that I am inclined
to doubt him." He exhaled a cloud of blue-grey smoke and
resumed, "I don't think a man's health depends so much on what
he does as on whether he wants to do it. I'm doing what I want to
do."

"That's all a man can ask of life," agreed McIntyre.

"How does the work look now, boys?"

"My end's in pretty good shape," Charlie answered. "We finished the second pressure tests on the new tanks and the fuel lines today. The ground tests are all done, except the calibration runs. Those won't take long—just the four hours to make the runs if I don't run into some bugs. How about you, Mac?"

McIntyre ticked them off on his fingers. "Food supplies and water on board. Three vacuum suits, a spare, and service kits. Medical supplies. The buggy already had all the standard equipment for strato flight. The late lunar ephemerides haven't arrived as yet."

"When do you expect them?"

"Any time—they should be here now. Not that it matters. This guff about how hard it is to navigate from here to the Moon is hokum to impress the public. After all, you can *see* your destination—it's not like ocean navigation. Gimme a sextant and a good radar and I'll set you down anyplace on the Moon you like, without cracking an almanac or a star table, just from a general knowledge of the relative speeds involved."

"Never mind the personal buildup, Columbus," Charlie told him; "we'll admit you can hit the floor with your hat. The general idea is, you're ready to go now. Is that right?"

"That's it."

"That being the case, I *could* run those tests tonight. I'm getting jumpy—things have been going too smoothly. If you'll give me a hand, we ought to be in bed by midnight."

"OK, when I finish this cigar."

They smoked in silence for a while, each thinking about the coming trip and what it meant to him. Old Harriman tried to repress the excitement that possessed him at the prospect of immediate realization of his lifelong dream.

"Mr. Harriman—"

"Eh? What is it, Charlie?"

"How does a guy go about getting rich, like you did?"

"Getting rich? I can't say; I never tried to get rich. I never wanted to be rich, or well known, or anything like that."

"Huh?"

"No, I just wanted to live a long time and see it all happen. I wasn't unusual; there were lots of boys like me—radio hams, they were, and telescope builders, and airplane amateurs. We had science clubs, and basement laboratories, and science-fiction leagues—the kind of boys who thought there was more romance in one issue of the *Electrical Experimenter* than in all the books Dumas ever wrote. We didn't want to be one of Horatio Alger's Get-Rich heroes either, we wanted to build space ships. Well, some of us did."

"Jeez, Pop, you make it sound exciting."

"It was exciting, Charlie. This has been a wonderful, romantic century, for all its bad points. And it's grown more wonderful and more exciting every year. No, I didn't want to be rich; I just wanted to live long enough to see men rise up to the stars, and, if God was good to me, to go as far as the Moon myself." He carefully deposited an inch of white ash in a saucer. "It has been a good life. I haven't any complaints."

McIntyre pushed back his chair. "Come on, Charlie, if you're ready."

"OK."

They all got up. Harriman started to speak, then grabbed at his chest, his face a dead grey-white.

"Catch him, Mac!"

"Where's his medicine?"

"In his vest pocket."

They eased him over to a couch, broke a small glass capsule in a handkerchief, and held it under his nose. The volatile released by the capsule seemed to bring a little color into his face. They did what little they could for him, then waited for him to regain consciousness.

Charlie broke the uneasy silence. "Mac, we ain't going through with this."

"Why not?"

"It's murder. He'll never stand up under the initial acceleration."

"Maybe not, but it's what he wants to do. You heard him."

"But we oughtn't to let him."

"Why not? It's neither your business, nor the business of this damn paternalistic Government, to tell a man not to risk his life doing what he really wants to do."

"All the same, I don't feel right about it. He's such a swell old duck."

"Then what d'yuh want to do with him—send him back to Kansas City so those old harpies can shut him up in a laughing academy till he dies of a broken heart?"

"N-no-o-o—not that."

"Get out there, and make your setup for those test runs. I'll be along."

A wide-tired desert runabout rolled in the ranch yard gate the next morning and stopped in front of the house. A heavy-set man with a firm, but kindly, face climbed out and spoke to McIntyre, who approached to meet him.

"You James McIntyre?"

"What about it?"

"I'm the deputy federal marshal hereabouts. I got a warrant for your arrest."

"What's the charge?"

"Conspiracy to violate the Space Precautionary Act."

Charlie joined the pair. "What's up, Mac?"

The deputy answered, "You'd be Charles Cummings, I guess. Warrant here for you. Got one for a man named Harriman, too, and a court order to put seals on your space ship."

"We've no space ship."

"What d'yuh keep in that big shed?"

"Strato yacht."

"So? Well, I'll put seals on her until a space ship comes along. Where's Harriman?"

"Right in there." Charlie obliged by pointing, ignoring McIntyre's scowl.

The deputy turned his head. Charlie couldn't have missed the button by a fraction of an inch, for the deputy collapsed quietly to the ground. Charlie stood over him, rubbing his knuckles and mourning.

"Damn it to hell—that's the finger I broke playing shortstop. I'm always hurting that finger."

"Get Pop into the cabin," Mac cut him short, "and strap him into his hammock."

"Aye aye, Skipper."

They dragged the ship by tractor out of the hangar, turned, and went out the desert plain to find elbow room for the takeoff. They climbed in. McIntyre saw the deputy from his starboard conning port. He was staring disconsolately after them.

McIntyre fastened his safety belt, settled his corset, and spoke into the engine-room speaking tube. "All set, Charlie?"

"All set, Skipper. But you can't raise ship yet, Mac—*She ain't named!*"

"No time for your superstitions!"

Harriman's thin voice reached them. "Call her the *Lunatic*—it's the only appropriate name!"

McIntyre settled his head into the pads, punched two keys, then three more in rapid succession, and the *Lunatic* raised ground.

"How are you, Pop?"

Charlie searched the old man's face anxiously. Harriman licked his lips and managed to speak. "Doing fine, son. Couldn't be better."

"The acceleration is over; it won't be so bad from here on. I'll unstrap you so you can wiggle around a little. But I think you'd better stay in the hammock." He tugged at buckles. Harriman partially repressed a groan.

"What is it, Pop?"

"Nothing. Nothing at all. Just go easy on that side."

Charlie ran his fingers over the old man's side with the sure, delicate touch of a mechanic. "You ain't foolin' me none, Pop. But there isn't much I can do until we ground."

"Charlie—"

"Yes, Pop?"

"Can't I move to a port? I want to watch the Earth."

"Ain't nothin' to see yet; the ship hides it. As soon as we turn ship, I'll move you. Tell you what; I'll give you a sleepy pill, and then wake you when we do."

"No!"

"Huh?"

"I'll stay awake."

"Just as you say, Pop."

Charlie clambered monkey fashion to the nose of the ship and anchored to the gimbals of the pilot's chair. McIntyre questioned him with his eyes.

"Yeah, he's alive all right," Charlie told him, "but he's in bad shape."

"How bad?"

"Couple of cracked ribs anyhow. I don't know what else. I don't know whether he'll last out the trip, Mac. His heart was pounding something awful."

"He'll last, Charlie. He's tough."

"Tough? He's delicate as a canary."

"I don't mean that. He's tough way down inside—where it counts."

"Just the same, you'd better set her down awful easy if you want to ground with a full complement aboard."

"I will. I'll make one full swing around the Moon and ease her in on an involute approach curve. We've got enough fuel, I think."

They were now in a free orbit; after McIntyre turned ship, Charlie went back, unslung the hammock, and moved Harriman, hammock, and all, to a side port. McIntyre steadied the ship about a transverse axis so that the tail pointed towards the sun, then gave a short blast on two tangential jets opposed in couple to cause the ship to spin slowly about her longitudinal axis, and thereby create a slight artificial gravity. The initial weightlessness when coasting commenced had knotted the old man with the characteristic nausea of free flight, and the pilot wished to save his passenger as much discomfort as possible.

But Harriman was not concerned with the condition of his stomach.

There it was, all as he had imagined it so many times. The Moon swung majestically past the view port wider than he had ever seen it before, all her familiar features cameo clear. She gave way to the Earth as the ship continued its slow swing, the Earth itself as he had envisioned her, appearing like a noble moon, many times as wide as the Moon appears to the Earthbound, and more luscious, more sensuously beautiful than the silver Moon could be. It was sunset near the Atlantic seaboard—the line of shadow cut down the coast line of North America, slashed through Cuba, and obscured all but the west coast of South America. He savored the mellow blue of the Pacific Ocean, felt the texture of the soft green and brown of the continents, admired the blue-white cold of the polar caps. Canada and the northern states were obscured by cloud, a vast low-pressure area that spread across the continent. It shone with an even more satisfactory dazzling white than the polar caps.

As the ship swung slowly around, Earth would pass from view, and the stars would march across the port—the same stars he had always known, but steady, brighter, and unwinking against a screen of perfect, live black. Then the Moon would swim into view again to claim his thoughts.

He was serenely happy in a fashion not given to most men, even in a long lifetime. He felt as if he were every man who has ever lived, looked up at the stars, and longed.

As the long hours came and went he watched and dozed and

dreamed. At least once he must have fallen into deep sleep, or possibly delirium, for he came to with a start, thinking that his wife, Charlotte, was calling him. "Delos!" the voice had said. "Delos! Come in from there! You'll catch your death of cold in that night air."

Poor Charlotte! She had been a good wife to him, a good wife. He was quite sure that her only regret in dying had been her fear that he could not take proper care of himself. It had not been her fault that she had not shared his dream, and his need.

Charlie rigged the hammock in such a fashion that Harriman could watch from the starboard port when they swung around the far face of the Moon. He picked out the landmarks made familiar to him by a thousand photographs with nostalgic pleasure, as if he were returning to his own country. McIntyre brought her slowly down as they came back around to the Earthward face, and prepared to land east of Mare Fecunditatis, about ten miles from Luna City.

It was not a bad landing, all things considered. He had to land without coaching from the ground, and he had no second pilot to watch the radar for him. In his anxiety to make it gentle he missed his destination by some thirty miles, but he did his cold-sober best. But at that it was bumpy.

As they grounded and the pumice dust settled around them, Charlie came up to the control station.

"How's our passenger?" Mac demanded.

"I'll see, but I wouldn't make any bets. That landing stunk, Mac."

"Damn it, I did my best."

"I know you did, Skipper. Forget it."

But the passenger was alive and conscious although bleeding from the nose and with a pink foam on his lips. He was feebly trying to get himself out of his cocoon. They helped him, working together.

"Where are the vacuum suits?" was his first remark.

"Steady, Mr. Harriman. You can't go out there yet. We've got to give you some first aid."

"Get me that suit! First aid can wait."

Silently they did as he ordered. His left leg was practically useless, and they had to help him through the lock, one on each side. But with his inconsiderable mass having a lunar weight of only twenty pounds, he was no burden. They found a place some fifty yards from the ship where they could prop him up and let him look, a chunk of scoria supporting his head.

McIntyre put his helmet against the old man's and spoke. "We'll leave you here to enjoy the view while we get ready for the trek into town. It's a forty-miler, pretty near, and we'll have to break out spare air bottles and rations and stuff. We'll be back soon."

Harriman nodded without answering, and squeezed their gauntlets with a grip that was surprisingly strong.

He sat very quietly, rubbing his hands against the soil of the Moon and sensing the curiously light pressure of his body against the ground. At long last there was peace in his heart. His hurts had ceased to pain him. He *was* where he had longed to be—he had followed his need. Over the western horizon hung the Earth at last quarter, a green-blue giant moon. Overhead the Sun shone down from a black and starry sky. And underneath the Moon, the soil of the Moon itself. He was on the Moon!

He lay back still while a bath of content flowed over him like a tide at flood, and soaked to his very marrow.

His attention strayed momentarily, and he thought once again that his name was called. Silly, he thought, I'm getting old—my mind wanders.

Back in the cabin Charlie and Mac were rigging shoulder yokes on a stretcher. "There. That will do," Mac commented. "We'd better stir Pop out; we ought to be going."

"I'll get him," Charlie replied. "I'll just pick him up and carry him. He don't weigh nothing."

Charlie was gone longer than McIntyre had expected him to be. He returned alone. Mac waited for him to close the lock, and swing back his helmet. "Trouble?"

"Never mind the stretcher, Skipper. We won't be needin' it. Yeah, I mean it," he continued. "Pop's done for. I did what was necessary."

McIntyre bent down without a word and picked up the wide skis necessary to negotiate the powdery ash. Charlie followed his example. Then they swung the spare air bottles over their shoulders, and passed out through the lock.

They didn't bother to close the outer door of the lock behind them.

TENDERFOOT IN SPACE

When this book was in process, Dr. Kondo asked me whether there were any stories of Robert's which had not been reprinted. On looking over the list of stories, I found that "Tenderfoot in Space" had never been printed in anything except when it originally appeared in Boys' Life. All copies in our possession had been sent to the UCSC Archives, so I asked them to Xerox those and send them to me, and found this introduction by Robert, which he had added to the carbon in the library before he sent it down there. I was completely surprised, and asked Dr. Kondo whether he would like to use it.

Here it is—Virginia Heinlein

This was written a year before Sputnik and is laid on the Venus earthbound astronomers inferred before space probes. Two hours of rewriting—a word here, a word there—could change it to a planet around some other star. But to what purpose? Would The Tempest be improved if Bohemia had a sea coast? If I ever publish that collection of Boy Scout stories, this story will appear unchanged.

Nixie is (of course) my own dog. But in 1919, when I was 12 and a Scout, he had to leave me—a streetcar hit him.

If this universe has any reasonable teleology whatever (a point on which I am unsure), then there is some provision for the Nixies in it.

I

"Heel, Nixie," the boy said softly, "and keep quiet."

The little mongrel took position left and rear of his boy, waited.

He could feel that Charlie was upset and he wanted to know why—but an order from Charlie could not be questioned.

The boy tried to see whether or not the policeman was noticing them. He felt lightheaded—neither he nor his dog had eaten that day. They had stopped in front of this supermarket, not to buy, for the boy had no money left, but because of a BOY WANTED sign in the window.

It was then that he had noticed the reflection of the policeman in the glass.

The boy hesitated, trying to collect his cloudy thoughts. Should he go inside and ask for the job? Or should he saunter past the policeman? Pretend to be just out for a walk?

The boy decided to go on, get out of sight. He signaled the dog to stay close and turned away from the window. Nixie came along, tail high. He did not care where they went as long as he was with Charlie. Charlie had belonged to him as far back as he could remember; he could imagine no other condition. In fact Nixie would not have lived past his tenth day had not Charlie fallen in love with him; Nixie had been the least attractive of an unfortunate litter; his mother was Champion Lady Diana of Ojai—his father was unknown.

But Nixie was not aware that a neighbor boy had begged his life from his first owners. His philosophy was simple: enough to eat, enough sleep, and the rest of his time spent in playing with Charlie. This present outing had been Charlie's idea, but any outing was welcome. The shortage of food was a nuisance but Nixie automatically forgave Charlie such errors—after all, boys will be boys and a wise dog accepted the fact. The only thing that troubled him was that Charlie did not have the happy heart which was a proper part of all hikes.

As they moved past the man in the blue uniform, Nixie felt the man's interest in them, sniffed his odor, but could find no real unfriendliness in it. But Charlie was nervous, alert, so Nixie kept his own attention high.

The man in uniform said, "Not so fast, boy."

Charlie stopped, Nixie stopped. "You speaking to me officer?"

"Yes. What's your dog's name?"

Nixie felt Charlie's sudden terror, got ready to attack. He had never yet had to bite anyone for his boy—but he was instantly ready. The hair between his shoulder blades stood up.

Charlie answered, "Uh . . . his name is 'Spot.'"

"So?" The stranger said sharply, "Nixie!"

Nixie had been keeping his eyes elsewhere, in order not to distract his ears, his nose, and the inner sense with which he touched people's feelings. But he was so startled at hearing this stranger call him by name that he turned his head and looked at him.

"His name is 'Spot,' is it?" the policeman said quietly. "And mine is Santa Claus. But you're Charlie Vaughn and you're going home." He spoke into his helmet phone: "Nelson, reporting a pickup on that Vaughn missing-persons flier. Send a car. I'm in front of the new supermarket."

They were taken to the local justice of the peace. "You're Charles Vaughn?"

Nixie's boy felt unhappy and said nothing.

"Speak up, son," insisted the old man. "If you aren't, then you must have stolen that dog." He read from a paper: ". . . accompanied by a small brown mongrel, male, well trained, responds to the name 'Nixie.' Well?"

Nixie's boy answered faintly, "I'm Charlie Vaughn."

"That's better. You'll stay here until your parents pick you up." The judge frowned. "I can't understand your running away. Your folks are emigrating to Venus, aren't they?"

"Yes, sir."

"You're the first boy I ever met who didn't want to make the Big Jump." He pointed to a pin on the boy's lapel. "And I thought Scouts were trustworthy. Not to mention obedient. What got into you, son? Are you scared of the Big Jump? 'A Scout is Brave.' That doesn't mean you don't have to be scared—everybody is at times. 'Brave' simply means you don't run even if you are scared."

"I'm not scared," Charlie said stubbornly. "I *want* to go to Venus."

"Then why run away when your family is about to leave?"

Nixie felt such a burst of warm happy-sadness from Charlie that he licked his hand.

"Because Nixie can't go!"

"Oh." The judge looked at boy and dog. "I'm sorry, son. That problem is beyond my jurisdiction." He drummed his desk top. "Charlie . . . will you promise, Scout's honor, not to run away again until your parents show up?"

"Uh . . . yes, sir."

"Okay. Joe, take them to my place. Tell my wife she had better see how recently they've had anything to eat."

The trip home was long. Nixie enjoyed it, even though Charlie's father was happy-angry and his mother was happy-sad and Charlie himself was happy-sad-worried. When Nixie was home he checked quickly through each room, making sure that all was in order and that there were no new smells. Then he returned to Charlie.

The feelings had changed. Mr. Vaughn was angry, Mrs. Vaughn was sad, Charlie himself gave out such bitter stubbornness that Nixie went to him, jumped onto his lap, and tried to lick his face. Charlie settled Nixie beside him, started digging fingers into the loose skin back of Nixie's neck. Nixie quieted at once, satisfied that he and his boy could face together whatever it was—but it distressed him that the other two were not happy. Charlie belonged to him; they belonged to Charlie; things were better when they were happy, too.

Mr. Vaughn said, "Go to bed, young man, and sleep on it. I'll speak with you again tomorrow."

"Yes, sir. Good night, sir."

"Kiss your mother goodnight. One more thing. Do I need to lock doors to be sure you will be here in the morning?"

"No, sir."

Nixie got on the foot of the bed as usual, tromped out a space, laid his tail over his nose, and started to go to sleep. But his boy was not sleeping; his sadness was taking the distressing form of heaves and sobs. So Nixie got up, went to the other end of the bed and licked away tears—then let himself be pulled into Charlie's arms and tears applied directly to his neck. It was not comfortable and too hot, besides being taboo. But it was worth enduring as Charlie started to quiet down, presently went to sleep.

Nixie waited, gave him a lick on the face to check his sleeping, then moved to his end of the bed.

Mrs. Vaughn said to Mr. Vaughn, "Charles, isn't there *anything* we can do for the boy?"

"Confound it, Nora. We're getting to Venus with too little money as it is. If anything goes wrong, we'll be dependent on charity."

"But we *do* have a little spare cash."

"Too little. Do you think I haven't considered it? Why, the fare for that worthless dog would be almost as much as it is for Charlie himself! Out of the question! So why nag me? Do you think I enjoy this decision?"

"No, dear." Mrs. Vaughn pondered. "How much does Nixie weigh? I . . . well, I think I could reduce ten more pounds if I really tried."

"What? Do you want to arrive on Venus a living skeleton? You've reduced all the doctor advises, and so have I."

"Well . . . I thought that if somehow, among us, we could squeeze out Nixie's weight—it's not as if he were a St. Bernard!—we could swap it against our weight for our tickets."

Mr. Vaughn shook his head unhappily. "They don't do it that way.

"Let me explain. Surely, it's weight; it's always weight in a space ship. But it isn't just my hundred and sixty pounds, or your hundred and twenty, nor Charlie's hundred and ten. We're not dead weight; we have to eat and drink and breathe air and have room to move—that last is expensive because it takes more ship weight to hold a live person than it does for an equal weight in the cargo hold. For a human being there is a complicated formula—hull weight equal to twice the passenger's weight, plus the number of days in space times four pounds. It takes a hundred and forty-six days to get to Venus—so it means that the calculated weight for each of us amounts to six hundred and sixteen pounds before they even figure in our actual weights. But for a dog the rate is even higher—five pounds per day instead of four."

"That seems unfair. Surely a little dog can't eat as much as a man? Why, Nixie's food costs hardly anything."

Her husband snorted. "Nixie eats his own rations and half of what goes on Charlie's plate. However, it's not only the fact that a dog does eat more for his weight, but also they don't reprocess waste with a dog, not even for hydroponics."

"Why not? Oh, I know what you mean. But it seems silly."

"The passengers wouldn't like it. Never mind; the rule is: five pounds per day for dogs. Do you know what that makes Nixie's fare? Over three thousand dollars!"

"My goodness!"

"My ticket comes to thirty-eight hundred dollars and some, you get by for thirty-four hundred, and Charlie's fare is thirty-three hundred—yet that confounded mongrel dog, which we couldn't sell for his veterinary bills, would cost three thousand dollars. If we had that to spare—which we haven't—the humane thing would be to adopt some orphan, spend the money on him, and thereby give him a chance on an uncrowded planet, not to waste it on a dog. Confound it; a year from now Charlie will have forgotten this dog."

"I wonder."

"He will. When I was a kid, I had to give up dogs more than once. They died, or something. I got over it. Charlie has to make up his mind whether to give Nixie away, or have him killed humanely." He chewed his lip. "We'll get him a pup on Venus."

"It wouldn't be Nixie."

"He can name it Nixie. He'll love it as much."

"But, Charles, how is it there are dogs on Venus if it's so dreadfully expensive to get them there?"

"Eh? I think the first exploring parties used them to scout. In any case they're always shipping animals to Venus; our own ship is taking a load of milk cows."

"That must be terribly expensive."

"Yes and no. They ship them in sleep-freeze of course, and a lot of them never revive. But they cut their losses by butchering the dead ones and selling the meat at fancy prices to the colonists. Then the ones that live have calves and eventually it pays off." He stood up. "Nora, let's go to bed. It's sad—but our boy is going to have to make a man's decision. Give the mutt away, or have him put to sleep."

"Yes, dear." She sighed. "I'm coming."

Nixie was in his usual place at breakfast—lying beside Charlie's chair, accepting tidbits without calling attention to himself. He had learned long ago the rules of the dining room: no barking, no whining, no begging for food, no paws on laps, else the pets of his pet would make difficulties. Nixie was satisfied. He had learned as a puppy to take the world as it was, cheerful over its good points, patient with its minor shortcomings. Shoes were not to be chewed, people were not to be jumped up on, most strangers must be allowed to approach the house (subject, of course, to strict scrutiny and constant alertness)—a few simple rules and everyone was happy. Live and let live.

He was aware that his boy was not happy even this beautiful morning. But he had explored this feeling carefully, touching his boy's mind with gentle care by means of his canine sense for feeling, and had decided from his superior maturity, that the mood would wear off. Boys were sometimes sad, and a wise dog was resigned to it.

* * *

Mr. Vaughn finished his coffee, put his napkin aside. "Well, young man?"

Charlie did not answer. Nixie felt the sadness in Charlie change suddenly to a feeling more aggressive and much stronger but no better. He pricked up his ears and waited.

"Chuck," his father said, "last night I gave you a choice. Have you made up your mind?"

"Yes, Dad." Charlie's voice was very low.

"Eh? Then tell me."

Nixie could feel anger welling up in the man, felt him control it. "You're figuring on running away again?"

"No, sir," Charlie answered stubbornly. "You can sign me over to the state school."

"Charlie!" It was Charlie's mother who spoke. Nixie tried to sort out the rush of emotions impinging on him.

"Yes," his father said at last. "I could use your passage money to pay the state for your first three years or so, and agree to pay your support until you are eighteen. But I shan't."

"Huh? Why not, Dad?"

"Because, old-fashioned as it sounds, I am head of this family. I am responsible for it—and not just food, shelter, and clothing, but its total welfare. Until you are old enough to take care of yourself I mean to keep an eye on you. One of the prerogatives which go with my responsibility is deciding where the family shall live. I have a better job offered me on Venus than I could ever hope for here, so I'm going to Venus and my family goes with me. It just happens, too, that your mother and I like to have you around." He drummed on the table, hesitated. "I think your chances are better on a pioneer planet, too—but, when you are of age, if you think otherwise, I'll pay your fare back to Earth. But you go with us. Understand?"

Charlie nodded, his face glum.

"Very well. I'm amazed that you apparently care more for that dog than you do for your mother and myself. But—"

"It isn't that, Dad. Nixie needs—"

"Quiet. I don't suppose you realize it, but I tried to figure this out. I'm not taking your dog away from you out of meanness. If I could afford it, I'd buy the hound a ticket. I'm forced to admit that I can't spare the money. But something your mother said last night brought up a third possibility."

Charlie looked up suddenly, and so did Nixie, wondering why the surge of hope in his boy.

"I can't buy Nixie a ticket, but it's possible to ship him as freight."

"Huh? Why, sure, Dad! Oh, I know he'd have to be caged up but I'd go down and feed him every day and pet him and tell him it was all right and—"

"Slow down! I don't mean that. All I can afford is to have him shipped the way animals are always shipped in space ships—in sleep-freeze."

Charlie's mouth hung open. He managed to say, "But that's—"

"That's dangerous. As near as I remember, it's about fifty-fifty whether he wakes up at the other end. But if you want to risk it—well, perhaps it's better than giving him away to strangers and I'm sure you would prefer it to taking him down to the vet's and having him killed."

Charlie grabbed the dog's ear. "All right, Dad," he said gruffly. "We'll risk it, if that's the only way Nixie and I can still be partners."

Nixie did not enjoy the last few days before leaving; they held too many changes. Any proper dog likes excitement but home is for peace and quiet. Things should be orderly there—food and water always in the same place, newspapers to fetch at certain hours, milkmen to supervise at regular times, furniture all in its proper place. But during that week all was change—nothing on time, nothing in order. Strange men came into the house (always a matter for suspicion), but worse yet they carried away pieces of furniture, and he, Nixie, was not even allowed to protest, much less give them the what-for they had coming.

He was assured by Charlie and Mrs. Vaughn that it was "all right" and he had to accept it, even though it obviously was not all right. His knowledge of English was accurate for a few dozen words but there was no way to explain to him that almost everything owned by the Vaughn family was being sold, given to friends, or thrown away, nor would it have reassured him.

By the night before they left, the rooms were bare except for beds. Nixie trotted around the house, sniffing places where familiar objects had been, asking his nose to tell him that his eyes deceived him, whining at the results. Even more upsetting than physical change was emotional change, a heady and not entirely happy excitement which he could feel in all three of his people.

There was a better time that evening, as Nixie was allowed to go to Scout meeting. Nixie always went on hikes and had formerly attended all meetings. But now he attended only outdoor meetings since an incident the previous winter—Nixie felt that too much fuss had been made about it—just spilled cocoa and a few broken cups and anyhow it had been that cat's fault.

But this meeting he was allowed to attend because it was Charlie's last Scout meeting on Earth. Nixie was not aware of that but he greatly enjoyed the privilege, especially as the meeting was followed by a party at which Nixie became comfortably stuffed with hot dogs and pop. Scoutmaster McIntosh presented Charlie with a letter of withdrawal, certifying his status and merit badges and asking his admission into any troop on Venus. Nixie joined happily in the applause, trying to outbark the clapping.

Then the Scoutmaster said, "Okay, Rip."

Rip was senior patrol leader. He got up and said, "Quiet, fellows. Hold it, you crazy savages! Charlie, I don't have to tell you that we're all sorry to see you go, but we hope you have a swell time on Venus and now and then send a postcard to Troop Twenty-Seven and tell us about it. We'll post 'em on the bulletin board. Anyhow, we wanted to get you a going-away present. But Mr. McIntosh pointed out that you were on a very strict weight allowance and practically anything would either cost you more to take with you than we had paid for it, or maybe you couldn't take it at all, which wouldn't be much of a gift."

Nixie's ears pricked. Charlie said softly, "Steady, boy."

"Nixie has been with us almost as long as you have. He's been around, poking his cold nose into things, longer than any of the tenderfoot Scouts and longer even than some of the second class. So we decided he ought to have his own letter of withdrawal, so that the troop you join on Venus will know that Nixie is a Scout in good standing. Give it to him, Kenny."

The scribe passed over the letter. It was phrased like Charlie's letter, save that it named "Nixie Vaughn, Tenderfoot Scout." It was signed by the scribe, the scoutmaster, and the patrol leaders and countersigned by every member of the troop. Charlie showed it to Nixie, who sniffed it. Everybody applauded, so Nixie joined happily in applauding himself.

"One more thing," added Rip. "Now that Nixie is officially a Scout, he has to have his badge. So send him front and center."

Charlie did so. They had worked their way through the Dog Care merit badge together while Nixie was a pup, all feet and floppy ears; it had made Nixie a much more acceptable member of the Vaughn family. But the rudimentary dog training required for the merit badge had stirred Charlie's interest; they had gone on to Dog Obedience School together and Nixie had progressed from easy spoken commands to more difficult silent hand signals, including some fancy ones invented by Charlie.

Charlie used them now. At his signal Nixie trotted forward, sat stiffly at attention, front paws neatly drooped in front of his chest, while Rip fastened the tenderfoot badge to his collar, then Nixie raised his right paw in salute and gave one short bark, all to hand signals.

The applause was loud and Nixie trembled with eagerness to join it. But Charlie signalled "hold and quiet," so Nixie remained silently poised in salute until the clapping died away. He returned to heel just as silently, though quivering with excitement. The purpose of the ceremony may not have been clear to him—if so, he was not the first tenderfoot Scout to be a little confused. But it was perfectly clear that he was the center of attention and was being approved of by his friends; it was a high point in his life.

But all in all there had been too much excitement for a dog in one week; the trip to White Sands, shut up in a travel case and away from Charlie, was the last straw. When Charlie came to claim him at the baggage room of White Sands Airport, his relief was so great that he had a puppish accident, and was bitterly ashamed.

He quieted down on the drive from airport to spaceport, then was disquieted again when he was taken into a room which reminded him of his unpleasant trips to the veterinary—the smells, the white-coated figure, the bare table where a dog had to hold still and be hurt. He stopped dead.

"Come, Nixie!" Charlie said firmly. "None of that, boy. Up!"

Nixie gave a little sigh, advanced and jumped onto the examination table, stood docile but trembling.

"Have him lie down," the man in the white smock said. "I've got to get the needle into the large vein in his foreleg."

Nixie did so on Charlie's command, then lay trembling quiet while his left foreleg was shaved in a patch and sterilized. Charlie put a hand on Nixie's shoulder blades and soothed him while the veterinary surgeon probed for the vein. Nixie bared his teeth once but did not growl, even though the fear in the boy's mind was beating on him, making him just as afraid.

Suddenly the drug reached his brain and he slumped limp.

Charlie's fear surged to a peak but Nixie did not feel it. Nixie's tough little spirit had gone somewhere else, out of touch with his friend, out of space and time—wherever it is that the "I" within a man or a dog goes when the body wrapping it is unconscious.

Charlie grabbed the doctor's arm and asked shrilly, "Is he dead?"

"No, of course not."

"I thought he had died."

"Want to listen to his heart beat?"

"Uh, no—if you say he's all right. Then he's going to be okay? He'll live through it?"

The doctor glanced at Charlie's father, back at the boy, then said, kindly. "Look, son. If I put your dog over on that shelf, in a couple of hours he'll be sleeping normally and by tomorrow he won't even know he was out. But if I take him back to the chill room and start him on the cycle—" He shrugged. "Well, I've put eight head of cattle under today. If forty percent are revived, it's a good shipment. I do the very best I can."

Charlie looked grey. The surgeon looked at Mr. Vaughn, back at the boy. "Son, I know a man who's looking for a dog for his kids. Say the word and you won't have to worry whether this pooch's system will recover from a shock it was never intended to take."

Mr. Vaughn, said, "Well, son?"

Charlie stood mute, in an agony of indecision. At last Mr. Vaughn said sharply, "Chuck, we've got just twenty minutes before we must check in with Emigration. Well? What's your answer?" Charlie did not seem to hear. Timidly he put out one hand, barely touched the still form with the staring, unseeing eyes.

Then he snatched his hand back and squeaked, *"No!* We're going to Venus, *both* of us!" He turned and ran out of the room.

The veterinary spread his hands helplessly. "I tried."

"I know you did, Doctor," Mr. Vaughn answered gravely. "Thank you."

The Vaughns took the usual emigrant routing: winged shuttle rocket to the inner satellite station, transshipment there to the great globular cargo liner Hesperus. The jumps and changes took two days; they would stay in the deepspace ship for twenty-one tedious weeks, falling in half-elliptical orbit from Earth down to Venus. The time was fixed, an inescapable consequence of the law of gravity and the sizes and shapes of the two planetary orbits.

At first Charlie was terribly excited. The terrific high-gravity boost to break away from Earth's mighty grasp was as much of a shocker as he had hoped; six gravities *is* shocking, even to those used to it. When the shuttle rocket went into free fall a few minutes later, utter weightlessness was as distressing, confusing—and exciting—as he had hoped. It was so upsetting that he would have lost his lunch had he not been injected with anti-nausea drug. Soon he began to enjoy floating around.

Earth, seen from space, looked as it had looked in color-stereo pictures, but he found that the real thing is as vastly more satisfying as a hamburger is better than a picture of one. In the outer satellite station, someone pointed out to him the famous Captain Nordhoff, just back from Pluto. Charlie recognized those stern, lined features, familiar from TV and news pictures, and realized with odd surprise that the hero was a man, like everyone else.

Takeoff in the big space ship *Hesperus* was smooth, and rather disappointing.

By order of the Captain, passengers could sign up for a "sightseeing tour." Charlie's chance came when they were two weeks out—a climb through accessible parts of the ship, a quick look into the power room, a longer look at the hydroponics gardens which provided fresh air and part of their food, and a ten-second glimpse through the door of the control room, all accompanied by a lecture from a bored junior officer. It was over in two hours and Charlie was again limited to his own, very crowded part of the ship.

The emigrants saw little of the ship's crew, but Charlie got acquainted with Slim, the emigrants' cook. Slim was called so for the reason that cooks usually are; he sampled his own wares all day long and was pear shaped.

Like all spaceships, the *Hesperus* was undermanned except for astrogators and engineers. And Slim could use a helper. Charlie's merit badge in cooking plus a willingness to do as he was told made him Slim's favorite volunteer assistant. Charlie got from it something to do with his time, sandwiches and snacks whenever he wanted them, and lots of knowledgeable conversation. Slim had not been to college but his curiosity had never dried up; he had read everything worth reading in several ship's libraries and had kept his eyes open dirtside on every inhabited planet in the Solar System.

"Slim, what's it like on Venus?"

"Mmm, pretty much like the books say. Rainy. Hot. Not too bad at Borealis, where you'll land."

Charlie had almost managed not to worry about Nixie, having told himself that there was nothing to worry about. They were a month past midpoint, with Venus only two weeks away, before he discussed it with Slim. "Look, Slim, you know a lot about such things. Nixie'll make it all right—won't he?"

"Hand me that paddle. Mmm, don't know as I ever ran across a dog in space before. Cats now, cats belong in space. They're clean and neat and help to keep down mice."

"Slim, you're changing the subject. How about Nixie? He's going to be all right, isn't he?"

"As I was saying, I don't have opinions about things I don't know. Happens I don't know dogs. Never had one as a kid; I was raised in a big city. Since then I've been in space. No dogs."

"Darn it, Slim! You're being evasive. You know about sleep-freeze. I know you do."

Slim sighed. "Kid, you're going to die someday and so am I. And so is your pup. It's the one thing we can't avoid. Why, the ship's reactor could blow up and none of us would know what hit us till they started fitting us with haloes. So why fret about whether your dog comes out of sleep-freeze? Either he does and you've worried unnecessarily or he doesn't and there's nothing you can do about it."

"So you don't think he will?"

"I didn't say that. I said it was foolish to worry."

But Charlie did worry; the talk with Slim brought it to the top of his mind, worried him more and more as the day got closer. The last month seemed longer to him than the four dreary months that had preceded it.

Eventually the Captain slowed his ship, matched her with Venus and set her in a parking orbit, alongside Venus's single satellite station. After transshipment and maddening delay the Vaughns were taken down in the winged shuttle Cupid into the clouds of Venus and landed at the north pole colony, Borealis.

So far he had had one glimpse outdoors—a permanently cloudy sky which never got dark and was never bright. Borealis is at Venus's north pole and the axis of the planet is nearly erect; the unseen Sun circled the horizon, never rising nor setting by more than a few degrees. The colony lived in eternal twilight.

The lessened gravity, nine-tenths that of Earth, Charlie did not notice even though he knew he should. It had been five months since he had felt Earth gravity and the *Hesperus* had maintained only one-third gravity in that outer part where spin was most felt. Consequently Charlie felt heavier than seemed right, rather than lighter—he had forgotten full weight.

Nor did he notice the heavy concentration (about 2%) of carbon dioxide in the air, on which Venus's mighty jungles depended. It had once been believed that so much carbon dioxide, breathed regularly, would kill a man, but long before space flight, around 1950, experiments had shown that even a higher concentration had no bad effects. Charlie simply did not notice it.

Charlie's father immediately got busy hunting living quarters and conferring with his employers. Charlie didn't see much of him.

Nine days after their arrival Charlie was sitting in the recreation room of the reception center, disconsolately reading a book he had already read on Earth. His father came in.

"They're going to try to revive your dog. You want to be there, don't you? Or maybe you'd rather not? I can go."

Charlie gulped. "I want to be there."

The room was like the one back at White Sands where Nixie had been put to sleep, except that in place of the table there was a cagelike contraption with glass sides. A man was making adjustments on a complex apparatus which stood next to the glass box and was connected to it.

Two other men came in carrying a glass tray with something brown on it. This was Nixie, limp and apparently dead. Charlie caught his breath.

One assistant moved the little body forward, fitted a collar around its neck, closed down a partition like a guillotine, jerked his hands out of the way as the other assistant slammed the glass door through which they had put the dog in, quickly sealed it. Now Nixie was shut tight in a glass case, his head lying outside the end partition, his body inside.

"Cycle!" As he said it, the first assistant slapped a switch and fixed his eyes on the instrument board and Doctor Zecker thrust both arms into long rubber gloves passing through the glass, which allowed his hands to be inside with Nixie's body. With rapid, sure motions he picked up a hypodermic needle, already waiting inside, shoved it deep into the dog's side.

"Force breathing established."

"No heart action, Doctor!"

The reports came one on top of the other. The doctor looked up at the dials, looked back at the dog and mumbled. He grabbed another needle. This one he entered gently, depressed the plunger most carefully, with his eyes on the dials.

"Fibrillation!"

"I can see!" he answered snappishly, put down the hypo and began to massage the dog in time with the ebb and surge of the "Iron Lung."

And Nixie lifted his head and cried.

It was more than an hour before the doctor let Charlie take the dog away. During most of this time the cage was open and Nixie was breathing on his own, but with the apparatus still in place, ready to start again if his heart or lungs should falter in their newly relearned trick of keeping him alive. But during this waiting time Charlie was allowed to stand beside him, touch him, soothe and pet him to keep him quiet.

At last the doctor picked up Nixie and put him in Charlie's arms. "Okay, take him. But keep him quiet; I don't want him running around for the next ten hours. But not too quiet. Don't let him sleep."

"Why not, Doctor?" asked Mr. Vaughn.

"Because sometimes, when you think they've made it, they just lie down and quit. Just keep him quiet, but not too quiet. Keep him awake."

Charlie answered solemnly, "I will Doctor. Nixie's going to be all right—I know he is."

Charlie stayed awake all night long, talking to Nixie, petting him, keeping him quiet but not asleep. Neither one of his parents tried to get him to go to bed. In a few days Nixie was as good as ever.

II

Nixie liked Venus. It was filled with a thousand new smells, all worth investigating, countless new sounds, each of which had to be catalogued. As official guardian of the Vaughn family and of Charlie in particular, it was his duty and pleasure to examine each new phenomenon, decide whether or not it was safe for his people; he set about it happily, and as the days passed he made many new friends. People were anxious to speak to him, pet him, feed him.

His popularity was based on arithmetic: Borealis had fifty-five thousand people but only eleven dogs; many colonists were homesick for man's traditional best friend. Nixie did not know this, but he had great capacity for enjoying the good things in life without worrying about why.

Charlie, once he was over first the worry and then the delight of waking Nixie, found Venus interesting, less strange than he had expected. From time to time he was homesick. But not for long. Venus became home. He knew now what he wanted to be: a pioneer. When he was grown he would head south, deep into the unmapped jungle, carve out a plantation.

The jungle was the greatest single fact about Venus. The colony lived on the bountiful produce of the jungle, was surrounded by the jungle, unceasingly fought the jungle. The land on which Borealis sat, buildings and spaceport, had been torn away from the hungry jungle only by flaming it dead, stabilizing the muck with gel-forming chemicals, and poisoning the land thus claimed—then flaming, cutting, or poisoning any hardy survivor that pushed its green nose up through the captured soil.

The Vaughn family lived in a large apartment building which sat on newly captured land. Facing their front door, a mere hundred feet away across scorched and poisoned soil, a great shaggy dark-green wall loomed higher than the buffer space between. But the mindless jungle never gave up. The vines, attracted by light—their lives were spent competing for light energy—felt their way into the open space, tried to fill it. They grew with incredible speed. One day after breakfast Mr. Vaughn tried to go out his own front door, found his way hampered. While they had slept a vine had grown across the hundred-foot belt, supporting itself by tendrils against the dead soil, and had started up the front of the building.

The police patrols of the city were armed with flame guns and spent most of their time cutting back such hardy intruders. While they had power to enforce law, they rarely made an arrest. Borealis was a city almost free of crime; the humans were too busy fighting nature in the raw to require much attention from policemen.

But the jungle was friend as well as enemy. Its lusty life offered food for millions and billions of humans in place of the few thousands already on Venus. Under the jungle lay beds of peat, still farther down were thick coal seams representing millions of years of lush jungle growth, and pools of oil waiting to be tapped. Aerial survey by jet-copter in the volcanic regions promised uranium and thorium when man could cut his way through and get at it. The planet offered unlimited wealth. But it did not offer it to sissies. Charlie found that out when he went to a Scout meeting.

Getting back in the Scouts was fun, but even Scouting held surprises. Mr. Qu'an, Scoutmaster of Troop Four, welcomed him heartily. "Glad to have you, Chuck. It makes me feel good when a Scout among the new citizens comes forward and says he wants to pick up the Scouting trail again." He looked over the letter Charlie had brought with him. "A good record. Star Scout at your age. Keep at it and you'll be a Double Star—both Earth and Venus. That's all."

"You mean," Charlie said slowly, "that I'm not a Star Scout here?"

"Sure you are. You'll always be a Star Scout, just as a pilot is entitled to wear his comet after he's too old to herd a spaceship. But let's be practical. Ever been out in the jungle?"

"Not yet, sir. But I always was good at woodcraft."

"Mmm . . . Ever camped in the Florida Everglades?"

"Well, no, sir."

"No matter. I simply wanted to point out that while the Everglades are jungle, they are an open desert compared with the jungle here. And the coral snakes and water moccasins in the Everglades are harmless little pets alongside some of the things here. Have you seen our dragonflies yet?"

"Well, a dead one, at school."

"That's the best way to see them. When you see a live one, better see it first—if it's a female and ready to lay eggs."

"Uh, I know about them. If you fight them off, they won't sting."

"Which is why you had better see them first."

"Mr. Qu'an? Are they really that big?"

"I've seen thirty-six inch wing spreads. What I'm trying to say, Chuck, is that a lot of men have died learning the tricks of this jungle. If you are as smart as a Star Scout is supposed to be, you won't assume that you know what those poor fellows didn't. You'll wear that badge, but you'll class yourself in your mind as a tenderfoot all over again, and you won't hurry to promote yourself."

Charlie swallowed it. "Yes, sir. I'll try."

"Good. We use the buddy system. You take care of your buddy and he takes care of you. I'll team you with Hans Kuppenheimer. Hans is only a Second Class Scout, but don't let that fool you. He was born here and he lives in the bush, on his father's plantation. He's the best jungle rat in the troop."

Hans turned out to be easy to get along with. He was quiet, shorter but stockier than Charlie, neither unfriendly nor chummy; he simply accepted the assignment to look after Charlie.

Charlie took Nixie to Scout meeting and had a lot of explaining to do about Nixie's badge. "Nixie is a Scout, too. The fellows in my troop back Earthside voted him into the troop. They gave him that badge. So Nixie is a Scout."

Mr. Qu'an raised his eyebrows and smiled. One of the boys said, "A dog can't be a Scout."

Mr. Qu'an laughed, "Well, if a Martian—who is certainly not a human being—can hold an office in Scouting as some do, I can't see how Nixie is disqualified simply because he's a dog. Seems to me you'll have to show that he can't or won't do the things that a Tenderfoot Scout should do also."

"Uh . . ." Alf grinned knowingly. "Let's hear him explain the Scout Oath."

Mr. Qu'an turned to Charlie. "Can Nixie speak English?"

"What? Why, no, sir—but he understands it pretty well."

The Scoutmaster turned back to Alf. "Then the 'handicapped' rule applies, Alf—we never insist that a Scout do something he can't do. If you were crippled or blind, we would change the rules to fit you. Nixie can't talk words . . . so if you want to quiz him about the Scout Oath, you'll have to bark. That's fair, isn't it, boys?"

The shouts of approval didn't sit well with Alf. He answered sullenly, "Well, at least he has to follow the Scout Law—*every* Scout has to do *that.*"

The Scoutmaster grinned and turned to Charlie. "Is Nixie trustworthy?"

"Well . . . he doesn't get on furniture even if you're not watching him—and he won't touch food unless he's told to, and uh—"

"I think that's enough. Is he loyal?"

"He's loyal to *me.*"

"Good enough. Helpful?"

"There isn't a whole lot he can do, I guess. He used to fetch newspapers in—but he can't do that here. He'll fetch anything you ask him to, if he understands what it is."

"'Friendly,' well, obviously. 'Courteous'—we'll pass him on that, seeing what he has put up with tonight. Kind?"

"He'll let a baby try to pull his tail off, or step on his face, and never snap or growl. He did used to be kind of rough on cats, but I taught him better."

"Obedient?"

"Want to see?" Charlie put him through hand signal orders, ending with Nixie standing at attention and saluting. The applause made Nixie tremble but he held it until Charlie signalled, "At ease."

"Take note of that, Alf," Mr. Qu'an said drily, "next time I have to speak to you twice. 'Cheerful'—we can skip that; I'm sure his grin isn't faked. 'Thrifty,' well, we can hardly expect him to have a savings account."

"He buries bones."

"I suppose that's the canine equivalent. Brave?"

"*I* think he is. I've seen him tackle a dog three times his size and chase it out of our yard, too, back home, back Earthside."

"Clean?"

"Smell him. He had a bath just yesterday. And he's perfectly housebroken."

"All that is left is 'Reverent' and I don't intend to try to discuss that with him. I rule that Nixie is at least as reverent as the rapscallions I've heard fuming around here when they didn't think I was listening. How about it, boys? Does he pass?"

Nixie was voted into Troop Four in his tenderfoot status unanimously—Alfred Rheinhardt, Tenderfoot, abstaining.

After the meeting the troop treasurer buttonholed Charlie. "You want to pay your dues now, Chuck?"

"Oh, yeah, sure—I brought some money."

"Good." The other Scout accepted payment. "Here's your receipt."

"Just mark it in your book."

"Take it. No tickee, no washee. I'm nasty about it—that's why they made me treasurer. Now about Nixie— You pay? Or do I ask him?"

The other boy was not smiling and Charlie could not decide whether or not he was joking. He decided to play it just as soberly. "I settle for Nixie. You see, he doesn't have pockets." He dug down in his diminished resources, managed to piece out enough to pay the same amount for Nixie. "Here."

"Thanks."

Charlie was secretly delighted at the transaction, though it had cost him. Nixie was no longer an "Honorary Scout," he was a *Scout*—he kept the Law and his dues were paid.

Nixie's eligibility to take part in all troop doings was not questioned thereafter until the first hike. Mr. Qu'an looked troubled when Charlie showed up with him. "You had better take Nixie home."

Charlie was upset. "But, Mr. Qu'an—Nixie always goes on hikes."

"No doubt, back Earthside. Charlie, I'm not being arbitrary. I don't want your dog to get hurt."

"He won't get hurt! He's real smart."

The Scoutmaster groaned. Hans Kuppenheimer spoke up. "I think Nixie could come along, Mr. Qu'an."

The Scoutmaster looked at Hans doubtfully. "You'll have your hands full with Chuck, since it's his first time out."

Hans kept silent; Mr. Qu'an persisted, "You'd have to look out for them both, you know."

Hans still kept quiet. "Well," Mr. Qu'an said slowly. "Nixie is a member of the troop. If you can take care of him and Charlie, too, I'll let him come this time."

"Yes, sir."

The Scoutmaster turned away. Charlie whispered, "Thanks, Hans. That was swell." Hans said nothing.

In the two weeks that had preceded the hike, Nixie had adopted Hans as another member of Charlie's family. Subject always to his first loyalty, he accepted the other boy, took orders from him, even worked to hand signals, which he had never done with anyone but Charlie. At first he did it to please Charlie, but in time he was doing so because it was right and proper in his doggy mind, as long as it was all right with Charlie.

So when the troop set out on the hike Nixie was almost as much at home with Hans as with Charlie. But before they reached the jungle at the edge of town Hans said to Charlie, "Better have him heel."

"Why? He likes to run around and poke his nose into things. But he always stays in earshot. He'll come if he's called."

Hans scowled. "Suppose he can't? Maybe he goes into bush and doesn't come out. You want to lose him?"

It was a long speech for Hans. Charlie looked surprised, then called, "Nixie! Heel!"

The dog had been supervising the van, but he obeyed at once. Hans relaxed, muttered, "Better," and placed himself so that the dog trotted between them.

When the jungle loomed over them, pierced here by a road, Mr. Qu'an held up his arm and called out, "Halt! Check watches." He held up his wrist and waited; everybody else did the same.

Jock Quentin, an Explorer equipped with two-way radio, spoke into his microphone, then said, "Stand by—oh nine one one."

"Anybody fail to check?" continued Mr. Qu'an. "All you with polarizers, establish base line."

Hans took out an odd-looking pair of spectacles with adjustable double lenses and a sighting device which snapped out. "Try it."

"Okay." Charlie accepted them cautiously. "Why establish base line if we are going to stay on marked roads?"

Hans did not answer and Charlie felt foolish, remembering that the time to learn how not to get lost was before getting lost. He put on the polarizers and tried to locate the Sun. "Base Line" is the direction of the Sun at noon from Borealis and is the prime meridian of Venus; to find it, you first find the Sun, then figure where the Sun will be at noon.

That direction is south, of course—but *all* directions from Borealis are "south"; the city lies on the north pole. The difficulty of telling directions on Venus is very great. The stars and the Sun are always invisible, covered by a thick, unchanging blanket of cloud. Neither magnetic compasses nor gyro compasses are any use at the poles, nor is there moss on the north side of trees, nor any shadows to read—Venus is not only the land that time forgot; it is also the place of no directions.

The mapmakers were forced to make new directions. Toward the Sun at noon was "base"; back the other way was "reverse." The two directions between these were "right demi" and "left demi." Charlie had wondered why in the world, since they were going to use four directions anyway, they simply didn't call them north, south, east, and west?—until he saw a polar map at school which did have all the old familiar directions on it and with a grid of the new system laid over it. Then he understood. What use was "east" when it meant going counterclockwise in a tight little circle? How tight a circle and which direction was "counterclockwise"?—unless you knew ahead of time exactly where you were. Why, even the Sun wouldn't help, even if you could spot it with a polarizer, because the Sun could be north, south, east, or west at any time of day, depending on where you happened to be.

So Charlie buckled down and learned the new squared-off system.

He put on Hans' polarizers and looked around. No light leaked around the guards of the spectacles and the glass in them seemed opaque. He knew that he should be able to pick out the Sun, because he knew that the light from the sky, dispersed by clouds, was polarized—made to wiggle up-and-down, or sideways—and that these spectacles were intended to sort out the two kinds of light. But he could see nothing.

He turned slowly, blind behind the spectacles.

Hey, it was getting brighter! "I got it!"

"False sun," Hans announced dispassionately.

"You're faced just backwards," Mr. Qu'an's voice told him. "That's the reflection of the Sun. Never mind . . . but that's a mistake you cannot afford to make even once out in the bush. So keep trying."

Abashed, Charlie kept turning. There it was again! False sun? Or the Sun itself? How far had he turned?

He turned until he was dizzy, seeing brightness, then darkness, several times—and at last realized that one brightness was noticeably brighter. Finally he stopped. "I'm looking at the Sun," he announced firmly.

"Okay," Hans agreed. "Jigger with it. Fine it down."

Charlie fiddled with the screw settings of the spectacles while swinging his head back and forth like a radar until he had the light blanked out to the smallest gleam he could detect. "That's about it."

"Hold your head still. Uncover your right eye. Then coach me on."

Charlie did so, found Hans standing thirty feet away from him, holding his Scout staff upright. He himself was staring down the gunsight fastened to the spectacles. "Come right a couple of feet."

"Okay." Hans marked the line thus established with a piece of string. "My turn. Note your time." He took the spectacles and very quickly established a line of his own; it differed somewhat from Charlie's. "Now figure your hour angle."

The time was nine-thirty . . . and the sun moved fifteen degrees each hour . . . two and a half hours to noon; that's thirty-seven and a half degrees . . . and each minute space on his watch was six degrees—

Charlie was getting confused. He saw that Hans had simply laid his watch on the ground and was laying out base line; Hans' watch had a twenty-four hour face, he had pointed the hour at the Sun and the XII spot then pointed along base line.

No mental arithmetic, no monkeying around—"Gosh, I wish I had a watch like that!"

"Don't need it," Hans answered without looking up. "Your watch is okay. Make yourself a twenty-four hour dial out of cardboard."

"Hey, that would work, wouldn't it? I wish I had one now."

Hans fumbled in his duffel bag. "Uh, I made you one." He passed it over without looking up—a cardboard circle, laid out in twenty-four equal sectors.

Charlie was almost speechless. "Gee! Nixie, look at that! Say, Hans, I don't know how to thank you."

"Don't want you and Nixie getting lost," Hans answered gruffly.

Using it, Charlie aimed nine-thirty along his line and restretched his string to match noon on the cardboard dial. Base line, according to his sighting, differed a little from that found by Hans. In the meantime two patrol leaders were moving down the line of boys, checking with a protractor against another line stretched at right angles. Mr. Qu'an checked Charlie's layout himself. "About nine degrees off. Not bad for a first try."

"Uh, which way am I wrong?"

"Left demi. Look at Hans' layout—he's dead on, as usual." The Scoutmaster raised his voice. "All right, gang! Bush formation, route march. Flamers out, right and left. Rusty on point, Bill on drag—shake it up!"

The road cut straight through the jungle. The clearing had been flamed back wider than the road so that the jungle did not arch over it. The column kept to the middle where the ground was packed by trucks running to and from outlying plantations. The flamers on the flanks, both of them Explorers, walked close to the walls of green and occasionally used their flame guns to cut back some new encroachment, whereupon a scavenger gang would move out, toss the debris back into the living forest, then quickly rejoin the column. Keeping the roads open was everybody's business; the colony depended on roads even more than had ancient Rome.

It began to rain. Nobody paid any attention; rain was as normal as ice in Greenland. Rain was welcome; it washed off ever-present sweat and gave an illusion of coolness.

Presently the Point (Rusty Dunlop) stopped, sighted back at Drag, and shouted, "Right demi fifteen degrees!"

Drag answered, "Check!" Point continued around the slight bend. They had left Borealis headed "south" of course, but that particular south had been base two-thirty right demi, to which was now added fifteen degrees clockwise. It was Point's duty to set trail, keep lookout ahead, and announce his estimate of every change in direction. It was Drag's business to have eyes in the back of his head (since even here the jungle was not without power to strike), keep count of his paces, and keep record of all course changes and the number of paces between each—dead reckoning navigation marked down in a waterproof notebook strapped to his wrist. Drag was picked for his reliability and the evenness of his strides.

A dozen boys were imitating both Point and Drag, and recording everything, in preparation for Pathfinder merit badges. Each time the troop took a breather, they each again established base direction—later on each would attempt to map where he had been, using only his notes.

It was just practice, since the road was surveyed, but practice that could determine later whether they lived, or died miserably in the jungle. Mr. Qu'an had no intention of taking a troop which included tenderfoot town boys not yet twenty Venus years old into untracked jungle, but some of the older boys did go alone into virgin bush; some were already marking out land they would claim and try to conquer. On their ability to navigate by dead reckoning through cloud-covered swamp and bush and rain-forest, and return to where they had started, depended both their lives and their future livelihoods.

Mr. Qu'an dropped back, fell in beside Charlie. "Counting paces?"

"Yes, sir."

"Where's your notebook?"

"Uh, it was getting soggy in the rain, so I put it away. I'm keeping track in my head."

"That's a fine way to wind up at South Pole. Next time bring a waterproof one."

Charlie didn't answer. He had wanted one, as he had wanted a polarizing sighter and many other things. But the Vaughn family was still scratching for a toe hold; luxuries would have to wait.

Mr. Qu'an saw his expression. "If convenient, that is," he went on gently. "I don't want you to count paces now anyhow. You can't

learn everything at once and today you can't get lost. I want you to
soak up junglecraft. Hans, you two move to the flank. Give Charlie
a chance to see what we are passing through and lecture him about
it—and for goodness' sake try to say more than two words at a
time."

"Yes, sir."

"And—" The Scoutmaster was interrupted by a shout from the
boss of the scavenger gang. "Mr. Qu'an! Squint's got a screwbug!"

The man muttered something bitterly, started to run. The two
boys followed. The gang had been moving a large branch, freshly
flamed down. Now they were clustered around one boy, who was
gripping his forearm. Mr. Qu'an burst into the group, grabbed the
kid by that arm, examined it.

He shifted his grip so that the skin was drawn tight at one spot,
whipped out his knife, dug the point into skin and, as if cutting a
bad spot out of an apple, excised a chunk of flesh. Squint screwed
up his face and tears came into his eyes, but he did not cry out.

The scavenger boss had his first-aid kit open; as the Scoutmaster
handed his knife to a boy near him, the gang boss placed a shaker
bottle in Mr. Qu'an's hand. The Scoutmaster squirted powder into
the wound, accepted a pressure patch and plastered it over the cut.
Then he turned sternly to the gang boss. "Pete, why didn't you do
it?"

"Squint wanted you."

"So? Squint, you know better. Next time, let the boy closest to
you get it—or cut it out yourself. It could have gone in another
half inch while I was getting to you. And next time be more careful
where you put your hands!"

The column was halted. Point, looking back, saw Mr. Qu'an's
wave, lifted his own arm and brought it down smartly. They
moved on. Charlie said to Hans, "What's a screwbug?"

"Little thing. Bright red. Clings under leaves."

"What do they do to you?"

"Burrow in. Abscess. Don't get 'em out, maybe lose an arm."

"Oh." Charlie added, "Could they get on Nixie?"

"Doubt it. 'Cept maybe his nose. We'll check him every chance
we get."

They were on higher and drier ground now; the bush did not go up
so high, was not quite as dense. Charlie peered into it, trying to
sort out details, while Hans kept up what he probably felt was a
lively discourse—such as: "Poison," "Physic," or "Eat those."

"Eat what?" Charlie asked once. He had looked where Hans had pointed, saw nothing resembling fruit, berries, or nuts.

"Sugar stick." Hans thrust cautiously into the brush, pushed aside a Venus nettle with his staff, and broke off a foot of brown twig. "Nixie! Get out of there! Heel!"

Charlie accepted half of it, took a bite when he saw Hans do so. It chewed easily. Yes, it did have a sweetish taste. Not bad!

Hans spat out pulp. "Don't swallow the cud—give you trouble."

"I wouldn't've guessed you could eat this."

"Never go hungry in the bush."

"Hans? What do you do for water? If you haven't got any?"

"Huh? Water all around you."

"Yeah, but *good* water."

"All water is good water—if you clean it." Hans' eyes darted around. "Find a filter ball. Chop off top and bottom. Run water through. I'll spot one, show you."

Hans found one shortly, a gross and poisonous-looking fungus. But when he started in after it he was told gruffly by the flamer on that flank to get back from the edge and stay there. Hans shrugged. "Later."

The procession stopped in the road clearing, lunched from rucksacks. Nixie, the educated dog who held American Kennel Club degrees of Utility Dog and Tracking Dog, skillfully sampled every lunch. After a rest they went on. Occasionally the troop moved aside to let some plantation family, mounted on a high truck with great, low-pressure bolster wheels, roll past on the way to a Saturday night in town. The main road led past narrow tunnels cut into the bush, side roads to plantations. Late in the afternoon they passed one; Hans hooked a thumb at it. "Home."

"Yours?"

"Half a mile in."

A couple of miles beyond, the troop left the road, started across country. But this was high land, fairly dry and semi-open, no worse than most forest back Earthside. Hans merely saw to it that Nixie stayed close at heel and cautioned Charlie, "Mind where you step—and if anything drops on you, brush it off quick."

They broke out shortly into a clearing, made camp, and started supper. The clearing was man made, having been flamed down, although a new green carpet had formed underfoot. Four corners of a rectangle were established with Scout staffs, then Jock Quentin, the troop's radioman, clamped mirrors to three of them.

After much fiddling he had a system rigged whereby the beam of a powerful flashlight bounced around the rectangle and back into a long tube which housed a photocell; the camp was now surrounded by an invisible fence. Whenever the beam was broken an alarm would sound.

Meanwhile other Scouts were lashing staffs together, three to a unit, into long poles. Rags were sopped with a sickly-sweet fluid, fastened to the ends and the poles were erected, one at each corner of the camp. Charlie sniffed and made a face. "What's that stuff?"

"For dragonflies. They hate it."

"I don't blame 'em!"

"Haven't seen one lately. But if they were swarming, you'd rub it on your hide and be glad of the stink."

"Hans? Is it true that a dragonfly sting can paralyze a man?"

"No."

"Huh? But they say—"

"Takes three or four stings. One sting will just do for an arm or a leg—unless it gets you in the spine."

"Oh." Charlie could not see much improvement.

"I was stung once," Hans added.

"You *were?* But you're still alive."

"Paw fought it off and killed it. Couldn't use my left leg for a while."

"Boy! You must be lucky."

"Unlucky. But not as unlucky as it was. We ate it."

"You *ate* it?"

"Sure. Mighty tasty. They are."

Charlie felt queasy. "You eat *insects?*"

Hans thought about it. "You ever eat a lobster?"

"Sure. But that's different."

"It sure is. Seen pictures of lobsters. Disgusting."

This gourmets' discussion was broken up by the Scoutmaster. "Hans! How about scaring up some oil weed?"

"Okay." Hans headed for the bush. Charlie followed and Nixie trotted after. Hans stopped. "Make him stay behind. We can't gather weed and watch him, too."

"All right."

Nixie protested, since it was his duty to guard Charlie. But once he understood that Charlie meant it, he trotted back and supervised campmaking.

The boys went on. Charlie asked, "This clearing—is it the regular Scout camp?"

Hans looked surprised. "I guess so. Paw and I aren't going to set a crop until we flame it a few more times."

"You mean it's *yours?* Why didn't you say so?"

"You never asked me." Presently he added, "Some planters, they don't like Scouts tromping around, maybe hurting a crop."

Oil weed was a low plant, resembling bracken. They gathered it in silence, except once when Hans brushed something off Charlie's arm. "Want to watch that."

While they were loading, Hans made quite a long speech: "Dragonflies, they aren't much. You hear them coming, you can fight 'em off. Even with your bare hands, 'cause they can't sting till they light. Won't sting anyway, 'cept when they're swarming— then just the females, ready to lay eggs." He added thoughtfully, "They're stupid, they don't know the eggs won't hatch in a man."

"They won't?"

"No. Not that it does the man any good, he dies anyway. But they think they're stinging a big amphibian, thing called kteela."

"I've seen pictures of kteela."

"So? Wait'll you see one. But don't let it scare you. Kteela can't hurt you and they're more scared than you are—they just look fearsome." He brushed at his arm. "It's little things you got to watch."

Oil weed burned with a clear steady flame; the Scouts had a hot dinner and hot tea. No precautions were taken against fire; of the many hazards on Venus, forest fire was not one. The problem was to get anything to burn. After they had eaten, Mr. Qu'an examined one boy in first-aid and artificial respiration; listening, Charlie found that there was much he must learn and unlearn, conditions were different. Then Rusty Dunlop broke out a mouth organ and they all sang. Finally Mr. Qu'an yawned and said, "Sack in, Scouts. Hard day tomorrow. Pedro Patrol, first watch—then rotate down the list."

Charlie thought he would never get to sleep. The ground under his ground cloth was not hard, but he was not used to sleeping with lighted sky in his eyes and he was acutely aware of strange noises in the bush around them.

He was awakened by a shout. "Dragons! Heads up, gang! Watch yourself!"

Charlie reached down, grabbed Nixie to his chest, then looked around. Several boys were pointing. Charlie looked and thought at first that he was seeing a helicopter. Suddenly it came into perspective and he realized that it was an enormous insect . . . unbelievably huge, larger than had been seen on Earth since the Carboniferous period, a quarter of a billion years ago. It was coming toward camp. Something about it—its wings?—made a whining buzz.

It approached the tall poles with the smelly rags, hesitated, turned away. Mr. Qu'an looked thoughtfully after it, and glanced at Hans.

"They're not swarming," Hans said. "Anyhow, that was a male."

"No doubt you're right. Still—double guard the rest of the night." He lay down.

The troop started back the next morning—"morning" by clock; Charlie, awakening stiff and sleepy to the same dull-bright changeless sky, felt as if he had napped too long but not well during an afternoon. They headed back toward town. Once on the cleared road, Hans left Charlie and looked up the Scoutmaster. He was back shortly, grinning. "Stay over night with me? You and Nixie?"

"Gee! Is it okay? Your folks won't mind?"

"They like company. You can ride in with Paw in the morning."

"It would be swell, Hans, but how about my folks? Do you suppose Jock could raise them on the portable?"

"Everything's okay. Mr. Qu'an'll phone 'em, and you can call 'em from my place."

When the troop reached the side road for the Kuppenheimer plantation. Mr. Qu'an ordered the two boys to head straight for the house and no monkey business—check in at once with Hans' parents. They solemnly agreed and left the troop. The side road was a dark tunnel; Hans hurried them through it. A few hundred yards farther on they came out into cultivation; Hans slowed down. "You okay?"

"Sure."

"Let's check Nixie."

Nothing seemed to have attached itself to Nixie and his wagging tail gave no evidence of distress; they went on. Charlie looked around with interest. "What are you cropping?"

"Jungle bread on the right. Once it's established, you don't have to worry about it, mostly; it smothers everything else. Other side is mutated bananas, they take more care."

Shortly they came to the house, on a rise and with no growth around it—a typical Venus settler's house, long and low and built of spongy logs and native bamboo. Hans' mother greeted Charlie as if he were a neighbor boy, seen daily, and patted Nixie. "He minds me of a hund I had in Hamburg." Then she set out banana cake, with mugs of coffee that were mostly milk. Nixie had his cake on the floor.

There were several kids around, younger than Hans but looking just like him. Charlie did not get them straight, as they talked even less than Hans did and hung back from Nixie—unlike their mother, they found him utterly strange. But presently, seeing how the monster behaved with Hans and their mother, they timidly patted him. After that, Nixie was the center of attention while they continued shyly to ignore Charlie.

Hans bolted his cake, hurried out. He was back a few minutes later. "Maw, where's the flamer?"

"Paw is using it."

Hans looked blank. "Well—we don't have to have it. Come on. Chuck." He carried two hefty machetes, and he handed one of them to Charlie.

"Okay." Charlie stood up. "Thanks, Mrs. Kuppenheimer."

"Call me 'Maw' "

"Hurry up, Charlie."

"Right. Say—how about that call to my folks?"

"I forgot! Maw, would you phone Mrs. Vaughn? Tell her Chuck is staying all night?"

"Yes, surely. What's your frequency, Charlie?"

"Uh, you have to call city exchange and ask them to relay."

"Jawohl. You boys run along."

They headed off through the fields. Nixie was allowed to run, which he did with glee, returning every thirty seconds or so to see that his charges had not fainted or been kidnapped in his absence.

"Where are we going, Hans?"

Hans' eyes brightened. "To see the prettiest plantation land on Venus!"

"It's mighty pretty, no doubt about it."

"Not Paw's land. *My* plantation."

"Yours?"

"Will be mine. Paw posted an option bond. When I'm old enough, I'll prove it." He hurried on.

Charlie realized shortly that he had lost his bearings, even though they were in a cultivated grove. "Hold it, Hans. Can I borrow your polarizer?"

"What for?"

"I want to establish base, that's what. I'm all mixed up."

"Base is that direction." Hans answered, pointing with his machete. "My polarizer is at the house. We don't need it."

"I just thought I ought to keep straight."

"Can't get lost. I was born on this piece."

"But I wasn't."

"Just keep your eyes open. We head for that big tree." Charlie looked, saw several big trees. "Over a ridge. Pretty soon we come to my land. Okay?"

"I guess so."

"I'll show you the bush way to establish base—polarizers are for townies." Hans looked around, his quick eyes sorting details. "There!"

" 'There' what?"

"Compass bug. Don't scare him."

Charlie looked, discovered a small beetlelike creature with striped wing casings. Hans went on, "When they fly, they take off right toward the Sun. Every time. Then they level off and head home—they live in nests." Hans slapped the ground by it; the little creature took off as if jet propelled. "So the Sun is that way. What's the time?"

"Ten-thirty, almost."

"So which way is base?"

Charlie thought. "Must be about there."

"Isn't that the way I pointed? Now you find one. Always one around, if you look."

Charlie found one, frightened it, watched it take off in the same direction as the first. "You know, Hans," he said slowly, "bees do something like that—fly by polarized light, I mean. That's the way they find their hives on cloudy days. I read about it."

"Bees? Those Earth bugs that make sugar?"

"Yes. But they aren't bugs."

"I'll never see one," Hans answered indifferently. "Let's go."

Presently they left cultivation, started into bush. Hans required Nixie to heel. Even though they were going up hill, the bush got thicker, became dense jungle. Hans led the way, occasionally chopping an obstacle. At last he stopped. "Trash!" he said bitterly.

"Trouble?"

"This is why I wanted the flamer. This bit grows pretty solid."

"Can't we chop it?"

"Take all day with a bush knife. Needs heat. Going to have to poison this whole stretch 'fore I get a road through, Paw's place to mine."

"What do we do?"

"Go around." Hans headed left. Charlie could see no track, decided that Hans must know his way by the contour of the ground. About half an hour later Hans paused and whispered, "Keep quiet. Nixie, too."

"What for?" Charlie whispered back.

"Good chance you'll see kteela, if we don't scare them." He went noiselessly ahead, with Charlie and the dog on his heels. He stopped. "There."

Charlie oozed forward, looking over Hans' shoulder—found that he was looking down at a stream. He heard a splash on his right, turned his head just in time to see spreading ripples. "Did you see him?" Hans asked in a normal voice.

"No."

"Shucks, he was right there. A big one. Their houses are just downstream. They often fish along here. Have to keep your eyes open, Chuck." Hans looked thoughtful. "Kteela are people."

"Huh?"

"They're people. Paw thinks so. If we could just get acquainted with them— But they're timid. Come on—cross here." Hans went down the bank, sat on muddy sand by running water and started taking his shoes off. "Mind where you sit."

Charlie did the same. Bare-footed and bare-legged, Hans picked up Nixie. "I'll lead. It's shallow here. Keep moving and don't stumble."

The water was warm and the bottom felt mucky; Charlie was glad when they reached the far side. "Get the leeches off," Hans commanded as he put Nixie down. Charlie looked down at his legs, was amazed to find half a dozen purple blobs, big as hens' eggs, clinging to him. Hans cleaned his own legs, helped Charlie make sure that he was free of parasites. "Run your fingers between your toes. Try to get the sand fleas off as you put your boots on, too—though they don't really matter."

"Anything else in that water?" Charlie asked, much subdued.

"Oh, glass fish can bite a chunk out of you, but they aren't poisonous. Kteela keep this stream clean. Let's go."

* * *

They went up the far bank, reached a stretch that was higher and fairly dry. Charlie thought they were going upstream; he was not sure. Hans stopped suddenly. "Dragonfly. Hear it?"

Charlie listened, heard the high, motor-like hum he had heard the night before. "There it is," Hans said quickly. "Hang onto Nixie and be ready to beat it off. I'm going to lure it."

Charlie felt that attracting its attention was in a class with teasing a rattlesnake, but Hans was already waving his arms. The fly hesitated, veered, headed straight for him. Charlie felt a moment of dreadful anticipation—then saw Hans take one swipe with his machete. The humming stopped; the thing fluttered to the ground.

Hans was grinning. The dragonfly jerked in reflex, but it was dead, the head neatly chopped off. "Didn't waste a bit."

"Huh?"

"That's lunch. Cut some of that oil weed behind you." Hans squatted down. In three quick slices he cut off the stinger and the wings; what was left was the size of a medium lobster. Using the chrome-sharp machete as delicately as a surgeon's knife, he split the underside of the exoskeleton, gently and neatly stripped out the gut. He started to throw it away, then paused and stared at it.

Charlie had been watching in uneasy fascination. "Trouble?"

"Egg sac is full. They're going to swarm."

"That's bad, isn't it?"

"Some. They swarm every three, four years." Hans frowned. "We better skip seeing my land. Got to tell Paw, keep the kids in."

"Okay, let's get started."

"Eat first. Ten minutes won't matter—not really swarming yet, else this one wouldn't have been alone."

Charlie started to say that he was not interested in lunch—not this lunch—but Hans was already starting a fire. What was left in the exoskeleton was clean milky-white meat, lean flying muscle. Hans cut out chunks, toasted them over the fire, salted them from a pocket shaker. "Have some."

"Uh, I'm not hungry."

"Crazy in the head, too. Here, Nixie!" Nixie had been waiting politely but with his nose quivering. He snapped the tidbit out of the air, gulped it down, waited still more eagerly while Hans ate the next bit.

It did smell good, and it looked good, when Charlie kept his mind off the source. His mouth began to water. Hans looked up. "Change your mind?"

"Oh—let me taste just a bite."

It reminded Charlie of crab meat. A few minutes later the exoskeleton was stripped too clean to interest even Nixie. Charlie stood up, burped gently, and said, "Ready?"

"Yeah." Hans frowned. "One thing I do want to show you—there's a way back that may be quicker than the way we came."

"What is it?"

Hans did not answer but headed off in a new direction. Charlie wondered how he had picked it out without a compass bug. Several minutes later they were headed down hill. Hans stopped. "Hear it?"

Charlie listened, seemed to pick out a soft roar under the ever-present multiple-voice of the jungle. "It's not a dragonfly?"

"Course not. You've got ears."

"Then what is it?" Hans simply led on. Presently they broke out into a clearing, or rather a room, for the jungle arched in overhead. It held a delightful, surprising waterfall; the muted roar was its song.

"Isn't that swell?"

"You bet," Charlie agreed. "Haven't seen anything so pretty in years."

"Yeah, it's pretty. That's not the point. My land is just above. Put a water wheel here, have my own power." Hans led his two friends down to it, began to talk excitedly about his plans. The roar was so great that he had to shout.

So neither one of them heard it coming. Nixie began to bark; Charlie turned his head and saw it at the last moment. "Hans! Dragon!"

Too late—it nailed Hans between his shoulderblades. It laid no eggs; Charlie killed it, crushed it with his bare hands. But Hans had already been stung.

Charlie wiped his trembling hands on his pants and looked down at his chum. Hans had collapsed even as Charlie had killed the thing; he lay crumpled on the ground. Charlie bent over him. "Hans! Hans, answer me!"

Hans' eyelids fluttered. "Get Paw."

"Hans, can you stand up?"

"Sorry—Chuck"—then very feebly, "My fault." His eyes stayed open but Charlie could get no more out of him.

Even in his distress Charlie's training stayed with him. He could not find Hans' pulse, so he listened for his heart, was rewarded and greatly relieved by a strong, steady flub-a-*dub!* . . . flub-a-*dub!*

Hans looked ghastly, but apparently it was true that they just paralyzed; they didn't kill.

But what to do?

Hans had said to get his father. Sure—but how? Could he find his way back to the house? Even if he could, could he lead them here? No, surely Mr. Kuppenheimer would know where the waterfall was that Hans planned to harness; the problem was just to find the house. Now let's see; back up that bank, then downstream through the bush. Was it actually downstream? Was this even the same stream they had forded? It must be; they hadn't crossed any watershed. Or had they?

Well, it had better be the same stream, else he was lost beyond hope. Back through the bush then, and across the stream—

How was he going to cut back in and hit the stream at the shallow place? That bush all looked pretty much alike.

Maybe it would be better to go downstream along the bank until he hit it. Then cross, find a compass bug, and strike off in the general direction of the plantation until he came to cultivated fields. He remembered which way base was when they had left cultivation; that would keep him straight.

Or would it? They had headed first for that place that couldn't be passed without a flamer—but where had they gone then? How many turns? Which way were they heading when he had not quite seen a kteela?

Well, he would just have to try. Surely he couldn't miss anything as big as a plantation. He looked down at Hans and decided that he couldn't leave him there. Nixie had been sniffing at Hans' still body; now he began to whine steadily. "Shut up, you!" Charlie snapped. "I've got too much trouble without that."

Nixie shut up. Charlie knelt and started wrestling the limp body into a fireman's carry, while wondering miserably whether or not Hans had told his mother where they were going. Or what good it would do if he had, since they weren't where Hans had intended to go.

"Heel, Nixie."

An indefinitely long time later Charlie lowered Hans to the ground in a fairly open place. It had taken only a short struggle to convince him that he could not carry Hans along the bank of the stream. A man might have been able to carve his way with a machete, but, while Charlie had two machetes, he could not swing a knife and carry Hans at the same time. He abandoned one by the waterfall, thinking that Hans could find it there another day; he was tempted to abandon both, as the one on his belt was heavy and got in his way, but he decided that he might have to have it; they had done plenty of chopping in getting there.

So he set out again, this time trying to retrace their steps through the bush, hoping to spot places they had chopped in coming there. But he never spotted such a sign; the living green maze had swallowed such puny marks.

After a long time he decided to go back to the familiar waterfall—he would stay there, nurse Hans, filter water for them all, and wait. Surely Mr. Kuppenheimer would eventually think of the waterfall.

Maybe he could keep an oil weed fire going, throw water on it and make some sort of a smoke signal.

So he turned back . . . and could not find the waterfall. Not even the stream.

He walked through something. He couldn't see it; there were branches in his face. But it clung to his legs like red-hot wires; he stumbled and almost dropped Hans in getting free of it. Then his leg went on hurting. The fiery burning dropped off a little but a numbness crept up his right leg.

He was glad indeed to put Hans on the ground at the first fairly open place he came to. He sat down and rubbed his leg, then checked Hans—still breathing, heart still beating . . . but out like a light.

Nixie sniffed Hans again, then looked up and whined inquiringly. "I can't help it," Charlie said to him. "He's a mess. I'm a mess. You're a mess, too."

Nixie barked.

"I will, I will . . . just as soon as I can move. Don't hurry me. How would *you* like to carry him for a while?"

Charlie continued to rub his leg. The pain was going away but the numbness was getting worse. At last he said to Nixie, "I guess we ought to try it, pal. Wait a second while I look for a compass bug—the way I figure it, we came mostly base, so I guess we ought to try to head reverse." He glanced at his wrist to see what time it was.

His watch had stopped.

But it *couldn't* stop—it was self winding.

Nevertheless it had. Perhaps he had banged it in the bush.

No matter, it had stopped. He looked for Hans' watch, thinking that it was easier to use as a compass dial than his own anyhow.

Hans was not wearing his watch, nor was it in any of his pockets. Whether he had left it at the house or whether it had fallen off in the bush did not matter; they had no watch between them. No use looking for a compass bug—for Charlie had no idea at all what time it might be. It seemed to him that he had been carrying Hans, fighting this dreary bush, for a week.

He almost admitted defeat at that moment. But he rallied, telling himself that if he went downhill he was bound to find the stream. Then he would find the ford or the waterfall, one or the other. He hauled himself into position to lift Hans, favoring his right leg.

He need not have bothered; his right leg would not support him.

The "pins and needles" in it were almost unbearable, as if he had sat much too long in a cramped position. But they would not go away as they always had in the past; nothing he could do would make that leg obey orders. He lowered his head against Hans and bawled.

He became aware that Nixie was licking his face and whining. He stopped his useless blubbering and raised his head. "It's all right, fellow. Don't you worry."

But it was not all right. While Charlie was no jungle rat, he did know that search parties could comb the area for weeks and not find them, could pass within feet of this spot and never see them. Possibly no human being had ever been where they were now; possibly no human would reach this spot in many years to come.

If he didn't use his head now, they would never get out.

Nixie sat patiently, watching him, trusting him.

"Nixie, this is up to you now, boy. You understand me?"

Nixie whined.

"Go back to the house. Fetch! Fetch Maw. Fetch anybody. Right now! Go back to the house."

Nixie barked.

"Don't argue with me. You've got to do it. Go home! Go back and fetch somebody."

Nixie looked dubious, trotted a few steps in the direction in which they had come, stopped and looked around inquiringly. "That's right! Keep going! Go back to the house! Fetch somebody! *Go!*"

Nixie looked sharply at him, then trotted away in a businesslike fashion.

Sometime later Charlie raised his head and shook it. Gosh! he must have gone to sleep . . . couldn't do that . . . what if another dragonfly came along . . . have to stay awake. Was Hans all right? Have to pick him up and get out of here . . . where was Nixie? "Nixie!"

No answer. That was the last straw. But he would have to get moving anyhow—

His leg wouldn't work . . . felt funny. "Nixie! *Nixie!*"

Mrs. Kuppenheimer heard the scratching and whining at the door, wiped her hands on her apron and went to it. When she saw what was there she threw her hands up. "Liebchen! What happened to you?" She knelt swiftly, picked up the dog and put him on her clean table, bent over him, talking to him and picking leeches from him, wiping blood away. "Schrecklich!"

"What happened to him, Mama?"

"I don't know." She went on working. But Nixie jumped out of her arms, charged straight for the closed door, tried to crash his way out—then leaped and clawed at it, howling.

Mrs. Kuppenheimer gathered him up and held his struggling body against her breast. "Gerta! Get Paw!"

"What's the matter with him, Mama?"

"Something dreadful has happened. *Run!*"

The Borealis council hall was filled with Scouts and older people. Hans and Charlie were seated in a front row, with Nixie on a chair between them. Hans had crutches across one knee; Charlie had a cane. Mr. Qu'an came down the aisle, saw them, and sat down as Charlie moved Nixie over to share his seat. The Scoutmaster said to Hans. "I thought you were through with crutches?"

"Maw made me bring 'em."

"I—" Mr. Qu'an stopped. An older man had just taken the head place at a table in the front of the hall at which were seated several other men.

"Quiet, please." The man waited. "This Court of Honor is met in special session for awards. It is our first duty tonight—and our proud honor—to award a lifesaving medal. Will Tenderfoot Scout Nixie Vaughn please come forward?"

"Now, Nixie!" Charlie whispered.

Nixie jumped off the chair, trotted forward, sat at attention and saluted, trembling.

DESTINATION MOON

Today, with space full of ships, colonies on the inner planets, and Earth's Moon so close that pilots on the Luna run sleep home nights, it is hard to imagine when "flying to the Moon" was a figure of speech for the impossible, when men who thought it could be done were visionaries, crackpots.
It is hard to realize the opposition they faced, to understand why they persisted, what they thought—
Farquharson, *History of Transportation,* III: 414

I

The Mojave Desert was gray with first morning light, but at the construction site lights were still burning in the office of the technical director. The office was quiet, save for petulant burbling of a pot of coffee.

Three men were present—the director himself, Doctor Robert Corley, Lincoln-tall and lean, Rear Admiral "Red" Bowles, regular navy retired, and Jim Barnes, head of Barnes Aircraft, Barnes Tool Works, other enterprises.

All three needed shaves; Barnes badly needed a haircut as well. Barnes was seated at Corley's desk; Bowles sprawled on a couch, apparently asleep and looking like a fat, red-headed baby; Doctor Corley paced the room, following a well worn pattern.

He stopped, and stared out the window. A thousand yards away on the floor of the desert a great ship, pointed and sleek, thrust up into the sky, ready to punch out through Earth's thick atmosphere.

Wearily he turned away and picked up a letter from the desk; it read:

Reaction Associates, Inc.
Mojave, California.
Gentlemen:
  Your request to test the engine of your atomic-powered rocket ship at the site of its construction is regretfully denied.
  Although it is conceded that no real danger of atomic explosion exists, a belief in such danger does exist in the public mind. It is the policy of the Commission—Corley skipped down to the last paragraph:—*therefore, test is authorized at the Special Weapons Testing Center, South Pacific. Arrangements may be*—

He stopped and shoved the letter at Barnes. "If we've got to test at Eniwetok, we've got to find the money to do it."

Barnes' voice showed exasperation. "Doc, I've told you the syndicate won't put up another dime; there is no other money to be found."

"Confound it—we should have government money!"

Barnes grunted. "Tell that to Congress."

Without opening his eyes Bowles commented, "The United States is going to stall around and let Russia get to the Moon first—with hydrogen bombs. That's what you call 'policy.'"

Corley chewed his lip. "It's got to be *now.*"

"I know it." Barnes got up and went to the window. The rising sun caught a highlight on the polished skin of the great ship. "It's got to be now," he repeated softly.

He turned and said, "Doc, when is the next favorable time to leave?"

"When we planned on it—next month."

"No, I mean this month."

Corley glanced at the wall calendar, dug into a bookcase for a well-thumbed volume, did a quick estimate. "Tomorrow morning —around four o'clock."

"That's it, then. We blast off tomorrow morning."

Admiral Bowles sat up with a jerk. "Blast off in an untested ship? Jim, you're crazy!"

"Probably. But now is the time—*now.* If we wait even a month, we will be tangled in some new snafu. That ship is ready, except for testing the power plant. So we'll skip the test!"

"But we haven't even selected a crew."

Barnes grinned. *"We're the crew!"*

Neither Corley nor Bowles answered. Barnes went on, "Why not? The takeoff is automatic. Sure, we agreed that we should have young men, fast reflexes, and all that malarkey—and every damned one of us has been trying to figure out a reason why he should be included. You, Red, you sneaked off to Moffeatt Field and took a pilot's physical. Flunked it, too. Don't lie to me; I *know.* And you, Doc, you've been hinting that you ought to nurse the power plant yourself—you've been working on your wife, too."

"Eh?"

"She wanted me to say that the syndicate would object to your going. Don't worry; I didn't agree."

Corley looked at him levelly. "I've always intended to go. She knows that."

"That's my boy! Red?"

Bowles heaved himself to his feet. "Shucks, Jim, I didn't bust that physical much—just overweight."

"You're in. I don't want an eager young beaver as co-pilot anyhow."

" 'Co-pilot?' "

"Want to rassle me for skipper? Red, I've meant to gun this crate myself ever since the day—Lordy, four years ago!—when you brought Doc to see me with a satchelful of blueprints." He drew a breath and looked around exultantly.

Bowles said, "Let's see. You for pilot; I'm co-; Doc is chief. That leaves nobody but the radarman. You can't possibly train a man in the electronics of that ship by tomorrow morning."

Barnes shrugged. "Hobson's choice—it has to be Ward." He named the chief electronics engineer of the project.

Bowles turned to Corley. "Does Ward hanker to go?"

Corley looked thoughtful. "I'm sure he does. We haven't discussed it." He reached for the phone. "I'll call his quarters."

Barnes stuck a hand in the way. "Not so fast. Once the word got out, the Commission has twenty-four hours in which to stop us."

Bowles glanced at his watch. "Twenty-one hours."

"Long enough, anyhow."

Corley frowned. "We can't keep it secret. We've got to load that ship. I've got to reach Dr. Hastings and get our ballistic calculated."

"One thing at a time." Barnes paused, frowning.

"Here's the plan: we'll tell everybody that this is just a dress rehearsal, but complete in all details, road blocks, rations, reporters, check-off lists, the works. Doc, you get the power plant ready. Red, you're in charge of loading. Me, I'm going into Mojave and phone Hastings. Then I'll phone the University and arrange for the big computer."

"Why drive twenty miles?" Corley protested. "Call from here."

"Because these wires are probably tapped—and I don't mean the F.B.I.! Aside from us three and Ward, Hastings is the one man who *must* know the truth—when he figures that ballistic, he's got to know it matters."

Barnes reached for his hat. "Doc, you can call Ward now—here I go."

"Wait!" said Bowles. "Jim, you're going off half cocked. You can at least find out from here where Hastings is. You may have to fly down to Palomar and get him."

Barnes snapped his fingers. "I *am* half cocked, Red. I forgot the most important item—the reason why I can't use my plane myself; I need it for the Resident Inspector." He referred to the project representative of the Atomic Energy Commission.

"Holmes? Why does *he* need your plane?"

"To get lost in. I'm going to persuade Ned Holmes to go to Washington and make one last plea for us to be allowed to test our engine here. He'll do it; turning us down wasn't his idea. Our boy Andy will fly him in my plane—and Andy will be forced down in the desert, forty miles from a phone. Very sad."

Corley grudged a smile. "Sounds like kidnapping."

Barnes looked innocent.

"Of course Holmes will put the Commission's seal on the power pile before he leaves."

"And we'll break it. Any more objections? If not, let's get Andy, Holmes, and Ward, in that order."

Admiral Bowles whistled. "Doc," he said, "that engine of yours had better work, or we will spend the rest of our lives in jail. Well, let's get busy."

II

The morning was well worn by the time Jim Barnes drove back to the construction site. The company guard at the pass gate waved him through; he stopped nevertheless. "Howdy, Joe."

"Morning, Mr. Barnes."

"I see the gate is open. Any orders from the front office?"

"About the gate? No. Somebody called and said today was dress rehearsal for the Big Boy." The guard hooked a thumb toward the ship, two miles away.

"That's right. Now listen; this dress rehearsal must be letter perfect. Keep that gate locked. Clear with me, or Admiral Bowles, or Doctor Corley himself before unlocking it."

"Gotcha, Mr. Barnes."

"Just remember that there are people who would do anything to keep that ship over there from leaving the ground—and they don't necessarily have foreign accents."

"Don't worry, Mr. Barnes."

But he did worry; corking up the gate still left fourteen miles of unguarded fence.

Oh, well—it was a risk that must be accepted. He drove on past the living quarters, through the circle of shops. The area swarmed with people, on foot, in trucks, in jeeps. Trucks were lined up at the entrance to the bull pen surrounding the ship itself. Barnes pulled up at the administration building.

In Corley's office he found Bowles, Corley himself—and Corley's wife. Corley looked harassed; Mrs. Corley was quite evidently angry. "Greetings, folks," he said. "Am I butting in?"

Corley looked up. "Come in, Jim."

Barnes bowed to Mrs. Corley. "How do you do, ma'am?"

She glared at him. "You! You're responsible for this!"

"Me, Mrs. Corley? For what?"

"You know very well 'what'! Oh you . . . you . . ." She caught her breath, then gave vent to one explosive word: "Men!" She slammed out of the room.

When the door had closed behind her, Barnes let his eyebrows seek their natural level. "I see she knows. You shouldn't have told her, not yet, Doc."

"Confound it, Jim. I didn't expect her to kick up a fuss."

Bowles faced around in his chair. "Don't be a fool, Jim. Doc's wife *had* to know—wives aren't hired hands."

"Sorry. The damage is done. Doc, have you put any check on phone calls?"

"Why, no."

"Do it. Wait, I'll do it." He stepped to the door. "Countess, call our switch board. Tell Gertie to switch all outgoing calls to you. You tell 'em firmly that outside lines are all in use, find out who it is, why they want to call, and whom—then tell the Director, Admiral Bowles, or me. Same for incoming calls."

He closed the door and turned back to Bowles.

"Your wife knows?"

"Of course."

"Trouble?"

"No. Navy wives get used to such things, Jim."

"I suppose so. Well, I got Hastings squared away. He says that he will be here with the tape not later than two in the morning. I've got a plane standing by for him."

Corley frowned. "That's cutting it fine. We ought to have more time to set up the autopilot."

"He says he can't promise it sooner. How about things here?"

"Loading is coming all right," answered Bowles, "provided the trucks with the oxygen aren't late."

"You should have flown it in."

"Quit jittering. The trucks are probably in Cajon Pass this minute."

"Okay, okay. Power plant, Doc?"

"I haven't broken Ned Holmes' seal on the atomic pile yet. The water tanks are filling, but they've just started."

He was interrupted by the telephone at his elbow. "Yes?"

His secretary's voice sounded in the room. "Your wife wants to call long distance, Doctor. I'm stalling her. Are you in?"

"Put her on," he said wearily. Mrs. Corley's words could not be heard, but her angry tones came through. Corley answered, "No, dear . . . That's right, dear. I'm sorry but that's how it is . . . no, I don't know when the lines will be free; we're holding them for calls placed to the east coast . . . no, you can't have the car; I'm using it. I—" He looked surprised and replaced the instrument. "She hung up on me."

"See what I mean?" said Barnes.

"Jim, you're a fool," Bowles answered.

"No, I'm a bachelor. Why? Because I can't stand the favorite sport of all women."

"Which is?"

"Trying to geld stallions. Let's get on with the job."

"Right," agreed Corley and flipped a key on his Teletalk. "Helen, call the electronics shop and tell Mr. Ward that I want to see him."

"Haven't you broken the news to him?" demanded Barnes.

"Ward? Of course."

"How did he take it?"

"Well enough. Ward is high strung. At first he insisted there wasn't time to get all the electronic gear ready."

"But he's in?"

"He's in." Corley stood up. "I've got to get back into the ship."

"Me, too," Bowles agreed.

Barnes followed them out. As they passed the desk of Corley's secretary she was saying, "One moment, puh*lease*—I'm ringing him." She looked up and pointed to Corley.

Corley hesitated. "Uh, uh," said Barnes, "if you let 'em tie you up on the phone, we'll never take off. I'm elected. Go on, you two. Get the buggy ready to go."

"Okay." Corley added to his secretary, "Got Mr. Ward yet?"

"Not in the electronics shop. I'm chasing him."

"I want him right away."

Barnes went back inside and spent an hour handling a log jam on the telephone. Personal calls he simply stalled on the excuse that the lines were needed for priority long distance calls. If a call was concerned with getting the ship ready to go, he handled it himself or monitored it. As best he could he kept the construction site an island, cut off from the world.

He straightened out a matter with the chief metallurgist, gave the accounting office an okay on some overtime of the week before, assured Associated Press that the "dress rehearsal" was worth full coverage, and gleefully extended an invitation to the Los Angeles Associated Civic Clubs to go through the ship— next week.

That done, he took Corley's dictaphone and began a memorandum to his business manager on how to close the project in case (a) the trip was successful, (b) the ship crashed. He planned to mark it to be transcribed the following day.

A call from Dr. Corley interrupted him. "Jim? I can't find Ward."

"Tried the men's wash rooms?"

"No—but I will."

"He can't be far away. Anything wrong in his department?"

"No, but I need him."

"Well, maybe he's finished his tests and gone to his quarters to catch some sleep."

"There's no answer from his quarters."

"Phone could be off the hook. I'll send someone to dig him out."

"Do that."

While he was arranging this, Herbert Styles, public relations chief for the project, came in. The press agent slumped down in a chair and looked mournful.

"Howdy, Herb."

"Howdy. Say, Mr. Barnes, let's you and me go back to Barnes Aircraft and quit this crazy dump."

"What's biting you, Herb?"

"Well, maybe you can make some sense out of what's going on. They tell me to get everybody in here by three A.M.—A.P., U.P., INS, radio chains, television trucks, and stuff. Then you lock the joint up like a schoolhouse on Sunday. And all this for a practice drill, a dry run. Who's crazy? Me or you?"

Barnes had known Styles a long time. "It's not a drill, Herb."

"Of course not." Styles ground out a cigarette. "Now—how do we play it?"

"Herb, I'm in a squeeze. We're going to take off—at three fifty-three tomorrow morning. If word gets out before then, they'll find some way to stop us."

"Who's 'they'? And why?"

"The Atomic Energy Commission for one—for jumping off with an untested power-pile ship."

Styles whistled. "Bucking the Commission, eh? Oh, brother! But why not test it?"

Barnes explained, concluding with, "—so we can't test it. I'm busted, Herb."

"Isn't everybody?"

"That isn't all. Call it a hunch, or anything you like. If we don't take off now, we never will—even if I had the dinero to test in the South Pacific. We've had more than our share of bad luck on this project—and I don't believe in luck."

"Meaning?"

"There are people who want this enterprise to fail. Some are crackpots; some are jealous. Others—"

"Others," Styles finished for him, "don't like the United States getting space travel first any better than they liked us getting the atom bomb first."

"Check."

"So what do you want to guard against? A time bomb in the ship? Sabotage of the controls? Or the Federal marshal with a squad of soldiers to back him up?"

"I don't know!"

Styles stared at nothing.

"Boss—"

"Yeh?"

"Item: pretty soon you've got to admit publicly that it's a real takeoff, for you've got to evacuate this valley. The sheriff and state police won't play games just for a drill."

"But—"

"Item: by now it is after office hours on the east coast. You're fairly safe from the Commission until morning. Item: any sabotage will be done on the spur of the moment, provided it isn't already built into the ship."

"Too late to worry about anything built into the ship."

"Just the same, if I were you, I would go over her with a toothpick. Any last minute stuff will be done with a wrench, behind a control panel or such—what they used to call 'target of opportunity.'"

"Hard to stop."

"Not too hard. There isn't anything that can be done to that ship down at its base, right? Well, if my neck depended on that heap, I wouldn't let anybody up inside it from now on, except those going along. Not *anybody,* not even if he carried a certificate of Simon-pure one-hundred-percentism from the D.A.R. I'd watch what went in and I'd stow things with my own little patty-paws."

Barnes chewed his lip. "You're right. Herb—you just bought yourself a job."

"Such as?"

"Take over here." He explained what he had been doing. "As for the press, don't tip them off until you have to make arrangements for the road blocks and evacuation—maybe you can keep things wrapped up until around midnight. I'm going up into that ship and—"

The telephone jangled; he picked it up. "Yes?"

It was Bowles.

"Jim—come to the electronics shop."

"Trouble?"

"Plenty. Ward has run out on us."

"Oh, oh! I'll be right over." He slammed the phone and said, "Take over, Herb!"

"Wilco!"

* * *

Outside, he jumped in his car and swung around the circle to the electronics shops. He found Bowles and Corley in Ward's office. With them was Emmanuel Traub, Ward's first assistant.

"What happened?"

Corley answered, "Ward is in the hospital—acute appendicitis."

Bowles snorted. "Acute funk!"

"That's not fair! Ward wouldn't run out on me."

Barnes cut in. "It doesn't matter either way. The question is: what do we do now?"

Corley looked sick. "We can't take off."

"Stow that!" Barnes turned to Bowles. "Red, can you handle the electronics?"

"Hardly! I can turn the knobs on an ordinary two-way—but that ship is *all* electronics."

"I'm in the same fix—Doc, *you* could. Or couldn't you?"

"Uh, maybe—but I can't handle radar and power plant both."

"You could teach me to handle power plant and Red could pilot."

"*Huh?* I can't make a nucleonics technician out of you in something like a matter of hours."

Barnes seemed to feel the world pressing in on him. He shook off the feeling and turned to Traub. "Mannie, you installed a lot of the electronic gear, didn't you?"

"Me? I installed all of it. Mr. Ward didn't like to go up the Gantry crane. He is a nervous type guy."

Barnes looked at Corley. "Well?"

Corley fidgeted. "I don't know."

Bowles said suddenly, "Traub, where did you go to college?"

Traub looked hurt. "I got no fancy degree but I carry a civil service classification of senior electronics engineer—a P-5. I did three years in the Raytheon labs. I had my ham license since I was fifteen, and I was a master sergeant in the Signal Corps. If it makes with electrons, I savvy it."

Barnes said mildly, "The Admiral didn't mean any harm, Mannie. What do you weigh?"

Traub shifted his eyes from one to the other. "Mr. Barnes—this is no rehearsal? This is it?"

"This is it, Mannie. We take off—" He glanced at his watch. "—in thirteen hours."

Traub was breathing hard. "You gentlemen are asking me to go to the Moon with you? Tonight?"

Before Barnes could answer, Bowles put in:

"That's it, Mannie."

Traub swallowed hard. "Yes," he said.

"Yes?" Barnes echoed.

"I'll go."

Corley said hastily, "Traub, we don't want to rush you."

"Director, take a look at my job application. I put down 'Willing to travel.'"

III

The great ship was ringed with floodlights spaced inside the bull pen. It was still framed by the skeleton arch of the Gantry crane, but the temporary anti-radiation shield which had surrounded its lower part down to the jets was gone; instead there were posted the trefoil signs used to warn of radioactivity—although the level of radiation had not yet become dangerously high.

But the power pile was unsealed and the ship was ready to go. Thirteen-fifteenths of its mass was water, ready to be flashed into incandescent steam by the atomic pile, to be thrown away at thirty thousand feet per second.

High up in the ship was the control room and adjacent air lock. Below the air lock the permanent anti-radiation shield ran across the ship, separating the pressurized crew space from the tanks, the pumps, the pile itself, and auxiliary machinery. Above the control room, the nose of the craft was unpressurized cargo space.

At its base triangular airfoils spread out like oversize fins—fins they would be as the ship blasted away; glider wings they would become when the ship returned to Earth with her tanks empty.

Jim Barnes was at the foot of the Gantry crane, giving last-minute orders. A telephone had been strung out to the crane; it rang and he turned to answer it.

"Mr. Barnes?"

"Yes, Herb."

"Sheriff's office reports road blocks in place and everybody out of the valley—it cost plenty cumshaw to clear the Idle Hour Guest Rancho, by the way."

"No matter."

"Everybody out, that is, but Pete the Hermit. He won't git."

"The old boy with the whiskers in that shack north of the gate?"

"The same. We finally told him the score, but it didn't faze him. He says he ain't never seen no ship take off for the Moon and he ain't planning to miss it, not at his age."

Barnes chuckled. "Can't blame him. Well, let him sign the release our own people sign. Tell him if he won't sign, the show won't take place."

"And if he doesn't sign?"

"Herb, I take off even if some damn fool is standing under the jets. But don't tell him."

"I got you. Now how about the press?"

"Tell them now—but keep them off my neck. And even with releases they stay in the blockhouse."

"I'll have trouble with the newsreel and television people."

"Remote control or nothing. Herd 'em in, you go in last and lock the door behind you. They can string all the wires into the blockhouse they need, but *nobody* stays inside the area unsheltered."

"Mr. Barnes—do you really think the blast will be that dangerous?"

Barnes' reply was drowned out by the bull horn from the blockhouse: "Attention! The last bus is now loading at the north entrance to the shop circle!"

Presently Styles resumed:

"Another call—you better take it, boss. Trouble."

"Who is it?"

"Commanding general at Muroc."

"Put him on." In a moment he was saying, "Jim Barnes, General. How are you?"

"Oh—hello, Mr. Barnes. I hate to buck you, but your man seems unreasonable. Is it necessary to ask us to keep radar crews up all night for your practice drill?"

"Mmm . . . General, isn't your tracking radar always manned anyhow? I thought this country had a 'radar umbrella' over it."

The general answered stiffly, "That's not a proper question, Mr. Barnes."

"I suppose not. Big difference between passing a law and getting appropriations to carry it out, isn't there?" He thought a minute. "General, suppose I guarantee blips on your tracking screens?"

"What do you mean?"

Barnes said, "General, I've known you since open cockpits. You've used a lot of my planes."

"You make good planes, Mr. Barnes."

"Tonight I want some cooperation. This is it, Whitey."

"Huh?"

"We blast off tonight. As long as you know, you can call White
Sands and make sure they track us, too. And Whitey—"

"Yes, Jim?"

"What with getting your crew organized and calling White
Sands it will be another hour before you can call Washington,
wouldn't you think?"

Silence persisted so long that Barnes thought he had been cut off,
then the general answered, "It might take that long. Anything
more you had better tell me?"

"No . . . that's enough. Except one thing; I'm going, Whitey.
I'm piloting it."

"Oh. Good luck, Jim."

"Thanks, Whitey."

As Barnes turned away, he saw a plane circling the area, its lights
blinking. The elevator creaked behind him; he looked up to see
Corley, Bowles, and Traub descending. Corley shouted, "Is that
Dr. Hastings?"

"I hope so."

The plane landed and a jeep drove up to it. A few minutes later
the jeep swung into the bull pen and up to the crane; Doctor
Hastings got out. Corley ran to meet him.

"Doctor Hastings! You have it?"

"Greetings, gentlemen. Yes, indeed." Hastings tapped a bulging
pocket.

"Give it to me!"

"Suppose we go into the ship? I'd like to discuss it with you."

"Jump aboard." The two savants mounted the elevator and
started up.

Admiral Bowles touched Barnes' sleeve. "Jim—a word with
you."

"Shoot."

Bowles indicated Traub with his eyes; Barnes caught the meaning and they moved inside. "Jim," Bowles asked in a whisper,
"what do you know about this man Traub?"

"Nothing that you don't. Why?"

"He's foreign born, isn't he? Germany? Poland?"

"Russia, for all I know. Does it matter?"

Bowles frowned. "There's been sabotage, Jim."

"The hell you say! What sort?"

"The earth-departure radar wouldn't function. Traub opened up the front, then called me over."

"What was it?"

"A pencil mark drawn between two leads. It—"

"I get you, a carbon short. Sabotage, all right. Well?"

"My point is, he found it too easily. How would he know right where to find it if he didn't do it himself?"

Barnes thought about it. "If Traub is trying to stop us, all he has to do is to refuse to go. We can't go without him—and he knows it."

"Suppose his object was not just to stop us, but to wreck the ship?"

"And kill himself in the bargain? Be logical, Red."

"Some of those people are fanatics, Jim. Beyond logic."

Barnes considered it. "Forget it, Red."

"But—"

"I said, 'Forget it!' Get on back in that ship and prowl around. Imagine that you are a saboteur; try to think where you would hide a bomb—or what you would wreck."

"Aye, aye, sir!"

"Good. Mannie!"

"Yes, Mr. Barnes." Traub trotted up; Barnes told him to go up and continue checking. The phone at the foot of the crane rang; it was Styles again.

"Boss? Just got a call from the pass gate. The deputy there is hooked by car radio with the deputies at the road blocks—"

"Good. Nice organizing, Herb."

"Not good! The north road block reports a car with a bailiff; he has a federal court order to stop the takeoff. They let him through."

Barnes swore softly. "Call the pass gate. Tell the deputy there to stop him."

"I did. He won't. He says he can't interfere with federal business."

"That tears it!" Barnes stopped to think. "Tell him to make almighty sure that the man is what he says he is. Tell him that the court order is almost certainly phony—which it is. Tell him to hold the man while he gets in touch with the sheriff's office and has the sheriff phone the judge who is supposed to have issued the described order."

"I'll try," Styles answered, "but suppose the order is kosher, boss? Hadn't I better just put the slug on him and dump him in a closet until the fireworks are over?"

Barnes weighed this. "No—you'd spend your life breaking rocks. Gain me all the minutes you can—then hightail it for the blockhouse. Is everybody clear?"

"Everybody but the car and driver for Mrs. Corley."

"How about Admiral Bowles' wife?"

"He sent her off earlier—the Admiral doesn't like ships watched out of sight."

"Bless his superstitious heart! Send Mrs. Corley's car into the pen. I'm going to button up around here."

"Roger!"

Barnes turned around to find Corley and Hastings descending. He waited, bursting with impatience. Corley spoke as they reached bottom. "Oh, Jim, I—"

"Never mind! Is everything okay up there?"

"Yes, but—"

"No time! Say good-bye to your wife, Doctor Hastings—good-bye, and thanks! Your plane's waiting."

"Jim," protested Corley, "what's the rush? It's—"

"No time!" A car swung in through the gate of the pen, came toward them. "There's your wife. Say good-bye and get back here. Move!" Barnes turned away and went to the crane operator. "Barney!"

"Yeah?"

"We're going up now—*for the last time.* As soon as we are off the crane, back it away. The safety stops are off the tracks?"

"Sure."

"Off entirely, or just moved back?"

"Off entirely. Don't worry; I won't run her off the rails."

"Yes, you will. Run the crane right off the end."

"Huh? Mr. Barnes, if I dropped the wheels into the sand, it would take a week to get her back on."

"Check. That's exactly what I want. After you do it, don't stop to explain; just run for the blockhouse."

The operator looked baffled. "Okay—you said it."

Barnes came back to the elevator. Corley and his wife were standing near her car. She was crying.

Barnes shaded his eyes against the floodlights and tried to see the road to the pass gate. The foundry cut off his view. Suddenly headlights gleamed around that building, turned onto the shop circle and came toward the bull pen entrance. Barnes shouted, "Doc! *Now!* Hurry!"

Corley looked up, then hastily embraced his wife. Barnes shouted, "Come on! Come on!"

Corley waited to hand his wife into the car. Barnes climbed onto the elevator and, as Corley reached it, pulled him aboard. "Barney! UP!"

Cables creaked and groaned; the platform crawled upward. As Mrs. Corley's car approached the gate the other car started in. Both cars stopped, then the strange car bulled on through. It gunned in second toward the crane and slammed to a stop; a man swarmed out.

He ran to the elevator; the platform was thirty feet above his head. He waved and shouted. "Barnes! Come down here!"

Barnes shouted back, "Can't hear you! Too much racket!"

"Stop the elevator! I've got a court order!"

The driver of the car jumped out and ran toward the crane control station. Barnes watched, unable to stop whatever was to come.

Barney reached behind him and grabbed a wrench; the driver stopped short. "Good boy!" Barnes breathed.

The elevator reached the airlock door; Barnes nudged Corley. "In you go!" He followed Corley, turned and lifted the gangway off the lip of the door, shoved it clear with his foot. "Barney! Get going!"

The crane operator glanced up and shifted his controls. The crane quivered, then very slowly crawled back from the ship, cleared it, and continued.

It backed still farther, lurched out of plumb, and trembled. Its drive motor squealed and stopped. Barney slid out of his saddle and loped away toward the gate.

IV

Time checks had been completed with Muroc, with White Sands and with their blockhouse. The control room was quiet save for the sighing of air-replenishing equipment, the low hum of radio circuits, and stray sounds of auxiliary machinery. The clocks at each station read 3:29—twenty-four minutes to H-hour.

The four were at their stations; two upper bunks were occupied by pilot and co-pilot; the lowers by power engineer and electronics engineer. Across the lap of each man arched a control console; his arms were supported so that his fingers were free to handle his switches without lifting any part of his body against the terrible weight to come. His head was supported so that he might see his instruments.

Traub lifted his head and peered out one of the two large quartz ports. "It's clouding up. I can't see the Moon."

Barnes answered, "Out where we're going there won't be any clouds."

"No clouds?"

"What do you expect, out in space?"

"Uh, I don't know. I guess I got most of my ideas about space travel from Buck Rogers. Electronics is my game."

"Twenty-three minutes," announced Bowles. "Skipper, what's the name of this bucket?"

"Huh?"

"When you launch a ship you have to name her."

"Eh, I suppose so. Doc, what do you say? She's your baby."

"Me? I've never thought about it."

"How," Bowles went on, "about calling her the *Luna?*"

Corley considered. "Suits me, if it suits the rest of you."

"The spaceship *Luna,*" agreed Barnes. "Sounds good."

Traub chuckled nervously. "That makes us 'the Lunatics.'"

"And why not?" agreed Barnes.

"Twenty minutes," announced Bowles.

"Warm her up, Doc. Check off lists, everybody."

"She's hot now," Corley answered. "If I increase the fission rate, I'll have to give her something to chew. Jim, I've been thinking. We could still test her."

"Huh?"

"Set her for a half-*g* lift, and clear her throat once—I've got her set for that."

"What's the point? She either works, or she blows up."

"Okay," Corley answered.

Traub gulped. "Could she blow up?"

"Don't worry," Corley reassured him. "The scale model ran an hour and twenty-three minutes before it blew up."

"Oh. Is that good?"

"Mannie," Barnes ordered. "Switch on 'Ground Pick-Up.' We might as well watch."

"Yes, sir." Above them was a large TV screen. Traub could hook it in to a scanner in the tail, another in the nose, or—as now—pick up an ordinary video channel. The screen lighted up; they saw their own ship, lonely and tall in the floodlights.

An announcer's voice came with the picture: "—this ship, the mightiest ever built, will soon plunge into outer space. Its flight was unannounced until tonight, its destination has not been revealed. Is this—"

The broadcast was interrupted by Herb Styles. "Mr. Barnes! Boss!"

Barnes leaned out and looked at Traub in the couch beneath. "Are you hooked in?"

"Just a sec—go ahead."

"What is it, Herb?"

"Somebody tearing down the road, heading this way."

"Who?"

"Don't know. We can't contact the north road block."

"Call the pass gate. Head 'em off."

"It's no longer manned. Hey—wait. North road block coming in." After a pause, Styles yelled, "Truck loaded with men—they crushed through and ran over a deputy!"

"Keep your shirt on," cautioned Barnes. "They can't reach us. If they hang around down below, it's their misfortune. I'm blasting on time."

Bowles sat up. "Don't be too sure, Jim."

"Eh? What can they do to us now?"

"What would six sticks of dynamite against one of the tail jacks do to this ship? Let's take off—now!"

"Before calculated time? Red, don't be silly."

"Blast off and correct later!"

"Doc—could we do that?"

"Eh? *No!*"

Barnes stared at the TV picture. "Mannie—tell blockhouse to sound sirens!"

"Jim," protested Corley, "you can't take off now!"

"Are you still set up to test? Half *g?*"

"Yes, but—"

"Stand by!" His eyes were fixed on the pictured scene outside; headlights came around the foundry, sped toward the pen. The moaning of sirens drowned out Corley's answer.

The truck was almost at the gate. Barnes' forefinger stabbed the firing button.

A whine of great pumps was blanked out by a roar they could feel in their bones. The *Luna* shivered.

In the TV screen a flower of white light burst from the tail of the ship, billowed up, blanketing the headlights, the buildings, the lower half of the ship.

Barnes jerked his finger back. The noise died out; the cloud changed from incandescent to opaque. In the silence Styles' voice came over the speaker. *"Great—Day—in the Morning!"*

"Herb—can you hear me?"

"Yes. What happened?"

"Use the bull horn to warn them off. Tell 'em to scram; if they come closer I'll fry them."

"I think you have."

"Get busy." He watched the screen, his finger raised. The cloud lifted; he made out the truck.

"Nine minutes," Bowles announced, calmly.

Through the speaker Barnes could hear a voice on the bull horn, warning the attacking party back. A man jumped down from the truck, was followed by others. Barnes' finger trembled.

They turned and ran.

Barnes sighed. "Doc, did the test suit you?"

"A mushy cutoff," Corley complained. "It should have been sharp."

"Do we blast, or don't we?"

Corley hesitated. "Well?" demanded Barnes.

"We blast."

Traub heaved a mournful sigh. Barnes snapped, "Power plant—shift to automatic! All hands—prepare for acceleration. Mannie, tell blockhouse, Muroc, and White Sands to stand by for count off at oh three five two."

"'Oh three five two,'" Traub repeated, then went on, "Ship, calling blockhouse, Muroc, White Sands."

"Power plant, report."

"Automatic, all green."

"Co-pilot?"

"Tracking on autopilot." Bowles added, "Eight minutes."

"Doc, is she hot as she'll take?"

"I'm carrying the fission rate as high as I dare," Corley answered, strain in his voice. "She's on the ragged edge."

"Keep her so. All hands, strap down."

Corley reared up. "Jim—I forgot to pass out the drop-sick pills."

"Stay where you are! If we get seasick, we get seasick."

"One minute, coming up!" Bowles' voice was harsh.

"Take it, Mannie!"

"Blockhouse—Muroc—White Sands. Ready for count off!" Traub paused; the room was still.

"Sixty! Fifty-nine—fifty-eight—fifty-seven—"

Barnes gripped his arm rests, tried to slow down his heart. He watched the seconds click off as Traub counted them. "Thirty-nine! Thirty-eight! Thirty-seven!" Traub's voice was shrill. "Thirty-one! *Half!*"

Barnes could hear sirens, rising and falling, out on the field. Above him in the TV screen, the *Luna* stood straight and proud, her head in darkness.

"Eleven!

"And ten!

"And nine!

"And eight!"—Barnes licked his lips and swallowed.

"Five—four——three——two—

"Fire!"

The word was lost in sound, a roar that made the test blast seem as nothing. The *Luna* shrugged—and climbed for the sky.

V

If we are to understand those men, we must reorient.
Crossing the Atlantic was high adventure—when Columbus
did it. So with the early spacemen. The ships they rode in
were incredibly makeshift.

They did not know what they were doing. Had they
known, they would not have gone.

Farquharson, *Ibid.,* III: 415

Barnes felt himself shoved back into the cushions. He gagged and fought to keep from swallowing his tongue. He felt paralyzed by body weight of more than half a ton; he strained to lift his chest. Worse than weight was noise, a mind-killing "white" sound from unbearable ultrasonics down to bass too low to be heard.

The sound Dopplered down the scale, rumbled off and left

them. At five effective gravities they outraced their own din in six seconds, leaving an aching quiet broken only by noise of water coursing through pumps.

For a moment Barnes savored the silence. Then his eyes caught the TV screen above him; in it was a shrinking dot of fire. He realized that he was seeing himself, disappearing into the sky, and regretted that he had not watched the blast-away. "Mannie," he labored, to say, "switch on 'View After.'"

"I *can't,*" Traub groaned thickly. "I can't move a muscle."

"Do it!"

Traub managed it; the screen blurred, then formed a picture. Bowles grunted, "Great Caesar's ghost!" Barnes stared. They were high above Los Angeles; the metropolitan area was map sharp, picked out in street lights and neon. It was shrinking visibly.

Rosy light flashed through the eastern port, followed at once by dazzling sunlight. Traub yelped, *"What happened?"*

Barnes himself had been startled but he strove to control his voice and answered, "Sunrise. We're up that high." He went on, "Doc—how's the power plant?"

"Readings normal," Corley replied in tongue-clogged tones. "How long to go?"

Barnes looked at his board. "More than three minutes."

Corley did not answer; three minutes seemed too long to bear. Presently Traub said, "Look at the sky!" Corley forced his head over and looked. Despite harsh sunlight the sky was black and spangled with stars.

At three minutes and fifty seconds the jets cut off. Like the first time, the cutoff was mushy, slow. The terrible weight left them gradually. But it left them completely. Rocket and crew were all in a free orbit "falling" upward toward the Moon. Relative to each other and to ship they had no weight.

Barnes felt that retching, frightening "falling elevator" feeling characteristic of no weight, but, expecting it, he steeled himself. "Power plant," he snapped, "report!"

"Power plant okay," Corley replied weakly. "Notice the cut-off?"

"Later," decided Barnes. "Co-pilot, my track seems high."

"My display tracks on," wheezed Bowles, "—or a hair high."

"Mannie!"

No answer. Barnes repeated, "Mannie? Answer, man—are you all right?"

Traub's voice was weak. "I think I'm dying. This thing is falling—oh, God, *make it stop!"*

"Snap out of it!"

"Are we going to crash?"

"No, no! We're all right."

"'All right,' the man says," Traub muttered, then added, "I don't care if we do."

Barnes called out, "Doc, get those pills. Mannie needs one bad." He stopped to control a retch. "I could use one myself."

"Me, too," agreed Bowles. "I haven't been this seasick since I was—" He caught himself, then went on. "—since I was a midshipman."

Corley loosened his straps and pulled himself out from his couch. Weightless, he floated free and turned slowly over, like a diver in slow motion. Traub turned his face away and groaned.

"Stop it, Mannie," ordered Barnes. "Try to raise White Sands. I want a series of time-altitude readings."

"I can't—I'm sick."

"Do it!"

Corley floated near a stanchion, grabbed it, and pulled himself to a cupboard. He located the pill bottle and hastily gulped a pill. He then moved to Traub's couch, pulling himself along. "Here, Traub—take this. You'll feel better."

"What is it?"

"Some stuff called Dramamine. It's for seasickness."

Traub put a pill in his mouth. "I can't swallow."

"Better try." Traub got it down, clamped his jaw to keep it down. Corley pulled himself to Barnes. "Need one, Jim?"

Barnes started to answer, turned his head away, and threw up in his handkerchief. Tears streaming from his eyes, he accepted the pill. Bowles called out, "Doc—hurry up!" His voice cut off; presently he added, "Too late."

"Sorry." Corley moved over to Bowles. "Criminy, you're a mess!"

"Gimme that pill and no comments."

Traub was saying in a steadier voice, "Spaceship *Luna,* calling White Sands. Come in White Sands."

At last an answer came back, "White Sands to Spaceship—go ahead."

"Give us a series of radar checks, time, distance, and bearing."

A new voice cut in, "White Sands to Spaceship—we have been

tracking you, but the figures are not reasonable. What is your destination?"

Traub glanced at Barnes, then answered, *"Luna,* to White Sands—destination: Moon."

"Repeat? Repeat?"

"Our destination is the Moon!"

There was a silence. The same voice replied, " 'Destination: Moon'— Good luck, Spaceship *Luna!"*

Bowles spoke up suddenly. "Hey! *Come look!"* He had unstrapped and was floating by the sunward port.

"Later," Barnes answered. "I need this tracking report first."

"Well, come look until they call back. This is once in a lifetime."

Corley joined Bowles. Barnes hesitated; he wanted very badly to see, but he was ashamed to leave Traub working. "Wait," he called out. "I'll turn ship and we can all see."

Mounted at the centerline of the ship was a flywheel. Barnes studied his orientation readings, then clutched the ship to the flywheel. Slowly the ship turned, without affecting its motion along its course. "How's that?"

"Wrong way!"

"Sorry." Barnes tried again; the stars marched past in the opposite direction; Earth swung into view. He caught sight of it and almost forgot to check the swing.

Power had cut off a trifle more than eight hundred miles up. The *Luna* had gone free at seven miles per second; in the last few minutes they had been steadily coasting upwards and were now three thousand miles above Southern California. Below— opposite them, from their viewpoint—was darkness. The seaboard cities stretched across the port like Christmas lights. East of them, sunrise cut across the Grand Canyon and shone on Lake Mead. Further east the prairies were in daylight, dun and green broken by blinding cloud. The plains dropped away into curved skyline.

So fast were they rising that the picture was moving, shrinking, and the globe drew into itself as a ball. Barnes watched from across the compartment. "Can you see all right, Mannie?" he asked.

"Yeah," answered Traub. "Yeah," he repeated softly. "Say, that's *real,* isn't it?"

Barnes said, "Hey, Red, Doc—heads down. You're not transparent."

Traub looked at Barnes. "Go ahead, skipper."

"No, I'll stick with you."

"Don't be a chump. I'll look later."

"Well—" Barnes grinned suddenly. "Thanks, Mannie." He gave a shove and moved across to the port.

Mannie continued to stare. Later the radio claimed his attention. "White Sands, calling Spaceship—ready with radar report."

The first reports, plus a further series continued as long as White Sands and Muroc were able to track them, confirmed Barnes' suspicion. They were tracking "high," ahead of their predicted positions and at speeds greater than those called for by Hastings' finicky calculations. The difference was small; on the autopilot displays it was hardly the thickness of a line between the calculated path and the true path.

But the difference would increase.

"Escape speeds" for rockets are very critical. Hastings had calculated the classical hundred-hour orbit and the *Luna* had been aimed to reach the place *where the Moon would be* four days later. But initial speed is critical. A difference of less than one percent in ship speed at cutoff can halve—or double—the transit time from Earth to Moon. The *Luna* was running very slightly ahead of schedule—but when it reached the orbit of the Moon, the Moon would not be there.

Doctor Corley tugged at his thinning hair. "Sure, the cutoff was mushy, but I was expecting it and I noted the mass readings. It's not enough to account for the boost. Here—take a look."

Corley was hunched at the log desk, a little shelf built into the space between the acceleration bunks. He was strapped to a stool fixed to the deck in front of it. Barnes floated at his shoulder; he took the calculation and scanned it. "I don't follow you," Barnes said presently; "your expended mass is considerably higher than Hastings calculated."

"You're looking at the wrong figure," Corley pointed out. "You forgot the mass of water you used up in that test. Subtract that from the total mass expended to get the effective figure for blast off—this figure here. Then you apply that—" Corley hesitated, his expression changed from annoyance to dismay. "Oh, my God!"

"Huh? What is it, Doc? Found the mistake?"

"Oh, how could I be so stupid!" Corley started frenzied figuring.

"What have you found?" Corley did not answer; Barnes grabbed his arm. "What's up?"

"Huh? Don't bother me."

"I'll bother you with a baseball bat. *What have you found?*"

"Eh? Look, Jim, what's the final speed of a rocket, ideal case?"

"What is this? A quiz show? Jet speed times the logarithm of the mass ratio. Pay me."

"And *you* changed the mass ratio! No wonder we're running high."

"Me?"

"We both did—my fault as much as yours. Listen; you spilled a mass of water in scaring off that truck load of thugs—but Hastings' figures were based on us lifting that particular mass *all the way to the Moon.* The ship should have grossed almost exactly two hundred fifty tons at takeoff; she was shy what you had used—so we're going too fast."

"Huh? I wasted reaction mass, so we're going too fast? That doesn't make sense." Barnes hooked a foot into the legs of the stool to anchor himself, and did a rough run-through of the problem with slide rule and logarithm table. "Well, boil me in a bucket!" He added humbly, "Doc, I shouldn't have asked to be skipper. I don't know enough."

Corley's worried features softened. "Don't feel that way, Jim. Nobody knows enough—yet. God knows I've put in enough time on theory, but I went ahead and urged you to make the blunder."

"Doc, how important is this? The error is less than one percent. I'd guess that we would reach the Moon about an hour early."

"And roughly you'd be wrong. Initial speed is critical, Jim; you know that!"

"How critical? When do we reach the Moon?"

Corley looked glumly at the pitiful tools he had with him—a twenty-inch log-log slide rule, seven place tables, a Nautical Almanac, and an office-type calculator which bore the relation to a "giant brain" that a firecracker does to an A-bomb. "I don't know. I'll have to put it up to Hastings." He threw his pencil at the desk top; it bounced off and floated away. "The question is: do we get there at all?"

"Oh, it can't be that bad!"

"It *is* that bad."

From across the compartment Bowles called out, "Come and get it—or I throw it to the pigs!"

But food had to wait while Corley composed a message to Hastings. It was starkly simple: OFF TRAJECTORY. USE DATA

WHITE SANDS MUROC AND COMPUTE CORRECTION
VECTOR. PLEASE USE UTMOST HASTE—CORLEY.

After sending it Traub announced that he wasn't hungry and
didn't guess he would eat.

Bowles left the "galley" (one lonely hot plate) and moved to
Traub's couch. Traub had strapped himself into it to have stability
while he handled his radio controls. "Snap out of it, man," Bowles
advised. "Must eat, you know."

Traub looked gray. "Thanks, Admiral, but I couldn't."

"So you don't like my cooking? By the way, my friends call me
'Red.'"

"Thanks, uh—Red. No, I'm just not hungry."

Bowles brought his head closer and spoke in low tones. "Don't
let it get you, Mannie. I've been in worse jams and come out alive.
Quit worrying."

"I'm not worrying."

Bowles chuckled. "Don't be ashamed of it, son. We all get upset,
first time under fire. Come eat."

"I can't eat. And I've *been* under fire."

"Really?"

"Yes, really! I've got two Purple Hearts to prove it. Admiral,
leave me alone, please. My stomach is awful uneasy."

Bowles said, "I beg your pardon, Mannie." He added, "Maybe
you need another seasick pill."

"Could be."

"I'll fetch one." Bowles did so, then returned again shortly with
a transparent sack filled with milk—to be exact, a flexible plastic
nursing cell, complete with nipple. "Sweet milk, Mannie. Maybe
it'll comfort your stomach."

Traub looked at it curiously. "With this should go a diaper and a
rattle," he announced. "Thanks, uh—Red."

"Not at all, Mannie. If that stays down, I'll fix you a sandwich."
He turned in the air and rejoined the others.

VI

The *Luna* plunged on; Earth dropped away; radio signals grew
weaker—and still no word from Hastings. Corley spent the time
trying endlessly and tediously to anticipate the answer he expected
from Hastings, using the tools he had. Traub stood guard at the
radio. Barnes and Bowles spent a lengthy time staring out the

ports—back at the shrinking, cloud-striped Earth, forward at the growing gibbous Moon and brilliant steady stars—until Bowles fell asleep in mid-sentence, a softly snoring free balloon.

Barnes nudged him gently toward his couch and there strapped him loosely, to keep him from cluttering up the cramped cabin. He eyed his own couch longingly, then turned to Traub instead.

"Out of there, Mannie," he ordered. "I'll relieve you while you catch some shut-eye."

"Me? Oh, that's all right, Skipper. You get some sleep yourself and I'll take a rain check."

Barnes hesitated. "Sure you don't want to be relieved?"

"Not a bit. I feel—" He broke off and added, "Just a minute," and turned to his controls. He was on earphones now, rather than speaker. He settled them in place and said sharply, "Go ahead, Earth."

Presently Traub turned to Barnes: "Chicago *Tribune*—they want an exclusive story from you."

"No, I'm going to sleep."

Traub reported Barnes' answer, then turned back. "How about the Admiral or Doctor Corley?"

"The co-pilot is asleep and Doctor Corley is not to be disturbed."

"Mr. Barnes?" Traub's manner was diffident. "Do you mind if they get one from *me?*"

Barnes chuckled. "Not at all. But stick them plenty."

As Barnes closed his eyes he could hear Traub dickering with some faceless negotiator. He wondered if Traub would ever get to spend the fee? What was a man like Traub doing up here anyhow, in a ship headed nowhere in a hell of a hurry?

For that matter, why was Jim Barnes here?

After his interview, Traub continued guarding the radio. Signals grew fainter and presently reduced to garble. The room was quiet, save for the soft murmur of the air replenisher.

After a long time the radio came suddenly to life—NAA, Washington, Traub soon learned, had rigged a reflector to beam directly at them. "Can you take code groups?" he was asked.

He assured them that he could. "Despatch for Rear Admiral Bowles," NAA rapped back at him. "Zero zero zero one: code groups follow—love, uncle, king, easy, roger—boy, able, dog, item, peter—" The groups continued for a long time.

"Doctor Corley!"

Corley looked around vaguely, as if awakening in a strange place. "Eh? Yes, Mannie? I'm busy."

"Doctor Hastings calling."

"Oh, fine," Corley acknowledged. "Slide out of there and let me take it."

They changed places with effort, bothered by weightlessness. Traub felt a touch on his arm. "What is it, Mannie?"

He turned; Barnes and Bowles had waked up and loosed themselves. "Howdy, Skipper. It's Doctor Hastings."

"Good!"

"Uh, Admiral—got something for you." Traub hauled out the code dispatch.

Bowles stared at it. Barnes remarked, "Race results?"

Bowles did not answer. He shoved himself toward the forward bulkhead, as far away as possible. He then took a thin book from an inner pocket, and started studying the message with the aid of the book. Barnes looked surprised but said nothing.

Hastings' report was short but not sweet. They would reach the Moon's orbit where planned, but more than fifty hours too soon—and would miss the Moon by more than 90,000 miles!

Barnes whistled. "Hot pilot Barnes, they call me."

Corley said, "It's no joke."

"I wasn't laughing, Doc," Barnes answered, "but there is no use crying. It will be tragic soon enough."

Traub broke in. "Hey—what do you mean?"

"He means," Bowles said bluntly, "that we are headed out and aren't coming back."

"On out? And out—out into outer space? Where the stars are?"

"That's about it."

"Not that," Corley interrupted, "I'd estimate that we would reach our farthest point somewhere around the orbit of Mars."

Traub sighed. "So it's Mars, now? That's not so bad, is it? I mean they say people live on Mars, don't they? All those canals and things? We can get another load of water and come back."

"Don't kid yourself, Mannie," Bowles said. "Just be glad you're a bachelor."

"A bachelor? Who said I was?"

"Aren't you?"

"Me? I'm a very domestic type guy. Four kids—and married fourteen years."

Corley looked stricken. "Mannie, I didn't know."

"What's that got to do with it? Insurance I've got, with a rocket experimentation rider. I knew this was no picnic."

Barnes said, "Mannie, if I had known, I wouldn't have asked you to go. I'm sorry." He turned to Corley, "When do we run out of water—and air?"

Corley raised his voice. "Please! Everybody! I didn't say we weren't going to get back. I said—"

"But you—"

"Shut *up*, Red! I said *this* orbit is no good. We've got to vector west, toward the Moon. And we've got to do it at—" He glanced at a clock. "Good grief! Seven minutes from now."

Barnes jerked his head around. "Acceleration stations, everybody! Stand by to maneuver!"

VII

The most treacherous maneuver known to space flight is a jet landing on an airless planet. Even today, it commands the highest pay, the most skilled pilots—

Farquharson, *Ibid.*, III: 418

For forty hours they fell toward the Moon. The maneuver had worked; one could see, even with naked eye, that they were closing with the Moon. The four took turns at the radio, ate and slept and talked and stared out at the glittering sky. Bowles and Traub discovered a common passion for chess and played off the "First Annual Interplanetary Championship"—so dubbed by the Admiral—using pencil marks on paper.

Traub won, four out of seven.

Some two hundred thousand miles out the *Luna* slid past the null point between Earth and Moon, and began to shape her final orbit. It became evident that the correction vector had somewhat overcompensated and that they were swinging toward the Moon's western limb—"western" as seen from Earth: the *Luna*'s orbit would intersect her namesake somewhere on the never-yet-seen far side—or it was possible that the ship would skim the far side at high speed, come around sharply and head back toward Earth.

Two principal styles of landing were possible—Type A, in which a ship heads in vertically, braking on her jets to a landing in one maneuver, and Type B, in which a ship is first slowed to a circular orbit, then stopped dead, then backed to a landing when she drops from the point of rest.

"Type A, Jim—it's simplest."

Barnes shook his head. "No, Doc. Simple on paper only. Too risky." If they corrected course to head straight in (Type A), their speed at instant of braking would be a mile and a half a second and an error of one second would land them 8000 feet above—or below!—the surface.

Barnes went on, "How about a modified 'A'?"

Modified Type A called for intentionally blasting too soon, then cutting the jets when the radar track showed that the ship hovered, allowing it to fall from rest, then blasting again as necessary, perhaps two or three times.

"Confound it, Jim, a modified 'A' is so damned wasteful."

"I'd like to get us down without wrecking us."

"And I would like us to get home, too. This ship was figured for a total change of twelve and a half miles per second. Our margin is paper thin."

"Just the same, I'd like to set the autopilot to kick her a couple of seconds early."

"We can't afford it and that's that."

"Land her yourself, then. I'm not Superman."

"Now, Jim—"

"Sorry." Barnes looked at the calculations. "But why Type A? Why not Type B?"

"But Jim, Type B is probably ruled out. It calls for decelerating at point of closest approach and, as things stand now, 'closest approach' may be contact."

"Crash, you mean. But don't be so damned conventional; you can vector into a circular orbit from any position."

"But that wastes reaction mass, too."

"Crashing from a sloppy Type A wastes more than reaction mass," Barnes retorted. "Get to work on a 'B'; I won't risk an 'A.'"

Corley looked stubborn. Barnes went on, "There's a bonus with Type B, Doc—two bonuses."

"Don't be silly. Done perfectly, it takes as much reaction mass as Type A; done sloppily, it takes more."

"I won't be sloppy. Here's your bonus: Type A lands us on this face, but Type B lets us swing around the Moon and *photograph the back side* before we land. How does that appeal to your scientific soul?"

* * *

Corley looked tempted. "I thought about that, but we've got too little margin. It takes a mile and a half of motion to get down to the Moon, the same to get up—three miles. For the trip back I have to save enough mass to slow from seven miles a second to five before we dip into the atmosphere. We used up seven to blast off—it all adds up to twelve. Look at the figures; what's left?"

Barnes did so and shrugged. "Looks like a slightly fat zero."

"A few seconds of margin at most. You could waste it on the transitions in a Type B landing."

"Now the second bonus, Doc," Barnes said slowly. "The Type B gives you a chance to change your mind after you get into a circular orbit; the straight-in job commits you beyond any help."

Corley looked shocked. "Jim, you mean go back to Earth *without landing?*"

Barnes lowered his voice. "Wait, Doc. I'd land on the Moon if I had enough in tanks to get down—and not worry about getting up again. I'm a bachelor. But there's Mannie Traub. No getting around it; we stampeded him. Now it turns out he has a slew of kids, waiting for poppa to come home. It makes a difference."

Corley pulled at his scalp lock. "He should have told us."

"If he had, we wouldn't have taken off."

"Confound it, things would have been all right if I hadn't suggested that you test the engine."

"Nonsense! If I hadn't scared those babies off with a blast, they probably would have wrecked the ship."

"You can't be sure."

"A man can't be sure of anything. How about Traub?"

"You're right—I suppose. Okay, we leave it up to Traub."

From the other end of the compartment Traub looked around from his chess game with Bowles.

"Somebody call me?"

"Yes," Barnes agreed. "Both of you. We've got things to decide."

Barnes outlined the situation. "Now," he said, "Doc and I agree that, after we get into a circular orbit and have had time to add up what's left, Mannie should decide whether we land, or just swing around and blast for home."

Bowles looked amazed, but said nothing.

Traub looked flustered. "Me? It ain't my business to decide. I'm the electronics department."

"Because," Barnes stated, "you're the only one with kids."

"Yes, but— Look here—is there really a chance that, if we landed, we wouldn't be able to get back?"

"Possible," Barnes answered and Corley nodded.

"But don't you *know?*"

"Look, Mannie," Barnes countered, "we've got water in the tanks to land, take off, and return to Earth—but none for mistakes."

"Yes, but you won't make any mistakes, will you?"

"I can't promise. I've already made one and it's brought us to this situation."

Traub's features worked in agonized indecision. "But it's not my business to decide!"

Bowles spoke up suddenly. "You're right; it's not!" He went on, "Gentlemen, I didn't intend to speak, because it never crossed my mind that we might not land. But now the situation demands it. As you know, I received a coded message.

"The gist was this: our trip has caused grave international repercussions. The Security Council has been in constant session, with the U.S.S.R. demanding that the Moon be declared joint property of the United Nations—"

"As it should be," Corlcy interrupted.

"You don't see the point, Doctor. Their only purpose is to forestall us claiming the Moon—*we,* who actually are making the trip. To forestall us, you understand, so that the United States will not be able to found a base on the Moon without permission— permission that is certain to be vetoed."

"But," pointed out Corley, "it works both ways. We would veto Russia establishing a base on the Moon. Admiral, I've worked with you because it was a way to get on with my life's ambition, but, to be frank, using the Moon as a rocket launching base—by *anybody*— sticks in my craw."

Bowles turned red. "Doctor, this is not an attempt to insure the neutrality of the Moon; this is the same double-talk they used to stop world control of atomics. The commissars simply want to tie us up in legalisms until *they* have time to get to the Moon. We'll wake up one morning to find Russia with a base on the Moon and us with none—and World War Three will be over before it starts."

"But—Admiral, you can't know that."

Bowles turned to Barnes. "Tell him, Jim."

Barnes gestured impatiently. "Come out of your ivory tower,

Doc. Space travel is here now—we did it. There is bound to be a rocket base on the Moon. Sure, it ought to be a United Nations base, keeping the peace of the world. But the United Nations has been helpless from scratch. The first base is going to belong to us—or to Russia. Which one do you trust not to misuse the power? Us—or the Politburo?"

Corley covered his eyes, then looked at Bowles. "All right," he said dully. "It has to be—but I don't like it."

Traub broke the ensuing silence with "Uh, I don't see how this ties in with whether we land or not?"

Bowles turned to him. "Because of this: the rest of that message restored me to active duty and directed me to claim the Moon in the name of the United States—as quickly as possible. We would have what the diplomats call a *fait accompli*. But to claim the Moon *I have to land!*"

Traub stared. "Oh. I see."

Bowles went on in a gentle voice, "Mannie, this goes beyond you and me, or even your kids. The surest way to make sure that your kids grow up in a peaceful, free world is to risk your neck right now. So we've *got* to land."

Traub hesitated; Bowles went on, "You see that, don't you? It's for your kids—and millions of other kids."

Barnes interrupted him. "Red—quit working on him!"

"Eh?"

"He'll make a free choice—after we've leveled off and looked the situation over."

"But, Jim, I thought we saw eye to eye. You told Doc—"

"Pipe down! You've stated your case, now quit trying to work him up into being a martyr."

Bowles turned bright red. "I must inform you, sir, that besides being returned to active duty I was given authority to commandeer this ship."

Barnes locked eyes with him. "You can take your authority and—do whatever you think proper with it. I'm skipper and will stay so as long as I'm alive." He looked around. "All hands—get ready for approach. Doc, go ahead with trial calculations, Type B. Mannie, warm up the pilot radar. Bowles!"

Finally Bowles answered, "Yes, sir."

"Rig the autocamera in the starboard port. We'll take a continuous strip as we pass around the far side."

"Aye aye, sir."

* * *

Traub leaned from his couch and peered out the starboard port. "It's just like the other side."

Barnes answered, "What did you expect? Skyscrapers? Co-pilot, how do you track?"

"Speed over ground—one point three seven. Altitude, fifty-one point two, closing slowly."

"Check. I project closest approach at not less than twenty-one—no contact. What do you get?"

"Closer to twenty, but no contact."

"Check. Take over orientation. I'll blast when altitude changes from steady to opening."

"Aye aye, sir!"

The *Luna* was swinging around the unknown far face of the Moon, but her crew was too busy to see much of the craggy, devil-torn landscape. She was nearing her closest approach, travelling almost horizontally. She was pointed tail first, ready to blast back from a top speed of a mile and a half a second to a circular orbit speed of a mile a second. At Barnes' order Bowles gave his attention to placing her axis precisely horizontal.

The television screen read "View Aft"; in its center was a cross mark lying over a picture of the mountainous horizon they were approaching. He jockeyed the ship against the reaction of the flywheel, then steadied her by gyros when one cross line held steady on the horizon.

Barnes set his controls on semiautomatic, ready both to fire and cut off with one punch of the firing button. Into his autopilot he fed the speed change he wished to achieve. Altitude dropped to forty miles, to thirty, to less than twenty-five. "Power plant," Barnes called out, "stand by for blasting!"

"Ready, Jim," Corley reported quietly.

"Electronics?"

"Everything sweet, Skipper."

Barnes watched ground speed with one eye, the radar altimeter with the other . . . twenty-three, it said . . . twenty-two . . . twenty-one and a half. . . .

Twenty-one point five . . . twenty-one point four—point four again—and again. Point five! and crawling up. His finger stabbed at the firing button.

The blast was fourteen seconds only, then it cut off, but in the same mushy fashion which it had before. Barnes shook his head to clear it and looked at his board. Altitude twenty-one point five; ground speed, one plus a frog's whisker—they were in orbit as planned. He sighed happily. "That's all for now, troops. Leave everything hot but you can get out of your hammocks."

Bowles said, "Hadn't I better stay and watch the board?"

"Suit yourself—but they won't repeal the law of gravitation. Doc, let's see how much juice we have left." He glanced at a clock. "We've got an hour to make a decision. It will be almost half an hour before Earth is in sight again."

"I don't like the way she cuts off," Corley complained.

"Quit fretting. I used to have a car that sounded its horn every time I made a left turn."

Bowles got a container of coffee, then joined Traub at the starboard port. They peered around the automatic camera and watched the moonscape slide past. "Rugged terrain," Bowles remarked.

Traub agreed. "There's better stuff going to waste in California."

They continued to stare out. Presently Bowles turned in the air and slithered back to his acceleration couch.

"Traub!"

Mannie came to the desk. "Mannie," Barnes said, pointing at a lunar map, "we figure to land spang in the middle of the Earthside face—that dark spot, *Sinus Medii.* It's a plain."

"You figure to land, then?"

"It's up to you, Mannie. But you'll have to make up your mind. We'll be there in about—uh, forty minutes."

Traub looked troubled. "Look, chief, you shouldn't—"

He was interrupted by Bowles' voice. "Captain! We are closing, slowly."

"Are you sure?"

"Quite sure. Altitude nineteen point three—correction: point two . . . closing."

"Acceleration stations!"

Barnes was diving toward his couch as he shouted. Traub and Corley followed him. As he strapped down Barnes called out, "Co-pilot—get a contact prediction. All hands, stand by for maneuvers." He studied his own board. He could not doubt it; they were in something less than a perfect circle.

He was trying to make a prediction from his display when Bowles reported, "I make it contact in nine minutes, Captain, plus or minus a minute."

Barnes concentrated. The radar track was jiggling as much as five or ten percent, because of mountains below them; the prediction line was a broad band. As near as he could tell, Bowles was right.

"What now, Captain?" Bowles went on. "Shall I swing her to blast forward?" A slight nudge would speed up the ship, in effect, lift her, permit her to *fall around* the Moon rather than curve down.

It would also waste reaction mass.

Nine minutes . . . nine hundred miles, about. He tried to figure how many minutes it would be until they raised Earth over the horizon, ahead.

Seven minutes, possibly—and Earth would be in sight. A landing at *Sinus Medii* was impossible but they still might land in sight of Earth without using more precious water to correct their orbit. "Mannie," he snapped, "we land in seven minutes—or we never land. *Make up your mind!*"

Traub did not answer.

Barnes waited, while a minute coursed by. Finally he said in a weary voice, "Co-pilot—swing to blast forward. All hands, prepare for departure."

Traub suddenly spoke up. "That's what we came for, wasn't it? To land on the Moon? Well, let's land the damn thing!"

Barnes caught his breath. "Good boy! Co-pilot, cancel that last. Steady ship for deceleration. Sing out when you see Earth."

"Aye aye, sir!"

"There's Earth!"

Barnes glanced up, saw Terra pictured in the TV screen, rising behind a wall of mountains. Bowles went on, "Better land, Jim. You'll never get over those mountains."

Barnes did not argue; their altitude was barely three miles now. He shouted, "Stand by. Red, start swinging as soon as I cut off."

"Right!"

"Fire!" He stabbed the button. This maneuver was manual, intended only to stop their forward motion. He watched his ground-speed radar while the ship shivered—nine-tenths . . . seven . . . five . . . four . . . three . . . two . . . one . . . six-hundredths. He jerked his finger off just before it dropped to zero and prayed that a mushy cutoff would equal his anticipation.

He started to shout to Bowles, but the ship was already swinging.

Earth and the horizon swung up in the TV screen and out of sight.

For a crawling ten seconds, while they fell straight down, the *Luna* crept into position for a tail-first landing. They were less than three miles up now. Barnes shifted scale from miles to feet and started his prediction.

Bowles beat him to an answer. "Contact in seventy-two seconds, Skipper."

Barnes relaxed. "See the advantage of a Type 'B' landing, Doc," he remarked cheerfully. "No hurry—just like an elevator."

"Quit gabbing and get us down," Corley answered tautly.

"Right," Barnes agreed. "Co-pilot, predict the blast altitude." His own hands were busy to the same end.

Bowles answered, "Jim, you going manual or automatic?"

"Don't know yet." Automatic firing was quicker, possibly more certain—but that mushy cutoff could bounce them like a pingpong ball. He steadied cross-hairs on his autopilot display and read the answer: Blast at five two oh feet. What do you get, Red?"

"Check." Bowles added, "That's less than three seconds blast, Jim. Better make it automatic."

"Tend to your knitting."

"My mistake."

Nearly forty seconds passed and they had fallen to eleven thousand feet before he decided. "Power plant, set for manual landing. Co-pilot, cover me at five hundred feet."

"Jim, that's too late," Bowles protested.

"You will be covering me all of a tenth of a second after I should fire."

Bowles subsided. Barnes grabbed a glance at the TV screen; the ground under them seemed level and there was no perceptible drift. He looked back at his board. "Correction—cover at five ten."

"Five ten—right."

The seconds clicked past; he had his finger poised over the button when Bowles shouted, "Jim—look at the screen!"

He looked up—the *Luna,* still carrying a trifle of drift, was now over a long crack, or rill—and they were about to land in it.

Barnes jabbed the button.

He let up at once; the *Luna* coughed to silence. The rill, canyon, or crevasse was still in sight but no longer centered. "Co-pilot— new prediction!"

"What happened?" Corley demanded.

"Quiet!"

"Prediction," Bowles chanted, "blast at—at three nine oh."

Barnes was adjusting verniers for his own prediction as Bowles reported. "Check," he answered. "Cover at three seven oh." He threw one glance at the TV screen. The crevasse was toward the edge of the screen; the ground below looked fairly smooth. Unquestionably the ship had a slight drift. All he could do was hope that the gyros would keep them from toppling. *"Brace for crash!"*

480—450—400— He jabbed the button.

The terrible pressure shoved his head back; he lost sight of the altimeter. He caught it again—190—150—125—

At "fifty" he snatched his finger away and prayed.

The jet cut off sloppily as always. A grinding jar slammed him more deeply into the cushions. The ship lurched like an unsteady top—and stayed upright.

Barnes found that he had been holding his breath a long time.

VIII

Columbus found a pleasant climate, rich land, docile natives. Nowhere in our System did explorers find conditions friendly to men—and nowhere was this more brutally true than on our nearest neighbor.

Farquharson, *Ibid.*, III: 420

Barnes felt dazed, as if wakening from a confusing dream. Bowles' voice recalled him to the present. "Jacks are down, skipper. Unclutch the gyros?"

He pulled himself together. "Check our footing first. I'll— Say! *We're on the Moon!"* Frantically he unstrapped.

"We sure are!" answered Bowles. "A fine landing, Jim. I was scared."

"It was terrible, and you know it."

"We're alive, aren't we? Never mind—*we made it.*"

Corley interrupted them. "Power plant secured."

Barnes looked startled. "Oh, sure. Traub, your department okay?"

Mannie answered weakly, "I guess so. I think I fainted."

"Nonsense!" Bowles reassured him. "Come on—let's look."

The four crowded at the portside port and stared out across an umber plain, baking under an unchecked sun, now not far from zenith. Miles away, jutting up into black, star-studded sky, were the peaks they had seen. In the middle distance was a single pock mark, a crater a mile or less across. Nothing else broke the flat desolation . . . endless, lifeless waste, vacuum sharp and kiln dry.

Traub broke the silence with an awed whisper. "Gosh, what a place! How long do we stay, Mr. Barnes?"

"Not long, Mannie." He tried to make his words carry conviction. "Doc," he went on, "let's check the mass ratio."

"Okay, Jim."

Bowles went to the starboard port; one glance through it and he sang out, "Hey—see this."

They joined him. Below was the dark chasm in which they had almost landed. It ran close to the ship; one jack almost touched the edge. Barnes looked down into its awesome depths and felt no regret about expending mass to avoid it.

Bowles stared at it. "I repeat, Jim, a fine landing."

"Too close for comfort."

Bowles pushed his face to the quartz and tried to see farther to right and left. "I'm turned around," he complained. "Which way is Earth?"

"Earth is east, of course," Corley answered.

"Which way is east?"

"Man, you certainly are confused. East is out the other port."

"But it *can't* be. We looked out there first and Earth wasn't in sight." Bowles crossed back to the other port. "See?"

Corley joined him. "That's east," he stated. "Look at the stars."

Bowles looked. "But something is screwy. I saw Earth before we landed, in the screen. You saw it, didn't you, Jim?"

"Yes, I saw it."

"You, Doc?"

"I was too busy. How high was it?"

"Just rising. But I *saw* it."

Corley looked at the sky, then at the mountains. "Sure, you did. And it's there—back of those mountains."

Barnes whistled tonelessly. "That's it. I've landed us a few miles too short."

Bowles looked whipped. "Out of line-of-sight," he said dully. "I could claim it until hell freezes—and I can't get the message back."

Traub looked startled. "We're cut off from Earth? But I saw it, too."

"Sure, you did," agreed Barnes, "you saw it while we had altitude. Now we're down too low."

"Oh." Traub looked out. "But it isn't serious, is it? Earth is back of those mountains—but it's in the east; it will rise after a bit. How fast does the Moon turn? Twenty-eight days and something?"

Barnes turned to Corley. "You tell him, Doc."

"Mannie—the Earth doesn't rise or set."

"Huh?"

"The Moon keeps the same face to the Earth all the time. From any one spot, the Earth doesn't move; it just hangs."

"Huh?" Traub raised his hands, stared at them; it could be seen that he was visualizing it, using his fists for Earth and Moon. "Oh—I get it." He looked dismayed. "Say, that's bad. That's really bad."

"Snap out of it, Mannie," Barnes said quickly. "If we can't contact Earth, we'll just have to wait until we get back." He said nothing about his own fears.

Bowles smashed a fist into a palm. "We've got to contact Earth! It doesn't matter whether we get back; four casualties is cheap. But to get a message through now—*this* message, that a United States vessel has landed and taken possession—can mean the salvation of the United States." He turned to Corley. "Doctor, we have enough power to lift us over those mountains, haven't we?"

"Eh? Why, yes."

"Then let's do it—now." He turned toward his couch.

"Hold it, Red!" Bowles stopped; Barnes went on, "If we make one lift and drop, to near those mountains, you know what that does to our chances of getting back."

"Of course! It's not important; we owe it to our country."

"Maybe so. Maybe not." Barnes paused. "If it turns out that we don't have enough juice left to break free of the Moon, I'll concede your point."

"Jim Barnes, we can't consider ourselves against the safety of our country."

"Speak for yourself, Red. Conceded that a claim to the Moon might help out the State Department this week—again it might not. It might stimulate Russia into going all out for space travel while the United States stumbles along as before, proud that we claimed it, but unwilling to spend real money to make it stick."

"Jim, that's sophistry."

"So? That's my decision. We'll try everything else first. You don't know you can't get a message through. Why don't you try?"

"When we're not in line-of-sight? Don't be silly."

"Earth is not far down behind those mountains. Find a place that *is* line-of-sight."

"Oh. Now you make sense." Bowles looked out at the mountains. "I wonder how far away they are?"

"Tell you in a moment," Traub offered. "Wait till I swing the soup bowl around." He started for his couch.

"Never mind, Mannie!" put in Barnes. "No—go ahead. It won't hurt to know. But I wasn't talking about the mountains, Red. They are too far away. But if you scout around, you may find a spot from which the mountains are low enough to let you see Earth. Or you might find some hills—we can't see all around from inside here. Mannie, is it possible to take out the radio and use it outside the ship?"

"Outside? Let me see— The transmitter is unpressurized; I guess I could jigger it. How about power?"

Bowles said, "Doc, how much cable can we dig up?"

Barnes cut in, "Find your spot, then we'll see what's needed."

"Right! Jim, I'll go out at once. Mannie, come with me and we'll find a spot."

"Outside?" Traub said blankly.

"Sure. Don't you want to be the first man to set foot on the Moon?"

"Uh, I guess so." Traub peered out at the blazing unfriendly surface.

Corley got an odd look; Barnes noted it and said, "One moment, Red. Doc is entitled to the honor of being first. After all, the Corley engine made it possible."

"Oh, sure! Doc can be first down the ladder. Let's all go."

"I'll go later," Barnes decided. "I've got work to do."

"As you wish. Come on, Doc."

Corley looked shy. "Oh, I don't have to be first. We all did it, together."

"Don't be modest. Into our suits—let's go!" Thoughts of military policy seemed to have left Bowles' mind; he was for the moment boyishly eager for adventure. He was already undogging the hatch that led down into the airlock.

Barnes helped them dress. The suits were modifications of high-altitude pressure suits used by jet pilots—cumbersome, all-enclosing skins not unlike diving suits and topped off with "goldfish bowl" helmets. The helmets were silvered except for the face plates; a walkie-talkie radio, two oxygen bottles, and an instrument belt completed the main features of a suit. When they were dressed but not helmeted, Barnes said, "Stay in sight of the ship and each other. Red, when you shift from tank one to tank two, git for home and don't dawdle."

"Aye aye."

"I'm going now." He gasketed their helmets, leaving Corley to the last. To him he said softly, "Don't stay long. I need you."

Corley nodded. Barnes fastened the doctor's helmet, then climbed up into the control room and closed the hatch. Corley waited until Barnes was clear, then said, "Check radios. Check instruments."

"Okay, Doctor," Traub's voice sounded in his earphones.

"Okay here," added Bowles.

"Ready for decompression?" They assented; Corley touched a button near the door; there came a muted whine of impellers. Gradually his suit began to lift and swell. The feeling was not new; he had practiced in their own vacuum chamber back at Mojave. He wondered how Traub felt; the first experience with trusting a Rube Goldberg skin could be frightening. "How are you doing, Mannie?"

"All right."

"The first time seems odd, I know."

"But it's not the first time," Traub answered. "I checked these walkie-talkies in the chamber at the job."

"If you gentlemen are through chatting," Bowles cut in, "you'll note that the tell-tale reads 'vacuum.'"

"Eh?" Corley turned and undogged the outer door.

He stood in the door, gazing north. The aching, sun-drenched plain stretched to a black horizon. On his right, knife sharp in the airless moonscape, was the wall of mountains they had grounded to avoid. He lifted his eyes and made out the Big Dipper, midnight clear above a dazzling, noonday desert.

Bowles touched his arm. "One side, Doc. I'll rig the ladder."

"Sorry."

Bowles linked the ends of a rope ladder to hooks outside the door. Finished, he kicked the ladder out. "Go ahead, Doc."

"Uh, thanks." Corley felt for the first rung. It was a clumsy business in the pressure suit. Finally he knelt, grasped the threshold, got a toe in and started down.

It was awkward, rather than hard work. Suit and all, he weighed less than forty pounds. He found it easier to lower himself by his

hands alone. He could not see below his chin, but the shape of the
ship let him know his progress. Finally he was even with the jets.
He lowered himself a bit more, felt for the ground—and kicked his
toe into the lunar soil.

Then he was standing on it.

He stood there a moment, his heart pounding. He was trying to
realize it, take it in, and found himself unable to do so. He had
lived the moment too many thousands of times in too many years
of dreams. It was still a dream.

A foot brushed his shoulder; he stepped back to avoid being
stepped on by Traub. Soon Bowles joined them. "So this is it," the
Admiral said inanely and turned slowly around. "Look, Mannie!
Hills! Not far away."

Corley saw that Bowles was looking under the jets to the south.
The plain was broken there with a sharp eruption of rock. Corley
touched Bowles' arm. "Let's get away from the ship. Here where
the jets splashed is probably a bit radioactive."

"Okay." Bowles followed him; Traub brought up the rear.

IX

Columbus had one motive; Queen Isabella had another—
                                        Farquharson, *Ibid.,* III: 421

On climbing back into the control room Barnes did not immediately get to work. Instead he sat down and thought. For the
last—two days, was it? three days? four days, really—he had had no
chance to collect his thoughts, drop his public mask and invite his
soul.

He felt unutterably weary.

He lifted his eyes to the mountains. There they stood, tall and
forbidding, witnesses that he had accomplished his driving purpose.

To what end? To let Corley explore the dark outer reaches of
science? To help Bowles insure the safety of western civilization—
or perhaps hasten a new crisis?

Or to make orphans of four kids whose old man was "a very
domestic type guy" but could be shamed into coming along?

No, he knew it had been because Jimmy Barnes had been small
for his age, clumsy with his fists, no decent clothes—so he had to
make more money, boss more men, build faster planes than

anyone else. He, James A. Barnes, had reached the Moon because he had never been sure of himself.

He wondered about Mannie's kids and his stomach was a rock inside him.

He threw off the mood and went to the radio controls keyed the walkie-talkie circuit and called out, "This is Jim Barnes, kiddies, coming to you by courtesy of 'SLUMP,' the Super soap. Come in, come in, wherever you are!"

"Jim!" Bowles' voice came back. "Come on out."

"Later," Barnes answered. "Where's Doc?"

"Right here," Corley answered. "I was just coming back."

"Good," said Barnes. "Red, I'll leave this switched on. Sing out now and then."

"Sure thing," Bowles agreed.

Barnes went to the desk and began toting up mass reserves. An orbit computation is complicated; calculating what it takes to pull free of a planet is simple; he had a rough answer in a few minutes.

He ran his hand through his hair. He still needed that haircut—and no barbers on *this* block. He wondered if it were true that a man's hair continued to grow after his death.

The hatch creaked and Corley climbed into the room. "Whew!" he said. "It's good to get out of that suit. That sun is really hot."

"Wasn't the gas expansion enough to keep you cool?"

"Not cool enough. Those suits are hard to get around in, too, Jim—they need a lot of engineering."

"They'll get it," Barnes answered absently, "but reengineering this ship is more urgent. Not the Corley engine, Doc; the controls. They aren't delicate enough."

"I know," Corley admitted. "That poor cutoff—we'll have to design a prediction for it into the autopilot, and use a feedback loop."

Barnes nodded. "Yes, sure, *after* we get back—and if we get back." He tossed his fingers at the scientist. "Hum that through."

Corley glanced at it. "I know."

"Red won't find a spot in line-of-sight with home; those mountains are infernally high. But I wanted him out of the way—and Mannie. No use talking to Red; he's going to get a posthumous Congressional Medal if it kills him—and us too."

Corley nodded. "But I'm with him on trying to contact Earth; I need it worse than he does."

"Hastings?"

"Yes. Jim, if we had enough margin, we could blast off and correct after radio contact. We haven't; if we get off at all it will be close."

"I know. I spent our ticket home, when I made that extra blast."

"What good would it have done to have crashed? Forget it; I need Hastings. We need the best orbit possible."

"Fat chance!"

"Maybe not. There's libration, you know."

Barnes looked startled. "Man, am I stupid!" He went on eagerly, "What's the situation now? Is Earth swinging up, or down?"

The Moon's spin is steady, but its orbit speed is not; it moves fastest when it is closest to Earth. The amount is slight, but it causes the Moon to appear to wobble each month as if the Man-in-the-Moon were shaking his head. This moves the Earth to-and-fro in the lunar sky some seven degrees.

Corley answered, "It's rising—I think. As to whether it will rise enough—well, I'll have to compute Earth's position and then take some star sights."

"Let's get at it. Can I help?"

Before Corley could reply Bowles' voice came over the speaker: "Hey! Jim!"

Barnes keyed the walkie-talkies. "Yes, Red?"

"We're at the hills south of the ship. They might be high enough. I want to go behind them; there may be an easier place to climb."

On the airless Moon, all radio requires line-of-sight—yet Barnes hated to refuse a reasonable request. "Okay—but don't take any chances."

"Aye aye, Skipper."

Barnes turned to Corley. "We need the time anyhow."

"Yes," Corley agreed. "You know, Jim, this isn't the way I imagined it. I don't mean the Moon itself—just wait until we get some pressurized buildings here and some decent pressure suits. But what I mean is what we find ourselves doing. I expected to cram every minute with exploring and collecting specimens and gathering new data. Instead I'll beat my brains out simply trying to get us back."

"Well, maybe you'll have time later—too much time."

Corley grudged a smile. "Could be—"

He sketched out the relative positions of Earth and Moon,

consulted tables. Presently he looked up. "We're in luck. Earth will rise nearly two and a half degrees before she swings back."

"Is that enough?"

"We'll see. Dig out the sextant, Jim." Barnes got it and Corley took it to the eastern port. He measured the elevations of three stars above the tops of the mountains. These he plotted on a chart and drew a line for the apparent horizon. Then he plotted Earth's position relative to those stars.

"Finicky business," he complained. "Better check me, Jim."

"I will. What do you get?"

"Well—if I haven't dropped a decimal point, Earth will be up for a few hours anyway three days from now."

Barnes grinned. "We'll get a ticker-tape parade yet, Doc."

"Maybe. Let's have another look at the ballistic situation first." Barnes' face sobered.

Corley worked for an hour, taking Barnes' approximation and turning it into something slightly better. At last he stopped. "I don't know," he fretted. "Maybe Hastings can trim it a little."

"Doc," Barnes answered, "suppose we jettison everything we can? I hate to say it, but there's all that equipment you brought."

"What do you think I've been doing with these weight schedules? Theoretically the ship is stripped."

"Oh. And it's still bad?"

"It's still bad."

Bowles and Traub returned worn out and just short of sun stroke. The Admiral was unhappy; he had not been able to find any way to climb the hills: "I'll go back tomorrow," he said stoutly. "I mean after we've eaten and slept."

"Forget it," advised Barnes.

"What do you mean?"

"We are going to have line-of-sight from here."

"Eh? Repeat that."

"Libration," Barnes told him. "Doc has already calculated it."

Bowles' face showed delighted comprehension. Traub looked puzzled; Barnes explained it.

"So you see," Barnes went on, "we'll have a chance to send a message in about seventy hours."

Bowles stood up, his fatigue forgotten. "That's all we need!" He pounded his palm exultantly.

"Slow down, Red," Barnes advised, "our chances of taking off look worse than ever."

"So?" Bowles shrugged. "It's not important."

"Oh, for Pete's sake! Drop the Nathan Hale act. Have the common decency to give a thought to Mannie and his four kids."

Bowles started to retort, stopped—then went on again with dignity. "Jim, I didn't mean to annoy you. But I meant what I said. It's not important to get back, as long as our message gets through. Our mistakes will make it easier for the next expedition. In a year the United States can have a dozen ships, better ships, on the Moon. Then no country would be so foolhardy as to attack us. *That* is important; we aren't."

He went on, "Every man dies; the group goes on. You spoke of Mannie's kids. You have no children, nor has Corley. Mannie has—so I know he understands what I mean better than you do." He turned to Traub. "Well, Mannie?"

Traub looked up, then dropped his eyes. "Red is right, Mr. Barnes," he answered in a low voice, "but I'd like to get home."

Barnes bit his lip. "Let's drop it," he said irritably. "Red, you might rustle up some supper."

For three days, Earth time, they labored. Bowles and Barnes stripped the ship—cameras, empty oxygen bottles, their extra clothing, the many scientific instruments Corley had hoped to use—Wilson cloud chamber, Geiger counter, a 12″ Schmidt camera and clock, still cameras, the autocamera, ultra- and infra-spectrographs, other instruments. Corley stayed at his desk, computing, checking, computing again—getting the problem in the best possible shape to turn over to Hastings. Traub overhauled his radio and lined up his directional antenna to the exact orientation at which Earth would appear.

The hour finally crept up to them. Traub was in his couch at the radio controls while the rest crowded at the eastern port. What they needed to say had been made one message:

A formal claim to the Moon, setting forth time and place of landing, a long and technical message to Hastings, and finally code groups supplied by Bowles. Traub would send it all out as one, many times if necessary.

"I see it!" It was Corley who claimed the distinction.

Barnes stared at the spot. "Your imagination, Doc; a highlight on the peaks." The sun was behind them, "afternoon" by local time; the mountains were bright in the east.

Bowles put in, "No, Jim. There's something there."

Barnes turned. "Start sending!"

Traub closed his key.

The message was repeated, with listening in between, time after time. An arc of Earth slowly, terribly slowly, crept above the horizon. No answer came back, but they did not despair, so little of Earth was as yet in sight.

Finally Barnes turned to Corley. "What does that look like, Doc? The part we can see, I mean."

Corley peered at it. "Can't say. Too much cloud."

"It looks like ocean. If so, we won't get a jingle until it's higher."

Corley's face slowly became horror struck. "What's the matter?" demanded Barnes.

"Good grief! *I forgot to figure the attitude.*"

"Huh?"

Corley did not answer. He jumped to the desk, grabbed the Nautical Almanac, started scribbling, stopped, and drew a diagram of the positions of Earth, Sun, and Moon. On the circle representing the Earth he drew a line for the Greenwich meridian.

Barnes leaned over him. "Why the panic?"

"That *is* ocean, the Pacific Ocean."

Bowles joined them. "What about it?"

"Don't you see? Earth turns to the east; America is moving away—already out of sight." Corley hurriedly consulted his earlier calculations. "Earth reaches maximum elevation in about, uh, four hours and eight minutes. Then it drops back."

Traub pushed up an earphone. "Can't you guys shut up?" he protested. "I'm trying to listen."

Corley threw down his pencil. "It doesn't matter, Mannie. You aren't ever going to be in line-of-sight with NAA."

"Huh? What did you say?"

"The Earth is faced wrong. We're seeing the Pacific Ocean now, then we'll see Asia, Europe, and finally the Atlantic. By the time we should see the United States it will have dropped back of the mountains."

"You mean I'm just wasting time?"

"Keep sending, Mannie," Barnes said quietly, "and keep listening. You may pick up another station."

Bowles shook his head. "Not likely."

"Why not? Hawaii may still be in sight. The Pearl Harbor station is powerful."

"Provided they have rigged a beam on us, same as NAA."

"Well, keep trying, Mannie."

Traub slipped his earphone back in place. Bowles went on, "It's nothing to get excited about. We'll be picked up anywhere." He chuckled. "Soviet stations will be listening to us shortly. They will be broadcasting denials at the same time stations in Australia are telling the world the truth."

Corley looked up. "But I won't get to talk to Hastings!"

Bowles said very gently:

"As I said, that isn't important in the long run."

Barnes said, "Stow it, Red. Don't get downhearted, Doc—there is a good chance that some other station will beam us. Keep trying, Mannie."

"Will you guys *please* shut up?"

He did keep trying over and over again; in the intervals he listened, not only to the beam frequency of NAA, but all over the dial.

More than eight hours later the last faint arc of Earth had vanished. No one had thought to eat and Traub had not left his post for any purpose.

They went on preparing to leave, but their hearts were not in it. Corley stayed at his desk, except for snatches of sleep, trying to make up by effort for the lack of fine tools. He set the departure ahead to give him more time. The aching, cloudless lunar day wore on and the sun sank to the west. They planned to risk it just at sundown. It was admitted by Corley—and by Barnes, who checked his figures—that the situation theoretically did not permit success. By the book, they would rise, curve around the Moon, and approach the border where the fields of Earth and Moon balance—but they would never reach it; they would fall back and crash.

It was also agreed, by everyone, that it was better to die trying than to wait for death. Bowles suggested that they wait a month until next sight of Earth, but arithmetic shut off that chance; they would not starve; they would not die of thirst—they would suffocate.

Bowles took it serenely; Traub lay in his bunk or moved like a zombie. Corley was a gray-faced automaton, buried in figures. Barnes became increasingly irritable.

As a sop to Corley, Bowles made desultory readings on the instruments Corley had not had time to use. Among the chores was developing the films taken on the flight across the back face. It had been agreed to keep them, they weighed ounces only, and it was desirable to develop them to prevent fogging by stray radioactivity. Barnes assigned Traub the task, to keep him busy.

Traub worked in the airlock, it being the only darkroom. Presently he came poking his head up through the hatch. "Mr. Barnes?"

"Yes, Mannie?" Barnes noted with satisfaction that Traub showed his first touch of animation since his ordeal.

"See what you make of this." Traub handed him a negative. Barnes spread it against a port. "See those little round things? What are they?"

"Craters, I guess."

"No, *these* are craters. See the difference?"

Barnes tried to visualize what the negative would look like in positive. "What do you think?"

"Well, they look like hemispheres. Odd formation, huh?"

Barnes looked again. "Too damned odd," he said slowly. "Mannie, let's have a print."

"There's no print paper, is there?"

"You're right; my error."

Bowles joined them. "What's the curiosity? Moon maidens?"

Barnes showed him. "What do you make of those things?"

Bowles looked, and looked again. Finally he asked, "Mannie, how can we enlarge this?"

It took an hour to jury-rig a magic lantern, using a pilfered camera lens. They all gathered in the airlock and Traub switched on his improvised projector.

Bowles said, "Focus it, for cripes' sake." Traub did so. The images of his "hemispheres" were reasonably distinct. They were six in number, arranged in a semicircle—and they were unnatural in appearance.

Barnes peered at them. "Red—you were a bit late when you claimed this planet."

Bowles said, "Hmmm—" Finally he emphatically added, "Constructions."

"Wait a minute," protested Corley. "They *look* artificial, but some very odd formations are natural."

"Look closer, Doc," Barnes advised. "There is no reasonable doubt. The question: were we a year or so late in claiming the Moon? Or millions of years?"

"Eh?"

"Those are pressure domes. Who built them? Moon people, long before history? Visiting Martians? Or Russians?"

Traub said, "Mr. Barnes—why not *live* Moon people?"

"What? Take a walk outside."

"I don't see why not. As soon as I saw them I said, 'That's where those flying saucers came from a while back.'"

"Mannie, there were no flying saucers. Don't kid yourself."

Traub said, doggedly, "I knew a man who—"

"—saw one with his own eyes," Barnes finished. "Forget it. That's our worry—there. They're real. They show on film."

"Forget Martians, too," Bowles said gruffly, "and any long-dead Moon people."

"I take it you go for Russians?" Barnes commented.

"I simply know that those films must be in the hands of military intelligence as soon as possible."

"Military intelligence? Ah, yes, on Earth—a lovely thought."

"Don't be sarcastic. I mean it."

"So do I."

From willingness to die, his mission accomplished, Bowles became frantic to live, to get back. It made him bitter that he himself had insisted on landing—with all-important new evidence even then latent in the ship.

He sweated out a possible scheme to get the films back to Washington and seized a time when Traub was out of the ship to propose it to Barnes. "Jim—could you get this ship back by yourself?"

"What do you mean?"

"You checked the figures. One man might make it—if the ship were lightened by the other three."

Barnes looked angry. "Red, that's nonsense."

"Ask the others."

"No!" Barnes added, "Four men came; four go back—or nobody does."

"Well, *I* can lighten ship, at least. That's my privilege."

"Any more such talk and it'll be your privilege to be strapped down till takeoff!"

Bowles took Barnes' arm. "Those films have *got* to reach the Pentagon."

"Quit breathing in my face. We'll make it if we can. Have you anything left to jettison?"

"Jim, this ship gets back if I have to drag it."

"Drag it, then. Answer my question."

"I've got the clothes I stand in—I'll jettison them." Bowles looked around. "Jettison, he says. Jim Barnes, you call this ship stripped. By God, I'll show you! Where's that tool kit?"

"Traub just took it outside along with other stuff."

Bowles jumped to the microphone. "Mannie? Bring back the hacksaw; I need it!" He turned to Barnes. "I'll show you how to strip ship. What's that radio doing there? Useless as a third leg. Why do I need an autopilot display? Yours is enough. Doc—get up off that stool!"

Corley looked up from his closed world of figures. He had not even heard the row. "Eh? You called me?"

"Up off that stool—I'm going to unbolt it from the deck."

Corley looked puzzled. "Certainly, if you need it." He turned to Barnes. "Jim, these are the final figures."

Barnes was watching Bowles. "Hold the figures, Doc. We may make a few revisions.

Under the drive of Bowles' will they stripped ship again, fighting against their deadline. Rations—*all* rations—men do not starve quickly. Radios. Duplicate instruments. Engineering instruments not utterly essential to blasting. The hot plate. Cupboards and doors, light fixtures and insulation; everything that could be hacksawed away or ripped out bodily. The ladder from control room to airlock—that was kicked out last, with three space suits and the rope ladder.

Bowles found no way to get rid of the fourth pressure suit; he had to wear it to stay alive while he pushed out the last items—but he found a way to minimize even that. He removed the instrument belt, the back pack, the air bottles, the insulating shoes, and stood there, gasping the air left in the suit, while the lock cycled from "vacuum" to "pressure" for the last time.

Three hands reached down and pulled him through the hatch. "Stations!" Barnes snapped. "Stand by to blast!"

They were waiting for the count off, when Traub reached up and touched Barnes' arm. "Skipper?"

"Yes, Mannie?"

Traub looked to see if the other two were noticing; they were not. "Are we really going to make it?"

Barnes decided to be truthful. "Probably not." He glanced at

Bowles; the Admiral's features were sunken; his false teeth had gone with the rest. Barnes grinned warmly. "But we're sure going to give it a try!"

The monument where the proud Luna *once stood is pictured in every schoolroom. Many trips followed, some tragic, some not, before space transportation reached its present safe operation. The spaceways are paved with the bodies and glorious hopes of pioneers. With accomplishment of their dream some of the romance has gone out of space.*

Farquharson, *Ibid.,* III: 423

SHOOTING
DESTINATION MOON

"Why don't they make more science fiction movies?"

The answer to any question starting, "Why don't they—" is almost always, "Money."

I arrived in Hollywood with no knowledge of motion picture production or costs, no experience in writing screen plays, nothing but a yen to write the first Hollywood picture about the first trip to the Moon. Lou Schor, an agent who is also a science fiction enthusiast, introduced me to a screen writer, Alford van Ronkel; between us we turned out a screen play from one of my space travel stories.

So we were in business—

Uh, not quite. The greatest single production problem is to find someone willing to risk the money. People who have spare millions of dollars do not acquire them by playing angel to science fiction writers with wild ideas.

We were fortunate in meeting George Pal of George Pal Productions, who became infected with the same madness. So we had a producer—*now* we were in business.

Still not quite— Producers and financiers are not the same thing. It was nearly a year from the writing of the screen play until George Pal informed us that he had managed to convince an angel. (How? Hypnosis? Drugs? I'll never know. If I had a million dollars, I would sit on it and shoot the first six science fiction writers who came my way with screen plays.)

Despite those huge Hollywood salaries, money is as hard to get in Hollywood as anywhere. The money men in Hollywood write large checks only when competition leaves them no alternative;

they prefer to write small checks, or no checks at all. Even though past the big hurdle of getting the picture financed, money trouble remains with one throughout production; if a solution to a special-effects problem costs thirty thousand dollars but the budget says five thousand dollars, then you have got to think of an equally good five thousand dollar solution—and that's all there is to it.

I mention this because there came a steady stream of non-motion-picture folk who were under the impression that thousand-dollar-a-week salaries were waiting for them in a science fiction picture. The budget said, "No!"

The second biggest hurdle to producing an accurate and convincing science fiction picture is the "Hollywood" frame of mind—in this case, people in authority who either don't know or don't care about scientific correctness and plausibility. Ignorance can be coped with; when a man asks "What does a rocket have to *push* against, out there in space?" it is possible to explain. On the other hand, if his approach is, "Nobody has ever been to the Moon; the audiences won't know the difference," it is impossible to explain anything to him; he does not know and does not want to know.

We had plenty of both sorts of trouble.

That the picture did not end up as a piece of fantasy, having only a comic-book relation to real science fiction, can be attributed almost entirely to the integrity and good taste of Irving Pichel, the director. Mr. Pichel is not a scientist, but he is intelligent and honest. He believed what Mr. Bonestell and I told him and saw to it that what went on the screen was as accurate as budget and ingenuity would permit.

By the time the picture was being shot the entire company—actors, grips, cameramen, office people—became imbued with enthusiasm for producing a picture which would be scientifically acceptable as well as a box office success. Willy Ley's *Rockets and Space Travel* was read by dozens of people in the company. Bonestell and Ley's *Conquest of Space* was published about then and enjoyed a brisk sale among us. Waits between takes were filled by discussions of theory and future prospects of interplanetary travel.

As shooting progressed we began to be deluged with visitors of technical background—guided missiles men, astronomers, rocket engineers, aircraft engineers. The company, seeing that their work was being taken seriously by technical specialists, took pride in turning out an authentic job. There were no more remarks of "What difference does it make?"

Which brings us to the third hurdle—the *technical* difficulties of filming a spaceship picture.

The best way to photograph space flight convincingly would be to raise a few hundred million dollars, get together a scientific and engineering staff of the caliber used to make the A-bomb, take over the facilities of General Electric, White Sands, and Douglas Aircraft, and *build* a spaceship.

Then go along and photograph what happens.

We had to use the second-best method—which meant that every shot, save for a few before takeoff from Earth, had to involve special effects, trick photography, unheard-of lighting problems. All this is expensive and causes business managers to grow stomach ulcers. In the ordinary motion picture there may be a scene or two with special effects; this picture had to be *all* special effects, most of them never before tried.

If you have not yet seen the picture, I suggest that you do not read further until after you have seen it; in this case it is more fun to be fooled. Then, if you want to look for special effects, you can go back and see the picture again. (Adv.)

The Moon is airless, subject only to one-sixth gravity, bathed in undiluted sunlight, covered with black sky through which shine brilliant stars, undimmed by cloud or smog. It is a place of magnificent distances and towering mountains.

A sound stage is usually about thirty feet high, and perhaps a hundred and fifty feet long. Gravity is Earth normal. It is filled with cigarette smoke, arc light fog, and dust—not to mention more than a hundred technicians.

Problem: to photograph *in a sound stage* men making a rocket landing on the Moon, exploring its endless vistas, moving and jumping under its light gravity. Do this in Technicolor, which adds a sheaf of new problems, not the least of which is the effect of extra hot lights on men wearing spacesuits.

The quick answer is that it can't be done.

A second answer is to go on location, pick a likely stretch of desert, remove by hand all trace of vegetation, and shoot the "real" thing. Wait a minute; how about that black and star-studded sky? Fake it—use special effects. Sorry; once blue sky is on Technicolor emulsion it is there to stay. With black-and-white there are ways, but not with color.

So we are back on the sound stage and we *have* to shoot it there. Vacuum clear atmosphere? No smoking—hard to enforce—high speed on all blowers, be resigned to throwing away some footage, and leave the big doors open—which lets in noise and ruins the sound track. Very well, we must dub in the sound—and up go the costs—but the air *must* be clear.

Low gravity and tremendous leaps—piano wire, of course—but did you ever try to wire a man who is wearing a spacesuit? The wires have to get inside that suit at several points, producing the effect a nail has on a tire, i.e., a man wearing a pressurized suit cannot be suspended on wires. So inflation of suits must be replaced by padding, at least during wired shots. But a padded suit does not wrinkle the same way a pressurized suit does and the difference shows. Furthermore, the zippered openings for the wires can be seen. Still worse, if inflation is to be faked with padding, how are we to show them putting on their suits?

That sobbing in the background comes from the technical adviser—yours truly—who had hoped not only to have authentic pressure suits but had expected to be able to cool the actors under the lights by the expansion of gas from their air bottles. Now they must wear lamb's wool padding and will have no self-contained source of breathing air, a situation roughly equivalent to doing heavy work at noon in desert summer, in a fur coat while wearing a bucket over your head.

Actors are a hardy breed. They did it.

To get around the shortcomings of padded suits we worked in an "establishing scene" in which the suits were shown to be of two parts, an outer chafing suit and an inner pressure suit. This makes sense; deep-sea divers often use chafing suits over their pressure suits, particularly when working around coral. The relationship is that of an automobile tire carcass to the inner tube. The outer part takes the beating and the inner part holds the pressure. It is good engineering and we present this new wrinkle in spacesuits without apology. The first men actually to walk the rugged floor of the Moon and to climb its sharp peaks, will, if they are wise, use the same device.

So we padded for wire tricks and used air pressure at other times. Try to see when and where we switched. I could not tell—and I saw the scenes being shot.

* * *

Now for that lunar landscape which has to be compressed into a sound stage—I had selected the crater Aristarchus. Chesley Bonestell did not like Aristarchus; it did not have the shape he wanted, nor the height of crater wall, nor the distance to apparent horizon. Mr. Bonestell knows more about the surface appearance of the Moon than any other living man; he searched around and found one he liked—the crater Harpalus, in high northern latitude, facing the Earth. High latitude was necessary so that the Earth would appear down near the horizon where the camera could see it and still pick up some lunar landscape; northern latitude was preferred so that Earth would appear in the conventional and recognizable schoolroom-globe attitude.

Having selected it, Mr. Bonestell made a model of it on his dining room table, using beaver board, plasticine, tissue paper, paint, anything at hand. He then made a pinhole photograph from its center— Wait; let's list the stages:

1. A Mount Wilson observatory photograph.
2. Bonestell's tabletop model.
3. A pinhole panorama.
4. A large blowup.
5. A Bonestell oil painting, in his exact detail, about twenty feet long and two feet high, in perspective as seen from the exit of the rocket, one hundred fifteen feet above the lunar surface.
6. A blownup photograph, about three feet high, of this painting.
7. A scenic painting, about four feet high, based on this photograph and matching the Bonestell colors, but with the perspective geometrically changed to bring the observer down to the lunar floor.
8. A scenic backing, twenty feet high, to go all around a sound stage, based on the one above, but with the perspective distorted to allow for the fact that sound stages are oblong.
9. A floor for the sound stage, curved up to bring the foreground of the scene into correct perspective with the backing.
10. A second back drop of black velvet and "stars."

The result you see on the cover of this issue. It looks like a Bonestell painting because it *is* a Bonestell painting—in the same sense that a Michelangelo mural is still the work of the master even though a dozen of the master's pupils may have wielded the brushes.

Every item went through similar stages. I was amazed at the thoroughness of preliminary study made by the art department— Ernst Fegte and Jerry Pycha—before any item was built to be photographed. Take the control room of the spaceship. This compartment was shaped like the frustrum of a cone and was located near the nose of spaceship *Luna*. It contained four acceleration couches, instruments and controls of many sorts, an airplane pilot's seat with controls for landing on Earth, radar screens, portholes, and a hatch to the air lock—an incredibly crowded and complicated set. (To the motion picture business this was merely a "set," a place where actors would be photographed while speaking lines.)

To add to the complications the actors would sometimes read their lines while hanging upside down in midair in this set, or walking up one of its vertical walls. Add that the space was completely enclosed, about as small as an elevator cage, and had to contain a Technicolor sound camera housed in its huge sound-proof box—called a "blimp," heaven knows why.

I made some rough sketches. Chesley Bonestell translated these into smooth drawings, adding in his own extensive knowledge of spaceships. The miniature shop made a model which was studied by the director, the art director, and the cameraman, who promptly tore it to bits. It wouldn't do at all; the action could not be photographed, could not even be seen, save by an Arcturian Bug-Eyed Monster with eyes arranged around a spherical 360°.

So the miniature shop made another model, to suit photographic requirements.

So I tore that one apart. I swore that I wouldn't be found dead around a so-called spaceship control room arranged in any such fashion; what were we making? A comic strip?

So the miniature shop made a third model.

And a fourth.

Finally we all were satisfied. The result, as you see it on the screen, is a control room which might very well be used as a pattern for the ship which will actually make the trip some day, provided the ship is intended for a four-man crew. It is a proper piece of economical functional design, which could do what it is meant to do.

But it has the unique virtue that it can be photographed as a motion picture set.

A writer—a fiction writer, I mean; not a screen writer—is never bothered by such considerations. He can play a dramatic scene inside a barrel quite as well as in Grand Central Station. His mind's eye looks in any direction, at any distance, with no transition troubles and no jerkiness. He can explain anything which is not clear. But in motion pictures the camera has got to *see* what is going on and must see it in such a fashion that the audience is not even aware of the camera, or the illusion is lost. The camera must see all that it needs to see to achieve a single emotional effect from a single angle, without bobbing back and forth, or indulging in awkward, ill-timed cuts. This problem is always present in motion picture photography; it was simply exceptionally acute in the control room scenes. To solve it all was a real *tour de force;* the director of photography, Lionel Linden, aged several years before we got out of that electronic Iron Maiden.

In addition to arranging the interior for camera angles it was necessary to get the camera to the selected angles—in this enclosed space. To accomplish this, every panel in the control room was made removable—"wild," they call it—so that the camera could stick in its snout and so that lights could be rigged. Top and bottom and all its sides—it came apart like a piece of Meccano. This meant building of steel instead of the cheap beaverboard-and-wood frauds usually photographed in Hollywood. The control room was actually stronger and heavier than a real spaceship control room would be. Up went the costs again.

Even with the set entirely "wild" it took much, much longer to shift from one angle to another angle than it does on a normal movie set, as those panels had to be bolted and unbolted, heavy lights had to be rigged and unrigged—and the costs go sky high. You can figure overhead in a sound stage at about a thousand dollars an *hour,* so, when in the movie you see the pilot turn his head and speak to someone, then glance down at his instruments, whereupon the camera also glances down to let you see what he is talking about, remember how much time and planning and money it took to let you glance at the instrument board. This will help to show why motion picture theaters sell popcorn to break even— and why science fiction pictures are not made every day. Realism is confoundedly expensive.

* * *

Nor did the costs and the headaches with the control room stop there. As every reader of *Astounding* knows, when a rocket ship is not blasting, everything in it floats free—"free fall." Men float around—which meant piano wires inside that claustrophobic little closet. It was necessary at one point to show a man floating out from his acceleration couch and into the center of the room. Very well; unbolt a panel to let in the wires. Wups! While a spaceship in space has no "up" or "down," sound stage three on Las Palmas Avenue in Hollywood certainly does have; supporting wires must run vertically—see Isaac Newton. To float the man out of the tight little space he was in would require the wires to turn a corner. Now we needed a Hindu fakir capable of the Indian rope trick.

The special effects man, Lee Zavitz, has been doing impossible tricks for years. He turned the entire set, tons of steel, on its side and pulled the actor out in what would normally be a horizontal direction. Easy!

So easy that the art department had to design double gimbals capable of housing the entire set, engineer it, have it built of structural steel, have it assembled inside a sound stage since it was too big to go through the truck doors. Machinery had to be designed and installed to turn the unwieldy thing. Nothing like it had ever been seen in Hollywood, but it did enable a man to float out from a confined space and, later, to walk all around the sides of the control room with "magnetic" boots.

This double gimbals rig, three stories high, put the control room set high in the air, so the carpenters had to build platforms around it and the camera had to be mounted on a giant boom—one so huge, so fancy, and so expensive that Cecil B. de Mille came over to inspect it. The camera itself had to be mounted in gimbals before it was placed on the boom, so that it might turn with the set—or the other way, for some special effects. This meant removing its soundproof blimp, which meant dubbing the sound track.

("Who cares? It's only money." Don't say that in the presence of the business manager; he's not feeling well.)

This was not the end of the control room tricks. Some of the dodges were obvious, such as making dial needles go around, lights blink on and off, television and radar screens light up— obvious, but tedious and sometimes difficult. Producing the effect of a ship blasting off at six gravities requires something more than sound track of a rocket blast, as the men each weigh over a thousand pounds during blast. Lee Zavitz and his crew built large inflated bladders into each acceleration couch. Whenever the jet was "fired" these bladders would be suddenly deflated and the actors would be "crushed" down into their cushions.

A thousand pounds weight compress the man as well as his mattress, which will show, of course, in his features. The makeup man fitted each actor with a thin membrane, glued to his face, to which a yoke could be rigged back of his neck. From the yoke a lever sequence reaching out of the scene permitted the man's features to be drawn back by the "terrible" acceleration. Part of what you see is acting by some fine actors, Dick Wesson, Warner Anderson, Tom Powers, John Archer; part was a Rube Goldberg trick.

The air suddenly escaping from the bladders produced a sound like that of a mournful cow, thus requiring more dubbing of sound track. The air had to be returned to the bladders with equal suddenness when the jet cut off, which required a compressed air system more complicated than that used by a service station.

The sets abounded in compressed air and hydraulic and electrical systems to make various gadgets work—to cycle the air lock doors, to rig out the exit ladder, to make the instrument board work—all designed by Zavitz. Lee Zavitz is the man who "burned Atlanta" in Gone With The Wind, forty acres of real fire, hundreds of actors and not a man hurt. I saw him stumped just once in this film, through no fault of his. He was controlling an explosion following a rocket crash. It was being done full size, out on the Mojave Desert, and the camera angle stretched over miles of real desert. From a jeep back of the camera Zavitz was cuing the special effects by radio. In the middle of the explosions the radio decided to blow a tube—and the action stopped, ruining an afternoon's work. We had to come back and do it over the next day, after a sleepless night of rebuilding by the special effects crew. Such things are why making motion pictures produces stomach ulcers but not boredom.

The greatest single difficulty we encountered in trying to fake realistically the conditions of space flight was in producing the brilliant starry sky of empty space. In the first place nobody knows what stars look like out in space; it is not even known for sure whether twinkling takes place in the eye or in the atmosphere. There is plausible theory each way. In the second place the eye is incredibly more sensitive than is Technicolor film; the lights had to be brighter than stars to be picked up at all. In the third place, film, whether used at Palomar or in a Technicolor camera, reports a point light source as a circle of light, with diameter dependent on intensity. On that score alone we were whipped as to complete realism; there is no way to avoid the peculiarities inherent in an artificial optical system.

We fiddled around with several dodges and finally settled on automobile headlight bulbs. They can be burned white, if you don't mind burning out a few bulbs; they come in various brightnesses; and they give as near a point source of light as the emulsions can record—more so, in fact. We used nearly two thousand of them, strung on seventy thousand feet of wire.

But we got a red halation around the white lights. This resulted from the fact that Technicolor uses three films for the three primary colors. Two of them are back to back at the focal plane, but the red-sensitive emulsion is a gnat's whisker away, by one emulsion thickness. It had me stumped, but not the head gaffer. He covered each light with a green gelatin screen, a "gel," and the red halation was gone, leaving a satisfactory white light.

The gels melted down oftener than the bulbs burned out; we had to replace them each day at lunch hour and at "wrap up."

There was another acute problem of lighting on the lunar set. As we all know, sunlight on the Moon is the harshest of plastic light, of great intensity and all from one direction. There is no blue sky overhead to diffuse the light and fill the shadows. We needed a sound-stage light which would be as intense as that sunlight—a single light.

No such light has ever been developed.

During the war, I had a research project which called for the duplication of sunlight; I can state authoritatively that sunlight has not yet been duplicated. An arc light, screened by Pyrex, is the closest thing to it yet known—but the movies already use arc lights in great numbers, and the largest arc light bulb, the "brute," is not nearly strong enough to light an entire sound stage with sunlight intensity—raw sunlight, beating down on the lunar set would have been equivalent to more than fifteen hundred horse power. There are no such arc lights.

We traced down several rumors of extremely intense lights. In each case we found either that the light was not sufficiently intense for an entire sound stage, or it was monochromatic—worse than useless for Technicolor.

We got around it by using great banks of brutes, all oriented the same way and screened to produce approximate parallelism. Even with the rafters loaded with the big lights almost past the safety point, it was necessary to use some cross lighting to fill gaps. The surface of the Moon had some degree of "fill" in the shadows by reflection from cliff walls and the ground; it is probable that we were forced to fill too much. We used the best that contemporary engineering provides—and next time will gladly use an atomic-powered simulation of the Sun's atomic-powered light.

The simulation of raw sunlight was better in the scenes involving men in spacesuits outside the ship in space, as it was not necessary to illuminate an entire sound stage but only two or three human figures; a bank of brutes sufficed and no fill was needed, nor wanted, since there was no surrounding landscape to fill by reflection.

The effect was rather ghostly; the men were lighted as is the Moon in half phase, brilliantly on one side, totally unlighted and indistinguishable from the black sky itself on the other side.

This scene in which men are outside the ship in space involved another special effect—the use of a compressed oxygen bottle as a makeshift rocket motor to rescue a man who has floated free of the ship. The energy stored by compressing gas in a large steel bottle is quite sufficient for the purpose. I checked theory by experiment; opening the valve wide on such a charged bottle gave me a firm shove. The method is the same as that used to propel a toy boat with a CO_2 cartridge from a fizz water bottle—the basic rocket principle.

We had considered using a shotgun, since everyone is familiar with its kick, but we couldn't think of an excuse for taking a shotgun to the Moon. Then we considered using a Very pistol, which has a strong kick and which might well be taken to the Moon for signaling. But it did not *look* convincing and it involved great fire hazard in a sound stage. So we settled on the oxygen bottle, which looked impressive, would work, and would certainly be available in a spaceship.

However, since we were still on Las Palmas Avenue and not in space, it had to be a wire trick, with four men on wires, not to mention the oxygen bottle and several safety lines. That adds up to about thirty-six wires for the heavy objects and dozens of black threads for the safety lines—and all this spaghetti must not show.

Each man had to have several "puppeteers" to handle him, by means of heavy welded pipe frames not unlike the cradles used by Tony Sarg for his marionettes, but strong enough for men, not dolls. These in turn had to be handled by block and tackle and overhead traveling cranes. Underneath all was a safety net just to reassure the actors and to keep Lee Zavitz from worrying; our safety factor on each rig was actually in excess of forty, as each wire had a breaking strength of eight hundred pounds. To top it off each man had to wear a cumbersome, welded iron, articulated harness under his spacesuit for attachment of wires. This was about as heavy and uncomfortable as medieval armor.

The setups seemed to take forever. Actors would have to be up in the air on wires for as long as two hours just to shoot a few seconds of film. For ease in handling, the "oxygen bottle" was built of balsa wood and embedded in it was a small CO_2 bottle of the fire extinguisher type. This produced another headache, as, after a few seconds of use, it would begin to produce carbon dioxide "snow," which fell straight down and ruined the illusion.

But the wires were our real headache. One member of the special effects crew did nothing all day long but trot around with a thirty-foot pole with a paint-soaked sponge on the end, trying to kill highlights on the wires. Usually he was successful, but we would never know until we saw it on the screen in the daily rushes. When he was not successful, we had to go back and do the whole tedious job over again.

Most of creating the illusion of space travel lay not in such major efforts, but in constant attention to minor details. For example, the crew members are entering the air lock to go outside the ship in free fall. They are wearing "magnetic" boots, so we don't have to wire them at this point. Everything in the air lock is bolted down, so there is nothing to spoil the illusion of no up-and-down. Very well—"Quiet, everybody! Roll 'em!"

"Speed!" answers the sound man.

"Action!"

The actors go to the lockers in which their spacesuits are kept, open them—and the suits are hanging straight down, which puts us back on Las Palmas Avenue! "Hold it! Kill it! Where is Lee Zavitz?"

So the suits are hastily looped up with black thread into a satisfactory "floating" appearance, and we start over.

Such details are ordinarily the business of the script girl who can always be depended on to see to it that a burning cigarette laid down on Monday the third will be exactly the same length when it is picked up on Wednesday the nineteenth. But it is too much to expect a script girl to be a space flight expert. However, by the end of the picture, our script clerk, Cora Palmatier, could pick flaws in the most carefully constructed space yarn. In fact, everybody got into the act and many flaws were corrected not because I spotted them but through the alertness and helpfulness of others of the hundred-odd persons it takes to shoot a scene. Realism is compounded of minor details, most of them easy to handle if noticed. For example, we used a very simple dodge to simulate a Geiger counter—we used a real one.

A mass of background work went into the flight of the spaceship *Luna* which appears only indirectly on the screen. Save for the atomic-powered jet, a point which had to be assumed, the rest of the ship and its flight were planned as if the trip actually were to have been made. The mass ratio was correct for the assumed thrust and for what the ship was expected to do. The jet speed was consistent with the mass ratio. The trajectory times and distances were all carefully plotted, so that it was possible to refer to charts and tell just what angle the Earth or the Moon would subtend to the camera at any given instant in the story. This was based on a precise orbit—calculated, not by me, but by your old friend, Dr. Robert S. Richardson of Mount Wilson and Palomar Mountain.

None of these calculations appears on the screen but the results do. The *Luna* took off from Lucerne Valley in California on June 20th at ten minutes to four, zone eight time, with a half Moon overhead and the Sun just below the eastern horizon. It blasted for three minutes and fifty seconds and cut off at an altitude of eight hundred seven miles, at escape speed in a forty-six-hour orbit. Few of these data are given the audience—but what the audience sees out the ports is consistent with the above. The time at which they pass the speed of sound, the time at which they burst up into sunlight, the Bonestell backdrops of Los Angeles County and of the western part of the United States, all these things match up. Later, in the approach to the Moon, the same care was used.

Since despite all wishful thinking we are still back on Las Palmas Avenue, much of the effect of taking off from Earth, hurtling through space and landing on the Moon had to be done in miniature. George Pal was known for his "Puppetoons" before he started producing feature pictures; his staff is unquestionably the most skilled in the world in producing three-dimensional animation. John Abbott, director of animation, ate, slept, and dreamed the Moon for months to accomplish the few bits of animation necessary to fill the gaps in the live action. Abbott's work is successful only when it isn't noticed. I'll warrant that you won't notice it, save by logical deduction, i.e., since no one has been to the Moon as yet, the shots showing the approach for landing on the Moon *must* be animation—and they are. Again, in the early part of the picture you will see the *Luna* in Lucerne Valley of the Mojave Desert. You know that the ship is full size for you see men climbing around it, working on it, getting in the elevator of the Gantry crane and entering it—and it *is* full size; we trucked it in pieces to the desert and set it up there. Then you will see the Gantry crane pull away and the *Luna* blasts off for space.

That *can't* be full size; no one has ever done it.

Try to find the transition point. Even money says you pick a point either too late or too soon.

The *Luna* herself is one hundred fifty feet tall; the table top model of her and the miniature Gantry crane are watchmaker's dreams. The miniature floodlights mounted on the crane are the size of my little fingertip—and they work. Such animation is done by infinite patience and skill. Twenty-four separate planned and scaled setups are required for each second of animation on the screen. Five minutes of animation took longer to photograph than the eighty minutes of live action.

At one point it seemed that all this planning and effort would come to nothing; the powers-that-be decided that the story was too cold and called in a musical comedy writer to liven it up with—*sssh!*—sex. For a time we had a version of the script which included dude ranches, cowboys, guitars and hillbilly songs on the Moon, a trio of female hepsters singing into a mike, interiors of cocktail lounges, and more of the like, combined with pseudoscientific gimmicks which would have puzzled even Flash Gordon.

It was never shot. That was the wildest detour on the road to the Moon; the fact that the *Luna* got back into orbit can be attributed to the calm insistence of Irving Pichel. But it gives one a chilling notion of what we may expect from time to time.

Somehow, the day came when the last scene had been shot and, despite Hollywood detours, we had made a motion picture of the first trip to the Moon. Irving Pichel said, "Print it!" for the last time, and we adjourned to celebrate at a bar the producer had set up in one end of the stage. I tried to assess my personal account sheet—it had cost me eighteen months work, my peace of mind, and almost all of my remaining hair.

Nevertheless, when I saw the "rough cut" of the picture, it seemed to have been worth it.

THE WITCH'S DAUGHTERS

Have no truck with the
    daughters of Lilith.
Pay no mind to the
    red-headed creatures.
Man, be warned by their
    sharp, white teeth;
Consider their skulls, and their
    other queer features.

They're not of our tribe, with their
    flame-colored hair;
They're no sib to us, with their
    pale, white skins;
There's no soul behind those
    wild green eyes
Man, when you meet one—
    walk widdershins!

When they die, they pop,
    like burst soap bubble
(Eight hundred years
    is their usual span).
Loving such beings
    leads only to trouble.
By Heaven, be warned,
    you rash young man!

August 1946

THE BULLETIN
BOARD

Our campus is not a giant, factory-size job with a particle accelerator and a two-hundred-man football squad, but it's chummy. The chummiest thing about it is the bulletin board in Old Main. You may find a stray glove fastened up with a thumbtack, or you can pick up a baby-sitting job if a married veteran doesn't beat you to it. Or you can buy a car cheap if you tow it from where it gave up. There are items like: "Will the person who removed a windbreaker from the Library please return same and receive a punch in the nose?"

But the main interest is the next four sections, "A-TO-G," "H-TO-L," "M-TO-T," and "U-TO-Z," for they are what we use in place of the U.S. Postal "Service" at enormous saving in postage. Everybody inspects his section before class in the morning. If there's nothing for you, at least you can see who does get mail and sometimes from whom. You'll look again at lunch time and before going home. A person with a busy social life will check the board six or seven times.

Mine isn't that busy but I frequently find a note from Cliff. He knows I like to, so he indulges me. It's *fun* to get mail on the board.

There was a girl I used to run across because we were both in "H-TO-L"—Gabrielle Lamont. I would say hello and she would say hello and there it stopped. Gabrielle was a sad one—not a total termite, but dampish. Her face had the usual features but she let them live their own lives, not even lipstick. She skinned her hair back and her clothes looked as if they had been bought in France. Not Paris—just France. There's a difference.

Which they probably were. Her father is in Modern Languages and he sent her three years to school in France. It did something. I don't think she ever had a date.

We both had eight o'clocks and she would check "H-to-L" every morning when I did and then go quietly away. There was never a note for her.

Until this one morning . . . Georgia Lammers, who is purely carnivorous, took a note off the board as Gabrielle came up. I heard this soft little voice say, "Excuse me. That's mine."

Georgia said, "Huh? Don't be silly!"

Gabrielle looked scared but she put out her hand. "Read the name, please. You've made a mistake."

Georgia snatched the note away. She is a junior and wouldn't bother to speak to me if Daddy weren't on the staff—but I'm not afraid of her. "Do it," I insisted. "Let's see the name."

Georgia stuck the envelope in my face and snapped, "Read it yourself, snoopy!"

"'Gabrielle Lamont,'" I read out loud. "Hand it over, Georgia."

"What?" she yelped, and looked at it. Her cheeks got very red. "Hand it over," I repeated.

"Well!" said Georgia. "Anybody can make a mistake!" She flung the note at Gabrielle and flounced off.

Gabrielle picked it up. "Thanks," she whispered.

"Usual Yellow Cab Service," I said. "A pleasure"—which it was. Georgia Lammers is popular in a cheap, plunging-neckline way, but not with me. She acts as if she had invented sex.

Gabrielle started getting mail every day—some in envelopes, some just with a thumbtack shoved through folds. I wondered who it was, but every time I saw Gabrielle she was alone. I decided it must be someone her father did not like so they had to use notes to arrange secret dates. I told Cliff so, but he said I had an uncontrolled romantic imagination.

Gabrielle got eleven notes that week and I got only four, all from Cliff. I pointed this out and he said I did not appreciate my blessings and he was going to ration me to three a week. Men are exasperating.

I came up one morning as Gabrielle was taking down a note; this Georgia Lammers was there. As Gabrielle left I said sweetly, "Nothing for you, Georgia? Too bad. Or was it Gabrielle's turn to swipe *your* note?"

Georgia sniffed and went into the Registrar's office, where she is a part-time clerk. I thought no more about it until after five, when I was waiting in Old Main for Daddy, intending to ride home with him.

There was nothing on "H-TO-L" for me, or for Gabrielle, or Georgia. Nobody was around so I sat down on the Senior Bench and rested my feet.

I jumped when I heard someone behind me, but it was only Gabrielle. She's a freshman, too, and anyhow she wouldn't tell. But I didn't sit down again—our senior committee thinks up fantastic punishments for ignoring their sacred privileges.

A good thing I didn't—Georgia came out of the office then. But she did not notice me; she went straight to "H-TO-L" and unpinned a note. I thought: Maureen, your memory is slipping; there was nothing for her a minute ago.

Georgia turned and saw me. She flushed and said, "What are you staring at?"

"Sorry," I said. "I didn't think there was a note for you—I just looked at the board."

She started to flare up, then she put on a catty smile. "Want to read it?"

"Heavens, no!"

"Go ahead!" She shoved it at me. "It's *very* interesting."

Puzzled, I took it. It was a blank sheet, nothing but creases and thumbtack holes. "Somebody is playing jokes on you," I said.

"Not on *me.*"

I turned it over. The address read: "Miss Gabrielle Lamont."

It finally soaked in that the address should have been "Georgia Lammers." Or should have been for Georgia to touch it. I said, "This note isn't yours. You have no right to it."

"What note?"

"This note."

"I don't see any note. I see a blank sheet of paper."

"But— Look, you thought it was a note to Gabrielle. And you took it down anyway."

Her smile got nastier. "No, I *knew* it wasn't a note. That's the point."

"Huh?"

She explained and I wanted to scratch her. Poor little Gabrielle had been sending notes to herself, just to get mail when everybody else did—and Georgia had caught on. Both girls had campus jobs which kept them late; Georgia had seen Gabrielle come in late a week earlier, look around, and pin up a note. Being a sneak, she had ducked out to find out to whom Gabrielle was writing—only to find that it was addressed to Gabrielle herself.

Poor Gabby! No wonder I had never seen her with anyone. There wasn't anyone.

Georgia licked her lips. "Isn't it a scream? That snip trying to make us think she's popular? I should write a real note on this—let her know that her public isn't fooled."

"Don't you dare!"

"Oh, don't be dull!" She pinned it up, putting the tack back in the same holes. "I'll let the joke ride until I think of something good."

I grabbed her arm. "Don't you touch her notes again or I'll—"

She shook me off. "You'll what? Tell her that you know her notes are phony? I can just see you!"

"I'll tell the Dean, that's what! I'll tell the Dean you've been opening Gabrielle's notes."

"Oh, yes? You looked at it, too."

"But you handed it to me!"

"Did I? My word against yours, sweetie pie."

"But—"

"And if you talk, the whole campus will know about Gabrielle's fake notes. Think it over." She marched off.

I was so quiet on the way home that Daddy said, "'Smatter, Puddin'? Flunk a quiz?"

I assured him that my academic status was satisfactory. "Then why the mourning?"

Before Daddy let me register he had warned me that the First Law of the Jungle for a professor's child was not to be a pipeline to the faculty. "But, Daddy, you're a professor."

"Student stuff, eh? Better sweat it out alone. Good luck."

I did not tell Mother either, because with Mother free speech is not just a theory. I did nothing but worry. Poor Gabrielle! She took her "note" down next morning, looking pleased—and I wanted to cry. Then I saw the smirk on Georgia Lammers' face and I felt like murder and mayhem. There was another "note" Friday and I wanted to shout to her not to touch it. I didn't dare. It was like a time bomb, watching Gabrielle's pitiful make-believe and knowing that Georgia meant to wreck it as soon as she thought up something nasty enough.

I was in the Registrar's office Monday, not to see Georgia, though I couldn't avoid her, but because I am a freshman reporter for the Campus Crier. One of my chores is getting up the "Happy Birthday" column. I thumbed through the files, noting dates from the coming Friday through the following Thursday. Gabrielle's name turned up for Friday and I decided to send her a birthday card, via the bulletin board, so for once she would have *real* mail. Next I listed Bun Peterson's name; her birthday was the same as Gabrielle's. Bun is president of the Student Council and head cheerleader and honorary football captain; it seemed a shame she had to have Gabrielle's birthday as well. I decided to get Gabrielle a really *nice* card, with a hanky.

As I finished Georgia picked up my list and said, "Who's getting senile?"

I said, "You are," and took it back.

She said, "Don't get too big for your beanie, freshman." She went on, "Going to the party for Bun Peterson?"—then added, "Oh, I forgot—it's upper classmen only."

I looked her in the eye. "A double choc malt against a used candy bar you aren't either!"

She didn't answer and I swaggered out.

It was a busy week. Junior sprained his arm, Mother was away two days and I kept house, the cat had to be wormed, and I typed a term paper for Cliff. I didn't think about Gabrielle until late Friday when I stopped by the board on the chance that there might be a note from Cliff. There wasn't, but there was another of Gabrielle's notes, in an envelope with her name typed. I realized with a shock that I had forgotten her birthday card.

I was wondering whether to get one and let her find it Monday, when I heard a *pssst!* It was Georgia Lammers, motioning me to come to the office. Curiosity got me; I went.

She pulled me inside; there was no one else in the outer office. "Keep back," she whispered. "If she sees anyone, she may not stop. She's due now—it's after five."

I shook her off. "Who?"

"Gabrielle, of course. Shut up!"

"Huh?" I said. "She's already been there. Her 'note' for Monday is up."

"A lot you know! Hush!" She crowded me into the corner, then peeked out.

"Quit shoving!" I said and looked out.

Gabrielle was pinning something up, her back to us. She saw the envelope with her name, took it down, and hurried away.

I turned to Georgia. "If you've monkeyed with one of her notes, I *will* go to the Dean."

"Go ahead—see how far it gets you."

"Did you touch that note?"

"Sure I did—I wrote it. What's wrong with that?"

She had me; anybody can send anyone a note. "Well, what did you say?"

"What business is it of yours? Still," she went on, "I'll tell you. It's too good to keep." She dug a paper out of her purse. It was a typewritten rough draft, full of x-outs and inserts; it read:

Dear Gabrielle,

Today is Bun Peterson's birthday—and we are giving her the finest surprise party this school has ever seen. We would like to invite everybody, but we can't—and you have been picked as one of the girls to represent the freshman class. We are gathering in groups and will descend on her in a body. Your group will meet at seven o'clock in the Snack Shoppe. Put on your best bib and tucker—and don't breathe a word to *anyone!*

The Committee

"It's a shabby trick," I said, "to invite her to another girl's party on her own birthday. You knew it was her birthday."

"What of it?"

"It's mean—but just like you. How did you get them to invite her? You aren't on the committee—are you?"

She stared, then laughed. "She's not invited to anything."

"Huh? You mean there's no party? But there *is.*"

"Oh, sure, there's a party for Bun Peterson. But that little snip won't be there. That's the joke."

It finally sank in. Gabrielle would go to the Snack Shoppe and wait—and wait—and wait—while the party she thought she had been invited to went on without her. "That strikes you as funny?" I said.

"That's just the beginning," this Lammers person answered. "About eight-thirty, when she is beginning to wonder 'Wha Hoppen?' a messenger will bring another note. It will be blank paper, just like those she sends to herself—then she'll *know.*" She giggled and wet her lips. "The little fake will have her comeuppance."

I started after her and she ducked back of the counter. "You're not allowed back here!" she yelped.

I stopped. "You'll have to come out some time. Then we'll find Gabrielle and you will tell her the truth—all of it!"

"Tell her yourself!" she snapped. Two boys drifted in and the Registrar came out of the inner office and Georgia became briskly official. I left.

Cliff was waiting at "H-TO-L"; I was never so glad to see him.

"Well," Cliff said a bit later, "phone her. Tell her she's been had and not to go to the Snack Shoppe."

"But, Cliff, I *can't!* That would be almost as cruel as the way Georgia planned it. Look—can't you get somebody to take her to Bun's party?"

Cliff wrinkled his forehead. "I don't see how."

"Cliff, you've got to!"

"Puddin', today is Gabrielle's birthday, too. Right?"

"Yes, yes—that's what makes it so mean."

"You don't want to send her to Bun's party. What we do is give her a surprise party of her own. Simple."

I stared with open-mouthed adoration. "Cliff—you're a genius."

"No," he said modestly, "just highly intelligent and with a heart of gold. Let's get busy, chica."

First I phoned Mother. She said, "Tonight, Maureen? I like to entertain your friends but—" I cut in with a quick up-to-date. Presently she said, "I'll check the deep freeze. Sommers Market may still be open. How about turkey legs and creamed mushrooms on toast?"

"And ice cream," I added. "Birthday parties need ice cream."

"But the cake? I'm short on time."

"Uh, we'll get the cake."

As I hung up Cliff came out of the other booth. "I got the Downbeat Campus Combo," he announced.

"Oh, Cliff—an *orchestra!*"

"If you can call those refugees from a juke box that."

"But how will we pay for it?"

"Don't ask—it was a promotion. They bid on Bun's party and got left, so they listened to reason. But I'm not doing well on guests, baby."

"You called your house?"

"Yes. A lot of the boys have other plans."

"You call again and tell those free loaders that they will never eat another Dagwood in my house if they are not *there,* on *time,* and each with a present. No excuses. This is total war."

"Aye aye, sir."

We went to Helen Hunt's Tasty Pastry Shoppe. Mr. Helen Hunt was just closing but he let us in. No birthday cake . . . not a baker in the place until four the next morning—sorry. I spotted a three-tier wedding cake. "Is that a prop?"

"Frankly, that's a disappointment. My wife and I each entered the same order."

"You're stuck with it?"

"Oh, we may get a wedding cake order unexpectedly."

"Eight dollars," I said.

He looked at the cake. "Ten dollars"—then added, "Cash."

I looked at Cliff. He looked at me. I opened my purse and he got out his wallet. We had six fifty-seven. Mr. Helen Hunt stared at the ceiling. Cliff sighed and unpinned his fraternity pin from my blouse, handed it over, and Mr. Helen Hunt dropped it into the cash register.

He took the little bride-and-groom off the cake, set candles around each tier, then fetched an icing gun. "What name?"

"Gabrielle," I replied. "No, make it 'Gabby'—G, A, double-B, Y."

I called Madame O'Toole from there. Madame bends hair for half the girls on the campus. She lives back of her beauty salon and agreed to be panting and ready at seven-fifteen. Fast driving let Cliff drop me at six-ten. Junior was stringing Christmas tree lights across the front porch and Daddy was moving furniture. Mother was swooshing like a restless tornado, a smudge of dirt on her cheek. I kissed Daddy but Mother wouldn't hold still.

I made three calls while the tub was filling, then dunked, put my face on, and inserted myself into my almost-strapless formal. Cliff honked at five minutes to seven; he looked swell in a tuxedo a little too small and the darling had two gardenia corsages, one for me and one for Gabrielle. We roared away toward the Snack Shoppe, hitting on all three.

We got there at seven-fifteen. I looked in and saw Gabrielle at a rear table, looking forlorn and nursing a half-empty coke. She was in a long dress which was not too bad but she had tried to use makeup and did not know how. Her lipstick was smeared, crooked, and the wrong color, and she had done awful things with rouge and powder. Underneath she was scared green.

I walked in. "Hello, Gabby."

She tried to smile. "Oh—hello, Maureen."

"Ready to go? We're from the committee."

"Uh—I don't know. I don't feel well. I'd better go home."

"Nonsense! Come on—we'll be late." We got on each side and hustled her out to Cliff's open-air special.

"Where is the party?" Gabrielle asked nervously.

"Don't be nosy. It's a surprise." Which it was.

Cliff pulled up at Madame O'Toole's before she could ask more questions. Gabrielle looked puzzled but her will to resist was gone. Inside I said to Madame O'Toole, "You have seventeen minutes."

Madame looked her over like a pile of wet clay. "Two hours is what I need."

"Twenty minutes," I conceded. "Can you do it?" Over the phone I had told her that she had to create Cleopatra herself, starting from zip.

She pursed her lips and looked the kid over again. "We'll see. Come along, child."

Gabrielle looked dazed. "But Maureen—"

"Hush," I said firmly. "Do exactly what Madame tells you."

Madame led her away. While we waited Cliff called the Deke house and the senior dorm and stirred out five more men and two couples. It was thirty minutes before they reappeared—and I nearly fainted.

Madame was wasted here—she belonged at the court of Louis Quinze.

And so did Gabrielle.

At first I thought she was wearing no makeup. Then I saw that it had been put on so skillfully that you thought it had grown there. Her eyes were eight times as big as they had been and looked like pools of secret sorrow—you know, a woman who has *lived*. Her hair was still brushed straight back but Madame had done it over. What had been a bun was now a chignon—"bun" wasn't the word. Her cheekbones were higher, too. And Madame had done something to the dress—it clung more and seemed more low-cut. Riding high on her shoulder was the corsage and her skin blended into the petals.

Instead of the beads she had been wearing there was a single strand of pearls resting where pearls love to rest. They must have been Madame's very own. They looked real.

Cliff gasped so I poked him to remind him not to touch. Gabrielle smiled timidly. "Do I look all right?"

I said, "Sister, Conover would shoot Powers for your contract. Madame, you're wonderful! Let's go, kids. We're late."

You can't talk when Cliff is driving, which was good. We got there at twenty past eight; our block was jammed and our house stood out in colored lights. Junior was on guard; he ducked inside.

Cliff took our coats; I gave Gabrielle a shove and said, "Go on in."

As she appeared in the living room the Downbeat boys hit it and they all sang:

"Happy birthday, dear Gabby!
"Happy birthday to you!"

And then I was almost sorry, for the poor baby covered her face and sobbed.

And so did I. Everybody began laughing and talking and shouting and the Downbeat Combo went into dance music, not good but solid, and I knew the party would do. Mother and I smuggled Gabby upstairs and I fixed my face and Mother shook Gabby and told her to stop crying. Gabby stopped and Mother did a perfect job fixing what damage had been done. I didn't know Mother owned mascara but I am always finding out new things about Mother.

So we went back down. Cliff showed up with a strange man and said, "Mademoiselle Lamont, permettez-moi de vous presenter M'sieur Jean Allard," which was more French than I knew he had.

Jean Allard was an exchange student that one of the boys had brought along. He was slender and dark and he fastened himself to Gabby—his English was spotty and *here* was a woman that spoke his language . . . that and Madame O'Toole's handiwork. He had competition; most of the stags seemed to want to get close to the new-model Gabby.

I sighed with relief and slipped out to the kitchen, being suddenly aware that I had missed dinner, a disaster for one of my metabolism. Daddy was there in an apron; he gave me a turkey leg. I ate that and a few other things that wouldn't fit on the plates.

Then I went back and danced with Cliff and some of the stags that had gotten crowded out around Gabby. When the orchestra took ten it turned out that Johnny Allard could play piano, and he and Gabby sang French songs—the kind that sound naughty, what with the eye-rolling, but probably aren't. Then we all sang *Alouette* which is more my speed.

Gabby was gaining a reputation as a woman of the world. I heard one ex–Boy Scout say, "You've *really* seen the Folies Bergère?"

Gabby looked puzzled and said, "Why not?"

He said, "Gee!" while his eyebrows crowded his scalp.

Finally we brought out the cake and everybody sang "Happy Birthday" again and Mother had to repair Gabby's face a second time. But by now Gabby could have washed her face and it wouldn't have mattered.

Professor Lamont arrived while we were killing the ice cream and cake—Daddy's doing. He and Jean Allard talked French, then I heard Jean ask him, in schoolbook English, for permission to call on his daughter. Doctor Lamont agreed in the same stilted fashion.

I blinked—Cliff never asked Daddy; he just started eating at our house, off and on.

Around midnight Doctor Lamont took his daughter home, loaded with swag. At the last minute I remembered to run upstairs and wrap up a new pair of nylons that would never fit Gabby but she could exchange them. So Gabby cried again and clung to me and got incoherent in two languages and I cried some, too. Finally everybody left and Cliff and Daddy and I tidied up the place, sort of. When I hit the bed, I died.

Cliff showed up next morning. We gloated over the party, at least I did. Presently he said, "What about Georgia?"

I said, "Huh?"

He said, "You can't leave it at this. It ought to be poisoned needles, or boiling lava, but the police are narrow-minded."

"Any ideas?"

He pulled out the bill for the cake. "I'd like to see her pay this."

"So would I! But how in the world?"

Cliff explained, then we composed the letter together, like this:

Dear Georgia,
    Yesterday was Gabrielle Lamont's birthday—and we gave her the finest party this school has ever seen. Too bad you were hanging around the Snack Shoppe while the fun was going on. But we know you would like to give her a present anyway—you

can still pay for the cake. Put on your best bib and tucker and trot around to Helen Hunt's. It was a surprise party, so don't breathe a word to *anyone!* (Nor shall we.)

The Committee

P.S. On second thought it will be more fun if you *don't* pay for the cake!

It wasn't anonymous; the bill had our names on it and we pinned it to the letter. I bet Cliff two hamburgers that she wouldn't knuckle under. I was wrong. Half an hour after it was delivered Helen Hunt phoned to say that Cliff could have his pin back, the mortgage was lifted.

Monday morning I was at the board earlier than either Cliff or Gabby. Gabby's poor little "note" was still pinned up, where she had put it Friday. I wondered what she would do; start pretending all over again?

I spotted her coming up the steps, walking alone and lonely, same as always—and again I wondered if it had done any good. Then somebody shouted, "Hey, Gabby! Wait a minute." She stopped and two boys joined her.

I watched her and then Cliff growled at my back, "Why the sniffles? Got a cold?"

I said, "Oh, Cliff! Give me your hanky and don't ask silly questions."

POOR DADDY

Mother is too busy for anything, except that she is always taking on more jobs. She can do them, too, and it never matters whether they're something that Grandmother would call "ladylike."

She practically built our new house—only it wasn't new when we moved into it. For about three months, turpentine flavor would show up in the butterscotch pudding, or Daddy would complain that he didn't mind not being able to use his electric razor while Mother was installing new wiring, but he *would* appreciate it if his other razor weren't used to skin insulation.

Mother wouldn't hear him; she'd be rebuilding the staircase, or something.

Eventually the house was finished, except for clearing out the garage so that the car could be kept inside, and covering the pipes in the new bathroom, and a few other things that Mother could do any day she had to wait for a pot roast to finish cooking. It left her with nothing to do, except teaching Sunday School and managing the Community Chest drive and seeing that Daddy changed his shirts and keeping up with her painting and the play she was writing.

Daddy suggested that she improve her mind, but Mother said nonsense, Daddy had all the mind the family needed. Daddy is fearfully learned about tribal customs and Yucatan culture and things like that. Besides, Mother pointed out that she had rerigged her bookrack so that it would go on the vacuum cleaner as well as over the sink, so she was already improving her mind. What she needed was exercise.

Daddy invited her to go fishing, but Mother said it wasn't exercise the way he did it, practically urging the fish not to disturb him. Daddy said the fish got plenty of exercise and who was he to insist on all the benefits? Daddy talks that way because the freshmen laugh.

Anyhow, that's why we took up figure skating.

Not Daddy—just Mother and Junior and me. Daddy said he had tried skating once and he had weak ankles, just go ahead and enjoy ourselves. He took out a family accident insurance policy and forgot the matter.

I liked figure skating, all but getting your pants wet if you take a tumble. I know why they call that other sort "dry" ice; the kind you skate on isn't. Junior liked it because he could go slamming around, bumping into people and being a nuisance to his elders. But Mother took to it as if all her life had been preparation for this consummation.

She never was good at school figures; Mother's style can't be limited to a little patch of ice barely big enough for a figure eight. But dancing she loved—she was doing tangoes and waltzes and beginning to boss things when our club organized an ice carnival, while I was still struggling with the Mohawk in the fourteen-step. The fourteenstep is the first dance you learn; I was hope-lessly outclassed by Mother, not a desirable thing, except that, as a result of my difficulties with the Mohawk, Cliff came into my life.

A Mohawk is not an Indian and neither is Cliff. A Mohawk is a transition from front to back while passing from one edge on one foot to a similar edge on the other foot. That doesn't seem clear—anyhow you skate forward as fast as you can and suddenly turn and skate backward. All this while your partner has his feet crossed, and you are in a close embrace, and while turning a corner that you can't see.

It would help to dislocate both knees. In fact, you can hardly avoid it. I explained it to Daddy and he said it didn't sound practical, except possibly in a wheel chair.

You may wonder why I persisted. Well, in the first place it was my battle with the Mohawk that caused Cliff to introduce himself and start teaching me. That was good. In the second place they say that love will cause a man to put up with a poor skating partner for ninety days—maybe six months, if it's true love. That was bad. The way I figured it I had a maximum of half a year in which to master that Mohawk—or put Cliff out of my life and devote myself to good works.

That Mohawk nearly stopped me, but Cliff was very patient. He said the trouble might be the fit of my boots, and got me some heel liners. I finally learned it after a fashion, and Cliff went on to teach me other things.

The Mohawk never bothered Mother. She was past it and learning the cut-off in the fox trot, which is even trickier, and zipping through seven or eight other dance patterns. Mother never actually danced well, but she could dance and she could hold up her partner in a pinch. Mother is little but tough. I am more a Junoesque type. She developed a bouncy style of her own. Our club professional gave up trying to smooth it out and let her learn new things as fast as she wanted to, which was just as well.

In March Daddy came to see the carnival and the dance that followed. He complimented Mother on the costumes, which she had made, of course. But the dancing afterward gave him pause. Mother is *very* popular on the ice—even Cliff would rather dance with her than with me. I suppose that it should have made Daddy proud to see how the mother of his progeny was sought after; instead he looked thoughtful. He remarked that the tango should be restricted to married couples, or at least considered tantamount to an engagement.

Mother said pish and tush.

Daddy dropped in at the rink and watched the dancing once or twice after that. When school closed he left on a long fishing trip and didn't urge Mother to go along, which worried me, but Mother said he was accepting the universe. Usually Daddy makes the universe accept him. It seemed odd. The importance of a stable family background for the adolescent is emphasized in all the textbooks, as well as in the more interesting works on psychology Daddy means to keep locked up; I decided I had better keep an eye on things.

Daddy sent back cards postmarked Green Mountain Falls, Colorado, and some fish packed in ice.

When he got back he showed an interest in skating and borrowed Mother's *Primer of Figure Skating.* One evening when Mother, Junior, and I returned from the rink, Daddy put down the book and announced, "Martha, I have concluded that figure skating is fundamentally simple."

Mother should have been wary. She said, "Yes, dear? That's nice," and sailed out to throw dinner together.

"Yes," he said, following her. "It is simple physics, primarily the conservation of angular momentum, plus laws relating to the acquirement of reflex patterns. Figure skating may be learned rapidly by analyzing each move, then being sure to do it correctly the first time. Anyone of adequate mentality should acquire the art in a short time."

"Hmm," said Mother. "I suppose you can apply these principles you've discovered?"

"Certainly," Daddy told her. "Skating is ordinarily taken up by the very young, whose habits of mental discipline are not formed. Or, conversely, by older people—but casually rather than systematically. I wish I had time to demonstrate it. However, the principles are clear from my analysis."

And that is why we all went to the rink the following Friday.

Mother started to pick out skates for Daddy. He waved her out of the skate shop. "I shall do this methodically," he said. "I'll see you all on the ice."

I've never seen Mother in such a dither. "Your father is such a child! Maureen, you help him when he steps on the ice—the mood he's in, he won't let me. Oh, dear! I wonder if I still know how to apply a traction splint?"

"Probably be his head, rather than his leg," I offered. It didn't console her.

I didn't get a chance to help, as he was met at the ice by Miss Swenson, our club professional. "I arranged by telephone for Miss Swenson's help, my dear," he said to Mother. With that he stepped down on his toe picks, just as it says in the book.

Miss Swenson flashed Mother a smile and said, "Don't worry, I'll take care of him."

Mother said, "Who said I was worried?" and skittered off. She looked mad.

Miss Swenson towed Daddy to the pen where the bunnies practice. Then she said sweetly to me, "Now, Maureen, go skate somewhere else. Just pretend your father isn't here at all." I can take a hint; I went back to my patch and practiced inside edges.

Mother joined me. "Is he all right?" she asked.

"Probably. Miss Swenson hardly ever maims them."

"I'll just skate down and see how they're making out."

"I wouldn't," I told her. "I got chased out. They don't want an audience."

Mother said, "They'll be too busy to notice me." She came back with her cheeks red and started doing loops like mad.

Presently the music started for dancing. Mother had ducked into the girls' room to restore her makeup and her confidence. The first dance was a fourteenstep.

Dad and Miss Swenson came out onto the dance floor. They actually lined up to start the dance with the others!

I closed both eyes. Dear heaven, I thought, don't let him do it. Oh, don't let him fall—they'll cut my poor Daddy to ribbons. The fourteenstep is awfully fast. If you fall down, it's just like being caught by traffic lights.

Finally I opened my eyes to see if I were going to be an orphan. Cliff skated up and said, "Skate this one, Puddin'?"

I said I might never skate again and tried to pick out Daddy. Finally I saw him, away down the ice. He was in the four-beat roll that carries you down the rink, and he was actually doing it—or sort of. I've seen circus bears that skated better, but he was still on his skates. I decided that Miss Swenson must be stronger than I'd thought.

There was still the corner to turn and it was coming at him. The ladies' Mohawk may forever remain my bugaboo, but the men's Mohawk is no slouch, and it comes right at the turn. I got ready to identify the body.

Then he was past it and Miss Swenson was faking to cover up the extra steps he took. He turned the corner without even missing the beat. I wanted to cheer but my throat was dry.

Mother showed up. "Where's your father, Maureen?" she demanded.

I pointed. They were swooping down the ice, and Daddy's roll was deeper this time.

It was the only time I've seen Mother start to faint. She managed to control it, but I had to grab her to keep her from sitting down suddenly on some very wet ice. The music stopped and Daddy skated up alone. "My dear," he said to Mother, "this next is a tango. Would you essay it with me?"

Mother grabbed him. "Charles!" she shrilled. "Get off this ice! You'll kill yourself—I don't know how that woman could take you out in that traffic!"

"Quiet, my dear," said Daddy. "I am unhurt. Will you tango with me, or shall I dance with my instructor?"

"You can't tango!"

"I have studied the pattern carefully. I expect to retain a semblance of the moves."

They tangoed. It wasn't good, but Daddy had not been woofing about memorizing the pattern. My own wasn't much better—I kept changing sides with Cliff at the wrong times, trying to watch.

We rode home in silence. I got Junior aside when we got home. "What did you think of Daddy's skating?" I asked.

"Huh? Dad's a terrible skater."

"Weren't you amazed that he could skate at all?"

"Why?" was all I could get out of him.

I didn't discuss it with Daddy until three days later, because it took that long to collect facts. I tackled him privately. "Daddy," I said, "something is worrying me."

"Well, Puddin'? Can I help?"

"Perhaps, since you are more experienced than I."

"Easy now! What are you leading up to?"

"Well, what would you think of a person who deceived someone?"

"It depends on the circumstances. For example, deception is justifiable around Christmas and before birthdays."

"Oh." I considered. "I don't know what category this belongs in."

"Well, spill it."

"Very well, then. It says in your logic text that when apparent facts lead to contradictions, each alleged fact should be tested. I have reason to believe that the sort of fish you sent home are not found in the lake at Green Mountain Falls."

"Who said they were? There are other places to fish."

"I suppose so. It occurred to me that both Green Mountain Falls and Broadmoor are suburbs of Colorado Springs."

"Go on."

"Broadmoor reminded me of the figure-skating school at the ice palace there each summer."

"Yes?"

"One conjecture led to another. I remembered that Miss Swenson teaches at the rink over in Centerville mornings, and that you don't have any morning classes at present."

"Hmm . . . Did Miss Swenson show any interest in your conjectures?"

"Oh, Miss Swenson is incorruptible! But, Daddy, George at the skate shop is not so difficult. Cliff got him to recall that some skates were shipped to him from Colorado Springs recently. For five dollars he thinks he could remember whose they were."

"Tell Cliff not to waste his money. What is your object in this snooping, young lady? Not something your mother thought of?"

"Oh, no, Daddy! Mother is baffled."

"Then why—"

"At first it was just curiosity. Since then, however—"

"Yes?"

"After I had the facts, I still couldn't see the *reason.* Why the mystery? Come clean, Daddy."

He stopped to load his pipe. "Put yourself in my place, Puddin'. Suppose the girl of your dreams was being chased after by a bunch of young bucks who could cut didos on the ice. What would you do?"

"Why, uh—I'd learn to skate," I answered automatically. I was dazed. Imagine it! Romance—jealousy!—at Daddy's age!

"Yes, but not in public. It wouldn't do to go stumbling around with your mother hovering over me and explaining how I wasn't the athletic type and wasn't it brave of me? I had to impress her."

"Oh. I see your point, Daddy."

I suppose that should have settled it, but I had one more thing in mind. "Oh, Daddy—"

"Yes, Puddin'?"

"I'm glad you comprehend the crucial symbolic importance skating can have in relationships between the sexes, because then you will understand—" I stopped. I couldn't tell him anything about Cliff because Cliff doesn't know yet that he's going to marry me. Men are so complicated.

Daddy raised his brows. "Understand what, Puddin'? And where did you get all those big words? Not from me, I trust."

"No—I mean, yes." I hesitated; this was going to be touchy. "Well, to get to the point, Daddy, during my investigations I examined your skates. They're awfully nice. If I had Stanzione boots and Olympiad blades like yours, I might make marvelously fast progress myself. Of course, I'd keep your grisly secret," I added hastily.

"Blackmail!" Daddy said. "Puddin', men have been shot at sunrise for less."

"I suppose so, Daddy."

"You are almost too big to spank."

"I'm glad you think so, Daddy. It makes everything simpler."

"I said *almost.* However, you're getting older and have heavier expenses. Suppose I raise your allowance. Then, if you need skates, I'll advance the cash and deduct it."

"This is a private arrangement, Daddy?"

He shook his head. "Say anything you like. You will have to judge moral problems for yourself."

Daddy is such a lamb.

GUEST OF HONOR SPEECH AT THE THIRD WORLD SCIENCE FICTION CONVENTION DENVER, 1941

THE DISCOVERY OF THE FUTURE

Here in my hand is the manuscript of a speech. If it works out anything like the synopses I have used, this speech will still be left when I get through.

Before I start, I want to mention an idea that might be fun. It was an innovation in political speaking introduced in California by Upton Sinclair that raised Cain with the ordinary run of political speakers: answering questions from the platform. But I want to put one reservation on it, and that is that questions should be in writing, with names signed, so we can read them into the mike so that I can have clearly in mind what the questions are.

During the course of the last day or so, I have gathered the impression that quite a number of people are interested in the background of my stories; and, in some cases, in my social and political ideas, economic ideas, etc.—some of which, but not all, shows in my stories. Some of them have evidenced an interest in my own personal background. So, if the question comes along, I will do my best to answer it, perhaps dodging the embarrassing ones a little.

To get to the talk itself: THE DISCOVERY OF THE FUTURE. I was told that there was no time limit, so I assumed that he wanted my usual three hour speech. Or, perhaps, we can just keep going until the hall is cleared.

Forry [Ackerman] told you that I have been reading science fiction for a long time. I have. I have been reading it as long as I could get hold of it, and I probably experienced much the same process most of you did: parental disapproval, those funny looks you get from friends, for reading "that kind of junk."

We here, the science fiction fans, are the lunatic fringe! We are the crazy fools who read that kind of stuff—who read those magazines with the outlandish machines and animals on the covers. You leave one around loose in your home and a friend will pick it up. Those who are not fans ask you if you really read that stuff, and from then on they look at you with suspicion.

Why do we do it? I think I know. This is an opinion, but it is probably why we like science fiction. It is not just for the adventure of the story itself—you can find that in other types of stories. To my mind it is because science fiction has as its strongest factor the single thing that separates the human race from other animals—I refer to a quality which has been termed "time-binding." With a hyphen. It's a term that may not have come to your attention. It is a technical term invented by Alfred Korzybski, and it refers to the fact that the human animal lives not only in the present, but also in the past and the future.

The human animal differs from all other animals *only* in this one respect. The definition includes both reading and writing. That is the primary technique whereby we are able to make records, to gather data and to look into the future. Other things we do that we think of as making us humans rather than animals— some animals have done at some time. They form governments. They invent machines. Some animals even use money. I have not seen them doing it, but I have heard reports that I believe to be credible. But time-bind they do not do, to anything like the extent that the human race does.

Time-binding consists of making use of the multitudinous records of the past that we have. On the basis of those records, the data we have collected directly and the data that we get from others by means of time-binding techniques, including reading and writing, we are able to plan our future conduct. It means that we have lived mentally in the past and in the future, as well as in the present. That is certainly true of science fiction fans.

I like the term Future Fiction that Charlie Hornig gave it. It seems to me a little broader than Science Fiction because most of these stories are concerned with the future—what will happen.

In taking the future into account, trying to predict what it will be, and trying to make your plans accordingly, you are time-binding. The child-like person lives from day to day. The adult tries to plan for a year or two at least. Statesmen try to plan for perhaps twenty years or more. There are a few institutions which plan for longer than the lives of men, as for example, the Smithsonian Institution and the Catholic Church, that think not in terms of lifetimes, but in centuries. They make their plans that far ahead, and to some extent, make them work out.

Science fiction fans differ from most of the rest of the race by thinking in terms of racial magnitudes—not even centuries, but thousands of years. Stapledon thinks in terms of . . . how many years? How far does his time scale go? I don't know: the figures mean nothing to me.

That is what science fiction consists of—trying to figure out from the past and from the present what the future may be. In that we are behaving like human beings.

Now, all human beings time-bind to some extent when they try to discover the future. But most human beings—those who laugh at us for reading science fiction—time-bind, make their plans, make their predictions, only within the limits of their personal affairs. In that respect, they may try to predict for a year or two, make plans, even try to predict for their entire lifetimes, but they rarely try to predict in terms of the culture in which they live. In fact, most people, as compared with science fiction fans, have no conception whatsoever of the fact that the culture they live in *does* change, that it *can* change. Even though they may believe it with the top of their minds, they don't believe it way back in the thalamus, in their emotions.

Our grandfathers thought the horse could never be replaced by the auto. Four years after the Wright brothers first flew, they were still trying to get the War Department to come out to look at the airplane. And when one Major General did take a look at an airplane flying, he remarked that it was a very interesting scientific toy, but, of course, it had no possible military application! That was just a short time ago, a very short time.

You will hear that sort of thing around you all the time. I made use, a while ago, of a quotation I would like to use again, from G. B. Shaw. Referring to Brittanicus in *Caesar and Cleopatra,* he said, "he is an outlander and a barbarian and he believes that the customs of his tribe are the laws of nature." That is what you are up against when you try to get most people to read science fiction. That is why they think you are crazy, because they believe that the customs of their tribe are the laws of nature, immutable and unchanging. They do not believe in changes.

Phrases like "There'll always be an England" are pleasant and inspiring at the present time, but *we* know better. There won't always be an England, nor a Germany, nor a United States, a Baptist Church, nor monogamy, nor the Democratic Party, nor the modesty taboo, nor the superiority of the white race, nor airplanes. Nor automobiles. They will go. They will be gone— we'll see them go. Any custom, institution, belief, or social structure that we see around us today will change, will pass, and most of those we will *see* change and pass.

In science fiction, we try to envision what those changes might be. Our guesses are usually wrong; they are almost certain to be wrong. Some men, with a greater grasp on data than others, can do remarkably well. H. G. Wells, who probably knows more (on the order of ten times as much, or perhaps higher) than most science fiction writers, has been remarkably successful in some of his predictions. Most of us aren't that lucky.

I do not expect my so-called *History of the Future* to come to pass. I think some of the trends in it may show up, but I do not think that my factual predictions as such are going to come to pass, even in their broad outlines.

You speak of this sort of thing to an ordinary man—tell him that things are going to change—he will admit it, but he does not believe it at all. He believes it just with the top of his mind. He believes in "progress." He thinks things will get a little bit bigger, and louder, and brighter, a few more neon signs. *But he does not believe that any actual change in the basic nature of the culture in which he lives, or its technology, will take place.*

Airplanes he thinks are all right, but those crazy rocket ship things! Why a rocket ship couldn't possibly fly. It hasn't got anything to PUSH on. That is the way he feels about it.

There will never be any rocket ships. That is all right for Buck Rogers in the funny papers. He does not believe that there could be rocket ships, nor does he believe that there will be things that will make rockets look like primitive gadgets that even the wildest of the science fiction writers have not been able to guess or think about. Rocket ships are about as far as I am willing to go because I have not got data enough to think about, to make a reasonable guess about the other forms of transportation or gadgets we may have.

But that same man did not believe in airplanes in 1910!

I have spoken primarily of mechanical changes because they are much easier to show, to point to, than the more subtle sociological changes, cultural changes, changes in our customs. Some of these can be pointed out. I would like to point out one of them right now. The word "syphilis" could not be used in public even as short a time as fifteen years ago.

Yet, as I used it here, I did not see any shock around the room—nobody minded it—even the *Ladies' Home Journal* runs articles on it. We are getting a little more civilized in that respect than we were twenty years ago. Our grandfathers considered that word indecent. They believed that things that were decent and indecent were subject to absolute rules, that they were laws of nature. The majority of people around us now believe that their criteria of decency and indecency are absolute, that they won't change, that there are some things that are *right* and some things that are *wrong*. They do not know enough about past history to be able to make any predictions about the future.

I could think of some rude words to use in that connection, words that are still rude now. I think it quite possible that twenty years from now on this same platform I could use those words and not produce any shock around the room.

For things *do* change. And words which we consider utterly indecent today may very possibly simply be used as tags, as terms with no emotional connotation to them, twenty years from now.

We happen to live in a period of sudden and drastic change in a good many of the things that happen to us. I think it is extremely important that we be prepared for that change and for that reason, I think that science fiction fans are better prepared to face the future than the ordinary run of people around them, because they believe in change.

To that extent, I think that science fiction, even the corniest of it, even the most outlandish of it, no matter how badly it's written, has a distinct therapeutic value because *all* of it has as its primary postulate that the world *does* change. I cannot overemphasize the importance of that idea.

Unless you believe that, unless you are prepared for it—as I know all of you are—you can't retain your sanity these days. When a man makes predictions and they keep failing to come true, time and again, he goes insane, functionally insane. It has been proved in laboratories time and again. It has been proved with respect to men, but I'll give an illustration with respect to animals.

The well-known experiment was performed with rats, an experiment in which a rat was disappointed in his predictions time and again. He went crazy. It happens to work the same way with men. Things do not necessarily work the same way with animals as they do with men, but in this case, there is data to prove it. The inability to believe in change makes absolutely certain that your prediction will disappoint you. That does not apply to this group, but it does apply to a great many people.

For that reason, I believe we are in a period in which large portions of the human race will be in a condition of, if not insanity, at least un-sanity. We see that over a large portion of the world today. I think we have seen it crawling up on us for a number of years. In 1929 we had the market crash and people jumped out of the window as a result of not being able to predict things which were perfectly obvious, written on the face of the culture, something that would happen.

The Depression came along, and the madhouses filled up again. Other only slightly less slap-happy individuals proceeded to be a bit unsane by concocting the most wildly unscientific schemes for making everybody rich by playing musical chairs. Not quite crazy—they could still find their way around and take street cars and not get lost, but not quite sane either. That can lead, if it goes on long enough, to a condition of mass insanity that none of us is going to like.

Nevertheless, we science fictionists, I think, are better prepared for it than others. During a period of racial insanity, mass psychoses, hysteria, manic depression, paranoia, it is possible for a man who believes in change to hold on, to arrest his judgment, to go slow, to take a look at the facts, and not be badly hurt. Things will probably happen to us, very unpleasant indeed, we can't separate ourselves from the matrix in which we find ourselves. Nevertheless, WE stand a chance, for I am very much afraid that a great many people of the type who laugh at us for dealing with this stuff, will not be able to hang on.

The important thing is to hang on to your sanity, to preserve sanity while it happens—no matter what bad things happen to the world. As individuals it may be difficult for us to do anything about it, even though all of us in our own ways, and according to our lights, are trying. But this series of wars that we find the world in now may go on for another five years, ten years, twenty years—it may go on for fifty years—you and I may not live to see the end of it.

I, personally, have hopes—wishful thinking—that it will terminate quickly enough so that I can pass the rest of my lifetime in comparative peace and comfort. But I'm not optimistic about it. During such a period, it is really difficult to keep a grip on yourself, but I think that we are better prepared to than some of the others.

I can speak more freely here than I could in a political meeting, because it's a highly selected group. I've known a good many science fiction fans, and I've observed, statistically, certain things about them. Most of them are young as compared with other groups, most of them are extremely precocious—quite brilliant. I'd be very much interested to see IQs run on a typical group of fans.

But, even without IQs I know that most of the people here are way above average in intelligence. I've had enough data on it to know. I'm not trying to flatter you, I'm not interested in that. I *am* interested in the fact that you have unusually keen minds. However, that lays us open, and I am including myself in this, lays us open to dangers that don't hit the phlegmatic, the more stolid. Unless we are able to predict, we are even more likely to be subjected to functional unsanities than those around us.

I'm preaching, sure. I know that. I could have filled a speech with wisecracks and with stories and anecdotes, but I feel very deeply about this. And if you can bear with me for a few minutes more, I still want to talk about it.

There's a way out, there's something that we can do to protect ourselves, something that would protect the rest of the human race from the sort of things that are happening to them, and are going to happen to them. It's very simple, and it's right down our alley: the use of the *scientific method.*

I'm not talking about the scientific method used in the laboratory. The scientific method can be used to protect ourselves from serious difficulties of other sorts—getting our teeth smashed in—in our everyday life, twenty-four hours of the day.

I should say what I mean by the scientific method. Since I have to define it in terms of words, I can't be as clear as I might be if I were able to make an extensional definition. But I mean a comparatively simple thing by the scientific method: the ability to look at what goes on around you. Listen to what you hear, observe, note facts, delay your judgment, and make your own predictions.

That's all there is, really, to the scientific method: to be able to distinguish facts from non-facts.

I used the term "fact." I used it in a technical sense, and I should say what I mean by a fact. A fact is anything that has happened before this moment, on July 4th, 1941. Anything that has already happened before this moment. Anything after this moment is a non-fact. Most people can't distinguish between them. They regard as a *fact* that they're going to get up and have breakfast tomorrow morning. They get the difference between facts and non-facts completely mixed up, and in particular, these days people are getting very mixed up between facts and theories, isms, ologies and so forth, so-called "laws of nature," depending on what year you happen to be speaking.

That distinction between fact and fiction, fact and non-fact, is of extreme importance to us now. It has even become a strong issue in the field of science fiction. Without referring to any movement by name, or any person by name, because I wish to make an illustration, I want to invite your attention to the fact that the science fiction field has been very much stirred up by a semipolitical movement which uses the word "fact" quite extensively. But it uses the word fact with reference to what they are—what they *predict* will happen in the future, and that's a non-fact. And any movement, institution, any theory, which does not make a clear and decided distinction between fact and non-fact, cannot by any stretch of the imagination be called a scientific movement. It simply is not because it does not use the scientific method. No matter how complicated their terminology may be, or how much they may use the *argot* of science.

I'm going to have to make an excursion here. I've wandered somewhat from the talk I had in mind.

I want to make another comment on science fiction and the fact that you and I have to put up with an awful lot of guff from people because of the orthodox point of view with which it is regarded.

I have never been able to understand quite why it is that the historical novel is the most approved, the most *sacred* form of literature. The contemporary novel is next so; but the historical novel, if you write an historical novel, that's *literature*.

I think that the corniest tripe published in a science fiction magazine (and some of it isn't too hot, we know that; some of my stuff isn't so hot) beats all of the *Anthony Adverse*s and *Gone With* *the Wind*s that were ever published, because at least it does include that one distinctly human-like attempt to predict the future.

One would think that the literary critics and the professors of English—those who make a business of deciding what is good and what is bad in literature—had some connection in their ancestry with the Fillyloo Bird. I think you know the Fillyloo Bird: he flew backwards because he didn't care where he was going, but he liked to see where he had been.

I want to mention the fashion in which the scientific method— just the matter of observing what goes on around you—observing it through your own eyes, instead of taking other people's opinions, reserving your judgments until you have enough data on which to make a judgment—can be of real use to you even now, quite aside from any possible worse period in history, in the coming history.

I mentioned that it can keep your teeth from getting knocked in; that's an important point. It can because you'll stay out of controversies and out of arguments that you would otherwise get into. If you are talking with a man who obviously does not bother to use the scientific method, or does not know how to use the scientific method, or does not know how to use the scientific method in his everyday life, you'll never get in an argument with him. You'll know there's no point in an argument with him, that you cannot possibly convince him. You can listen—and you'll get some new data from him—and you'll be better able to predict thereafter, if on no other point than the fact that you'll be better able to predict what his reactions will be.

There are other advantages, in the way of keeping yourself cooled down, so you can be a little happier. For example, a man who uses the scientific method cannot possibly be anti-Semitic. I have made that an illustration because it has caused a lot of trouble in the world lately. Why can't he be anti-Semitic? For a very simple reason: he doesn't have enough data, consequently he hasn't formed an opinion. No matter how long he lives he can't hate all Jews, and unless he knows all Jews, he can't hate all Jews, because he doesn't form an opinion unless he has data. It is possible for him to hate an individual Jew as it's possible for him to hate an individual Irishman or Rotarian or man or woman.

But he can't possibly be anti-Semitic. He can't hate all capitalists, he can't hate all unions, he can't hate all women—you can't be a woman-hater, not if you use the scientific method. You can't possibly: you don't know all women. You don't even know a large enough percentage of the group to be able to form an opinion on what the whole group may be!

By the same reasoning, it's very difficult for him to hate at all; and if you can just manage to keep hate out of your life (or a good portion of it—I can't keep it *all* out of my life myself. I've got to sit down and whip myself about the head and shoulders to get myself calmed down at times—but you can help yourself with this method)—if you can keep hate out of your life, you can keep from getting your teeth knocked in. You can keep out of a lot of difficulties and take care of yourself in a better fashion.

A man who uses the scientific method cannot possibly believe that all politicians are crooks, for he knows that one datum destroys the generalization. I'll give you one datum on that point: Senator George Norris, whether you like him or not, is a saint on earth. Whether you agree with his opinions or not, he's not a bad man.

And because he's never entirely certain of his own opinions on any subject, a man using the scientific method stays out of arguments, keeps himself from the emotional upsets that cause you to lose sleep and upset your stomach. You get such things as herpes—oh, I'm not an M.D., but there are plenty of functional disorders that a man can avoid, can very well avoid.

Here's a rough picture of the scientific man in everyday life. Such a man stands a better chance of living through our period to a ripe and happy old age, in my opinion. But I wish to make plain that the use of the scientific method does not depend on any formal education in science. It is an attitude and point of view and not a body of information. You need have no formal education at all to use the scientific method in your everyday life. I am not disparaging the body of scientific information that has been gathered by specialists or the equally enormous body of historical and sociological data that is available. Unfortunately, we can't get very much of it. But you can still use the scientific method, whether you've had a lot of education or not, whether you've had time to gather a lot of personal data or not.

With respect to the acquisition of scientific training, I've heard people around fan clubs remark, "I wish I knew something about mathematics," or "I wish I understood something about physics." Complaints that they're not fully appreciating some of the stories because they don't have enough specialized information. Some subject was too hard, or they weren't able to go far enough in school. I greatly sympathize with that.

I'm not trying to play it down or anything of the sort. It's very much of a regret to me that I'm not at least twins and preferably triplets, so that I could have time to study the various things that I'm interested in. And I know that a lot of you have felt the same way—that life is just too—not too short, but too narrow—we don't have room enough, time enough, to get around and learn all the things that we want to, and it is almost impossible for us to get a full picture of the world.

Surprising, that the data actually is available. God knows that no one can even hope to cover even a small corner of the scientific world these days. I think there's a way out of the dilemma, however, a fair one for us, and a better one for our children. It's the creation of a new technique to cover just that purpose. Men who might be considered encyclopedists, or interpreter-synthesists, I like to call them, men who make it their business to find out what it is the specialists have learned, and then apply it to the rest of us in consolidated form so that we can have, if not the details of the picture, at least the broad outlines of the enormous, incredibly enormous, mass of data that the human race has gathered. The facts behind us, the things that have happened before this moment, so that we can be better able to predict for ourselves, plan our lives after this moment.

There's only one synthesist who has really made such an attempt up to the present time, and I'm very pleased that it happens to be possibly the greatest of the science fiction writers: H. G. Wells. Wells perhaps didn't do a good job of it—good Lord! he didn't have a *chance* to; he had nobody before him, he did the pioneer work. He started it. But H. G. Wells, in his trilogy, *The Outline of History, The Science of Life* and *The Work, Wealth, and Happiness of Mankind,* is, so far as I know, the only writer who has ever lived who has tried to draw for the rest of us a full picture of the whole world, past and future, everything about us, so we can stand off and get a look at ourselves.

It will be better in the future. Nevertheless, it was great work, the fact that he *did* it, that he tried at all. A wonderful work. Because he had done that kind of work, that he tried to do that kind of work for the rest of us, is the reason to my mind why his scientific fantasies are more nearly accurate in their predictions than those of, oh, myself, and various other commercial writers in the field. I don't know as much as H. G. Wells: I probably never will know as much as H. G. Wells—my predictions *can't* be as accurate.

But, after considering H. G. Wells' trilogy, it occurred to me that it would be amusing, to me at least, and I hope to you, for me to mention some books by assorted writers that, to a certain extent, help to fill in the gaps in the picture. And—to a certain extent, help to make up the lack of a broad comprehensive scientific education, which no one, not even Sc.D.s and Ph.D.s can really have.

For example, in mathematics, is there one book which will help the non-mathematician, the person who hasn't specialized in it and made it his life work, to appreciate what mathematics is for? I've run across such a book; it's called *Mathematics and the Imagination* by Kasner and Newman. You don't have to have any mathematical education to read it. To my mind, it's a very stimulating book, a very interesting book, and when you've finished reading it, you at least know what the mathematicians are doing and why.

Among other things, you will discover—and this runs entirely contrary to our orthodox credos—that mathematics is not a science. Mathematics is not a science at all—it's an aspect of symbology, along with the alphabet. That there is no such thing as *discovering* mathematics, for example. Mathematics is invented; it's an invented art, and has nothing directly to do with science at all, except as a tool. And yet you will hear the ordinary layman speaking time and again of mathematics as a science. It just plain is not because it has no data in it; purely inventions, every bit of it, even the multiplication tables. Yes, *2 × 2 is 4* is an invention in mathematics, not a fact.

There are other such books. In physics, there is Eddington's *Nature of the Physical World,* I think one of the most charming books ever written, one of the most lucidly and brilliantly written books. It gives a beautiful background to modern physics. It's approximately fifteen years old, so in order to cover a lot of the things that are currently being used for fiction in the science fiction field, you would need to supplement that. The book I got for my own purpose to supplement it—because, you see, I'm not a professional physicist, I'm an engineer—to help to bring it up to date, is White's *Classical and Modern Physics,* published in 1940. It is about the latest book-bound thing on modern physics that I know of.

There are later things in such publications as *Physical Review* and *Nature,* but this goes up to and including the fission of uranium. It includes nuclear physics, and it delighted me to find the thought that, very likely when we got around to it, we'd find life on other planets. A very stimulating thing to get from a profession-al scientist, particularly in the field of *physical* sciences. I picked that book because White is an associate of Lawrence in the nuclear laboratory at Berkeley. In other words, he is in on the ground floor, he knows what he's talking about. It's modern physics, 1940, the best up to that time.

So far as astronomy is concerned, I've never seen anything that surpassed, for a popular notion of the broad outlines of the kind of physical world we live in, than John Campbell's series that appeared in *Astounding.* They started in 1936, and ran on for fifteen or sixteen issues, his articles on the solar system. I've always been sorry that Campbell did not go on from there and cover stellar astronomy, galactic astronomy, and some of the other side fields. But, even at that, anybody who has read through that series by Campbell on the solar system will never again have a flat-world attitude, which most people do have. Not in the science fiction field, of course—I mean not among fans of science fiction.

(I speak many times as if the human race were divided into two parts, as it *may* be; people who love science fiction, and people who don't. I think you will be able to keep sorted out which ones I'm talking about. I hope so.)

In the field of economics, an incomplete science, but neverthe-less one that you can't possibly ignore, I think the most illuminat-ing book I've ever read is one by Maurice Colburn, called *Economic Nationalism.* The title won't give any suggestion of what the contents are, but that is simply the tag by which it is known.

Jim Farley's *Behind the Ballots* is probably as nice a job of recording actual data in politics as I've ever seen; however, politics—I'd never recommend that people read books in the political field.

Go out and take a look *yourself.* Everything else you hear is guff.

I saved for the last on that list of the books that have greatly affected me, that to my mind are key books, of the stuff I've plowed through, a book which should head the list on the *must* list. I wish that everyone could read the book. There aren't many copies of it, and everyone can't, nor could everyone read this particular book. All of you could—you've got the imagination for it. It's *Science and Sanity* by Count Alfred Korzybski, one of the greatest Polish mathematicians when he went into the subject of symbology and started finding out what made us tick, and then worked up in strictly experimental and observational form from the preliminary work of E. T. Bell.

A rigor of epistemology based on E. T. Bell [break in transcript here—some words lost] . . . symbology of epistemology. The book refers to the subject of semantics. I know from conversation with a lot of you that the words epistemology and semantics are not unfamiliar to you. But because they may be unfamiliar to some, I'm going to stop and give definitions of those words.

Semantics is simply a study of the symbols we use to communicate. General Semantics is an extension of that study to investigate how we *evaluate* the use of those symbols. Epistemology is the study of *how* we know *what* we know. Maybe that doesn't sound exciting. It is exciting, it's very exciting. To be able to delve back into your own mind and investigate what it is you know, what it is you *can* know, and what it is that you *cannot possibly* know, is, from a standpoint of intellectual adventure, I think, possibly the greatest adventure that a person can indulge in. Beats spaceships.

Incidentally, any of you who are going to be in Denver in the next five or six weeks will have an opportunity, one of the last opportunities, to hear Alfred Korzybski speak in person. He will be here at a meeting (similar to this) of semanticians from all over the world; McLean from Los Angeles, and Johnson from Iowa, and Reisser from Mills College and Kendig and probably Hayakawa from up in Canada—the leading semanticians of the world—to hear Korzybski speak.

It is much better to hear him speak than it is to read his books. He's limited by the fact that he's got to stick to the typewriter, to the printed word, but when he talks, when he talks, it's another matter! He gestures, he's not tied down with his hands to the desk the way I am, he walks, stumps all around the stage, and waves his hands, and when he's putting quotation marks on a word, he puts them on . . . [illustrates, audience laughs]. And you really gather what he means. Incidentally, he looks like Conan Doyle's description of Professor Challenger if Professor Challenger had shaved his beard. Dynamic character.

You may not like him personally, but he's at least as great a man as Einstein, at least, because his field is broader. The same kind of work that Einstein did, the same kind of work using the same methods, but in a much broader field, much closer to human relationships. I hope that some of you will be able to hear him. I said that this will be one of the last chances, because the old man's well over seventy now. As he puts it, "I vill coagulate someday, I vill someday soon, I vill coagulate" which is the term he uses for dying.

He speaks in terms of colloidal chemistry. Properly, it's appropriate. He won't last much longer. In the meantime, he's done a monumental piece of work that H. G. Wells did in the matter of description, and the two together are giants in our intellectual horizon, our intellectual matrix today, that stick up over the rest like the Empire State Building.

I started out to talk primarily about science fiction and I got off on some of my own hobbies. It's a luxury to me not to be held down by a plot and a set of characters. Here I can say anything I like and not be bothered.

I myself have been reading science fiction since Gernsback started putting it out in the *Electrical Experimenter*. Then I read it in *Argosy* and I dug up all that I could out of the Kansas City Public Library. Every member of my family had a library card; there were seven of us, so I could bring home quite a number of books at one time. I wear glasses now as a result. I never had any particular notion of writing it until about two years ago when a concatenation of peculiar circumstances started me writing. I happened to hit the jackpot on the first one, so I continued writing. It amazed me to discover that people gave money away for doing things like that—it beats working.

It's likely that I won't be writing very much longer. With the way things are shaping up, I'll probably have other things I'll have to do, as will others here, whether we like it or not. But I hope to be a fan of science fiction for at least fifty years if I can hold myself together that long and keep from getting my teeth kicked in.

All I really want to do is to hang around as long as I can, watch the world unfold, see some of the changes—what they really are—that suits me.

GUEST OF HONOR SPEECH AT THE XIXth WORLD SCIENCE FICTION CONVENTION SEATTLE, 1961

THE FUTURE REVISITED

Madame Chairman, Banquet Chairman, members of the World Science Fiction Convention, friends—protocol now requires that I make a speech.

I don't know why this is so. I'm quite sure that nothing I can say tonight can compete with the entertainment offered last night.

There will be a question period. But right now, under a precedent established at the First World Science Fiction Convention, I am expected to produce some Big Thoughts giving clear evidence of a Deep Thinker.

It has been just twenty years since the last time I did this. A good interval, I think—it gives time for a new generation of fans to grow up and thereby reduces the likelihood that discrepancies between the Deep Thoughts on the first occasion and the Deep Thoughts on the next occasion will show up—it lets me speak freely.

Is there anyone here tonight who was at the Denver Convention in 1941? Do you recall what I said on that occasion?

You see? That shows you what one gets for deep thoughts. My subject twenty years ago was THE DISCOVERY OF THE FUTURE. My subject tonight is THE FUTURE REVISITED—and we'll check up a little, not too closely, on whether what I said twenty years ago still makes sense.

If you all will be so gracious as to invite me again, twenty years from tonight, I'll be happy to accept. 1981, that will be—I can't accept for 1984; Big Brother will be watching.

We might hold the 1981 convention on the Moon, at Luna City. I understand that there are very few conventions on the Moon—and these affairs have been growing more and more unconventional over the years—so we should call it Looneycon.

My subject in 1981 will be—obviously—THE FUTURE . . . WHATEVER BECAME OF IT?

But it may be more practical—more in accordance with the wishes of the authorities—for us to hold the 1981 Convention in some small garden city of the future located on the Arctic Ocean in the far north of Siberia.

We can call it the SlaveCon.

I went back and reread that speech of twenty years ago in order to see just what slips I would have to cover up or explain away tonight.

I found that it was not going to be necessary to cover up—largely because I had been too cagey to make very many specific predictions. However, I did make two hard-nosed predictions.

I predicted that the years immediately following 1941 would be a period of great and radical change . . . change so great that most people would not be able to understand it, assimilate it, cope with it—and that the whole world would start behaving irrationally—crazy.

Does anyone want to dispute that it has? If so, I won't argue—I'll simply refer them to the headlines in tonight's paper.

I also said that science fiction fans, because they were interested in the future and believed in change, would not be so shocked by these drastic changes we have all seen these past twenty years and thereby stood a better chance of not going crazy when the rest of the world did.

I can't prove that I was correct in this prediction—or pious hope—by referring you to the headlines. But—I can't see that science fiction fans are one whit crazier than they were twenty years ago.

The second firm prediction I made in 1941 was a dead cinch, no harder than predicting tomorrow's sunrise—at least it seems that easy, looking back instead of forward. I said that the series of wars the world was in would go on for five, ten, twenty, possibly fifty years—

Now look at the damned thing, twenty years later! Anybody here with a transistor radio? Will you keep it tuned to Conelrad, please?

Let's update that prediction tonight. Things are even worse tonight than they looked in 1941, with World War II already raging and Pearl Harbor only weeks away. 1941 looks like the Good Old Days now— There is no peace in the future for any of us . . . even the youngest here.

In prophesying tonight I am going to be less cagey, more specific, than I was in 1941—although not so specific as to try to guess tomorrow's headlines. In the wisely cynical words of L. Sprague de Camp: "It does not pay a prophet to be too specific."

But, as William Lindsay Gresham said, "You'll never get rich prophesying gloom." But I'm not trying to get rich tonight; I'm trying to make some hard-headed predictions—and I'm sorry to say that my crystal ball does not have very many nice things in it—not for the rest of this century.

So, for any of you who don't want to hear bad news, this is a good time to slide out the side door.

Wishful thinking—it would be so much pleasanter to indulge in wishful thinking. Do you remember a story, in *Astounding* I think, three or four years ago—"The Cold Equations"? One of the most nearly perfect science fiction stories ever written—and one of the most bloodcurdling.

Remember it? A sweet young girl, stowed away on a space ship. Lots of stories have started this way . . . and they usually end with a romance between the pilot and the sweet young stowaway, with a lavish ration of cops and robbers in between before he gets her.

This one didn't. No cops and robbers, no romance. The Cold Equations—the laws of nature—said that she had to be jettisoned —*killed*—to permit that space ship to land.

And she *was* killed. There wasn't any other possible answer.

By 1980 a solid world government, guaranteeing permanent peace and civil liberty to all, even to the citizens of those nations that choose to remain socialistic, a concerted effort by all nations to control population and raise living standards for all. Cancer conquered, and all the diseases of poverty and filth being brought under control as we devote the effort to world public health that we now devote to armaments and war, a thriving colony on the Moon, and a base on Mars, cheap and easy space travel . . . plenty to eat for everybody—that is what I would like to predict tonight. How I would love to live in such a world!

The Cold Equations say No.

I'll never see such a world. I'll be doing well to stay alive to my natural span.

And so will *you.*

Because one-third of us here in this room will die in the near future.

H-bombs? Probably *not* H-bombs. But there are lots of other ways to die besides H-bombs, some of them much nastier than blast or radiation burns. Such as being waylaid and killed by your next door neighbor because you have food. Or he thinks you have.

Or starving slowly in a slave camp. Oh, it can happen! There was a member of my family who was a wealthy woman in 1941—in 1942 she was in a concentration camp. She's dead now, the camp killed her—*very* slowly. Her husband is dead, too, but not the same way. He was a military P.O.W.—they took him out and lined him up along with eight hundred others and machine-gunned them.

Oh, yes, there are some things worse than H-bombs and fallout—and some of us here tonight are going to get intimately acquainted with them . . . in the near future.

How near? Probably not this week. The logic of war today is such that it is most exceedingly unlikely to break out in the middle of a crisis. In this new sort of war the real crisis never stops—and the poorest time to start the hot war is in the middle of a cooked-up crisis such as the one we are in tonight. The hot war is much more likely to break out—if it ever does break out, which is not the likeliest alternative—after a period of sweetness and light, of "peaceful coexistence," with no hint of warning.

So, if you want to make a trip around the world, even visit Berlin, or Moscow, go right ahead and don't worry. You'll be at least as safe as you are at home. So do it—live it up! Have fun.

> *Gather ye rosebuds while ye may*
> *Old Time is yet a-flying*
> *For while we're all still here today*
> *Some morrow we'll be dying.*

Of all the possible futures ahead of us for the rest of this century most of them encompass the destruction of the United States of America as the political entity we know and with the death of at least 50- or 60,000,000 of her citizens. Our country destroyed and one third of us dead—you—and you get it—so long, Ted—honey, you're too young to die!

Well, I've lived a full life—and the Cold Equations apply to me as much as to anyone. With any luck I'll be the first man on my block to glow in the dark—but with bad luck I'll have to go the hard way.

The secret of correct prediction is to shun wishful thinking and coldly believe the Cold Equations. Shun pessimistic thinking, too—as I am doing and as I shall presently prove to you. Treat the world the way a research scientist treats a problem—examine the data, try to organize, try to predict coldly and logically. Not what you *want* to have happen—but what *can* happen and what is most *likely* to happen—and then, and *only* then, what you yourself can do about it, to make things easier or better or safer for you and your kids.

You don't cope with a cancer by forgetting it, and hoping it will go away.

You don't avoid a traffic accident by closing your eyes.

Ninety percent of the possible futures ahead of us fall into two groups, none of them good.

All other possibilities—call it ten percent, I simply mean some small and unlikely fraction of the things that can happen to us; the remaining possibilities represented by this arbitrary ten percent are such wild chances as the sun going nova soon, or flying saucers landing on the White House lawn and in Red Square followed by the Galactic Overlords taking us under their benevolent wings— God, how many times have I read that story! Read it?—I've written it!

Or Nikita Khrushchev suddenly being converted to Christianity and volunteering for Mr. Kennedy's Peace Corps.

All you can say for those possibilities is that they are, none of them, physically *impossible*—but don't stay awake waiting for them.

The remaining nine chances out of ten, the probable futures, break into two parts. The first part—I won't say "first half"; there is no way to estimate the percentages—the first part is the blowup, the catastrophe, the one most science fiction stories have been written about or assumed as a condition, present or past, for the sixteen years since Hiroshima—I mean World War III, all-out and with all the trimmings, from H-bombs on Seattle and New York and fifty other targets to biological warfare and any other nastiness your imagination cares to contrive—and you can be sure that if your imagination picked the wrong choices, what *will* happen will be still nastier.

This first part, World War III, splits logically into two subdivisions: one in which we win, one in which we lose. Some people like to add a third case here, in which both the U.S. and the U.S.S.R. are so crippled that neither one wins—but that is not truly a third situation—because in that case China wins.

All I want to point out at the moment is that something on the order of one third of us die, no matter who wins. Not one third of the Russians—one third of *us*.

Or do we? Let me make a quick check. Will any of you here who have already built and stocked a fallout shelter please hold up your hands?

I expected it—I've asked this same question of a number of widely varied audiences; very few Americans are prepared to stay alive while the fallout cools down. Nor am I criticizing, please note that *my* hand did not go up. My wife and I have no fallout protection of any sort. I'm not proud of it, I'm not ashamed of it—I'm simply in the same boat as almost everybody else and have paid as little attention to the warnings.

I'm not preaching, I'm not urging you to hurry home and start filling sand bags and bottling water. This is how it *is*. We are not now prepared to live through a heavy attack—and those figures of a third or maybe a half of us dead *stand*—unless we do prepare. If we do; and from what I've seen of American temperament I doubt if we will prepare.

The other part that makes up the ninety percent of all of our possible futures is simpler, slower—and just as deadly in the long run. In due course, with no more than minor brush wars unfelt by any but the poor blokes who get killed in them, the United States will find itself in a situation where the simplest, easiest, and safest thing to do will be to surrender. Maybe it won't be called surrender—maybe it will be called a "realistic accommodation" by the editorial writers that year—or a "treaty of non-aggression with commercial agreements for mutual trade"—or anything. The name doesn't matter; the idea is that the Kremlin will be giving the orders here rather than Washington.

Death then comes to many of us with that whimper rather than the big bang and, of course, not nearly as quickly. But just as thoroughly. The laddies who liquidated the trouble in the Ukraine, and used tanks on the school boys of Budapest, won't hesitate to liquidate the bourgeois mentality here. You can ask yourself, most privately, whether or not you are of the temperament to live through this—and *I* don't want to know the answer!

But my own estimate of the average American Joe Blow is such that I expect the long-term casualties if we surrender to be at least as high as the casualties in all-out war. We've been free a long time, we won't take kindly to chains, a lot of us; they will have to liquidate, one way or another, quite a large portion of us before we will be docile.

But it will be slower and not nearly so spectacular. Just nastier—

That's all. That fills up the entire ninety percent of probable futures for us. All the other possibilities lie in that ten percent or less which are wildly unlikely.

"Now, wait a minute! There's one more. If we can just manage to avoid an all-out war—"

I can hear you saying it. I rather suspect that we *will* manage to avoid an all-out war. That is our most probable future. The Kremlin doesn't want war—God knows the Russian people don't want war although they won't have any choice, either way—and most Americans are most reluctant to face the prospect of a real war—how many of you have built fallout shelters?—that's proof. And I must admit that I am selfish enough to enjoy peace, such as it is, as long as it lasts. It is possible, though not too probable, that I will die of natural causes before this slower defeat overtakes us.

Let me define it. The remaining possibility is that, if we avoid an all-out World War III, that in time the Communist Axis would reform internally, cease to be aggressive and imperialistic, cease to menace us and the rest of the world, start being a peaceful, socialistic neighbor, something like Sweden. Or that, if we just wait long enough and avoid war, the Russian people themselves and the Chinese people will rise up, throw off their oppressors— and save us the headaches.

Okay, it's physically possible, we must add it to the list.

But *not* in the ninety percent.

This must be placed over in the fraction of wildly unlikely possibilities, along with the Galactic Overlords and Nikita Khrushchev learning to sing "Jesus, Lover of my Soul."

Anything else is wishful thinking at its sorriest.

Over and over again since my wife and I returned from the Soviet Union last year, people have said to us, almost pleadingly, "Don't you think that, in time, as they get more consumer goods and improve their standard of living, that the Russians will—"

No, I don't think it!

The first and most important thing to learn about Communists is that they behave like Communists.

Communism is a religion, an extremely moralistic and utterly engrossing religion. Do you think that you could possibly wean a Catholic priest away from his faith by offering him an improvement in his standard of living?

Preposterous! And, believe me, a devout Communist cannot be seduced with sirloin steaks and Cadillacs. Or Zims.

The *first* thing to learn about Communists in order to understand them—and thereby guess how the frog will jump—is that *Communists are not villains!*

Let me repeat it like a radio commercial: Communists are *not* villains!

They are devout, moral, very moralistic, kind, humane, and utterly convinced—by *their* standards! And they live by *their* standards!

Even Nikita Khrushchev, the butcher of the Ukraine and Hungary, is not a villain—not in his own mind. His conscience is clear and his motives are pure. He feels no more guilt for anything he has done than did the Grand Inquisitor of Spain in the time when the Inquisition was at its roughest—and for exactly the same reason: Nikita does what he does for the highest of moral reasons—by *his* standards.

Until you learn this one thing about Communists you have no chance of reading and understanding the Cold Equations.

Communists are nice people, almost all of them. They are sincere, they are true believers—and they won't be seduced by sirloin steaks. I have been in six Communist countries and in eight of the so-called Republics of the Soviet Union—in much travel over many years. I know many, many Communists, know them and like them. Like them? Of all the major peoples on this planet the Russians and the Chinese are the most like us, the ones I like best—and it is a matter of deep sorrow to me that these sweet and warm-hearted people should be elected by the logic of history to be our antagonists.

I wish you all could know them as well as I do—and I wish you could have the tremendous advantage, as I had, of having a wife who had gone to the tremendous effort of learning to speak Russian fluently before we went there.

This is impossible for most people, I know—I was lucky. Nevertheless it is possible to learn something intellectually of how the Communist mind works by studying, hard and sympathetically, Dialectical Materialism, the history of Communism and other aspects of Marxism-Leninism.

Know your enemy—the first law of war.

If the American people and in particular American political leaders took the trouble to try to learn the mind and methods and *high moral standards* of their enemy, we would not behave as foolishly as we do.

We might even save the lives of a third or more of our people.

To understand him on *his* terms— Not on ours, not on our bourgeois, capitalistic, democratic, almost anarchistic terms—but to learn what *he* thinks of himself—and why. Learn that Russians love their country, are loyal to their own form of government mostly—probably a higher percentage than of Americans loyal to their government, honestly believe that Communism is the salvation of mankind—if we learned these things, we wouldn't rely on Mr. Micawber's solution and wait for something to turn up.

However, I don't see one chance in ten thousand of Americans —enough Americans—getting to know the mind of the enemy well enough to realize this. Won't happen. Instead, we will go right on applying our own rather fuzzy and good-hearted humanitarianism and will go on applying to Communists our own parochial and rather naive standards—and will go on misunderstanding him and continue to be utterly surprised when he acts like a Communist.

It will likely be the ruin of us. Only in the rather unlikely chance of us stumbling into a war—and winning it at a cost almost too dreadful to visualize—can I see anything but ruin ahead.

However, if any of you, as individuals, want to understand the years ahead, just remember this: the key to it all is Communists are not villains.

Not that this will do our country any good—because the vast majority of us will go on thinking of Communists either as devils, or as poor stupid clunks who can be seduced by sirloin steak. And this misconception is going to ruin us and kill many of us.

But it isn't all bad—

Bear in mind that our ancestors outlived the saber-tooth tiger, lived through the Black Death. The human race isn't washed up yet and won't be. Forget *On the Beach;* the future isn't that bleak. If a third of us will die, that still means that two-thirds of us will live—and the loss won't matter to the human race. This, our race,

is appreciating at the rate of 160,000 humans per day now—
60,000,000 Americans can be replaced in how long? A year and
ten days—

Oh, most of them will be Chinese rather than Americans—but
is this bad?

Only for us. It may well be an improvement; the Chinese have
been raised in fortitude for centuries . . . whereas we have been
living pretty high on the hog and keep alive our poorest stock.
Racially and genetically it may well be an improvement for a third
of us to be killed off.

That doesn't mean we have to like it.

I'm merely saying let's not feel too tragic about it simply because
it's us—racially we aren't all that important.

And do remember that this little group here tonight can't do
much about it, one way or another. This wouldn't be the place to
attempt to start political action to try to change things anyhow; we
here represent too many highly divergent viewpoints—including,
I would guess from the size of the group, at least a handful of
devout, convinced, and non-villainous Communists.

No, tonight we are simply examining what is likely to happen in
the future.

Twenty years ago I urged the convention audience to prepare
themselves against the shock of change, so that they could roll with
the punch, be as happy as circumstances permitted—and increase
their chances of survival.

That still applies, twenty years later. Nobody will live through
the extremely rough period ahead of us, a period that probably will
see the end of our national history, by getting the jitters, flipping
his lid, or being overcome by the horror of it all.

The period ahead of us is guaranteed not to be boring.

I said that science fiction fans apparently had not changed in
twenty years. That is not quite true of many science fiction writers.
Or perhaps it is the editors, since I am judging by the stories I see
in print.

Twenty years and more ago science fiction writers (as it seems to
me) were much more free swinging. The worlds they wrote about
were dangerous and they never apologized for it—whereas today
many sf writers seem to write sweet little stories about a bucolic
culture after the blowup with everyone determined never to let the
scientists get out of hand again—so help me, to read many of the
sf stories today you would think that Lord God Almighty

made a terrible mistake when He invented radioactivity and that it was up to the human race, as instructed by sf authors, to correct His error.

But take a look back twenty-odd years ago. The worlds of Doc Smith's space epics make the prospects of World War III look like a tea party. Nor was he alone. John Campbell, in his space sagas, always described scenes just as rough—and so did Jack Williamson. Those were terrible and terrifying universes—yet their characters charged in undismayed, against any odds—scattering blood over thousands and millions of parsecs.

It seems to me that most of the writers today have fallen sick of the jitters. An all-out space battle, with beams flashing and planets destroyed in the backlash is just too horrible for them to think about.

Many of the sf writers today seem to have acquired a permanent nervous breakdown during and after World War II. Some of the things that science fiction long predicted have come to pass—and now they're scared silly.

I don't understand it.

Look, friends, the only possible way to enjoy life is not to be afraid to die. A zest for living requires a willingness to die; you cannot have the first without the second. The '60s and '70s and '80s and '90s can be loaded with the zest for living, high excitement, and gutsy adventure for any truly human person.

"Truly human"? I mean you descendants of cavemen who outlasted the saber-tooth, you who sprang from the loins of the Vikings, you whose ancestors fought the Crusades and were numbered the Golden Horde. Death is the lot of all of us and the only way the human race has ever conquered death is by treating it with contempt. By living every golden minute as if one had all eternity—

About fifty years ago when I was a small child a thing happened in my home town which made a permanent impression on me. My family lived in Kansas City then; there is a large park in the south of town, Swope Park. Almost every Sunday in good weather we would ride the street car out there and enjoy the park. Through the park runs—or did run, then—a railroad track, the Katy line. There were half a dozen places where one could cross the track on foot.

A man and his wife were walking in Swope Park one Sunday, started across those tracks, and she stepped on a switching juncture, got her foot caught in it—stuck tight.

Nothing to panic about, there were no trains in sight and that line carried only a couple of trains a day.

But she found that she could not pull it out even with her husband's help—and there was no one else around.

They both worked away at it for several minutes when a stranger came along, a man, and now all three of them strained and pulled.

No luck—and now they heard a train coming.

Too late to flag it down—too late to do anything—save continue to try to get her foot out of there.

Of course both the husband—and the stranger who had happened along—could have saved themselves easily.

But they didn't. Neither gave up, both men kept trying and were still trying as the train hit them.

The wife and the stranger were killed at once; the husband lasted just long enough to tell what happened and died before he could be moved.

The woman had no choice. The husband had a choice but acted as a husband should.

But what about the stranger?

No one would have blamed him if he had jumped clear at the last moment at which he could have saved himself. After all, in sober fact, the woman could not be saved—it was too late. She was not his wife, not his responsibility—she was a total stranger; we don't know that he ever learned her name.

But he didn't jump back. He was leaning over, pulling at this stranger's leg with all his strength when the locomotive hit him. He used the last golden moments of his life, the last effort his muscles would ever make, still trying to save her.

I don't know anything about him. I didn't see it happen and when the crowd gathered—amazing how fast a crowd can gather even in a lonely spot once an accident happens. My parents got me quickly back and away from there to keep me from seeing the mangled bodies. So all I really know about it is what I can recall from hearing my father read aloud the account in the Kansas City *Star*.

I don't even know the stranger's name. The newspaper described him as about twenty-eight, I think it was, and a "laborer." Probably that means "hobo" as he was walking along the tracks. It is possible that this married couple who died with him would never, under other circumstances, have met him formally, might not have been willing to sit down and eat with him.

I don't know. I'll never know anything about him—except how

he chose to spend the last five minutes of his short life . . . and how he elected to die.

But that is really quite a lot and I've thought about it many times since. Why did he do what he did? What did he think about in those last few rushing minutes when the train bore down on them? Or did he think about anything save the great effort he was making? Was he afraid? If he was, what inner resources did he draw on to offset that fear with ultimate courage?

We can't know. All we know is that, with no flags flying, no bands playing, no time to prepare his soul for the ordeal—he did it.

And the only conclusion I have ever been able to reach is this: This is how a man lives. And this is how a *man* dies.

His caveman ancestors have good reason to feel proud of him—and this is why the caveman's children are reaching out to the stars—and will *reach* the stars.

Would it have made a difference if some other man—or woman—had happened along in place of this nameless stranger? Did inexorable fate bring this hero to his appointed triumph? Or was it coincidence so wild that an author would be ashamed to use it that a man with the necessary courage happened to be walking along that railroad track?

I don't think any of these things are true. I suggest that it really didn't matter much in the outcome which human being happened along. I have great respect for the race of which I now have the honor to be a member—and I think that the chances are at least seven out of ten that *any* stranger with the same gutsy abandon would have done the same thing. You here in this room. Anybody—

This is not a tale about how a man happened to die in Swope Park on a Sunday afternoon back when Taft was President. This is a story for any year about how a *man . . . lives.*

The next ten, twenty, thirty, forty years will offer exceptional and rewarding opportunities for busy, happy, and adventurous living—to men and women who are not inclined to worry too much about just how *long* they will live.

It is possible that these many opportunities for a busy but short life will come as a result of us fighting and winning World War III, then trying to occupy the U.S.S.R. Let us say that this will be a very interesting experience and that at least some of the natives will not take kindly to being occupied—as Hitler learned and as

Khrushchev himself learned in the Ukraine—and let us note also that atomic weapons are very little use against an underground—and then let it go at that.

But I do not see us as the most likely winner. If we lose the war—or surrender without fighting—there will be, here in America, a long, long period of underground resistance. It will be both the most tragic and the proudest era in our history.

But not necessarily an unhappy one for those who choose to fight. Happiness does not come from sirloin steaks and Cadillacs —nor does hardship and danger mean unhappiness to those who choose it voluntarily. These are not the circumstances under which people commit suicide.

Nor will occupation of the United States necessarily be too uncomfortable for the survivors who choose not to resist. Oh, it will be different all right—but probably more like Czechoslovakia than like poor Poland. Life under Communism actually isn't so awfully difficult for most people—just dreary—unless you happen to be terribly fond of marching and group calisthenics.

But life for the underground resistance fighters will be most difficult—but not dreary. And it will be a great day for the 4-F, and the female warrior, and the over-age warrior. No bureaucratic piffle about flat feet or underweight or poor eyes or underage or overage—or even a growing cancer—this is a game with no rules and any number can play. Women will be just as welcome as men—a rifle or a knife wielded by a girl kills just as dead as one in the hands of a professional soldier. Besides that, women, especially if they are young and pretty—or either one—have weapons at their disposal in this sort of irregular fighting that we men simply don't have.

It will be a glorious and tragic period and it will go on for a long, long time.

If any of you here think that you might decide to join the underground when the time comes, rather than simply knuckle under and do as you are told, you may want to give it some thought and a certain amount of preparation ahead of time. In the first place you obviously can't take part in it unless you manage to live through WWIII—if they hold it. I won't discuss how to do this, as it is really very simple and the instructions are available at any Civil Defense office—unless, of course, you are at ground zero of a direct hit, a factor which renders all other considerations academic.

Besides dodging fallout, you may want to stash away some weapons and some ammunition—it will save you from having to steal them barehanded from Russians or Chinese afterwards—time-wasting and chancy. I won't go into the matter of what weapons or how much ammunition, either, except to say that if you happen to live in a state which has a registration law on guns, then buy your weapons in some other state, sneak them home, and hide them against *der Tag*—because the very first thing a military provost does is to go to the local records, find out who has guns, send squads around to pick them up—or shoot those who fail to surrender them.

You will want to learn how to make grenades and bombs in your own kitchen, too. Ask almost any chemist—my wife Ginny, or Isaac Asimov, or Will Jenkins, or Tom Scortia.

But most of all you will want to study—ahead of time—how to fight and stay alive. Your object will be to cause one of the conquerors to die for *his* country—not the other way around—and this sort of irregular fighting is a high art.

Fortunately there are books, excellent books. Here are three: *New Ways of War* by Tom Wintringham, *Guerrilla Warfare* by Yank Levy, and *The War of Guerrilla* by Che Guevara.

All three of these books are by Communists—and you can't possibly find better teachers anywhere.

If you can't lay hands on one of these, there is a book *Kill or Get Killed,* by an American colonel, Rex Applegate, just published by Stackpole this year. I don't know how good it is—and I do know that these three Communist books are good—but it may be easier to buy and it is well recommended.

This advice is just a footnote in hope that if you do decide to join in, it might keep you alive—a bit longer, at least. And if you do—good luck to you! Good hunting! Maybe we'll even run across each other some day—if we're both lucky, long enough.

It will be the most glorious and tragic period in our history—and it will go on for a long, long time.

But I am forced to say that it will not succeed. This is almost certain. Because *no* underground anywhere in history has ever managed to throw off their conquerors—without help from outside.

And we aren't going to have any help. Not any.

So in time, all of us who resist will be killed—or be captured and shipped off to slave labor camps. There is no hope of winning.

You won't have any more chance than that nameless stranger did when he chose to stick it out and be killed by that locomotive. All in this world that joining the underground has to offer is a chance to live as a *man*—and be happy as long as you are alive.

However, to some people that is quite a lot.

I think it behooves every one of us to take out his soul and examine it carefully—and decide just what sort of person he is—before the chips are down. You'll save yourself a lot of grief.

There are only two rational points of view; this is an either-or situation. Either you believe in your heart: "Give me Liberty or Give me Death"—

—or, your viewpoint is: "I'd rather be Red than dead."

No tertium quid. No middle ground. It's that nonexistent middle ground the wishful thinkers are looking for when they ask, "Don't you really think that the Russians, as they get more consumer goods and more cultural exchange with those of us in the free world, that they will—" and the rest of that nonsense.

This conflict will be resolved. Not because we wish it, but because Communists behave like Communists—and they will change, in the words of Nikita Khrushchev, when shrimps learn to whistle.

So find out where you stand—don't tell me, tell yourself.

This is a good time to say a word in praise of one of the greatest minds of this century—Bertrand, Lord Russell. A mind like a computer, utterly logical. I won't repeat his arguments—go look them up. Because no one has ever stated the arguments for pacifism and surrender more logically and more cogently.

I can't disagree with him in any way. The man makes sense.

My only difference with him is the total disagreement of starting from a different set of unarguable values. I honor and respect Lord Russell . . . because he knows where he stands and why and has the courage to stare open-eyed at the consequences of his own moral values.

But I have no use at all for the wishful thinker who makes himself believe that, if he just closes his eyes to it, the horrid things will all go away.

So examine your souls. "I'd rather be Red than dead"—nobody can argue with that. If you've got it in you to knuckle under and be one of the sheep—to be a collaborator, find it out *now*. It can save you a lot of grief in the future.

You can still build your fallout shelter, live through it—

surrender without resistance and save your own life and the lives of your children. If you've got talent for not fighting City Hall, you can even make a pretty good thing of it—perhaps better than you have now.

Only one minor drawback. Some dark night you may encounter a neighbor who is still bull-headedly attached to an older slogan: "Give me Liberty or Give me Death"—and in his stiff-necked way, *resents* your collaboration.

He may cut your throat. He *will* cut your throat!—if you are careless.

This is really sad. It really is. I mean it. A pacifist doesn't want to cut anybody's throat, not anybody. When he says, "I'd rather be Red than dead," he means it—but he doesn't mean any harm to anyone else.

It is most unfair that he should find himself trapped between two groups of fanatics, both of which are quite willing to cut throats between the soup and the entree—with no loss of appetite.

But that's how it is. This is no world for wishful thinkers and our immediate future has almost no place for a pacifist in it. It's not fair at all, but—your neighbor who now comes to your cocktail parties will, sometime before long—cut your throat.

He's a mean bastard and he just doesn't understand pacifists. He thinks they look better with their throats cut. And there are so many of him and so few of the People's Police that, chances are, he'll manage it—before the police get him.

It just . . . isn't . . . *fair!*

Perhaps this is a good time for me to stop and interpolate a statement on my own behalf. I have been forced to realize that, in the minds of many people—including some of you here tonight—I am a dirty war-mongering beast who wants to sprinkle fallout over innocent babes.

By the standards of antagonists I suppose the most I can plead is *nolo contendere.*

Which is the same as pleading guilty.

Yes, I would rather risk fallout on innocent babies, with chuckly smiles and dimpled knees—than see the United States of America surrender to this monstrous evil.

But my wishes in the matter will not be consulted—and I am not indulging in wishful thinking tonight. I think our most probable future is surrender without a fight. No radioactive fallout. Just slavery.

I happen to think that it is better to risk fallout for a baby than to risk slavery for it. But, again, my opinion won't be asked. I also think there are prices too high to pay to save the United States.

Conscription is one of them. Conscription is slavery—and I don't think that any people or nation has a right to save itself at the price of slavery for anyone—no matter what name it is called. We have had the draft for twenty years now; I think this is shameful. If a country can't save itself through the volunteer service of its own free people, then I say: Let the damned thing go down the drain!

I don't like suppression of the truth for any reason. I think the word "classified" stinks!

I do not think that a group of people is justified in locking up a human being. If I had my way, all jails and prisons would be torn down, utterly abolished!

I was not born with these opinions and I did not form them lightly. I say these things as a man who has, in the past, marked documents "Confidential" or "Secret," a man who has given orders to conscripts, as a man who has sentenced his fellow men to prison. I don't like any of it.

All three of these things have to do with why I despise Communism—but I will mention only the factor I despise most. I hate Communism most for its cold-blooded murder of the *truth!*

"Pravda" doesn't mean "truth." Pravda means whatever serves the world Communist revolution.

Let me tell you how this works in practice.

Thanks to George Orwell the grisly idea of unpersons and revised history is well known. Perhaps some of you thought that he was exaggerating.

While in the U.S.S.R. I tried very hard to find some trace of John Paul Jones. This should have been easy, as his career is unique; he founded both the American Navy and the modern Russian Navy.

But John Paul Jones has been sunk without a trace. I asked about him repeatedly, not only from guides who supposedly are trained in Russian history—and who *are* trained in it, of the revised sort—but also of professors of history, curators of historical museums and such. Not one of them had ever heard of him, he's an unperson.

Kerensky—Dr. Kerensky was President of Russia after the Tsar was overthrown and before Lenin came along. He is still living, in Palo Alto. I was unable to find anything about Kerensky in any Russian museum. I asked about him, and yes, they had heard of him—and changed the subject. He is becoming an unperson . . .

as soon as there is no one left alive who remembers him. All visible traces of him are gone.

Trotsky—Lenin and Trotsky were a team, like Khrushchev and Bulganin, in the early years of the U.S.S.R. While we were there the U.S.S.R. was holding a great Lenin celebration; among other exhibits were hundreds and hundreds of news photographs from the early days of Communist Russia. I looked them all over carefully trying to find Trotsky's unmistakable face, searching especially in group pictures of the Central Committee, pictures of the various ministers on official occasions.

Not one picture—Trotsky is an unperson. He exists only in the memories of those old enough to remember the early twenties.

In contrast, please note that Benedict Arnold, Aaron Burr, Jefferson Davis, Robert E. Lee, and other persons on the losing side in rebellions in our history are still in our history books.

I asked about several of the Russian heroes of WWII, such as Budënny and Timoshenko. Nobody knew or cared what had become of them—when a man drops out of the news in Russia, that's that.

Let me recount one recent news story—as reported in the Soviet Union: the U-2 incident.

You all remember it. A U-2 plane piloted by a civilian employee of the CIA—an American spy—came down in some fashion near Sverdlovsk in Siberia . . . and this marked the end of four years of aerial spying conducted by the CIA.

But here's how we got the story. On 5 May last year Mrs. Heinlein and I were in Alma-Ata, Kazakhstan, in the Soviet Union. Alma-Ata is almost unbelievably remote—it is in the middle of a restricted territory—slave camps and rocket launching sites in a vast semi-desert—3,000 miles inside the Iron Curtain, and a few miles from the Red China border. It is north of Sinkiang, north of Tibet, north of the Himalaya Mountains, northeast of Afghanistan, and almost exactly in the geometrical center of the great Asian land mass.

Not a good place to buy American newspapers.

However, we got the news orally, from a local Commie boss. Khrushchev made a speech that day and gave the official Communist version; this local boss ordered us into his office and gave it to us.

An American military plane had been shot down at 65,000 feet while attempting to cross the Afghanistan frontier into the U.S.S.R.—and let that be a lesson to us. The first attempt had been nailed right at the border and that was what would happen to any other American military plane that tried such aggression.

Khrushchev's speech was for internal consumption only—and please note the discrepancies between what was fed to the Russian people and what did happen. The incident now takes place 1,500 miles south of where it happened, right at the border. It is the first such incident, rather than the last of many, over four years. Soviet military might have smeared the attempt at once and at 65,000 feet.

(We may never know how and why that plane reached the ground. But for a number of physical, engineering reasons, it was *not* shot down at 65,000 feet by rocket fire.)

This is how history is revised, à la *Nineteen Eighty-Four*.

Two days later we saw pictures of the supposed wreckage in *Komsomolskaya Pravda*—and I pointed out to our guide that a radio installation does not fall 65,000 feet and reach the ground without a mark on it. I merely made her angry—she insisted that their newspapers "never print anything but the truth—never!"

Shortly thereafter we were in Kiev, waiting for a plane. Some Americans there asked us where we had been, where we were going; Mrs. Heinlein told them that we were now going to Vilno—and in answer to more questions, she explained that Vilno was the capital of Lithuania, one of the Baltic republics taken over by the U.S.S.R. about twenty years earlier.

A Russian translator, a young woman about twenty-three, was in the waiting room some distance away; she overheard this—and rushed over and butted in. With shrill indignation she informed us and the others that Mrs. Heinlein was *lying!*—that Lithuania had *always* been part of the Soviet Union!

Mrs. Heinlein shrugged and told her she was wrong and turned her back on her.

We went to Lithuania. Lithuania is a lovely country, very beautiful, and it had a very high native civilization and culture before the Communists came—Lithuania was far ahead of the barbaric giant east of it. It had its own literature and language and its industry was far ahead of that of the Soviet Union, especially its electrical industry.

A gentle, beautiful, and delightful place, even today—as long as you don't notice that all of the boss jobs there are held by Russians—not Lithuanians.

It is probably unnecessary to point out that the young woman was utterly mistaken and that Mrs. Heinlein was 100 percent correct—after all Lithuania lost its freedom so recently that the free Lithuanians—exiles and refugees—still maintain their national legation in Washington. The rape of Lithuania—and Estonia and Latvia, and the attempted rape of Finland—is still fresh in the minds of many of us and the facts are well and widely known throughout the world.

Except behind the Iron Curtain.

This is no accident, of course. On June 6th, 1941, after most elaborate preparations, the secret police swooped down and deported *all* of the Lithuanian national leaders of every sort—some 60,000 in a country of less than 3,000,000—and loaded them like cattle and shipped them east to such far-distant places as Kotlas and Vorkuta.

Thereafter it took about a year for the underground resistance to get organized.

However, it makes me solemnly proud to say that even this lopping off of all their leadership has not killed the Lithuanian spirit—they are *still* fighting and the Russian conquerors are still having an uneasy time of it. The Terror still shows in that country, a visitor can't miss it—whereas it doesn't show in Russia itself, nor even in the Ukraine. It is my guess that little Lithuania will never stop fighting its conquerors. I hope we do as well.

Since what happened to Lithuania is a preview of what will probably happen to us, let's stop a moment to see just how utterly the truth has been raped concerning Lithuania. Lithuania was a nation, a people, and a culture when Russia was merely peasant villages, serfs ruled over by illiterate barbaric chieftains. In the fourteenth century the Lithuanian Empire stretched right across Europe, from the Baltic to the Black Sea, Danzig to Odessa, an area greater than France, Germany, and England today—and controlled all the trade routes. Russia wasn't even a country then; they were a bunch of local tribes all paying tribute to the Tatar Khanate in the south. But you won't learn this in Russia today!

But a small people—the Lithuanians were never numerous—has trouble maintaining its independence in a country having no natural barriers. In time, Poland, Germany, and Russia all fought over little Lithuania and Napoleon crushed through it twice. In 1795 the Tsar annexed it and held it for 123 years, to 1918, during which time the Tsars tried, with extreme harshness—and without success—to extinguish Lithuanian nationalism, language, and culture. They rubbed out the name "Lietuva" and lumped it in as part of "Northwest Territory." In 1863 the Russians exiled 9,000 Lithuanian leaders to Siberia and imported Russians to fill all government jobs, closed the Roman Catholic schools, and forbade the Lithuanian language to be printed or taught—and note how closely this resembles what the Communists have done to them this generation, and are still doing.

But neither the Tsars nor the Communists were successful; harsh measures merely stimulated the underground. The Lithuanians have been free during most of their history, they were free and independent only twenty-two years ago and they have not forgotten their great history. They have never stopped fighting, they are fighting tonight—somewhere in Lithuania right this moment, some Russian or some collaborator is having his throat cut.

But, far from being "always a part of the Soviet Union" Lithuania fought the Russian Communists during the disorders that followed the collapse of the Tsarist Empire—fought them to a standstill and the Soviets signed a peace treaty in 1920, guaranteeing to respect Lithuanian independence and promising to pay indemnities—these promises were worth what Communist promises always are worth; nevertheless Lithuania remained free until World War II, at which time, by a combination of pressure and trickery, the U.S.S.R. took them over without a fight. How is it that this Russian girl in Kiev holds such a distorted view of history? The most ironical—and the most chilling—aspect of this incident was that she was *sincere.* She was certain that she was speaking the truth—and that Mrs. Heinlein was a liar, a capitalist, aggressor liar, intentionally spreading false stories about her beloved country.

How?

Well, in the first place people in the U.S.S.R. don't travel much—a trip such as most of you have made to come to this convention is impossible. A Soviet citizen has to use his passport and get a visa from the police to make a trip like that from Tacoma to Seattle. It is extremely unlikely that this young woman in Kiev had even been in Lithuania. She knows only what she is told—she knows less about her own country than I do, she's traveled less in it.

In the second place every word, every source of information available to her has been government controlled—books, magazines, television, radio, newspapers, *everything.* It is almost impossible to describe this; it has to be experienced—but it feels a little like being smothered in cotton wool. It is a very odd feeling and it overtakes one after only a few days in the Soviet Union. I can't describe it, put it over emotionally . . . but try to imagine a situation in which every textbook, novel, magazine, you name it, is published by the Government Printing Office, every editor is a political employee—and censor. Imagine, if you can, a situation in which fan magazines could not *possibly* be printed—putting out a fan mag would be a certain way to land in Siberia.

The effect on me of this atmosphere was such that when I first got outside I at once bought every newspaper and newsmagazine that I could lay hands on—French, American, British, German—and read them *all,* at once, thirstily.

This girl grew up under such conditions.

But the last and most important factor is that it starts so young. In the Soviet Union babies are placed in a kindergarten when they are only a few weeks old, while mom goes back to work.

Let me describe one. We visited the Forty Years of October Collective Farm, a large place with a school system, so they said, of 800 children—probably true since we were shown one of four schools on the farm and it did have about 200 kids in it.

We were taken into a kindergarten class, perhaps thirty boys and girls five or six years old—they had not yet learned to read. They gave a little performance for us—a little girl recited a poem, a little boy delivered a memorized prose recitation, the class sang a song. The children were healthy and clean and well dressed and happy and it was all very charming indeed, much like a parallel welcome to a visitor in one of our own kindergartens.

After we were outside and temporarily out of earshot of any of the local people, Mrs. Heinlein asked me if I had understood it; I admitted that I had caught only half a dozen words—I do not speak Russian—ordering a meal or directing a taxi driver is my outside limit.

"Well," she answered, "the little girl was reciting the life of Lenin, the little boy gave a speech about the Seven Year Plan, and the song the class sang was about how we must all fight to preserve our revolution."

And these were just little baby kids, who had not yet learned to read!

So let's not blame that young woman in Kiev. She was a nice, patriotic, earnest kid, saying what she honestly believed was the truth. I'm sorry that I was annoyed with her—as I certainly

was!—even at the time the row took place. Given other circumstances, I'm sure I could be friends with her.

I could never be friends with the Communist bosses who fed her
these lies and who have made it impossible for her to learn the
truth about Lithuania—or any other aspect of history. Their
cold-blooded suppression of the truth is, in the long run, more
damnable in its effects than anything else they have done.

About noon on May fifteenth, the day before the abortive Paris
Summit Conference, Mrs. Heinlein and I were going downhill
from the castle which dominates the lovely city of Vilno. Coming
uphill were a dozen-odd Red Army cadets; we stopped and
chatted, answered their questions, showed them our passports.

Presently one of them, who seemed to be in charge, asked us if
we had heard about the new Russian space ship?

No—we had been away from news lately. Tell us.

It just happened that morning—the cadet gave me lift-off time,
perigee, apogee, period, and even *now*—he illustrated with a
gesture—a Russian cosmonaut is circling the Earth!

All the other cadets nodded agreement to everything he said and
sometimes added details.

I congratulated them on their country's wonderful scientific
achievement—with a frozen smile and a sick feeling in my
stomach. We talked a bit more about it, then they went on up the
hill and we went down.

That afternoon we tried very hard to buy a copy of *Pravda*. None
were available anywhere—and this is like not being able to buy the
New York *Times* in New York City.

We tried to listen to the Voice of America—jammed more
heavily than we had ever heard it jammed.

We did listen to the Voice of Moscow—Mrs. Heinlein told me
that it did report the rocket—but just as one of the sputniki, no
mention of a passenger.

That evening our guide joined us to go to the ballet—and she
immediately told us that the cadet had been mistaken, it was not a
rocket ship with a man in it—just a dummy. The cadet had
misunderstood.

Well, perhaps so . . . but, if so, all those dozen or more cadets
were mistaken exactly the same way.

Remember the date, May fifteenth. This is the rocket on which
they admitted, a few days later, having trouble with the retrojets;
they fired in the wrong attitude and they could not bring it down.
It is also the one concerning which the New York *Herald-Tribune*

published the cartoon: "Dummy to base! What's this about 'not returning'?"

That rocket is still up there, it may have passed overhead while we ate dinner. Is there a dead Russian in it? Is there an "unperson" in the sky?

I don't know. Under the Communist system it is never possible to get the facts. The truth is dead—murdered—and the official version, the pravda, is that which advances the world Communist revolution.

But I wonder what our own history will be, say fifty years from now? Will it turn out that there never was a Cold War, never was a Korean War—and that the United States and other free countries voluntarily joined up as people's republics immediately after Mother Russia's glorious and unassisted victory in the Great Patriotic War of 1940-45? Will Plymouth Rock and Jamestown be dropped out of history books in favor of the Russian colonies which (in fact) existed in California and Alaska?

What new unpersons will there be? Edison? Einstein? Eisenhower?

I don't know, I can't guess. I simply know that when the government controls every word that is printed, every idea that is taught in school, history is no longer a record of the past but is a changeable thing, whatever is convenient to the government.

And I am strongly of the opinion that our most likely future is a Communist World State. This is not a certainty—but it is the strongest of the probabilities.

But it isn't all bad, our future. If World War III holds off for a number of years, or never occurs at all—as I think is very probable—the immediate future will be tremendously exciting.

Landing on and occupation of the Moon—oh, certainly! That could happen before the end of this year, 1961—although not by us, of course. Landings on Mars? Almost certain. How long? Five years? Ten years? Let's put it this way: almost all of us here tonight should live to see it. It is not even especially unlikely that some person now in this room will, before the 1960s are over, walk the dead sea bottoms of Barsoom.

Of course you may not like it; it is possible that the one of us here tonight who reaches Mars may not get there as a member of the United States Air Force—or "Space Force." The Russians have a well-established habit of sending their most cantankerous political prisoners to colonize very remote and exceptionally difficult and dangerous places—and I see no reason why the dawning age of space should change this habit.

However, if by any wild chance I myself am tapped for a corrective labor colony on Mars, I shall do my damndest to enjoy it, every golden moment. It is a chance that almost all of us science fiction fans would have given our eye teeth and our left arms up to the shoulder to get—and by damn! if the chance comes my way, I'm not going to curse my luck.

Mars!

Think of it! It's going to happen to somebody and it might be one of us. Shucks, if my wife can learn Russian, I guess I can learn it too. If I have to. If it is part of the price for going to Mars!

Travel to the planets is just one of the obvious things in Pandora's Box. Any of you who have been wringing your hands over the horrors of modern war had better massage them and get ready to wring them much harder.

Most of the worrying today seems to be over H-bombs and fallout. Listen, friends, H-bombs and fallout are going to be the very least of your worries.

I don't think that the Russians are going to hit us with H-bombs—unless they do it almost at once, which seems to me most unlikely. H-bombs destroy too much—and they don't want to ruin this country; they just want to own it. And fallout is too indiscriminate.

Something like the neutron bomb, which kills without fallout and without destroying things like steel mills and railroads, would suit them much better.

If they were loaded for bear with neutron bombs in ICBMs, they might be mightily tempted to quit sparring with us and let us have it, with both barrels—in which case there is little to worry about; a corpse does little worrying.

Another change, just over the hill, is that the so-called nuclear bomb club, now consisting of us, the Soviets, France, and Britain, is, very shortly, before the '60s are over, going to become about as exclusive as the Benevolent and Protective Order of Elks. All of the little nations are going to have them, too. If the war in Algeria lasts another ten years—and it has already lasted ten years—the Algerian Arabs are going to be using them.

They will even be in private hands. I can't venture to guess what

degree of anarchy we will have when a Brave New World Al
Capone has pony A-bombs . . . but don't be surprised when it
happens.

But don't blame me for it—*I* don't know how to make A-
bombs. It is just that this development is clearly in the cards.

There is an even fancier—and simpler—type of atomic weapon
coming up: The californium bullet, fired in an ordinary rifle, or
something much like it and weighing no more—a bullet of
fissionable material that reaches critical mass on impact and goes
off as a small A-bomb.

However, atomic weapons are not the ultimate in nastiness. It is
customary these days to speak of ABC weapons, meaning atomic,
biological, and chemical—and we tend to forget the second two.

Biological weapons? Diseases tailor-made for deadliness and for
ease of distribution—say a virus that can be put into New York
City's water system and won't be destroyed by processing nor
detected by ordinary methods of analysis. That's just a sample and
I'll pass on—but please note its beautiful simplicity compared
with H-bombs and ICBMs.

Chemical warfare? Both Russia and the United States have tons
and tons of nerve gas stockpiled—why use H-bombs? But why use
nerve gas? The biochemists, as mild and nearsighted and harmless
as physicists looked thirty years ago, are now talking about
chemical weapons, gases or aerosols, that, instead of killing, will
simply turn a man into a helpless slave by confusing him, breaking
his grip on reality—brother, when they start doing that the "Crazy
Years" are really here!

But ABC isn't the end of the alphabet. We must add both "W"
and "X"—"W" stands for weather and I won't elaborate as all of
you have read stories about melting the ice caps, causing a
crop-failure, drought, etc. Weather control is now in the fine
finished state that aeronautics was in 1906. Only a very rash
person will now guess what may come out of weather control.

"X," as always, stands for "unknown." Exactly as atomic
weapons were unknown and undreamed of—save by a few crazy
science fiction fans and writers only twenty-five years ago—

—and things are moving faster now. Much faster.

However, I don't consider any of these, even "X," the ultimate
weapon. The ultimate weapon was invented in pre-history. It is a
kitchen knife in the hands of a determined man—who is fed up.

Don't ever underrate this weapon. It is far more dangerous than all the ABCWX weapons put together—and there will be a big place for it in all of the next forty years. And thereafter, as long as any of the human race is still alive and still human.

But let's not talk about weapons. I am a short-time pessimist—but a long-time optimist. I don't think the human race is going to kill itself off. Why, I rather doubt if we are even going to indulge in one of those third-of-the-population-dead wars. And remember this: once the human race is established on more than one planet and, especially, in more than one solar system, there is no way now imaginable to kill off the human race. Instead we'll spread with that enormous speed described in Asimov's stories and wind up in a Galactic culture like that in Doc Smith's yarns.

Star travel? Sure, we'll have star travel—probably before the end of this century . . . in the lifetimes of many here tonight. The outstanding fact of 1961 is not H-bombs—but the hurtling speed of advancing technology. There are several things which indicate that we should and probably will have real star ships in that time—things that say it just as loudly as Dr. Goddard's first little rocket said that space ships of some sort were coming.

It won't solve the population pressure problem—and perfect contraception won't solve that either. But star ships *will* mean more human beings on other planets—very quickly—than on Earth, even though Earth is still more crowded.

Power, transportation, star ships, medicine, long life—never mind the individual predictions. The most significant single fact today is that ninety percent of all the scientists who ever lived in all history are alive right now—and working—and producing. We are doubling our knowledge every few years and the rate keeps going up. Predictions? Make your own. Pay no attention to the predictions of almost all of the professional scientists; by nature they are very conservative in their predictions and they have almost always been wrong—on the short side. The important fact is not what they *expect*—but the fact that they are alive and working. To get a better notion of the scale of the changes in the next few decades take the very wildest stuff being printed as fiction in science fiction magazines—

—then *square* it!

If you miss, it will be on the conservative side.

Brother, the joint is really jumpin'.

Will we encounter intelligent life elsewhere in the universe? This is almost a philosophic speculation, since we don't have enough data yet—but if I am crowded into a corner, I will answer flat-footedly that I expect us to find it almost as quickly as we have star travel. Soon, in other words.

If it turns out that we are the only life in the universe, it will be, to me, the most startling thing possible.

I have saved the most optimistic and happiest prediction for the last.

This century of revolution was bound to happen, even if Karl Marx had never lived. I rather think it will destroy democracy, probably all over the globe, for quite a long time.

But democracy and freedom, pleasant and sweet as they are to those of us who have learned to cherish them—cherish them so much that we are willing to die for them—nevertheless are not things essential to human life and progress; these are recent inventions—

—and don't give me any guff about the Greek city states; those states were founded on slavery.

Freedom and democracy we can lose . . . and then regain them in time. Not in your time and mine, probably—but when the human race needs these factors, we'll use them again.

But there is one very important factor which is growing all over this planet along with and as a direct result of this uncomfortable and dangerous century of revolution we are sweating out.

Reading and writing!

As of now, more than sixty percent of the human race cannot read or write. But as a direct result of all these revolutions people are learning to read and write who never did before.

Everywhere! It is one of the benefits—perhaps the only benefit —of Communism. But don't discount it; it is terrifically important.

A man who learns to read and write is half-way to freedom by that one fact.

What road he takes we can't guess. But eventually he, or his children or his children's children, will get there. The Communist bosses, instead of fighting it, are helping this process along—and they can't afford to change it, even if they see the danger to themselves in it, because no system these days can *afford* to try to reverse this and reinstitute illiteracy. The competition is too tough; *any* other system whose people are literate would displace them.

So note the twentieth century down as a century of tragedy and war and death—but also please note that it is the century in which the human race finally learned to read and write. More people will learn to read and write in the next forty years than in all the thousands of years in history.

I firmly predict that this will be the most important historical fact about this, our century.

I see that I have overstayed my welcome and I want to thank the committee for having arranged to have you all chained to your chairs—had you not been a captive audience you would have walked out long back. I ask your pardon for having discussed so many grim things—but it is not possible to speak sensibly about our tragic era without talking grimly about grim things. I didn't plan it that way; I just work here—on this planet, I mean.

So thank you all. I'll see you in Siberia in 1981.

Or maybe on Mars.

GUEST OF HONOR SPEECH

Rio de Janeiro Movie Festival
1969

In 1969, Robert was invited to a film festival in Rio de Janeiro and asked to make an introductory talk at the French Embassy Theater, when Destination Moon *was shown there. This speech is a tribute to Irving Pichel for his work on the picture, and to George Pal (who was present at the film festival) for allowing Mr. Pichel to do his work as he needed to. Following this talk, there was a showing of the motion picture.*
—Virginia Heinlein

Thank you, Mr. Blank. Cinematography is the greatest art medium the human mind has as yet ever developed, the most flexible, the most versatile of all artistic media. With film, plus sound and color and special effects it can do everything that any of the historic media could do—plus many things utterly impossible for other media.

But it has two drawbacks—it is usually terribly expensive—the budget for Kubrick's and Clarke's *2001* sounds like the national debt of a small nation—and it usually takes hundreds or thousands of people to make one film.

Now this doesn't suit artists.

Especially it does not suit writers, who are a bad-tempered breed at best. We shut ourselves up alone to work and snarl at anyone who interrupts us—especially anyone unfortunate enough to be married to a writer.

So most writers don't want to write for films; it forces them out of their self-imposed solitary confinement and requires them to adjust to real human beings . . . instead of the much more tractable imaginary people who live in their typewriters. I hate to write scripts myself (and have avoided doing any but a very few of them) because I know with dreadful certainty what will follow, after the first draft of the script is written.

But the first shortcoming of cinema is that "Creativity Is Not Divisible." That is the title of my talk—and I stole it, from a man now dead, God rest his gallant soul. It is the title of an essay on the nature of artistic creation, written by Irving Pichel, director of *Destination Moon*—and I shall steal much more from his essay before I sit down.

Creativity truly can*not* be divided. Every film which turns out to be an artistic success (most of them are not, as we all know too well) is invariably the creation of one man—usually the director, often the producer, once in a blue moon the writer. Creative art is *never* produced by the committee system. Never. Even when it may seem so from outside, even when others, perhaps thousands of others, take part in the work, it is always the genius of one man. In building a cathedral, it is the architect—not the stone cutters.

Permit me one concrete example— In traveling the continent of Europe, you will see or have seen so many square meters of Rubens' paintings that it is clearly evident that no one man would have time to paint them all. Yet they all are Rubens. How? Rubens' design—his cartoon, his palette—with an unknown number of Rubens' students laboring under the master's firm discipline. So . . . all Rubens, every one, no matter who applied which brush stroke.

In counterpoint to this imagine a symphony orchestra attempting to make music while two or more people wave batons—one trying to play Wagner, a second baton wielder trying simultaneously to lead them in the beautiful "Blue Danube," and a third is fiercely determined to force them into rock and roll.

A horrible thought. Let's forget it.

Yet there are many people who honestly feel that this is the way, indeed the only way, to make a moving picture.

Why, there are even bankers in New York who think they can direct pictures out in Hollywood by remote control.

Mama mia! *Boje moi!*

George Pal protected us from this sort of insanity. Himself a great creative genius—you are about to see several films George

Pal produced so let me name one, possibly greater than any of these, which George not only produced but wrote and directed and edited and created the special effects—practically everything but sweep out the sound stage—*The Tulips Shall Grow,* a picture for which he received a special royal award from Her Majesty the Queen of the Low Lands.

But in making *Destination Moon* George Pal elected to exercise his genius in another way: He hired as director an artist of great integrity, then stepped back and let him work, did not joggle his elbow or engage in back-seat driving. Instead he protected Irving Pichel from such art-destroying distractions while taking on his own shoulders all the other horrible problems of making a motion picture.

In Irving Pichel George had made a wise choice. Mr. Pichel was near the end of his life then—and a busy life it had been— legitimate stage actor—Irving knew all of Shakespeare so well that he could play any male Shakespearean role with only a brief refresher. But he was not limited to Shakespearean roles; some of the older ones of you here may remember Irving Pichel as a great Caesar in George Bernard Shaw's *Caesar and Cleopatra.* Then he was a film actor—director—producer. And a cultured, gallant, and generous gentleman—a good husband, a loving father, an indulgent grandfather—a gourmet, a judge of fine wines, a discriminating critic of music, an omnivorous reader in almost every branch of human knowledge—a true Renaissance Man, Irving would have been right at home in Florence in its great years—indeed, he could even handle a sword with skill and grace.

"They don't hardly make 'em no more!"

Or to put it in words Irving himself might have used: "—we shall not look upon his like again."

But a great architect does require skillful stonecutters; George Pal assembled some good ones. I cannot mention them all— I shan't even name the actors; when I shut up you will hear them speak for themselves. But some I must mention. Lee Zavitz, whose special effects won *Destination Moon* an "Oscar." Lee was a magician who could make *anything* appear on screen. In the filming of *Gone With the Wind* Lee Zavitz burned the city of Atlanta—forty acres of it with a huge mob scene and Lee started and stopped that fire three times without hurting a single person. Watch especially for the free-fall scenes both in and outside the space ship, note how closely they re-semble the space walks of today's news twenty years later and the free-fall television scenes from Apollo 8's mission at Christ-mas time—and, since you know that these shots are faked on a sound stage, try to find the wires that support the actors in free fall. A hint—they are *not* where you would expect them to be. And look carefully at the high-acceleration scenes; they are amazingly like some news photographs which appeared re-cently. If you want to know how Lee did it, ask George or me—afterwards.

I must add that some of the special effects that won that Oscar were created by George Pal himself—wearing his other hat. I won't tell you which ones; we don't want you to know until later. Then you can ask George, or me.

But this picture would have been impossible without the astronomical paintings of Chesley Bonestell—I felt so strong-ly about this that I told Mr. Pal that, if we could not get Ches-ley Bonestell, we should give up the project entirely. True. At that time twenty years ago Mr. Bonestell was the only man in the entire world who could paint an astronomical paint-ing with scientific accuracy and in such perfect detail that it could not be told from a color photograph. Now that we have entered the Space Age several other artists have learned this difficult skill. But in those days there was only one—Bone-stell.

Several people have asked me about him here at the Festi-val and assumed that he was dead. I am happy to say that he is very much alive, eighty years old this year, painting as much as ever and just as accurately—when he does die (there is no sign that he ever will but when he does) I expect him to take at least three more perfect brush strokes after he is pronounced dead.

On Christmas day three months ago Chesley drove sixty miles through a rain storm to have Christmas dinner with us, and we watched Apollo 8 live on television. Sometimes dreams do come true.

I've talked too long; let me quickly sketch how this film came to be. I don't often do work other than for money—but in 1947 I became possessed by an urgent longing to see a motion picture made about space travel—a realistic, scientifically accurate pic-ture. It was a foolish dream then, as I had no money, knew nothing about making motion pictures (and only very little more now); I am a novelist not a screenwriter.

But I had this wild dream and I just had to do something about it. In 1948 I found time to go to Hollywood: there I found a novel of mine about a trip to the Moon, adapted it into a screen story, then we went looking for a producer as crazy as we were.

Eventually we found him—George Pal.

(Oh, I admit he doesn't look crazy—he's feeling much better now. But this was twenty years ago.)

Then came the really hard part, financing the production. George Pal's problem— Find an investment banker willing to risk large sums of money on a Technicolor feature picture about a *trip to the Moon?*

Ridiculous! Everybody knows that space flight is impossible. It's just for comic books and for cheap Saturday morning films intended only for very young children who don't know any better. (Remember, this was twenty years ago.)

I don't know how George managed it—it was none of my business. But I understand from rumors that he was required to put both his soul and the pound of flesh nearest his heart as just part of the collateral for this wild scheme.

(Eventually the film was a success and they let him have his soul back, undamaged. I'm not sure about the pound of flesh. But not money. This picture made a great deal of money—but not for George Pal and not for me. But we realized our dream.)

Several scripts later Irving Pichel was brought into the production—and the first thing he did was to sit down and re-write the script. Now this is proper—"Creativity is *not* divisible." Although you may note several writing credits, mine among them but none for Irving Pichel, in fact every line of dialog, every piece of business, is exactly as Irving Pichel decided it must be. Oh, many lines are exactly as I wrote them— but only because they suited Irving Pichel. He pulled all the thousands of details in together, a single work of art by one artist. All the rest of us, actors and specialists, simply carried out his will.

But let me show you how wisely he did this. He never told Chesley Bonestell how to paint, nor Lee Zavitz how to accomplish a mechanical effect; he had the best in them and he trusted them. I was the technical and scientific adviser, a job for which *I* am qualified. But Pichel himself was no scientist; his degree—from

Harvard—was in English literature, and he did not know whether I was competent or a phony.

Early in the shooting he questioned some space flight technical point I insisted on. But it happens that one of Irving's sons is a rocket engineer, a graduate of California Institute of Technology. So I told him: "Don't take my word for it. Tonight, telephone your son and put the same question to him"—which Irving did . . . and from then on to the very end my word was law on all scientific and technical matters; no time was ever wasted on arguments. Irving would require me to make a decision, then used his authority to enforce it. If there are any errors in science or engineering in this picture, they are my errors—because Pichel trusted his staff.

(In fact, this film has stood up quite well on that point. Now, twenty years later, the only gadget shown in it which we do not as yet have is the atomic rocket engine . . . and that is in the R&D stage and most of us here today will live to see it realized.)

Pichel intentionally kept the film low in key and documentary in tone, with almost no plot. The big problem, as he saw it, was to make space flight believable—in 1949—and he tossed out many scenes both before and after shooting which added nothing to that single purpose. The result is a fictional story which looks like a documentary . . . and in which the leading "man" turns out to be a piece of machinery—the space craft.

In so doing, he made believers out of the whole company, most of whom started in thinking that the project was crazy—but what the hell, a day's work is a day's work. He pulled us together, we all caught the fever, the dream of space—and we ended up as a band of brothers.

Eventually it was done—we were tired but happy. George Pal gave a giant cocktail party on the *Moon* set and we relaxed and laughed and gossiped and were happy.

As my wife Ginny and I were leaving the party late that night she said to me, "Did you meet Dorothy Lamour?"

I said, *"What? She* was there?"

"Why, yes. I was chatting with her for about forty-five minutes."

There followed a longish silence, moody on my part.

I still have never seen Dorothy Lamour, much less chatted with her. Spaceships are wonderful but people remain more important than any machine, no matter how big or marvelous.

I still hope to go to the Moon someday . . . and to meet Dorothy Lamour.

And now, guests and friends, I give you George Pal's *Destination Moon,* directed by Irving Pichel, and produced twenty years ago when space travel was still only a dream.

GUEST OF HONOR
SPEECH AT THE
XXXIVth WORLD
SCIENCE FICTION
CONVENTION

MidAmeriCon, Kansas City—5 September 1976

One of the interesting things about the writing of Robert Heinlein was his versatility. He tried many genres, including detective stories, horror, sword and sorcery, fantasy, science fiction, as well as trying his hand at stories for boys and girls.

His favorite writing, of course, was science fiction, as it was his favorite reading. He began to read science fiction when he was a boy, borrowing his siblings' library cards in order to bring home as many books as possible. He read the Tom Swift stories, Verne, Wells, and in the 1920s he found a magazine which was one of the early science fiction ones—Hugo Gernsback's Electrical Experimenter.

Following his retirement from the Navy in 1934 for physical disability, he looked around for some sort of a career to fill the rest of his life—he was only twenty-seven years old at that time. He tried silver mining, but his backer was killed, and he turned to selling real estate. During the Depression, no one was buying houses—or at least, very few could afford them. Then he tried politics, running for the California State Assembly. He lost, by one vote per precinct.

Then his luck changed. He tried writing a story for one of the pulp magazines. It sold, and he wrote some more. Some of those sold, too, and Robert had found a way to fill his lifetime.

After World War II, during which he worked as an engineer for the Navy, as he was not allowed to return to active duty, he decided to make a try for the bigger markets than the pulp magazines he had been regularly writing for. Some stories sold to major markets— The Saturday Evening Post, *a juvenile novel to Scribner's, and he did a "classic" film,* Destination Moon.

Offers poured in, and Robert was able to choose which assignments he would take. It was his desire to do one juvenile book each year and one adult novel, plus such shorter items as pleased him to do. Despite all the acclaim for his juveniles and adult novels, requests to speak here and there, offers for articles, motion picture offers and so on, Robert remained a modest man, referring to himself as "a minor celebrity."

This book contains several stories, some speeches which have been mildly edited for smoother reading, and some assessments of Robert's work. Perhaps I should take the audience into my confidence about the 1976 speech in Kansas City. It is not up to Robert's usual standard. The reasons were double; an attendance of 4,000-5,000 people was expected at MidAmeriCon—and Robert was upset about his inability to meet that many people during the course of the convention. So he set up a special reception for blood donors, to limit the number.

This soon became oversubscribed, because of limitations in the size of the rooms available. So we added another, then another. Arrangements had to be made for the rooms, refreshments, and guards and so on. Together Robert and I made out the invitations, and kept the lists. We were so busy that Robert never had time to prepare his Guest of Honor speech! Another, family reason also intervened. Remember, please, that Kansas City was where many members of Robert's family lived. And his elder brother kept turning up with bushels of books for Robert to sign (in his free time!!!)

His agent, Lurton Blassingame, came to what was his first science fiction convention, and he wanted to give a luncheon in our suite during the festivities. If we were tired, it was with good reason! And Robert's speech was never prepared—there just was never the time to do that. So the talk was rather more informal than he would have wished.

—Virginia Heinlein

* * *

[Introduction] There is one way I want to close our session this afternoon—you know. . . . [Continuous applause.]

[Speaker: Robert A. Heinlein] What are we going to do for a finale? However, I will take advantage of this—make use of this for one thing. There are probably very few people in science fiction who know that Wilson Arthur Tucker is actually my son . . . [Applause.] Of course, the nickname, "Bob," might have given you some clue there . . . [Laughter.] . . . that's one reason why I go by Robert. But you can see the resemblance. It may look better on him—a little better—"Son, why did you grow a beard?" [Laughter.]

I have had no opportunity to find him; and really all I am familiar with in this hotel are the kitchens and the under passageways and the freight elevators . . . [Laughter.] With the aid of the Dorsai and Patricia Cadigan, I have managed to find my way through the catacombs—by following them. But I have Wilson Arthur Tucker within reach here, now, and please, son, would you autograph these books for me? . . . [Wild applause and laughter.]

This one is *A Procession of the Damned* by Wilson Tucker . . . [Laughter.] And here we have *Ice and Iron,* and again it says Wilson Tucker. And this one—this may have been done by a ghost; I don't know. It is called *The Long Loud Silence.* [Applause.]

And then I had one other difficulty—I searched through five hotels last night until my feet were tired, and I was unable to return some items that I was supposed to give back. [Much laughter.] . . . my epaulets . . . Is Patia von Sternberg in the room? Is Patia von Sternberg here? . . . Is there someone here on the closed circuit television who knows where she is? [Laughter.] She may need them at a later time. [Laughter and applause.] If she is not here, is there someone who knows her well enough to assure me they will be returned to her? I can't see anything beyond these lights. Is there someone down here? Ah! Thank you. [Applause.]

Can you hear me back there? Can you still hear me back there? [Answer: YES!] The thing looks like a cobra. [Laughter.] I don't know any way to answer my friends. I just hope they meant it . . . and thank you . . . thank you all!

Mr. Tucker brought this in ten minutes early. I agreed that I would not speak more than thirty minutes, so on a pro-rate of that as close as I can do it in my head without one of those little "punch things," I will set this for twenty-five minutes. [Applause and laughter.] Now, when this goes "ping" that's a period. All done. Pow!

"It's Great to be Back!" [Applause.] Before I left Kansas City fifty-one years ago, my best friend took me to dinner in the biggest, fanciest hotel west of the Mississippi—the Meuhlebach. [Applause.] I did not expect to return in this fashion. I went off to be a Naval Officer.

There's a long, long list of writers who became writers because that was all they could do. And there is very little use for an Ordnance Engineer or Gunnery Officer in the midst of a Depression, when he is in such shape that he can't take an eight-hour-a-day job. So, like Robert Louis Stevenson, H. G. Wells, and a long list, I became a writer because that was the only way I could see that I could make money without actually stealing. [Applause and laughter.]

The first time I spoke as a Guest of Honor in 1941, my subject was "The Discovery of the Future," and about all I had to say in too many thousands of words, was to expect the unexpected—change, change, lots of change.

Perhaps the most useful thing to the reader of science fiction is that he is not as subject to future shock as other people. [Applause.] On that occasion, I made a certain number of predictions—one of those was as easy as looking down the street, seeing the streetcar coming . . . (we had them here then; the principal change I've seen in Twelfth Street is that they have taken the streetcars out of the middle of the street) . . . seeing the streetcar coming and predicting that it was going to arrive. About the only prediction I made in 1941 was that we were about to get into a major war. [Laughter.] I won on that one. [Laughter.]

I would rather have lost. [Applause.]

By the way . . . "everything is up-to-date in Kansas City and they built a skyscraper seven stories high" . . . those of you staying in any of the convention hotels, step out on Baltimore, look to the north, you will see the street blocked by that same skyscraper, seven stories high—about as high as a building ought to go—that the song talks about. If you haven't noticed it yet, as is the case with some of you, you have yet to see daylight in Kansas City. [Laughter and applause.]

Before you leave, step out on Baltimore and have a look, because although it has been nearly three-quarters of a century since that building was built, it is still a magnificent edifice, even though it is surrounded by things that dwarf it; like the description in H. G. Wells when the sleeper awakes when he speaks of St. Paul completely dominated by this great megalopolis of his imagination. That is the way that skyscraper, seven stories high, looks now, but it is still beautiful. [Applause.] If you have been seeing only the night in Kansas City, I hope you have seen some of its nightlife, because this is the place from which show business starts.

A great many people have regarded this as a "great place to be from." [Laughter.] Jean Harlow [Applause] . . . I used to deliver the *Kansas City Journal* to the Carpentiers, whose daughter Harlean Carpentier, later was to be Jean Harlow. On up the street from where I lived was the home of the Powells. Their son, William Powell, had already left. [Applause.] He went to the same high school I did; the same high school Sally Rand went to . . . [Applause.] Her name was Billie Beck in those days. William Powell was about twelve to thirteen years senior to me in that high school, but belonged to the same Central Shakespeare Club.

I was in that club, and took part in the Literary Contest there, primarily in public speaking for one reason, and that was because I was then, and am still, a stammerer. Do I have any brothers or sisters here who also stutter or stammer? I can't see out there—are there any? [Applause.] I can't see your hands—Yell! [Answers.]

Very well then—all of you . . . [Laughter] . . . all of you who are not troubled with stuttering or stammering, if I stop and whistle, go ahead and laugh . . . it doesn't bother me and it shouldn't bother you because that will break the stammer and I can go ahead. That is also the reason for pauses in the voice. [Applause.]

Also from Kansas City—Noah Beery, Wallace Beery, oh, the list is endless . . . half of show business comes from Kansas City, and anyone who thinks that writing science fiction is not show business is out of their . . . No, I can't say that . . . [Laughter.]

Speaking of one thing that science fiction is, though, I want to meet the chap who said you could write science fiction without science.

This reminds me of a cartoon in the *New Yorker* which appeared about 1928, in which a clerk is saying, "Now here is an excellent gin, non-alcoholic, of course." [Laughter and applause.] Anyone who thinks science fiction can be written without science deserves to go and room with the person who thinks that historical novels can be written without a knowledge of history. [Applause.] But it also has to be fiction—it has to be a story. [Aside:] There is only one thing I am unsure about—whether I collapse first, or civilization collapses first. [Laughter.] Ginny and I have been in sort of a rush for some time now.

On the plane coming out, there was a man over here, next aisle, who was going [here Robert swings his head from one side to the other, slowly]. I said to him, "Just a moment, sir, excuse me—I'm a clinical psychologist—why are you going like this?" [Swings head slowly from side to side again.] He answered me, "Why . . . do . . . I . . . do . . . like . . . this?" And I answered, "Yes, why do you do like that?" He answered me, "This is . . . how . . . I . . . tell . . . time." [Laughter.] So I said to him, "What time is it?" He said, "It is now exactly 3:23." I said, "It's 3:31!" He said, "It is?" [At this point Robert swung his head side to side, fast.] [Laughter and applause.]

That's the shape Ginny and I have been in for quite some time now. We've been not quite catching up. We felt somewhat in the predicament of the man who got to be twenty-one before he had his first birthday. You all know about this . . . it happened that he was born on the 29th of February, 1896—so along comes 1897 and he's got no birthday . . . '98, '99, 1900, what happens then? No leap year! He missed that one. Along came 1904, and his parents who were in what we now call the Foreign Service, but was then the Consular Service and Ambassadorial Service, were stationed in Russia, just at the time the transition was made so that in moving from the Julian calendar to the Gregorian calendar, he got wiped out again. [Laughter.] Well, being in a family that moved around in that fashion, he then should have had one in 1908. They crossed the date line . . . [Laughter] . . . going west— which puts me in mind that Ginny's (how old are you now?)— well, in any case, she had a birthday—her birthday matches up with that of Shakespeare—since she won't tell me how old she is, but it is the same day of the year. We were coming from Tasmania to Pearl Harbor, and we stopped in at New Caledonia, where I wanted to look into some operations—matters with some medical interests I was concerned with, and also to look over an airstrip that my brother had built there in the 1940s, which caused the departure from New Caledonia to Pearl Harbor to go "slaunchwise"—it's never a perfect great circle and the navigator happened to be a close friend of mine . . . we had made several voyages in the same ship . . . and I said "George" (science fiction fan, by the way) . . . I said, "George, what day are we crossing the date line?" He said, "Well . . ." So I said, "Isn't it just about April

22nd?" He thought about it and said, "I think it might be." He saw me a few hours later with a big grin on his face, and he said, "Yes, it turns out to be April 22nd." So, sure enough, we crossed the dateline on April 22nd. So Ginny got to be two years older that year—this year! She won't tell me how old she is, but whatever it is she is two years older than she was last year. [Laughter.] [Ed. note by VH—It was a put-up job!]

But this wasn't nearly as complicated as the situation of the man who, through no fault of his own, found himself simultaneously married to both of his grandmothers. [Much laughter.] But I wanted to get back—this chap who was missing out on the birthdays . . . he kept having these things happen to him. It happened to him again in such a fashion that he finally got up, missed his sixteenth birthday, and he was twenty years old before he had his first birthday cake. Now do you put one candle on it at that point, or what??? [Laughter.]

In 1941, I did predict a war . . . that wasn't very hard to do. Along came 1961. I predicted a war again. And I did have some mistaken ideas about that as to when it would happen. But this is the 200th Anniversary of this, our Republic, and all of that time, while we tend to think of peace as a normal condition, if you will look into the actual history of this country, you will find that we have been fighting in 199 of those years. For example, the late war in Korea was the second war we had with Korea, not the first. Go look it up—you will find that I am speaking accurately. It surprised me the first time I saw the battle-torn flags at the Naval Academy when I went there as a Plebe from Kansas City. 199 years in which we have been fighting—only one year of nominal peace.

People worry about whether or not there is going to be an H-bomb or an A-bomb war. Certainly there is going to be one—there's going to be more than one! Don't kid yourselves. There will be wars—but the human race thrives on trouble. We're built for it—that's what we're good for. We wouldn't know how to get along without it. We are also going on out to the stars. [Applause.]

I don't know what language will be used as a working language in that first star ship—I would like it to be English, but that may be as much local patriotism as it is for me to be very happy for me to be back in my old home town.

My wife and I were traveling in the U.S.S.R. some eighteen years ago, I think it was, and at that time it was—we hit there at such a time that we were in Moscow at the time of the U-2 incident, but Gospodin Khrushchev kept it quiet, and by the time he decided what to do about it, we were out north of the Himalayas, about 2,500 kilometers from the U.S. Consul, with no other tourists around. At that point it was announced, and it felt very lonely. But things quieted down after a bit and we found ourselves in Riga where we were entertained by the Union of Soviet Writers. Now, all during the trip we had been toasted here, there and yon—on collective farms or anywhere; the toast would always be to Khrushchev, Mr. Eisenhower, "Miru Mir," Peace to the World, and every time they found that Ginny could speak fluent Russian, they always decided that she was of Russian descent, and I would explain, "No, no, nothing of the sort." She had learned it at night school at the University of Colorado, and that she had studied it very hard, and that was why she could speak Russian so well—in fact, we had a saying in our country that the optimists were learning Russian and the pessimists were learning Chinese. [Much laughter and applause.]

Well, I think that accounts for why I was out on my timing in my last prediction. On even-numbered days I get up in the morning and say, "Thank God for Russia," and on odd-numbered days I get up and say, "Thank God for China." It's something like this—Trojan point balance. As long as all three points are there, it stays in an uneasy, but nevertheless stable balance. I don't know how long that might last, but don't kid yourself that there will not be war. And don't kid yourself that there will not be survivors. The most ridiculous statement I have ever heard is one that was attached to a splinter political party: "Peace and Freedom." You can have peace, or you can have freedom, but you don't get both at once. [Applause. Booing.]

Yes, I heard both the applause and the boos. The only way a man can be free is by an utter willingness to fight with the outright viciousness of one of Larry Niven's Kzin.

The only peace that a man ever gets is the peace of the grave, and sometimes those who fight get it too, but this is the primary function of what otherwise is a genetically spoiled female—wait a minute—thank God—not his primary function . . . his secondary function is to fight in defense of women and children. [Booing and applause.]

Yes, I can hear the boos, too. And to those of you who booed, presently you will find that I am right. . . . [Laughter.] A great many of us are going to have only two choices—either not to fight and die, or to fight and die; but nevertheless, there will be survivors. I learned that from Willy Ley—a great and wise man, Willy. He said, "Robert, there are always survivors—no matter how bad it is, there are always survivors." . . . and that is how the human race develops. That fits right in with this business of going on out to the stars. The human race is going to break again into two pieces: Homo Terrans and (I can't get the Latin straight now—got my Latin expert down there and I won't attempt to)—but "Man of the Stars." It's going to be the same sort of situation that we had starting here from Westport Landing—on out to Westport and on out to the tracks across the Kansas prairie. I don't know which way I am oriented here—which way is north? Somebody local point out north for me. I am facing north?—all right. And they went off this way—there was an expression about it at that time: "The cowards never started and the weaklings died on the way." And that is what will happen to the human race with respect to going on out into space.

And I think one of the happiest things that happened to this convention was to have Viking II land, successfully! [Applause.] Right in the middle of it! [Applause.] And then there was this matter of—I made one other bad prediction when I was asked to do so in 1950—I got mixed up on some. I said we would cure cancer, make a breakthrough on housing, surely by this time. I was dead wrong. Between various special interests, most of the United States is still living in houses that could have been built just as well and sometimes better in the Roman Empire. [Applause.] They have the most modern electronic devices housed in things that are little better than masonry tents. [Applause.] [Timer pinged.]

Good night. [Applause.]

PART II
National Air and Space Museum Heinlein Retrospective— 6 October 1988

epoch-making movie *Destination Moon,* he helped inspire the
Nation to take its first step into space and onto the Moon. Even
after his death, his books live on as testimony to a man of
purpose and vision, a man dedicated to encouraging others to
dream, explore and achieve.

Signed and sealed at Washington, D.C.
this sixth day of October
Nineteen Hundred and Eighty-Eight
/s/James C. Fletcher
Administrator, NASA

Mrs. Heinlein took the rostrum and, in lieu of a speech, read This I
Believe *by Robert A. Heinlein.*

THIS I BELIEVE

[originally recorded in 1952 for Edward R. Murrow's *This I
Believe.*]

I am not going to talk about religious beliefs but about matters
so obvious that it has gone out of style to mention them. I believe
in my neighbors. I know their faults, and I know that their virtues
far outweigh their faults.

Take Father Michael down our road a piece. I'm not of his creed,
but I know that goodness and charity and loving kindness shine in
his daily actions. I believe in Father Mike. If I'm in trouble, I'll go
to him.

My next-door neighbor is a veterinary doctor. Doc will get out
of bed after a hard day to help a stray cat. No fee—no prospect of a
fee—I believe in Doc.

I believe in my townspeople. You can knock on any door in our
town saying, "I'm hungry," and you will be fed. Our town is no
exception. I've found the same ready charity everywhere. But for
the one who says, "To heck with you—I got mine," there are a
hundred, a thousand who will say, "Sure, pal, sit down."

I know that despite all warnings against hitchhikers I can step to
the highway, thumb for a ride and in a few minutes a car or a truck
will stop and someone will say, "Climb in Mac—how far you
going?"

I believe in my fellow citizens. Our headlines are splashed with
crime yet for every criminal there are 10,000 honest, decent,
kindly men. If it were not so, no child would live to grow up.

*T*he evening event to honor Robert Anson Heinlein in conjunction with the posthumous awarding of the NASA Medal for Distinguished Public Service, the highest NASA civilian award, began with Mr. James Sharp of the Museum outlining the program. After the awarding of the Medal, there were short speeches by five panelists, which were followed by a brief questions-and-answers period. Then, the movie Destination Moon, based on the work of Robert Heinlein, was screened; the movie had been made available through the courtesy of its owner, Mr. Wade Williams of Kansas City.

The five-hundred-plus capacity Langley Theater of the museum overflowed its capacity and some guests had to view the proceedings on a video screen in an adjacent room. Mr. Sharp introduced Dr. Noel Hinners, Associate Deputy Administrator, the third highest ranking official at NASA.

Dr. Hinners pinned the Medal on Mrs. Robert A. Heinlein after reading the citation below:

The National Aeronautics and Space Administration
Awards to Robert Anson Heinlein
the
NASA
DISTINGUISHED PUBLIC SERVICE MEDAL

In recognition of his meritorious service to the Nation and mankind in advocating and promoting the exploration of space. Through dozens of superbly written novels and essays and his

Business could not go on from day to day. Decency is not news. It is buried in the obituaries, but it is a force stronger than crime. I believe in the patient gallantry of nurses and the tedious sacrifices of teachers. I believe in the unseen and unending fight against desperate odds that goes on quietly in almost every home in the land.

I believe in the honest craft of workmen. Take a look around you. There never were enough bosses to check up on all that work. From Independence Hall to the Grand Coulee Dam, these things were built level and square by craftsmen who were honest in their bones.

I believe that almost all politicians are honest . . . there are hundreds of politicians, low paid or not paid at all, doing their level best without thanks or glory to make our system work. If this were not true we would never have gotten past the 13 colonies.

I believe in Rodger Young. You and I are free today because of endless unnamed heroes from Valley Forge to the Yalu River. I believe in—I am proud to belong to—the United States. Despite shortcomings from lynchings to bad faith in high places, our nation has had the most decent and kindly internal practices and foreign policies to be found anywhere in history.

And finally, I believe in my whole race. Yellow, white, black, red, brown. In the honesty, courage, intelligence, durability and *goodness* of the overwhelming majority of my brothers and sisters everywhere on this planet. I am proud to be a human being. I believe that we have come this far by the skin of our teeth. That we *always* make it just by the skin of our teeth, but that we will always make it. Survive. Endure. I believe that this hairless embryo with the aching, oversize brain case and the opposable thumb, this animal barely up from the apes will *endure*. Will *endure* longer than his home planet—will spread out to the stars and beyond, carrying with him his honesty and his insatiable curiosity, his unlimited courage and his noble essential decency.

This I believe with all my heart.

Mrs. Heinlein's recitation of "This I Believe" was so moving that she received a standing ovation.

Mr. Sharp then introduced the editor of this book, Yoji Kondo, as the moderator for the panel discussion to follow. The panel consisted of Tom Clancy, L. Sprague de Camp, Jerry Pournelle, Charles

Sheffield and Jon McBride. (Jim Sharp's introduction of Y. Kondo is a bit embarrassing—too flattering—for him to quote and is therefore omitted.)

After thanking Mr. Sharp, Yoji Kondo began with the following comments.

It is auspicious that this event takes place at the time of America's return to space. The success of the Space Shuttle mission over the past week is a fitting tribute to Robert Anson Heinlein, the grandmaster of science fiction, an engineer, a soldier, a gentleman and a man of noble vision, whom we also know as The Man Who Sold the Moon.

Robert Heinlein did not want his friends to mourn his death— there was no funeral for him. His remains were cremated and ashes strewn over the Pacific from a U.S. Navy ship with full military honors.

I think this is an appropriate way to celebrate the life and the works of Heinlein. This is not *a good-bye to Heinlein for he will continue to live in our mind through his magnificent books, which have been translated into every major language on this planet.*

I am supposed to be introducing the panelists but am not sure why. Surely, they are all well known to you. I will go through the motion, however, just in case there are E.T.s in the audience masquerading as humans.

SPEECHES BY THE PANELISTS

Author Tom Clancy has been an avid fan of Robert Heinlein's. A graduate of Loyola College in Baltimore, he is the author of the best-selling books The Hunt for Red October, Red Storm Rising, Patriot Games, *and* The Cardinal of the Kremlin. *A few weeks ago, I noted that all four of his books were on the* New York Times' *best-seller list. This must be an unprecedented record.*

Tom Clancy

Earlier this year I unexpectedly met the widow of Louis L'Amour. I'm not the most articulate person in the world, but for once I did manage to express myself properly. I told her, "I lost a friend."

Also this year, everyone in this room lost another friend. I know

I did. Both men were giants, both were part of our country's collective voice. Both men were American originals.

Mr. L'Amour wrote mainly about the past, and Mr. Heinlein wrote mainly about the future. But in a larger sense, both men wrote about our heritage. They wrote about values—American values. They wrote about people—Americans. The arenas of their fiction were very different, but the people who played in those arenas were the same. So was the message.

They wrote about freedom. They wrote about individual men and women who made their own way, and forged their own destiny. They wrote about people who fought for their individual identity, but never lost sight of their part of the social contract. They wrote about people for whom freedom was a cherished possession, but a possession that carried both price and responsibility. The price of freedom, as each of the masters recognized, is often blood. The responsibility of freedom is always respect for the rights of others.

For both men, this message was repeated in every book. The message was always conveyed positively, but always with grace and skill—and humor.

These were men who understood life. These men were teachers, but they were better than most members of that profession—they must have been, because their students paid for the lessons, and never fell asleep in class. These were men who told the world about America, and told Americans about themselves.

I, too, am a novelist. I do not write science fiction because I'm not sufficiently grounded in the sciences. People praise my imagination, but next to Bob Heinlein—well, in any comparison with the Grand Master, I have to come off second best. He taught me; I didn't teach him.

But I think I know what drove him. Mr. Heinlein once wrote that he entered the writing profession because he found it the best way to make money without working. That's a fine example of his humor. Red Smith put it another way: "Writing's easy. You just sit in front of a typewriter and open a vein."

Every book and every story begins in the writer's mind with a two-word question: "What if?" Once we ask ourselves that first question, something within us forces us to find the answer. If situation X happens, how will people react to it?

What will they think?

What will they do?

How will they cope?

How will they prevail?

What makes Mr. Heinlein a part of the American literary tradition is that his characters do prevail. His work reflects the fundamental American optimism that still surprises our friends around the world. As Mr. Heinlein taught us, the individual can and will succeed. The first step in the individual's success is the perception that success is possible. It is often the writer's task to let people know what is possible and what is not, for as writing is a product of imagination, so is all human progress.

What if?

If you can ask the question, you can answer it. That is Mr. Heinlein's lesson to us.

He wrote about the future because the future is where all of us will live. He carried on a tradition that stretches back to Jonathan Swift, and Jules Verne, the first SF author I read—in third grade—but he did it our way, the American way.

He wrote about technology—as I am often accused of doing— but in the one similarity between us, he recognized that technology is merely another word for tool. Technology is not what drives human progress. Ideas do. Ideas design the tools, and ideas direct their use.

I suppose Mr. Heinlein's most important message to us is that technology matters less than how we make use of it. What we become will be determined not by the tools we hold in our hands, but by the ideals we hold in our minds. Not by what we have, but by who we are and what we choose to be.

Mr. Heinlein is called the father of "hard" science fiction. The machines he included in his stories, however, were never as hard or as real his characters. Tools change over time. People do not. Truths do not. Principles do not. Certainly Bob Heinlein's principles never did.

Ladies and gentlemen, we meet in the best possible place to remember a giant. The Smithsonian Institution grew out of the bequest of a British subject, just as our country's principles grew from the writings of Edmund Burke and Adam Smith. This Institution is dedicated to remembering the past—how we got here, and what brought us here. But the contents of this building remind us that what brought us here are merely vehicles—tools. We built them to take us toward a goal. We rode them only part of the way. What matters is the goal, and we need other vehicles to go further on the way. We will build those vehicles, and their designs will come from the minds of men and women who know that there is yet a way to go. The path to that goal is marked by the vision of individual men and women who show all of us the direction.

We will never quite make it to that goal. At the end of each rainbow lies the beginning of another. But Bob Heinlein knew that the fun was in the trying, and the real accomplishment is in keeping our eyes on the future and our feet on the ground; in asking the right questions, and finding the right answers. Most of all, he told us that if we never forget who and what we are, then we alone will choose our future. And that's the point, isn't it? What distinguishes man from the animal, and the free man from the slave is that where our bodies go, our minds have already been. We follow the footsteps our minds have made for us. And so often there is one mind that defines the path for the imagination of us all.

Bob Heinlein helped to create the first science fiction movie I ever saw, *Destination Moon,* which was also the first truly serious attempt to describe a trip to the moon. It seems to me that there are some mementos of a similar trip in this building. You know, Bob Heinlein made footsteps big enough for a whole country to follow. And it was our country that did it. He wouldn't have had it any other way.

There are a lot of writers who will carry on Bob Heinlein's work. Some of them are right here with us. But I think the best news of all is that there are people in this room who will make the Master's words live—really live—because our country will inevitably proceed down the path marked by the ideas of Bob Heinlein. That's legacy enough for any man. He showed us where the future is. It's our job to go and make it.

Kondo's remarks after Clancy's speech:
I must disagree with Tom Clancy. I think his latest book, The Cardinal of the Kremlin, *is first class science fiction as well as an exciting adventure-mystery novel.*

Author L. Sprague de Camp was born in 1907 in New York. He was trained as a physicist at Caltech and later as an engineer for his master's degree at Stevens Institute of Technology and has been writing science fiction and fantasy for half a century with numerous fine books to his credit. During World War II, he served as a Lieutenant Commander in the Navy Reserve and worked in the

Navy laboratory in Philadelphia, where Robert Heinlein also worked. He and his wife Catherine met Robert Heinlein a couple of years earlier and had since been his friends. Sprague is the author or co-author of about one hundred books, ranging from science fiction and fantasy to history and popular science and technology. His best known novel is perhaps Lest Darkness Fall. *He has received many honors, including the Grand Master Nebula Award and the Grand Master of the World Science Fiction Convention.*

L. Sprague de Camp

Robert Anson Heinlein began writing soon after I did, but he quickly outdistanced me, both in quantity and, I suspect, quality as well. He and I belonged to that period of science fiction, in the late 1930s, now called the Golden Age. We, along with Asimov, del Rey, Russell, Sturgeon, and Van Vogt, all entered the field at that time and came under the influence of John W. Campbell, the famous editor of *Astounding Stories.* On his visits from California to New York, Robert Heinlein became an intimate of the Campbells.

I met Robert around 1940, either at one of Fletcher Pratt's naval war-game parties in New York or at the Campbells' apartment in New Jersey. We became close friends after he and I went to work at the Philadelphia Naval Base in 1942.

As I daresay you all know, Heinlein was a retired regular officer in the U.S. Navy. The Navy had retired him early in his career for medical reasons, and for the same reasons refused to put him back into uniform after Pearl Harbor. But Robert, in whom the fire of patriotism burned brightly, was determined to promote the war effort in any way he could.

Robert had kept up with his Annapolis classmate, A. B. Scoles, then the newly appointed director of the Materials Laboratory of the Naval Aircraft Factory, later the Naval Air Material Center. Scoles enlisted Heinlein as a civilian engineer in his facility.

I had been trained as an engineer at California Tech but had never really practiced that profession because of the great Depression of the 1930s. Early in 1942 I applied to the Navy and received a commission in the Reserve.

Meanwhile Scoles thought: Why not get some of Heinlein's writing colleagues, with technical backgrounds, who had been so glibly creating space ships and death rays, put them to work in the Matericals Laboratory, and see waht they could do?

In the spring of 1942, Heinlein aggranged a meeting in New York with Scoles, John Campbell, himself, and me. Campbell decided to stay with his editorial job. Scoles arranged to have me, when I finished Naval Training School at Dartmouth, assigned to his unit. He also persuaded Asimov, then writing his way through Columbia University, to join the Laboratory as a civilian chemist.

So for three and a half years Asimov, Heinlein, and I, along with scores of other technical people, navigated desks and fought the war with flashing slide rules. It must have irked Bob to see me, green to Navy ways and never much of an organization man anyway, running about with pretty gold stripes on my sleeves. But he was a good sport about it, and I am sure that his advice saved me from making a bigger ass of myself than I otherwise would have. Robert was ultra-conscientious in carrying out what he deemed his patriotic duty, and so close-mouthed that I never did learn what sort of projects he worked on.

In 1979 Charles Berlitz, inventor of the mythical Bermuda Triangle, coauthored a book, *The Philadelphia Experiment,* later used as the basis for a movie. The book asserted that during the Hitlerian War, the Navy experimented with rays and vibrations to make a warship invisible. The experiment, he wrote, succeeded all too well. As a result, the destroyer escort *Eldridge* popped through the fourth dimension and reappeared at the Norfolk Navy Yard, 200 miles away. Then it popped back, leaving the crew in a nervous state for which I can scarcely blame them.

When this nonsense appeared, a fan wrote saying: Aha! Now I know what you, Heinlein, and Asimov were up to at the Navy Yard! I had to reply: Sorry, but there was no such experiment. But I am sure that an invisibility project would have been more fun than running endless tests on hydraulic valves, windshield de-icers, and trim tab controls for naval aircraft.

Heinlein and Asimov worked in other sections of the Laboratory on equally realistic problems. Being close personal friends, we got together, with our ladies, on weekends when we could spare the rationed gasoline. Now and then our gatherings were enlivened by visits from other writers-turned-warriors, such as Sgt. Jack Williamson.

When the war ended, Heinlein and I at once returned to writing, while Asimov was drafted into the Army and made corporal and sharpshooter by the end of his hitch. We next saw the Heinleins in 1950, when Catherine and I took our nine-year-old son West. In Hollywood, Robert showed us through the George Pal studio. There we saw the models used in making the movie *Destination Moon,* based on Robert's novel for young adults, *Rocket Ship Galileo.*

Later meetings with Robert occurred mainly at conventions, although we briefly visited Bob and Virginia in Colorado and later in the futuristic house they built in Santa Cruz, California. We also corresponded.

Robert had tried several occupations between the time the Navy retired him and his entry into freelance writing. One was an attempt at silver mining. Another was as an active political worker in California, for the Democratic Party. His political orientation then was quite different from the emphatic conservatism that he later embraced. His change took place mainly, I think, around 1960, when he and Virginia were touring the Soviet Union at the time that Francis Powers, the U-2 spy-plane pilot, was shot down. Virginia can tell you of the unpleasant experience that befell the Heinleins.

Nobody denies Robert's having, during his writing career, become the Number One man in American imaginative fiction. His stories are immensely readable and carry one along, even when one disagrees with some of the opinions expressed. His work is always full of interesting ideas, for he had one of the most brilliant, razor-keen minds that it has been my privilege to know.

During his last decades, of the many novels he wrote, some received mixed reviews. The explanation is that he was always trying out something new; so these works were experimental. And it is the nature of the experiments that they don't always work. One of them, *Stranger in a Strange Land,* created a stir when word got around that Charles Manson, the leader of the Manson murder gang, had been inspired by that Heinlein novel. When the rumor reached Heinlein, he sent a lawyer to look into it. The lawyer reported that Manson was only semiliterate, never read much of anything, and had never heard of Heinlein or his book.

So I remember Robert, not as the famous, adulated, erudite writer, but as a longtime friend who passionately loved his country, struggled with ill health, was kind and loyal to his friends, and was always delightful and stimulating company.

* * *

Author Jerry Pournelle has known Robert Heinlein since the sixties. He has a bachelor's, a master's and a doctorate in physics, psychology and political science. He was also an artillery officer in the Army. Among many other things, Jerry is a former President of the Science Fiction Writers of America and Chairman of the Citizens' Advisory Council on National Space Policy. He has written a large number of science fiction books, including The Mercenary, King David's Spaceship *and* Prince of Mercenaries. *With Larry Niven, he has written several bestsellers, including* Lucifer's Hammer, The Mote in God's Eye, *and* Footfall. *His latest [in 1988] book with Larry Niven and Steven Barnes is* The Legacy of Heorot.

Jerry Pournelle

On a high hill in Samoa there is a grave. Inscribed on the marker are these words:

> *"Under the wide and starry sky*
> *Dig the grave and let me lie.*
> *Glad did I live and gladly die*
> *And I laid me down with a will!*
>
> *"This be the verse you grave for me—*
> *Here he lies where he longed to be,*
> *Home is the sailor, home from the sea,*
> *And the hunter home from the hill.'"*

These lines appear another place—scrawled on a shipping tag from a compressed-air container, and pinned to the ground with a knife.

That shipping tag is not yet on the Moon. It will be.

Some years ago when the United States flew spacecraft instead of endlessly re-designing them, I had the extraordinary fortune to be sitting with Robert A. Heinlein in the cafeteria at Cal Tech's Jet Propulsion Laboratory during the landing of the Viking probe to Mars. We were in the cafeteria because, while I had both press and VIP credentials, Mr. Heinlein did not. I had brought him to JPL because I thought he belonged there; but there hadn't been time to get him credentials, so the NASA authorities ordered him out of the Von Karman Center.

I was outraged, and wanted to make a scene, but Robert would have none of that. He trudged up the hill to the cafeteria.

There is sometimes justice in this world. At the moment our first spacecraft landed on Mars, most of the network news cameras were in the cafeteria trained on Mr. Heinlein, rather than down in the center recording what NASA's officialdom thought they should be watching.

On Sunday, May 8, Robert A. Heinlein died peacefully during a nap. Like one of his beloved cats, when it was time he left us without fuss. He was cremated and his ashes scattered at sea from a warship. If we want to take his ashes to the Moon, we will have to take a pint of seawater. I think he'd find that acceptable.

Mr. Heinlein began writing science fiction before World War II, at a time when most strategists thought that battleships would dominate naval warfare and the battleships' analog fire control system was the most advanced computer technology in the world, when the Norden bombsight was top secret technology. After the war, while Dr. Vannevar Bush was telling Congress that the US would never be threatened by intercontinental missiles, Robert Heinlein gave us *Space Cadet* and *Universe.*

He wrote the outline of his "future history" in 1940–41. He was ridiculed for predicting in that history that the first rocket to the Moon would fly as early as 1976—and that it would usher in a "false dawn" followed by a long hiatus in space travel during the "crazy years" of mass psychosis toward the end of the twentieth century. Alas, some of that is chillingly accurate.

Robert Heinlein had as much to do with creating our future as any man of this century. It was not remarkable that the science reporters for the networks chose to follow him to exile in the cafeteria. They, like most of JPL's scientists and engineers, would never have been there if his stories had not called them to study and learn so that they could make his dreams a reality. His stories have caused more young people to choose careers in science and engineering than all the formal recruitment pitches ever tried.

He created our future in other ways. His stories made us ready, convinced us that it could be done. Robert Heinlein was truly *The Man Who Sold the Moon.*

Twenty years ago, Robert Heinlein took the time to review the first novel of a young space scientist turned professor turned novelist. My novel. Five years later, he read the first draft of *The Mote In God's Eye* and sent us a seventy page single-spaced critique that has more about how to be a successful writer than all the creative writing courses ever taught.

I owe a great part of whatever success I've had as a writer to help and encouragement Robert Heinlein gave me over the past thirty years. I once asked him how I could pay him back. His answer was simple: "You can't. You pay it forward."

He changed our lives in many ways. His dreams prepared the way for space flight. We are all in his debt.

No debt was ever easier to pay. Indeed, it costs nothing, because we get back tenfold everything we invest.

We can pay Robert Heinlein forward by keeping the dream alive: A dream of an endless frontier where free people know no limits and knowledge has no bounds.

Ad Astra and Goodbye.

Author Charles Sheffield has known Robert Heinlein since 1979. He was born in England in 1935 and received a Ph.D. in theoretical physics from Cambridge University. He is Chief Scientist of Earth Satellite Corporation and a past president of the American Astronautical Society and of the Science Fiction Writers of America. He is the author of eighty scientific papers and the best-selling popular science books Earth Watch, Man on Earth, *and* Space Careers. *He has published seven science fiction novels, including* Proteus Unbound, The Web Between the Worlds, *and* Between the Strokes of Night, *and sixty short stories [as of 1988].*

Charles Sheffield

I've been reading Heinlein for over forty years. I suspect that a lot of you, like me, started when you were ten to fifteen years old and have been doing it ever since.

There is perhaps one slight difference between my reading and yours, in that I was reading as a teenager and as a young man in Britain. It wasn't until the mid-1960s that I came to the United States and started to read *about* Heinlein, rather than simply seeking out his stories. That's when I found to my amazement that he was described in U.S. writings as a very American writer, in fact as a "quintessentially American author." Not only that, people keep on saying the same thing today.

I was surprised when I ran across that point of view, because I had felt, simply from reading Heinlein, that he was a quintessentially *British* author. His spelling was a little odd in places, and he had certain curious or unfamiliar turns of phrase, but he was clearly British to my mind.

Of course when you read as a teenager you don't think nationality. You pull out the *ideas.* So I want to mention some of the ideas which led me at the time, and to this day, to the view of Heinlein the Englishman.

The first one is almost an outrage. It is the sea. The British have always considered that they owned the sea: an island nation, Drake and the Spanish Armada, Nelson and Trafalgar. And yet Robert Heinlein's works are permeated by the sea. Not only that, he took the sea to space. Many of the things that he described in space draw directly from Navy tradition. I later found that this was not an accident. Mr. Heinlein was a graduate of the U.S. Naval Academy and had served at sea. But long before I knew that, I was enormously taken with the fact that here was a man who had a *feeling* for the ocean world, and could somehow get across into science fiction, into stories that were not about Earth seas but about space, the same feelings—of immensity, of loneliness, of tradition, of comradeship.

The second thing that I drew out of Mr. Heinlein's works was a very strong sense of history. I hope that I will not be misunderstood if I say that Europeans tend to consider that Americans are a little short on history. In a country settled less than five hundred years ago by its principal current occupants, and founded as a nation only just over two centuries ago, there seems to most Europeans, with a thousand year or a two thousand year perspective, to be just not much history about. As Santayana said, those who cannot remember the past are condemned to repeat it. I would like to offer an alternative to that: Only someone who really understood history, and the long-term sweep of human development, could have written a consistent future history. No one has ever succeeded in that enterprise as well as Robert Heinlein; and of course, he did it first. He could do so because he had read and understood the lessons of history.

The third thing, which I have to name carefully, and which I draw again directly from his works, is the importance of what I will call *ritual* in human affairs. Ritual can easily be given wrong connotations, but what I am referring to is the importance to life of family, of traditions, and—to use a word which is much diminished in esteem these days—of discipline. Those qualities, and their importance to human events, are very obvious when you read Mr. Heinlein's works. They permeate the content.

The fourth notion drawn in the works of Heinlein, something which again may seem unpopular today, is the idea that *competence is good.* There's nothing wrong with being a polymath. You don't have to be bad at one thing, you can be good at many things. When you read Heinlein, he doesn't write about idiots, fumbling their inadequate way through the world to achieve nothing. And why should he? Others are doing that. Too many novels today have as their message: "Let me take you in this book from the squalid, dull, and meaningless life that you live, to the squalid, dull, and meaningless life that I live." Heinlein would have none of that. He believed that there is nothing wrong with being competent. That's one of the most important lessons he offered (but never rammed down your throat; he taught more subtly than that).

The fifth thing that is implicit in his works is something that I again think of as very British. It's the notion of *justice and fair play;* the idea that, despite setbacks and good or bad luck, people will ultimately achieve their just deserts. In Heinlein stories, the Universe itself can be cruel. He never underestimates the danger that, if you goof in the wrong place and at the wrong time, Nature will not give you a second chance. You'll be part of history. But Heinlein stories also say that there are in this world (and all others) good guys and bad guys, and the good guys will finally win, and the bad guys, driven by greed or vanity or hate or lust for power, should and will finally lose. This is a moral position, and Heinlein's works never lack morality (which, as he clearly pointed out, has little or nothing to do with the conventional definition of *morals,* so often preoccupied as they are with the sexual customs of a particular age).

The sixth quality I want to mention again requires that we use a word diminished and depreciated in much of today's discourse. It is *patriotism.* Patriotism is not, thank Heaven, a uniquely American phenomenon. It is also not the mindless attitude of "My country, right or wrong." It is love for the homeland, in the form of the desire to improve it and make it as good as it can be. No nation can be improved from the outside. Patriotism is determination to make improvements *from within,* to do it for yourself, to accept criticism from without only to make those improvements, and to resist external coercion. The people of every nation want to make their country cleaner, stronger, and a better place for the next generation. The quality of patriotism in its finer form is seen in every land around the world. As Robert Heinlein often made clear, it should not be confused with imperialism, which is conceptually its opposite, nor with a refusal to listen to criticism. Patriots listen to and evaluate all criticism; but they make up their own minds. This idea, of thoughtful independence and of loyalty to one's own kind (species, nation, town, and family) runs through the corpus of Heinlein writing.

Where does this lead us? I could use everything that I have said, and a dozen other points drawn from Heinlein works, to assert again that Robert Heinlein is an essentially English or at least British author. Except that others are here, and have other views. Yoji Kondo will surely stand up to disagree with me, and say, No, no. Robert Heinlein is an essentially *Japanese* author.

I will not argue. Mr. Heinlein was an American original. That is undeniable, and it is foolish to dispute it. At the same time, he was a truly international author.

So to readers in the United States, I say only this: You can, justifiably, claim a large share of Robert Heinlein; but half a billion readers around the world will not permit you a monopoly.

Kondo's comments after Sheffield's speech:
I am sorry, Charles, but I never had the opportunity to think of Robert Heinlein as a Japanese author since I started reading Heinlein after my arrival in the U.S. in 1960. On the other hand, the first science fiction movie I ever saw (in 1950) was Destination Moon *by Heinlein, although I was not aware of the significance of that name at the time. I journeyed two hundred miles to see the movie and it was well worth every mile that I traveled.*

Robert Heinlein was proud that he had served in the Navy until discharged for physical disability. I am very happy to introduce Captain Jon McBride of the U.S. Navy, who has also been an astronaut since 1979. His son, Richard, also is a Navy officer. Captain McBride is the recipient of numerous medals and honors both from the Navy and NASA, including the Defense Superior Service Medal. He flew sixty-four combat missions in Vietnam. He was the pilot of Space Shuttle mission that flew exactly four years ago. He was to have been the commander of the Shuttle mission in March 1986, immediately after the Challenger flight in January. He currently serves as NASA Assistant Administrator for Congressional Affairs.

Jon McBride

Thank you Yoji, very much. Jerry, I'm much like you this evening. I thought we were going to sit down here and have a panel discussion, so I don't have any prepared remarks. But I do have a lot of thoughts I'd like to share with you before we do conduct our panel. I do feel very close to Robert Heinlein. I feel like he's right here in the room with me.

You know there are a lot of milestones in astronauts' lives which may inspire or instill them to go out and do whatever it is that they do. Of course I can remember Sputnik, which generated it all—started back in 1957. I was in high school at the time, and watching and experiencing Sputnik and shortly thereafter, Telstar. And then we began our Mercury program. We selected our first seven astronauts—trained them to fly in Mercury. We did our Gemini program which utilized a two-man capsule. This led us to Apollo, the three-man capsule which carried six crews of Americans to the surface of the Moon. So we Americans can take great pride in the fact that we've had twelve of our American sons walk on the face of the Moon starting in 1969. Which, believe it or not, we celebrate our twentieth anniversary of in 1989. It just doesn't seem that long. We had our Skylab in the seventies, which was a very successful mission; Apollo-Soyuz, a joint effort between ourselves and the Soviet Union; and, of course, we are now actively involved in our Space Shuttle program, which is the heartbeat of America's Space Program, I think.

And what's not so surprising to me is that most of these things Robert Heinlein saw. He had this vision. If you read a lot about Robert Heinlein you'll see that many of these things he saw back in the thirties and the forties. He envisioned this trip to the Moon. Women flying in space. Believe it or not, he was one of the first people to predict that.

So as I wander back to my childhood, and I think even before Sputnik or Telstar or Mercury or Gemini—all those things, I can remember being an eight-year-old back in the hills of West Virginia, going down to the local theater on a Saturday morning and watching *Destination Moon*. I think that was one of the things that got me started. I went out and started building rockets myself. Experimenting. My mother allowed me to build a laboratory down in my basement in West Virginia. And, unfortunately, we had some accidents down there a couple of times [laughter from the audience]. But like Robert and others here in the audience, we pressed on and made something. And I think that's what Robert was all about.

You know, I can't think of a better or more fitting place for all of us to share this evening than here in the Air and Space Museum. Where else can you look back over thirty or forty or fifty years of aerospace history and bring it right up to date? And we're all right here where it happened. You can go out there and see the visions of Robert and share them with us this evening.

So it's truly a pleasure for me, Yoji; and I appreciate the opportunity to come over here and share in this evening. I'm kind of at a disadvantage because I'm probably the only panelist who never was a close personal friend of Robert. But it's not like I don't feel like I was a close personal friend of his, because I certainly do. He made great contributions to our society, to our science fiction, and in fact, to the reality of our Space Program that we're living with today.

So thank you for inviting me. It's a pleasure to be a part of such a distinguished panel. And now I'm ready to answer questions if everyone else is. Thank you.

SPEECHES BY THE SPECIAL GUESTS

After each speech, there was an enthusiastic applause. Before proceeding with brief panel discussions, Kondo invited two special guests to say a few words.

Author Catherine Crook de Camp, or Mrs. L. Sprague de Camp, had known Robert Heinlein, with her husband, for half a century. Born in New York City, she received her B.A. from Barnard College and pursued graduate education at Columbia and other universities. She was a teacher for a number of years but, once she found out how much fun it was to write, she started collaborating with her husband. Together, they have published a number of fantasy books. She will share with us a woman's sensitive reminiscences of Heinlein.

Catherine Crook de Camp

Other people may remember Robert Heinlein as the premier SF writer of this century or as a world-renowned personality—a man whose vision foresaw the conquest of outer space. But I remember him as he was before Time and the sheer brilliance of his mind wrought their transformations upon him. The Second World War had begun when in 1942 Sprague volunteered for the Naval Reserve, got a commission as a Lieutenant, and set off for the naval training school in New Hampshire. Before leaving, he told me to find an apartment in the Philadelphia suburbs as he would later be assigned to the Naval Base there.

It was a daunting assignment, as thousands of other families were at that time converging on the Philadelphia Naval Base, but Robert—we often called him Bob in those days—and his then wife Leslyn offered to put me up when I went on this house-hunting safari.

So, never having met them, I took a train to Lansdowne, and on a rainy July afternoon I timidly rang a doorbell. The door was answered by a handsome young man with a clipped moustache and an athletic build. It was mutual admiration at first sight. With the advice and support of the Heinleins, I found an attic apartment just two short streets away and moved in books, beds, and baby, just one day before Sprague returned in his blue uniform with gold stripes on the sleeves.

Most Saturday afternoons during the War years, the Heinleins spent with us, strolling on the lawn of the mansion whose attic sheltered us, or sharing rationed meals with other families in the neighborhood. It was a small, closely knit community in those lean years, when even the half-gallon of gasoline we needed to visit the city-bound Asimovs had to be carefully hoarded. Even then Bob was adamant about conserving our national resources. He would make us walk two miles, toddler and all, to share a snack with some other Annapolis family.

Bob was so intensely patriotic that while he was working for the government, he revealed nothing about his work except that it was classified. To this day we do not know exactly what he did.

Always a stickler for good manners, Bob made his displeasure known when people overstepped the bounds of civilized behavior. To friends, however, he was always generous, warm and helpful. He often helped the de Camps to acclimate themselves to naval ways at, say, the Officers' Club, so we could make friends with the regular naval officers who tended to look down their noses at mere reservists. When, later in the War, Bob moved down into the center of the city, he often invited us in to meet distinguished visitors to Philadelphia, many of whom were writers in civilian life. And he never once showed any animosity toward Sprague because of his officer's status, although it must have been hard, at times, for an Annapolis graduate to wear civvies when a rank amateur sported the gold stripes of a Lieutenant Commander.

Within a week of the end of the War, the Heinleins headed West. For some years, we heard little from Bob, because he was not one to air his troubles. Then we learned that, in 1947, he had divorced Leslyn in California and had begun the lonely year of waiting decreed by the courts. As soon as he was free, he eloped with Virginia to Raton, New Mexico; and so in 1948 began a happy, loving, interdependent marriage that lasted forty years.

Ginny was just the sort of companion Robert needed, as I realized the first time I met her. A well-balanced, hard-working, gracious young woman, she was totally dedicated to Robert's welfare. Her love and care, without a doubt, added many years to his life.

Ginny was also, and still is, a loyal friend to the de Camps. She entertained us when we took our nine-year-old son Rusty to Los Angeles to see the sets for *Destination Moon,* and some years later when we visited the Heinleins, with our younger son Gerry, in Colorado Springs. Because their house was home to several Persian cats, and Sprague is violently allergic to cat dandruff, Ginny gave an elegant cocktail party in her garage.

Eventually, when Colorado proved unsuitable for Ginny's health, Bob built a unique, circular house in Santa Cruz County, California. Here they lived for twenty years, and here were written many of the books that enhanced Bob's reputation.

On this fence-enclosed property, Bob and Ginny built a guest house, untouched by feline paw, because they hoped the de Camps would come to visit and they wanted us to be secure from allergies. Such care of friends is seldom undertaken by even one's dearest companions. I must admit that we were grateful.

Then early in 1988, Ginny and Bob decided to move to a smaller place in California. When he had to part with much of his library, Bob told me, the only works he kept with him were the books inscribed to him by the de Camps. We are very proud and deeply touched by his decision.

The last telephone call I made to Robert Heinlein was about a month before he died, while he was at home between two hospital stays. His voice seemed resonant and almost young that evening as we recalled the many happy times we'd shared. He described the splendid vistas from the windows of his new home as he looked towards his beloved sea. Finally, Bob and I said how much we'd always loved each other and always would. It was a heart-to-heart recap of forty-six years of tender friendship. And when there was nothing left to say, I sat beside the silent phone and wept.

Postscript: just a month later, a U.S. Naval vessel carried Bob's ashes out to the sea he had always loved and scattered them on the waves.

There are three guests here who came all the way from Japan for this ceremony. One of them, author Koichiro Noda, has published over a hundred books in science fiction and on the space program, including the translation of Heinlein's Citizen of the Galaxy. *Author Tetsu Yano, who will speak now, has been translating Heinlein books for the past few decades, contributing significantly to the immense popularity of Heinlein in Japan. He is also a science fiction writer in his own right.*

Tetsu Yano

Forty some years ago, I was fighting a war in the Pacific as a foot soldier. I was a sergeant in the Japanese Army and am proud to have been a sergeant because Robert Heinlein dedicated his *Starship Troopers* to all the sergeants of the world.

After the war, I worked in the American Army Headquarters in Kyoto, an ancient capital, which was one of the few cities in Japan that had been spared the ravages of the fire-bombing. General Lawrence Heinlein, Mr. Heinlein's elder brother, was also there as a young officer of the occupying forces, although I was not aware of it at the time.

One of my jobs there was to tend the boiler room. There were stacks of old books and magazines to burn in the furnace. Among them were numerous science fiction magazines. I had lost all my books during the war and had little money then to buy new ones. I wanted to and had to read something. Despite my lack of proper education in English, I found science fiction magazines quite readable. I became particularly inspired by the stories written by Robert Heinlein and Anson McDonald (Heinlein's pseudonym). His exhilarating tales gave me the will, hope and courage to go on living in the devastations of the postwar Japan.

Robert Heinlein was my teacher and benefactor. I learned English reading his stories and became a translator. It has been an honor to translate many of Heinlein's books into Japanese.

[*Overcome by his emotions, Mr. Yano breaks into tears.*]

I have a text for my speech here but am unable to read it. I cannot speak any more. Sayonara, Sensei! Goodbye, Master!

The audience, sharing this extraordinary public expression of grief by Mr. Yano, gives thunderous applause.

After the speeches by the two special guests, the five panelists and the moderator returned to the stage to discuss the future of the space program and to answer questions from the audience. It was followed by the showing of Robert Heinlein's Destination Moon. *Although the movie was made two decades before the actual Apollo II mission to the Moon, it was so captivating that one could have heard a pin drop.*

PART III
Tributes to
Robert A. Heinlein

RAH: A MEMOIR

Poul Anderson

Poul Anderson was born in 1926 in Bristol, Pennsylvania, to Scandinavian parents, who gave him the unique spelling of his first name. He majored in physics at the University of Minnesota but was writing fiction already before his graduation. A winner of numerous honors, including Hugo and Nebula awards, Poul has written some ninety books. Although he is best known for his science fiction novels, he has also written historical, mystery, contemporary and other types of books and articles. His books include Tau Zero, The Avatar, The Man Who Counts, *and* Orion Shall Rise. *From 1972 to 1973 he was president of the Science Fiction Writers of America. He once won a knighthood for prowess in medieval combat at a meeting of the Society for Creative Anachronism. Travel, hiking, sailing, sketching, carpentry, cuisine and conversation are among his favorite activities.*

Enough people with far better qualifications will have explained what Robert A. Heinlein meant to the world that there is no call for me to try. Let me rather write more personally, about the part he played in this one life. In itself that is of no importance to anybody else, but perhaps in a small way it can help show what a profound influence he was in the lives of many thousands—quite likely millions.

My first encounter with him was at the age of fourteen. Newly introduced to science fiction and thoroughly hooked, but living on a farm where the nearest town was small and had nothing like an adequate newsstand, I had scraped together the money for a couple of magazine subscriptions. Now the September 1941 *Astounding* arrived. To this day the dazzlement has not faded. It featured Isaac Asimov's "Nightfall." It included Malcolm Jameson's "Admiral's Inspection," Alfred Bester's "Adam and No Eve," the opening section of L. Sprague de Camp's lively article on Hellenistic science, "The Sea King's Armored Division," a peculiar and somehow disturbing story, "Elsewhere," by somebody named Caleb Saunders . . . and the final installment of *Methuselah's Children*.

That's a terrible way to come upon a novel. Nevertheless I was enthralled. Mentions in the letter column suggested that Robert Heinlein was a major writer. He proved it anew in the next issue, with "Common Sense." I couldn't wait for more.

I had to, though. His byline would not reappear for years. Luckily, there was this other fellow, just as brilliantly inventive, by the name of Anson MacDonald. That October number also contained his "By His Bootstraps." Presently came grim "Goldfish Bowl," captivating *Beyond This Horizon*—the first novel of manners I ever read—and provocative "Waldo." That was all. It seemed MacDonald too had more urgent things to do after Pearl Harbor than write science fiction. I found a couple of stories by one Lyle Monroe in lesser magazines and treasured them. A long time went by before I learned who these gentlemen really had been.

By then I'd left the farm. Through secondhand stores and the occasional anthology, I had accumulated everything overtly by Heinlein. I reveled in it, studied it, thought about it, damn near memorized it. Already as a kid I'd recognized that here was something very special. Though scarcely a man of the world yet, I'd become better able to understand what that something was.

He could tell a flaming hell of a story, in crisp and vigorous language. The ability wasn't unique, of course; but there was no mistaking a Heinlein work for anybody else's. He was a fountainhead of new ideas. They ranged from concepts as bold and basic as a future in which heredity was controllable to details as fine as the dress styles in that future. Always I'd be amazed, and then realize that, yes, sure, this is how it logically would be. He knew people, all sorts of people, and had the gift of making them come alive for the reader. A large part of that was his basic realism, his experience of how society works. Naive though I still was, I saw that this wasn't the wish-fulfillment politics of most science fiction, it was genuine, it was what would most likely happen in the context of a particular story.

Excited discussion of Heinlein's work was a significant part of what my friends and I did. And then one day we picked up the latest *Saturday Evening Post,* and there in that sanctum of bourgeois respectability stood "The Green Hills of Earth." The rest is literary history.

As a footnote to that, I'd become a writer myself, and inevitably took much inspiration from him. Among other things, I helped myself to his device of fitting various stories into a common time line, so that they illuminated each other and the civilization itself was a kind of ongoing protagonist. My series came nowhere near measuring up to his, and eventually I dropped it, but I'd learned a lot. To this day, surely, many a colleague acknowledges Heinlein as his or her Mentor figure.

He never minded imitations, nor the outright use of a motif he had introduced. That has always been considered legitimate in science fiction, a writer seeing further possibilities in somebody else's thought and developing them. Examples include Fritz Leiber's *Gather, Darkness!,* derived from "'If This Goes On'"— and *Sixth Column,* and my *Operation Chaos,* derived from "Magic, Inc." I took the liberty of dedicating the latter to him and his wife Virginia; he replied with a gracious and humorous letter which still resides within my file copy.

Indeed, he was quite frank about his own sources. When somebody asked him if David Gerrold's "Star Trek" script "The Trouble With Tribbles" wasn't a ripoff of the Martian flatcats in *Red Planet,* he answered that no, it certainly was not; both harked back to Ellis Parker Butler's turn-of-the-century "Pigs Is Pigs." On other occasions he declared that what any writer does to get an idea is file off the serial number, change the body lines, and give it a new paint job.

A wee bit disingenuous, maybe—he was much too intelligent not to be aware of the extent of his originality—but kindly. I have never heard that he ever snubbed or set himself above any colleague, even the most obscure pulpster. We were all his lodge brothers and sisters.

Critics were different. "I have nothing against critics," he once said in a letter. "I just don't think they should be allowed to ride in the front ends of streetcars." Pretentiousness and incompetence, like indecisiveness, disloyalty, and incivility, were objects of his contempt.

My wife Karen and I first met him in the mid-1950s. He and Virginia were visiting Berkeley, California and called on Anthony Boucher, who invited us over. We arrived in awe. He soon had us at our ease. Karen then wore her hair long, down her back almost to her waist, and happened to be in a dress with a wide skirt. I remember him smilingly observing how much she resembled Alice. Well, that day she was in Wonderland!

Later, for a while, she published an amateur magazine. It was good enough to draw contributions from professionals besides myself, and she ventured to put him on the mailing list. As a matter of policy, he never directly responded or gave material to such things. Had he done so for a single one, he would immediately have been deluged. However, he took the trouble to comment now and then on this, and allowed his remarks to appear anonymously. It's hard to imagine a finer compliment, and obviously these words were the high point of any issue.

We next met the Heinleins at that all-time best of world science fiction conventions, Seattle, 1961, where he was guest of honor. Throughout that long weekend he was the embodiment of graciousness and friendliness to all. Only once in my life have I encountered a man who could be equally courtly; it has to come by nature as well as practice. Regardless, Robert Heinlein called himself a country boy who had never quite gotten the mud off his boots, and he treated every human being who deserved consideration as his equal. In Seattle, as at similar events elsewhere, he was not content to be feted and adored. He laid in a lot of refreshments at his own expense and invited one and all to his suite for what became a wildly enjoyable party. I noticed him unobtrusively but carefully getting the name of each bellhop engaged in serving, and thereafter addressing that person by it, with a full measure of dignity. Otherwise he sat at the poolside by day or in his open lanai till late at night—God in a yellow bathrobe!—accessible to anyone. His formal speech was almost shockingly forceful; but that fitted the pattern. He assumed we were worthy of sharing his deepest concerns. The following day he was again relaxed and witty.

You find that humor in his stories, dry and sharp as a well-aged Monterey jack cheese, when it isn't so subtle that it escapes the notice of many. It crackled in his letters and his conversation, too. There at the convention, enjoying the magnificent but rare sight of Mt. Rainier's snowpeak in the sky, he related that once while in the Navy he'd been stationed in Seattle; after six weeks, he woke up one morning and found that overnight they'd put up the biggest damn mountain he'd ever seen. Until a few years ago, my place of residence, Orinda, California, had its own post office and zip but no legal existence, being unincorporated. "I believe in Orinda code in the higher or philosophical sense," said he, "as I believe in Oz."

Plain old country boy? The Heinleins traveled over most of this planet, keenly observing its multifariousness, its splendors and squalors, triumphs and tragedies. But that is documented elsewhere, perhaps most notably in his *Expanded Universe.*

He didn't lack showmanship, either. At the next world convention, Chicago, 1962, *Stranger in a Strange Land* received the Hugo award for best novel. It was about to be presented in absentia when he himself appeared, as if out of the blue. "My wife has gotten tired of dusting these things," he said. But that evening he threw the same kind of open party as in Seattle.

Earlier in the proceedings, Theodore Sturgeon, that year's Guest of Honor, had made a speech about science fiction people he had known. When it came to Heinlein, Sturgeon spoke of encouragement, advice, an unsolicited but much needed loan of money with no demand that it ever be repaid if that would be inconvenient, and, most meaningful—Sturgeon had been suffering a dreadful case of writer's block—a long list of suggested plots for stories. I vividly recall "the ghost of a kitten, trying to find its way home through eternity." The Heinleins loved cats and always had at least one. I have heard of various other acts of kindness, such as giving Philip K. Dick a typewriter when Phil was completely on his uppers; but since Heinlein never mentioned them, one can only feel certain that they were many.

"This," said Sturgeon after describing the kitten story, "from the mechanical, chrome-plated Heinlein." Afterward I told Robert and Virginia about his tribute. Mainly they laughed and wondered what they'd do with a mechanical, chrome-plated Heinlein. Stand it in the hall for a hatrack?

Remember, he had outraged a lot of softheads by publishing *Starship Troopers* and issuing calls for the Republic to prepare against what he saw as a clear and present danger. It had made him represent everything that the flower children of the '60s—that "low dishonest decade," to borrow Auden's phrase for the '30s—claimed to oppose. Ted Sturgeon was somewhat of a pacifist himself, but he could see past the advocacy to the human being, and the friendship continued for as long as both lived. No, longer; Heinlein gave a helping hand to Sturgeon's widow.

I never joined in the idiot cries of "fascist!" It was plain that the society of *Starship Troopers* is, on balance, more free than ours today. I did wonder how stable its order of things would be, and expressed my doubts in public print as well as in the occasional letters we exchanged. Heinlein took no offense. After a little polite argument back and forth, we both fell into reminiscences of Switzerland, where he got the notion in the first place. He went on to describe some construction work he was doing in his garden, hauling and placing stone like Robinson Jeffers.

We had met again in December 1961. That year the American Association for the Advancement of Science held its convention in Denver, quite an experience in its own right. Since the Heinleins then lived in Colorado Springs, Karen and I had asked if we might pay a call on them afterward. A short visit was all we had in mind; what we got was an invitation to spend a couple of days. They picked us up at the airport and drove us to their home, we walked in—and there hung the original painting of blind Rhysling beside the Grand Canal on Mars. The house was not only charming; designed by him, it was a marvel of efficiency. The hospitality we received was almost overwhelming. Besides joining a large dinner party the Heinleins gave at the opening of a new restaurant in town, we had a private evening with them, which turned into a long and unforgettable night. They didn't even protest when I got to the stage of trying to sing *"Die Beiden Grenadiere."*

We saw the fallout shelter they had installed, and later recognized it in *Farnham's Freehold*. However, already by then the furore over *Starship Troopers* had diminished. *Stranger in a Strange Land* was out, and the paradox arose that the author found himself proclaimed a guru. It was not a role he wanted. On the contrary, preserving the privacy that the Heinleins valued so much became a problem that would plague them through all the years to come. Scruffy characters kept showing up out of nowhere, demanding to share water and expecting to be fed and housed. To refuse went deeply against the grain, but self-protection soon grew necessary. After moving to California they were forced to surround their property with a chain link fence; but the gate would always open for friends.

I visited Colorado Springs once more, alone, to give a lecture at the Air Force Academy. That evening at the Heinleins' was a quiet one, full of good talk.

Meanwhile something had happened that could have been distressful, were they not such civilized people. I'd been doing research for a factual book on nuclear war, an attempt to explain to the general public what it could bring about and how complex and difficult such concepts as "deterrence" actually are. It opened my eyes to the full range of possibilities; and in those days that war looked probable. I expressed my horror in a letter to Heinlein. It must have been written unclearly, for he thought I'd gone over to the "anything else would be better" side. His response was gentle, but told me in unmistakable terms that if this was how I felt, I should campaign for unilateral disarmament, refuse to pay taxes, help picket defense installations, and otherwise put myself on the line. He would fight me every step of the way, but he would respect me.

I replied by return mail that this wasn't my meaning at all. I abhorred war; so did he. I knew a nuclear one would, at best, be a totally unprecedented catastrophe; so did he. Nevertheless, there were things still worse. His thinking had, in fact, helped guide mine. He accepted this. From then on I was proud to stand with him in eternal hostility to Communism and every other form of tyranny over the mind of man. Sometimes I disagreed about this or that detail—perhaps increasingly so as the years passed and the world changed—but no matter.

After all, various of his own opinions had evolved with time and experience, as they will for anyone who's alive between the ears. It would be presumptuous to try spelling out in detail what he believed, but the basics are clear enough. He prized freedom, though he knew it is bounded by duty, decency, and common sense, and cannot long exist without them. He honored woman-kind, but never imagined that the only difference between the sexes is in the plumbing. Once in a letter he said that the ultimate obscenity in totalitarianism is its interference with the relation-ships of love. The first obligation is always to children, for they are the future; and, while he was wryly aware of the flaws in our species, it is *our* species and so lays claims upon us. Likewise, he recognized the imperfections of the United States of America, he spoke warmly of many foreigners, including Russians, but his patriotism he never compromised.

In short, what he stood for, some would call old-fashioned, and others would call the wisdom of the race. On matters of religion he was, as far as I know, silent. Whatever creed he held was nobody else's affair.

If these recollections say little about Virginia Heinlein, it is because she is still, happily, with us, and keeps the same wish for privacy. Suffice that throughout their many years together she was his full partner, as strong and intelligent in every way as himself. (He remarked once with a grin that during World War II, when they were both in naval service, she was his superior officer.) By assuming most of the time-consuming, spirit-consuming burdens of their business, she made it possible for him to write unhampered; and so we are all in her debt. I hope it is not out of line for me to set down what both of them were candid about, that eventually the thin air of Colorado Springs affected her health and compelled them to move. At sea level she quickly regained robustness. After a while in Washington State, they bought land near Santa Cruz, California, and he designed a new house for them. It was quite unlike the old one, because this was another kind of territory, but it fitted equally well into its environment.

We visited them there in 1966, together with our twelve-year-old daughter, on our way south. Our car broke down before we arrived. Virginia drove miles to fetch us at the garage. Robert was recovering from an operation, and since work had barely started on the house, they were in temporary quarters. Just the same, they put us up, showed us around, grilled steaks, next day entertained us as heartily till our car was ready—and afterward our daughter shared the dedication of *Podkayne of Mars* with another young girl. It meant the world to her.

In the years that followed, we managed to drop in a few more times, and saw the place according to the way they had dreamed of and worked for it. In 1976 we joined them in an all-night vigil at the Jet Propulsion Laboratory in Pasadena until, line by line, Viking One displayed the first-ever images from the surface of Mars before his eyes. A few months later in Kansas City, he was again Guest of Honor at the world science fiction convention; they gave a stylish reception ("Put on your hurtin' shoes," he had written) to promote his new cause of blood drives at these events. A high point occurred when the telephoned news came in that Viking Two had successfully landed, and everybody cheered; but the most delightful to us was meeting an old friend of Robert's, Sally Rand.

The Heinleins only graced our home once, at an all-day party for a lot of people. Contact with them gradually became infrequent, to our regret. It was simply that the drive between Orinda and Santa Cruz—later, Carmel—is not negligible, we didn't want to be pushy, and they, after all, had their own lives to lead. When we did meet it was cordially, but others were present who also had a call on their attention.

These occasions were mostly gatherings related to the space program. The last couple of times I went alone, down to Los Angeles, to lend my services at meetings of the Citizens' Advisory Council on National Space Policy. They took place in the mansion of Larry and Marilyn Niven and were largely masterminded by Jerry Pournelle. They were unofficial and informal, but discussion was serious between scientists, engineers, military officers, government administrators, politicians' representatives, businessmen, and so on, down to us writers and such-like ordinary types. "Down" and "ordinary" are the wrong words as regards Robert Heinlein, though. When he voiced his opinions, everybody, repeat, everybody listened with respect. The recommendations of the group reached high circles in Washington—including, at least in précis form, the White House—and may have had some effect. What we offered was ideas for keeping America active in space, that promised land toward which he had been so powerful a leader.

Yet what I most remember are conversations in the evenings after sessions, three or four of us sitting in a motel room over a drink or two, quietly talking. His thoughts ranged as widely as ever, with the same wit and humanity as always. And I remember the morning after the final meeting, when everybody was homebound, saying goodbye for what would be the last time.

JIM BAEN'S RAH STORY

Jim Baen

Jim Baen came into the science fiction world first as the Managing Editor of Galaxy *and* Worlds of If *and then Editor in Chief of those magazines. After having served as senior editor at Ace Books, he joined Tor Books as vice president. He then had an opportunity to form his own company, Baen Books, and became its president. His firm has specialized in hard-core science fiction novels, although he also publishes fantasy books. In his various capacities as editor and publisher, he became acquainted with and became friends with Robert Heinlein. He is the only publisher whose appreciation appears in this volume.*

Anyone admitted to Robert's friendship felt immediately at the center, but truth be known, there were others closer than I—the Pournelles, the Andersons, the de Camps, his entire graduating class at Annapolis—but both he and his wonderful wife Ginny were fond of me, and I know that they found me marvelously sympatico as compared to the generality of New York publishing types. (Robert once mentioned that Ginny and I were the only two anarcho-syndicalists of his immediate acquaintance—bomb-throwers at heart if not in deed.) In any event, here is a short anecdote that was *not* written for this volume, but as a reply on an electronic bulletin board (The Byte Information Exchange, BIX to those who use it), complete with Message Header. It was written in response to a question regarding my familiarity with one of Robert's titles.

Actually, I *edited Expanded Universe.* There's a story behind
that, of Robert's remarkable generosity of spirit, and perhaps his
disinclination to have a favor to himself not returned with a
larger one. Here's the story.

In 1977 I had just become the Executive Editor for SF at Ace.
While reviewing various pending matters I noticed that we still
had one Heinlein title. (The previous administration had lost
several others.) I noted further that it had a royalty rate of four
percent, half or less of what Robert's new books got at the time.
Well Robert had always been a special hero to me and I didn't
like keeping half his money. I also thought it was incredibly
stupid.

So I approached Tom Doherty, then my boss and mentor, and
proposed that we unilaterally raise the royalty on *The Worlds of
Robert A. Heinlein* to eight percent, suggesting that aside from its
being right and proper it would be worth it in PR. He agreed. A
month later at that year's Worldcon (Florida it was, the
Fountainbleau), I marched up to The Great Man (Ginny was
there too, of course), didn't quite salute or click my heels, said
"Sir, Ace Books has raised your royalty rate to eight percent
without expectation of any quid pro quo thank you very much,
Sir." Jerky little half-bow, about face, and I'm outa' there.

(At least that's my memory of what I did—an Outside Observer
might have reported that the "march" was a shamble and the
clipped statement a mumble accompanied by an ingratiating
smirk. But I digress.)

Anyway, a few months later Robert's new agent, Eleanor Wood,
called me, apparently in great pain. The cause of the pain was
that Robert, it seems, wanted to *expand The Worlds of RAH* for
Ace—and had dictated a take-it-or-leave-it additional advance of
15K. That dictation was not for *us,* but for Eleanor; she knew
she could have squeezed some respectable multiple of $15K out
of us, but was under strict instructions to offer the work for that
amount, whence the pain. So we made the deal, several old
stories from Robert's trunk to pack into a new and improved

Worlds, which I retitled *Expanding Universe* and Robert retitled *Expanded Universe.*

But wait! There's more. RAH proceeded to spend fifty hours on the phone with me in conversations that started out being about the new stories and articles but ranged widely. The result of those conversations was about 40K of absolutely new unpublished RAH for the volume. (When Eleanor heard about *that* her pain was magnified a thousandfold.)

Our 15K volume has aged well. Eleanor now has that fiction/fact collection on the block—12 years after initial publication—for a medium six figures.

Now *that's* how a true gent responds to an act of spontaneous good will. Trouble is, I was totally outclassed; no way I could respond in kind. But note the dedication page on *New Destinies.*

REMEMBERING ROBERT HEINLEIN

Greg Bear

Greg Bear, born in San Diego in 1951, had seen many parts of the world, such as Japan and the Philippines, by the time he was twelve, thanks to his father, who was in the Navy. He started writing science fiction at an early age and sold his first short story when he was fifteen. He has been writing and publishing science fiction regularly since he was twenty-three. A winner of Hugo and Nebula awards, his novels include Hegira, Blood Music, Eon *and* The Forge of God. *Greg lectured frequently in San Diego schools and has also worked as a professional illustrator. His hobby interests include astronomy, physics and history. Since 1983, he has been married to Astrid Anderson Bear, the only daughter of Poul Anderson. He served from 1988 to 1990 as President of the Science Fiction Writers of America.*

The last time we heard from Bob, he was calling to recommend that we urge former ambassador Jeane Kirkpatrick to run for the Republican Presidential nomination. Astrid took the phone call. A few months later, he was dead.

The first time I heard from Robert Heinlein, I was eight or nine years old, and he called to me from the cover of a library book I saw in the house of a friend, Mike Tucker. Mike was ten or eleven and a little more advanced in his reading than I. The book was *Red Planet*. I didn't really believe that authors existed back then, although I was writing stories of my own and folding them into manilla chapbooks. *Red Planet*'s brilliant red cover, depicting a boy in a zebra-striped Mars suit, caught my eye, however, and I checked out the book and read it. *Red Planet* was the first real science fiction novel I encountered.

It sunk a depth-charge into my soul.

I had known before then that there was something called science fiction, but I had encountered it mostly in movies and in Tom Swift Jr. novels.

I read more Heinlein. I accidentally dropped a copy of *Have Space Suit—Will Travel* while reading in the bathtub that year, pulled it out soaking wet, and returned it to the library after it had dried. With a sympathy reserved for younger readers, they did not fine me.

Soon, I was off to Kodiak, Alaska, where my father was stationed as a naval meteorologist. The Kodiak naval station library had a rich selection of hardback SF, mostly from the 1950s; I soon learned that paperbacks were available and received by mail, from the publishers and bookclubs and from my grandmother, books by Edgar Rice Burroughs and Andre Norton and Doc Smith and Poul Anderson and L. Sprague de Camp and Brian Aldiss. I was off and running.

But Heinlein was there first. He was legendary. In early high school, I called him Hen-line. I soon learned better. I read most of what he had written.

When I attended my first science fiction convention in 1966, for a brief twenty minutes or so, I became aware of the phenomenon called fandom. In 1968 I went to Baycon and stayed for the duration, meeting John W. Campbell, Harlan Ellison, Lin Carter, Harry Harrison, Bjo Trimble, John Brunner, and Lord knows who all else. I had already met Ray Bradbury and begun a long correspondence with him. I bought Panshin's *Heinlein in Dimension* at Baycon, and learned that Heinlein didn't appreciate that book, or being analyzed in general.

I still hadn't met Heinlein. That happened at Caltech six or seven years later, after I'd published several stories and written my first salable novel (not to be sold for another three years). Heinlein was on a panel with a number of impressive science fiction writers, including Harry Harrison, Robert Silverberg, David Gerrold, and Jerry Pournelle.

I spoke briefly with Heinlein, who seemed tired, and I offered up a copy of *Time Enough for Love* for his autograph. I didn't like most of the book. Still, it was Heinlein, and it was a bestseller. Heinlein's courtly manner and sharp wit impressed me. Here was a genuine giant, and he spoke to youngsters with courtesy and tolerated their impudent remarks with congeniality even when he was tired. I next saw him at a distance at MidAmeriCon in Kansas City in 1976, where he was accompanied by his wife Virginia and by World's Fair fan dancer Sally Rand, who had gone to high school with him.

Having absorbed the undoubted classics, I did not read all of his later books. Nevertheless, when we crossed paths at an ABA gathering in Anaheim, I was floored when Heinlein remarked that he had read my novel *Strength of Stones,* and thought it was pretty good.

In 1979, I sat next to Bob and Ginny briefly at the Jet Propulsion Laboratory to witness incoming Jupiter pictures. He was doing much better now; fully alert and conversant, he had recovered from carotid bypass surgery, which added years to his life. He balanced a cane between his legs, bouncing it back and forth in his hands. "I used to wonder why old men did this with their canes," he said. "Now I know. It's so they won't forget them when they stand up." Young man in aging body.

It was in 1983 that I first had a chance to see Heinlein in person for hours at a time, to work with him, to become acquainted with this man who had made a decisive impression on my younger soul. Jerry Pournelle had invited me to a meeting of the Citizens Advisory Council on National Space Policy, hosted by Larry and Marilyn Niven in Tarzana. My father-in-law, Poul Anderson, was there, as well as scientists, politicians, rocket engineers, and other writers. It was a heady meeting; I still hadn't made much of a mark on the field, but I was working—really *working*—with brilliant and well-known people, Heinlein included. I learned a lot there, and even though I was one of two people present who claimed to be liberals, I was invited back. (So was the other.)

Much of what I learned was incorporated in my novel, *Eon,* which I had been working on for some years already.

We met at these council sessions several times, and to my enormous pride, I came to realize that Heinlein regarded me as a peer. To my delight, he had recently written a novel I thoroughly enjoyed: *Job: A Comedy of Justice.* As a connoisseur of James Branch Cabell, I couldn't help but relish Heinlein's vision of heaven and religion. (Some of Heinlein's sexual attitudes, expressed in the context of satire, were troublesome; but then, he had been zinging us with bizarre sexual situations for over thirty years.

Is seemingly casual rape [in *Friday*] and incest [in *Job*], devoid of emotional overtones, any stranger than the genealogy of "All You Zombies"?)

I was able to express my appreciation, and to tell him what he had done for me as a youth, and as a writer. At the last of these meetings where Heinlein was present, there was concern expressed by one of the younger attenders that he might not get into space in his lifetime. Heinlein, seated in the Nivens' living room, humphed, "You think *you're* worried."

It does not matter—certainly not now—that Heinlein and I would have disagreed on many substantial issues. The same could have been true of any number of others who have helped shape my thinking. Throughout my life, it has been my good fortune to be influenced by people who don't mind being disagreed with, who practically insist upon it; who believe that it adds to the interest of life.

The important relationship here was the passing of energy, not spin or charge; we agreed on enough very important issues to find common ground, and to work together.

What we agreed on is what Heinlein first impressed on me when I read *Red Planet:* the necessity for moral commitment, for a belief in the power of imagination, for a constant resurgence of hope against incredible odds, and the basic goodness and survivability of humanity despite all evidence to the contrary. Contra nihilism; we agreed that the rational mind must make a stand against nothingness, cheerfully, perhaps pessimistically, but never cynically.

In late April 1990, Charles Brown held a San Francisco Nebula banquet party at his house. He brought out a copy of the first Bluejay edition of *Eon* and said he thought I should have it. I thanked him, hoping he wasn't giving up his own copy, and dismissing me from his library. "Open it," he said. I did.

It had belonged to Robert A. Heinlein, and it was signed by him, with his stamp and the Bonny Doon Road address.

Perhaps I was able to return to Bob some of what he had given to me.

RECALLING ROBERT ANSON HEINLEIN

J. Hartley Bowen, Jr.

J. Hartley Bowen, Jr. was supervisor at the Navy laboratory in Philadelphia where Robert A. Heinlein served the country during World War II. Despite his discharge on physical disability from the Navy in 1933, Heinlein volunteered to serve in uniform when the war broke out but was assigned instead to work as a civilian engineer performing research to aid the war efforts.

Having been a reader of science fiction since the early issues of *Amazing Stories* in 1926, the name of Robert A. Heinlein was not unknown to me when he appeared in the offices of the Aeronautical Materials Laboratory of the Naval Aircraft Factory in Philadelphia in early 1942. I had been hired as a junior engineer in July 1939 when the total personnel of AML was approximately twenty and the hiring of a new person was an event. Expansion began after war broke out in Europe in September 1939 and by the time Bob Heinlein arrived we were expanding rapidly into two new buildings.

I was not greatly impressed when Bob reported for work; after all I was now a newly promoted supervisory chemist with my own technical and management headaches and he was assigned to a different part of the laboratory. He had come to AML, as I recall, because he had been at the Naval Academy at the same time as Commander A. B. Scoles who was Assistant Chief Engineer (Materials) and head of our laboratory in 1942. Bob had previously had active duty in the Navy after graduation from the Academy and after a few years left the Navy for health reasons. His natural patriotism urged him toward work in the war effort and he entered the civil service at AML.

However, I soon got to know Bob as a friend and often table-mate at lunch even though our work areas were unrelated. At one point in time Bob served as a sort of personnel man for the laboratory, and also as a kind of one-man grievance committee. During the war period there was a continuous state of organized chaos in the laboratory because of rapidly changing technical requirements, priorities, and personnel shortages. I recall very well that Bob Heinlein was a constantly stabilizing influence. One must realize that the engineering staff was a mix of old time civilians, new college graduates, and naval officers with ranks ranging from ensign to commander. It was almost inevitable for conflicts to arise when young officers were assigned to supervise civilians twice their age and with much greater technical experience. Because of his unique background mix of officer/civilian experience, Bob Heinlein sensed the emotions around him and often helped heal breaches among us. I recall in particular many times he intervened gently but firmly in problems involving my immediate boss (a civilian of twenty-five years experience) and very junior naval officer/project engineers; with the result that amicable conditions resulted.

Bob Heinlein was a most worthy addition to the Aeronautical Materials Laboratory. His technical competence, managerial ability, and ability to relate to others placed him in a class by himself. For sheer entertainment there was nothing to compare with sitting at lunch with Bob Heinlein, Sprague de Camp, and Isaac Asimov; the latter being a member of my technical area of work.

After the war I remained with the laboratory and retired after thirty-three years as Technical Director of the laboratory. In 1954 my wife and I were on a trip for the Navy to California and we added a vacation which included a stop at Colorado Springs and a very delightful evening visit with Bob and Virginia. I was fascinated by the house he had designed and I incorporated some features in my own place later. I never again saw Bob but corresponded and followed his writings. Among my favorites were *Stranger in a Strange Land,* "The Roads Must Roll," *Farnham's Freehold,* and most of all *Friday.*

I am honored to be able to contribute my thoughts about this great man who was truly a Citizen of the World.

ROBERT HEINLEIN

Arthur C. Clarke

Arthur C. Clarke's name is often heard in the same breath with Robert Heinlein's. He was born in England in 1917 and was educated there. A recipient of numerous awards, he is known as the author of Childhood's End, Imperial Earth, *and* Rendezvous with Rama, *among numerous other works. Many of his books and short stories relate the exciting possibilities of human adventure into space. The epic 1968 movie* 2001: A Space Odyssey *was a collaborative work between Stanley Kubrick and Arthur C. Clarke. Having served as president of the British Interplanetary Society, he is also known as the first person to suggest the idea of geosynchronous satellites for communications. He has been a resident in Sri Lanka for the past few decades and serves as chancellor of the University of Moratuwa. He has also played a leading role in the founding and operation of the International Space University.*

My first meeting with Bob and Ginny Heinlein was in 1952, on my initial visit to the United States as a result of selling *The Exploration of Space* to the Book-of-the-Month Club. I don't recall how I originally contacted Bob—probably through correspondence as a result of the movie *Destination Moon,* if not at an earlier date.

Anyway, when they heard that I was coming to the States, he and Ginny invited me to visit them in their self-designed, high-tech house at 1776 Mesa Avenue, Broadmoor, Colorado Springs (one of the few addresses I have never forgotten!)

It was a memorable visit, because not only did I have the privilege of meeting the Heinleins and their neighbours, but I also saw some of the most spectacular scenery in the US; the "Garden of the Gods" made a particular impression on me. Most unforgettable was our ascent of Pikes Peak by funicular, and the subsequent drive down by car.

I must admit that I did not realize what a sacrifice of working time and energy Bob and Ginny were making to entertain an unknown (and occasionally, I'm sure, uncouth) Britisher. I shall always be grateful to them for their kindness and hospitality.

Many years later, when I was lecturing at the Air Force Academy, I took the opportunity of revisiting 1776, and reviving happy memories. I told the current residents that I had once been a guest of their distinguished precursors.

The Heinleins must have been very sad to abandon their mile-high house, after Ginny was diagnosed as suffering from altitude sickness. However, they quickly bounced back, and built an even more impressive residence at a slightly lower altitude—Santa Cruz, California. Here, I again had the pleasure of staying with them, and also of meeting Chesley Bonestell, who dominated the space-art scene as thoroughly as Bob did the space fiction scene, and for the same period of over thirty years.

It gave me great satisfaction when, in 1980, Bob and Ginny paid a one-day visit to Sri Lanka on a 'round-the-world cruise. I chartered a plane to fly them over the southern part of the island, and showed them some of my favourite locations—including the Great Basses Lighthouse, scene of *The Treasure of the Great Reef.* Almost ten years later, in March 1990, I flew back over the same route and recalled with nostalgia that day we spent together.

When I wrote my "Science Fictional Autobiography" *Astounding Days,* I naturally had to include a tribute to Bob—and here is an extract from it, under the, alas, now all-too-appropriate heading "Requiem"—

Requiem

In the very month that War broke out in Europe, John Campbell printed an inconspicuous little story called "Life-Line." The blurb reads: "A new author suggests a means of determining the day a man must die—a startlingly plausible method!"

Plausible or not, "Life-Line" is still a good read. One Dr. Pinero invents an electrical device that can measure the

extension of an individual's track in four-dimensional
space-time, by detecting the discontinuities at each end, much as
engineers can pin-point a break in an undersea cable. He can
thus locate the moments of birth—and of death.

The impact on the Life Insurance companies is, of course,
shattering, and they Take Steps to put Dr. Pinero out of business.
He sits down to a good meal and calmly awaits the arrival of
their enforcers; having already consulted his own machine, he
knows that there is nothing else to be done. . . .

The story is smoothly written, and packs quite a number of
punches. During the next three years, Campbell's "new author"
contributed an astounding (sorry about that) *twenty* stories to the
magazine, including three serials. His name: Robert A. Heinlein.

"Life-Line," short though it is, already hints at some of the
preoccupations which would provide Heinlein with themes for
the rest of his career—e.g. mortality, and big business *versus* the
individual. Others were developed during the next two years in a
creative debut unmatched since the advent of Stanley Weinbaum.
And, unlike that brief Nova, Heinlein was to dominate the
science fiction sky for the next half century, and effect a
permanent change upon the pattern of its constellations.

Four months later (January 1940) he was back with a story
which remains one of his best-loved—"Requiem." Now that we
have watched whole armies of technicians working round the
clock at Cape Canaveral, the idea of a couple of barnstorming
rocket pilots giving $25 rides in a secondhand spaceship at a
country fair is more than a little comic. (Come to think of it,
when did you last see a barnstorming *aeroplane?* I haven't, since
my maiden flight from a field outside Taunton at the age of ten.)

Heinlein's protagonist is D. D. Harriman, an aging millionaire
who has made his fortune in the space business—but is not
allowed to leave Earth because of his heart condition. So he hires
the two owners of a beat-up, mortaged rocket ship to take him as
a passenger (one jump ahead of the bailiffs—just as in
Destination Moon) and dies happily in the dust of Mare
Imbrium, the most magnificent of the lunar "seas." Over his
grave are inscribed the lines that R. L. Stevenson wrote for his
own epitaph:—

Here he lies where he longed to be
Home is the sailor, home from the sea,
And the hunter home from the hill.

* * *

"Requiem," dated though it may be, is a moving story. And, on rereading it after many years, I have just discovered something that has given me quite a shock. The first "D." in D. D. Harriman stands for—*Delos.* Bob Heinlein chose better than he knew, when he selected that magic name; for, as I have good reason to remember, the Greek island of Delos is the reputed birthplace of Apollo.

As is now rather well known, my last encounter with Bob was, unfortunately, not a happy one. It was a private meeting to promote the Strategic Defence Initiative, better known as "Star Wars," and I—perhaps not too tactfully—criticized some of the more extreme claims of certain Star Warriors* (e.g. "putting an umbrella over the United States"!). Bob was much upset, and accused me of meddling in affairs which did not concern me— though I would have thought that SDI should concern *everybody* on the planet!

I'm not going to revive this argument—which hopefully history has already bypassed—but will add that there are a lot of things in SDI which *should* be done: see Freeman Dyson on this depressing subject.

Though I felt sad about this incident, I was not resentful, because I realized that Bob was ailing and his behaviour was not typical of one of the most courteous people I have ever known. I'm happy to say that friendly communications were later resumed, through Ginny's good offices.

Goodbye, Bob, and thank you for the influence you had on my life and career. And thank you too, Ginny, for looking after him so well and so long.

---

*Once neatly categorized to me by America's greatest experimental physicist as "very bright guys with no common sense."

ROBERT HEINLEIN

Gordon R. Dickson

Gordon R. Dickson was born in 1923 in Edmonton, Alberta, Canada with a Canadian engineer father and an American school teacher mother. He learned to read at the age of four years. After his father's death, his mother returned to the U.S. with Gordon and his younger brother. Gordon Dickson entered the University of Minnesota at the age of fifteen. During World War II, he served in the U.S. Army. He returned to the University and received his B.A. in Creative Writing; his instructors in literary composition included Sinclair Lewis and Robert Penn Warren. After doing graduate work, he started writing professionally in 1950. He has had no other occupation since, which makes his career rather unique. Dickson's major work is the Childe Cycle *multivolume series. Among the most popular in the* Childe Cycle *are perhaps his* Dorsai *warrior series. He served as President of the Science Fiction Writers of America in its early years and has taught in a number of writers' workshops. His latest book is* The Dragon Knight. *His hobbies include astronomy and history.*

Whenever an author who has touched many people dies, the source from which his or her stories emerged is effectively walled up forever. What he or she did cannot be duplicated after their death, any more than it could be duplicated while they were alive.

No writer has had more pastiches written about his characters than Conan Doyle, in the case of Sherlock Holmes and Watson. Some of these pastiches have been excellent—but they fall short of the power of stories by Doyle, himself, brought to life again. They are not *more* Conan Doyle.

So that when an author ceases to write because he or she is no more there to write, what is felt is not merely the loss of an old friend, but a certain part of the reader which has been touched by that writing; and now knows it is touched no more. In essence, a part of the reader has died with the writer.

As I have mentioned in other places and on other occasions, I first met Robert Heinlein at a convention. My memory fails to give me the exact date and time; but it was after I had begun writing science fiction, which would put it somewhere in the 1950s.

So, while time and the name of that convention are lost forever to my memory, the moment of meeting is not. I remember I was standing talking to Isaac Asimov, while Robert was up on a small stage or dais, surrounded by other people eager to talk to him. For some reason, speaking with Isaac, I referred to Robert and Isaac said to me, "Have you met him?"

I'm not exactly sure what I answered. Something to the effect that I hadn't, but didn't want to intrude now in what was going on at the moment.

Isaac, without saying anything more, took me by the elbow, led me up to the group—which parted for him and therefore for me—and led me up to Robert, saying "Robert, this is Gordon Dickson."

"Oh—" answered Robert Heinlein. And again my memory fails me as to his exact words, but he responded to my name as one he recognized; and as we talked it turned out that he had read the science fiction I had written.

I was, of course, very flattered. Like a multitude of people even then, I was in awe of Robert's abilities as an author, and deeply impressed that he should find what I wrote interesting.

I had always been and still am, fascinated by how other writers achieve the results they do with the written word. I have said on occasion that I never yet encountered a published writer who does not do at least one thing that I cannot do and would never be able to do.

This, of course, is because creativity expressed in this manner is such a completely individual thing that an author cannot even describe it to himself in full, let alone to other people; so that, ironically, writers tend not to talk about the creative elements of their work, but only—and even this at rare intervals—about the craft of it. The craft is something that can be described in words.

The spark that sets the reader alight cannot. It is unique with each author; and that is why I say that when one of them, like Robert, ceases to write his readers experience an element of his death.

That experience, of course, becomes even greater when the exiting author is a personal friend, as Robert became to me over the years that followed; with our all-too-infrequent, but rewarding, meetings when we were at the same convention together. It is a strange thing to come to know an author you have greatly admired also as a human being. In all cases in my experience, and not limited to those who are famous and also personal friends, admiration for their work ends up being paralleled by an admiration for each of them as an individual.

I use the word parallel deliberately. During the '80s, and even before, but primarily during the '80s, we who were publishing our writing were bombarded by frequent questionnaires from people trying to reconcile the work of a particular author—or the work of authors in general—with what they were as people. There was a great attempt to link what was found in the writing with the personality of the author, and his characters with individuals he knew.

Needless to say, this was a futile business; and, since most of us who wrote intuitively recognized it as a futile business from the beginning, the filling out of the questionnaires became an unjustifiable intrusion on our work time. Many of us ended up simply returning the unanswered questionnaires with a note to the effect that there was no point in our filling them out; or simply dropping the questionnaire in the waste basket and ignoring it.

This may seem like very harsh treatment to someone who was honestly interested in trying to make the identification that was attempted by the questionnaire. But the point was that it was an effort in the wrong direction. No writer uses a person they know in whole as a character in a work of fiction.

He or she cannot; because this would limit the author to what the person's characteristics actually were. It would force the author to build the story around that person, instead of molding elements of him or her into the story, adapting them to the story's needs.

Actually, the successful characters that appear in stories almost necessarily include elements, even wisps, of people that the author has encountered. But this is simply the similar use of places and things. An author may want to use a wingback chair in a story, and his use may be stimulated by memory of a wingback chair that he knows or remembers—but the chair in the story is a chair recreated to fit the requirements of the story, not merely a verbal equivalent of the original in photographic reproduction.

So, the attempt to make a conscious reconcilement of character and writing is an impossible one. Yet, in the case of what I have been writing about here, Robert's work and Robert as a person, there are identities that a friend may come to recognize over time. Not characters, not settings, but the colors of character and emotions.

All authors, as I pointed out earlier, do unique things that no one else can do in their writing. This is pure creativity; and it is a type of magic that is entirely individual, entirely indescribable. We can point to it and name it, but that is all.

Robert had a remarkable narrative ability. If an author writes well, the reader quickly falls through the words he or she is reading and begins to experience the story as if he or she were living it. The ability to make the reader do this varies from author to author; but Robert was superb at it. Where others might take anywhere from a couple of pages to a chapter or more to draw the reader completely and wholly into "experiencing," rather than merely "reading," the story, Robert could involve them in it completely within the first few paragraphs, if not with the first sentence.

His strength in this area was so great that it was the equivalent of what I have been told was once demonstrated on a late night TV show—an actor, challenged to prove the old adage that a really good actor could hold his audience merely by reading the phone book to them, said it was so. He proceeded to take a phone book and demonstrate the fact. Not merely the studio audience, but those watching the program at home were caught up in his recitation of the names from the page before him. He was able to move them emotionally merely by the way in which he read the names aloud.

The ability to do this sort of thing is never something that can be explained merely in terms of the craft of acting. It goes beyond that craft into a sort of individual and personal genius, which is unmatchable by anyone else. It can be duplicated by another actor, but only by his own, different genius in his own different, unique way.

The same is true of people in pictorial art and in music. Beyond craft there is art. And art depends upon this untouchable, indescribable unique creativity.

Yet it is creativity which comes from and is also a part of the whole person who writes successfully. Robert, like every other writer, was in a sense what he wrote; and to the elements of what he was as a person, names can be given. He was a very strong man—strong in the sense of attitude and belief. He was strong in what he knew and in what he knew he knew.

He was very much his own man. He was a person of deep loyalties and affections, and at the same time someone who was completely unhesitating in calling a spade a spade. He lived in a world of loyalties, obligations, manners, and an unhesitating facing of facts. The result was that he could be devastatingly outspoken when the need called for it, as in one of his letters to his editor of *Astounding* magazine, John Campbell, himself a man of strong pattern.

To Campbell on one occasion Robert wrote: *"So far as I have observed you, you would no more think of going off half-cocked, with insufficient and unverified data with respect to a matter of science than you would stroll down Broadway in your underwear. But when it comes to matters outside your specialties you are consistently and brilliantly stupid. You come out with some of the Goddamnedest flat-footed opinions with respect to matters which you haven't studied and have had no experience, basing your opinions on casual gossip, newspaper stories, unrelated individual data, out of matrix, armchair extrapolation and plain misinformation—unsuspected because you haven't attempted to verify it . . ."*

At the same time Robert showed the remarkable sensitivity necessary to writers who can touch readers so strongly as he was able to do. It was a sensitivity linked to another necessary quality in one who would write well—a fascination with all aspects of human beings and their lives.

He had fenced for the Naval Academy, during his four years there prior to graduation. His weapon was sabre. In later years when he and Virginia visited Germany, he was able to be introduced to a student dueling society (by then illegal but still quietly in existence) and be given a chance to cross sabres with the *schlagemeister* or "fencing instructor" of the society.

He told me about it afterwards.

"My wrists," he told me, "were always extremely strong. That was always my great advantage in sabre fencing. But when I crossed swords with the *schlagemeister* the difference between my strength and his in the wrist was so great I could barely feel his blade."

What he was referring to, of course, was that one of the ways a fencer measures the strength and intent of his opponent is by keeping a firm pressure of his own blade against that of the opponent. The sabre used in the dueling society bouts was an equivalent of the heavy German cavalry sabre. The normal modern fencing sabre is much lighter. Naturally after years of fighting with the heavier weapon the *schlagemeister* had developed unimaginable wrist strength.

Nowhere that I know of, does this appear in Robert's writing as a straight retelling of the incident itself. But the understanding he gained by the encounter, in deepening his general store of experience, inevitably deepened his writing as well, though in a way that it would be impossible to analyze.

I say this only because I have had similar experiences in which the emotion of discovering something entirely unexpected has fed into the emotion that later helped create the pattern of a story—and may unconsciously have affected other of my writing without my realizing it.

Another advantage in Robert's case of his desire to reach out and experience human elements that could be useful in his understanding of people, and therefore his effectiveness in portrayal of them, was an occasion in which he and Virginia were in Tahiti and they watched a firewalking ceremony.

This is a semi-religious rite in which people one by one walk barefoot over red-hot glowing coals for some distance down a narrow trench and, if their faith is great enough emerge at the far end without any sign of that great heat having burned the soles of their feet. Rash visitors in the past, tourists learn, have occasionally dared to try the firewalking and hopped off immediately with feet that had already started to swell to double their size.

Again, he had experienced. Once more, doing so had added to what he already knew and what therefore increased the reservoir from which he wrote.

Something like this may be more understandable to non-authors, if they look at the multitude of writers who have gone out of their way to know unusual experiences like this; and who have also been able to take a remarkable grip upon the reader's imagination, though seldom with a direct use of that experience as they knew it.

The experimentation is, in some way that we do not have the words to pin down, one of the strong requirements of the mind that can make real a creatively conceived story.

Writers occasionally do make direct and obvious use of their own personal background in telling their stories. The writing of Jack London is an immediate example. But the great majority do not. Even though that background is the source from which they draw the strengths of the stories they do write.

Isaac Asimov's academic background was in organic chemistry; and he taught biochemistry for a number of years at the college level.

None of his memorable novels are centered in chemistry. But it would be a mistake for example, not to recognize his improvement in correctness and plausibility in his novelization of the movie *Fantastic Voyage,* over that of the movie itself, was strongly fed by the depth of his knowledge of the human body. Not to speak of the advantages from his knowledge in other areas, for Asimov has the most wide ranging mind of any writer of the twentieth century, as the hundreds of nonfiction books he has written testify.

In the end the writer who has reached the artistic level and is given the publication he deserves, has an opportunity to reach out and affect more other human beings than anyone in any occupation except that of an unusually strong religious leader. That touching is part of, and continues to be a hallmark of his work throughout his working life time.

Yet the unknowable, indescribable spark that moves his writing from the area of craft to art remains an innate mystery in him; and on all others who write comparably memorable books of fiction.

Still, there can be no doubt that it is there. We are moved by it in their work; and we find it in them as people. Robert Heinlein was many things; it is impossible to encompass all he was in words, but there is one word in particular, unusual even among writers, but which can be applied to Robert, particularly, in his life as in his work.

Robert Heinlein was noble.

So is his work—inescapably. Every great writer is true to himself or herself because they cannot be otherwise. As a result, what they write resonates to what they are. It is this resonation that stays with us unmistakably after we finish the book, close it and put it down. It is also what touches us, alters us and stays with us through the rest of our own lives.

ROBERT A. HEINLEIN AND US

Joe Haldeman

Born in Oklahoma in 1943, Joe Haldeman grew up in several diverse locations in the U.S., such as Puerto Rico and Alaska. After receiving a B.S. degree in astronomy at the University of Maryland, he served in the Central Highlands of Vietnam as a combat engineer. He then pursued graduate work in computer sciences for a couple of years but dropped out to write. Among the many books he has written, The Forever War *and* Hemingway Hoax *are probably the best known. The former story was based on his personal experience as a soldier in Vietnam. He has received numerous honors, including Nebula and Hugo awards. He currently teaches science fiction writing and literature at M.I.T. one semester each year, splitting his residence between Florida and Massachusetts. In his spare time, he indulges in "omnivorous" reading, cooking, casino gambling, amateur astronomy, bicycling, fishing, canoeing, swimming, snorkeling, drawing and painting, gardening and guitar playing.*

It feels presumptuous for me to write an appreciation of Robert Heinlein, since there are so many people around who knew him more or less well during the half century he presided over American science fiction, and I knew him hardly at all. But it's also true that no man, including my own father, had as great an effect on my own eventual vocation (not a word I'm comfortable using, but it is more accurate than "job"), and I know there are dozens of women and men in the same position: most of the people below a certain age who write "hard" sf, and quite a few who write the other stuff. Let me claim to be writing this short memoir for all of us, then, and apologize for (and weakly justify) its personal nature by hoping that some of the anecdotes are representative of other people's long-distance relationships with this strange and important man.

I've just turned forty-five, so it was about thirty-seven years ago that Mrs. Chappars, my kindly and wise fourth-grade teacher, saw that I was drawing spaceships when I should have been paying attention to arithmetic, and instead of punishing me, loaned me a copy of *Red Planet*. I think I read it over one breathless weekend, and then read it again. Then I found out you could get more of this great stuff by looking under "Heinlein" at the library. (Nazis on the Moon! Galactic Empires! Interplanetary intrigue! Alien invaders! Wow!)

Heinlein was the first author I sought out, but here's a curious memory for someone who wound up being a writer: I didn't at first realize the name belonged to a person. I thought it was a kind of brand name, like Campbell's Soup. Campbell's Superman, he was, but I didn't know about that at the time.

Of course the library wasn't enough. I could save up my paper-route and poker quarters and buy new Heinleins at the drug store or slightly shabby ones at the Estate Book Shop. I compared notes with friends and we traded the duplicate used ones like baseball cards, a good *Puppet Masters* for an okay *Man Who Sold the Moon* missing two stories plus a beat-up *Day After Tomorrow*.

In that strange summer between eighth and ninth grade, between early puberty and desperate puberty, I learned to type by copying *The Green Hills of Earth*. I made what I thought were improvements. Critics accuse a lot of us of doing that for a living.

Starship Troopers came out when I was a senior in high school; *Stranger in a Strange Land* when I was a freshman in college. It was perfect timing for a generation poised facing a decade of war and rebellion. Many a late-night-to-dawn dormitory gabfest was fueled by the motley grab-bag of ideas in those two books.

I studied the short stories in *Green Hills of Earth, The Menace From Earth,* and *The Man Who Sold the Moon.* To ease off my senior year course load, I took a writing course, and wrote two blatantly Heinleinesque short stories, both of which later sold. (A couple of years before, I'd started a novel about a lunar colony that threatened to fling boulders at Earth. I was forty or fifty pages into it when *If* began serializing *The Moon is a Harsh Mistress.* We'd even used the same lunar launch site, proving conclusively that both of us could read a map. I said the hell with this writing business.)

Meanwhile the draft intervened. We were allowed two books in our Basic Training kit; I took *Cyrano de Bergerac* and *Glory Road.* A copy of *Green Hills* went to Vietnam with me. Once in a really dark hour, when it looked as if none of us would survive the year (three out of thirteen did), I wrote a long letter to Heinlein, thanking him for this and that. I carried it around for a while and eventually pitched it, not wanting to embarrass an old man or myself. He was about sixty then; not so old, as it turned out.

An odd parallel between his life and mine emerges here. He wanted to be a Navy man, but was disabled by tuberculosis and reluctantly left the service. I wanted to be an astronaut, through NASA's Scientist-as-Astronaut program, but came back from Vietnam so thoroughly shot up that I would never be the athletic stable intellectual type they were looking for.

Both of us wound up writing science fiction, ostensibly for the money. Heinlein did all kinds of neat things first—mining, running for office, architecture, real estate—and all I actually did was turn my back on graduate school. But he hadn't had Heinlein to use as an example. Just write every day and keep sending them out, and if you have any talent, sooner or later you'll make a living at it.

I first met him at a Nebula Banquet, in 1975, when he was named the first Grand Master. I was too shy to go to his table and introduce myself. Incredibly, he came to *me;* he walked over and shook my hand and said "I like your stuff." My wife says it was a week before my feet touched the floor. When I won the Nebula the next year, for *The Forever War,* his letter of congratulations meant more than the award itself.

He could be downright mushy about women and children and animals and the land, but about death he was, according to occasion, sarcastic or mystical or hard-boiled; no foolish consistencies. I wouldn't dishonor his memory or trivialize his passing by dragging out banal sentimentalities. Every science fiction writer knows how profoundly he or she was affected by the man, embracing or rejecting his style and substance. He was central to this small universe, and for a long time, anyone who enters it will have to deal with him.

THE RETURN OF WILLIAM PROXMIRE

Larry Niven

Larry Niven was born in 1938 in Los Angeles. He entered Caltech in 1956 but flunked out after discovering a bookstore packed with used science fiction magazines. He eventually received a B.A. in mathematics with a minor in psychology from Washburn University. Caltech's loss was Washburn's gain. However, since the university was hit by a tornado a month after his graduation, it might be difficult now to establish how outstanding his academic performance was. One might surmise it, however, from an honorary Doctor of Letters degree that he received in 1984 from that university. His first published story was "The Coldest Place" in Worlds of If. *Among numerous honors, he has won Hugo and Nebula awards. Perhaps the most popular of his books are* Ringworld *and its sequels. His collaborative works with Jerry Pournelle* The Mote in God's Eye, Lucifer's Hammer, Oath of Fealty, *and* Footfall *have been phenomenally successful.*

Through the peephole in Andrew's front door the man made a startling sight.

He looked to be in his eighties. He was breathing hard and streaming sweat. He seemed slightly more real than most men: photogenic as hell, tall and lean, with stringy muscles and no pot belly, running shoes and a day pack and a blue windbreaker, and an open smile. The face was familiar, but from where?

Andrew opened the front door but left the screen door locked. "Hello?"

"Doctor Andrew Minsky?"

"Yes." Memory clicked. "William Proxmire, big as life."

The ex-Senator smiled acknowledgment. "I've only just finished reading about you in the *Tribune,* Dr. Minsky. May I come in?"

It had never been Andrew Minsky's ambition to invite William Proxmire into his home. Still— "Sure. Come in, sit down, have some coffee. Or do your stretches." Andrew was a runner himself when he could find the time.

"Thank you."

Andrew left him on the rug with one knee pulled against his chest. From the kitchen he called, "I never in my life expected to meet you face to face. You must have seen the article on me and Tipler and Penrose?"

"Yes. I'm prepared to learn that the media got it all wrong."

"I bet you are. Any politician would. Well, the *Tribune* implied that what we've got is a time machine. Of course we don't. We've got a schematic based on a theory. Then again, it's the new improved version. It doesn't involve an infinitely long cylinder that you'd have to make out of neutronium—"

"Good. What would it cost?"

Andrew Minsky sighed. Had the politician even recognized the reference? He said, "Oh . . . hard to say." He picked up two cups and the coffee pot and went back in. "Is that it? You came looking for a time machine?"

The old man was sitting on the yellow rug with his legs spread wide apart and his fingers grasping his right foot. He released, folded his legs heel to heel, touched forehead to toes, held, then stood up with a sound like popcorn popping. He said, "Close enough. How much would it cost?"

"Depends on what you're after. If you—"

"I can't get you a grant if you can't name a figure."

Andrew set his cup down very carefully. He said, "No, of course not."

"I'm retired now, but people still owe me favors. I want a ride. One trip. What would it cost?"

Andrew hadn't had enough coffee yet. He didn't feel fully awake. "I have to think out loud a little. Okay? Mass isn't a problem. You can go as far back as you like if . . . mmm. Let's say under sixty years. Cost might be twelve, thirteen million if you could also get us access to the proton-antiproton accelerator at Washburn University, or maybe CERN in Switzerland. Otherwise we'd have to build that too. By the way, you're not expecting to get younger, are you?"

"I hadn't thought about it."

"Good. The theory depends on maneuverings between event points. You don't ever go backward. Where and when, Senator?"

William Proxmire leaned forward with his hands clasped. "Picture this. A Navy officer walks the deck of a ship, coughing, late at night in the 1930s. Suddenly an arm snakes around his neck, a needle plunges into his buttocks—"

"The deck of a ship at sea?"

Proxmire nodded, grinning.

"You're just having fun, aren't you? Something to do while jogging, now that you've retired."

"Put it this way," Proxmire said. "I read the article. It linked up with an old daydream of mine. I looked up your address. You were within easy running distance. I hope you don't mind?"

Oddly enough, Andrew found he didn't. Anything that happened before his morning coffee was recreation.

So dream a little. "Deck of a moving ship. I was going to say it's ridiculous, but it isn't. We'll have to deal with much higher velocities. Any point on the Earth's surface is spinning at up to half a mile per second and circling the sun at eighteen miles per. In principle I think we could solve all of it with one stroke. We could scan one patch of deck, say, over a period of a few seconds, then integrate the record into the program. Same coming home."

"You can do it?"

"Well, if we can't solve that one we can't do anything else either. You'd be on a tight schedule, though. Senator, what's the purpose of the visit?"

"Have you ever had daydreams about a time machine and a scope-sighted rifle?"

Andrew's eyebrows went up. "Sure, what little boy hasn't? Hitler, I suppose? For me it was always Lyndon Johnson. Senator, I do not commit murder under any circumstances."

"A time machine and a scope-sighted rifle, and me," William Proxmire said dreamily. "I get more anonymous letters than you'd believe, even now. They tell me that every space advocate day-dreams about me and a time machine and a scope-sighted rifle. Well, I started daydreaming too, but my fantasy involves a time machine and a hypodermic full of antibiotics."

Andrew laughed. "You're plotting to do someone good behind his back?"

"Right."

"Who?"

"Robert Anson Heinlein."

All laughter dropped away. "Why?"

"It's a good deed, isn't it?"

"Sure. Why?"

"You know the name? Over the past forty years or so I've talked to a great many people in science and in the space program. I kept hearing the name Robert Heinlein. They were seduced into science because they read Heinlein at age twelve. These were the people I found hard to deal with. No grasp of reality. Fanatics."

Andrew suspected that the Senator had met more of these than he realized. Heinlein spun off ideas at a terrific rate. Other writers picked them up . . . along with a distrust for arrogance combined with stupidity or ignorance, particularly in politicians.

"Well, Heinlein's literary career began after he left the Navy because of lung disease."

"You're trying to destroy the space program."

"Will you help?"

Andrew was about to tell him to go to Hell. He didn't. "I'm still talking. Why do you want to destroy the space program?"

"I didn't, at first. I was opposed to waste," Proxmire said. "My colleagues, they'll spend money on any pet project, as if there was a money tree out there somewhere—"

"Milk price supports," Andrew said gently. For several decades now, the great state of Wisconsin had taken tax money from the other states so that the price they paid for milk would stay *up*.

Proxmire's lips twitched. "Without milk price supports, there would be places where families with children can't buy milk."

"Why?"

The old man shook his head hard. "I've just remembered that I don't have to answer that question any more. My point is that the government has spent far more taking rocks from the Moon and photographs from Saturn. Our economy would be far healthier if that money had been spent elsewhere."

"I'd rather shoot Lyndon. Eliminate Welfare. Save a *lot* more money that way."

"A minute ago you were opposed to murder."

The old man did have a way with words. "Point taken. Could you get us funding? It'd be a guaranteed Nobel Prize. I like the fact that you don't need a scope-sighted rifle. A hypo full of sulfa drugs doesn't have to be kept secret. What antibiotic?"

"I don't know what cures consumption. I don't know which year or what ship. I've got people to look those things up, if I decide I want to know. I came straight here as soon as I read the morning paper. Why not? I run every day, any direction I like. But I haven't heard you say it's impossible, Andrew, and I haven't heard you say you won't do it."

"More coffee?"

"Yes, thank you."

Proxmire left him alone in the kitchen, and for that Andrew was grateful. He'd have made no progress at all if he'd had to guard his expression. There was simply too much to think about.

He preferred not to consider the honors. Assume he had changed the past; how would he prove it before a board of his peers? "How would I prove it *now?* What would I have to show them?" he muttered under his breath, while the coffee water was heating. "Books? Books that didn't get written? Newspapers? There are places that'll print any newspaper headline I ask for. 'Waffen SS to Build Work Camp in Death Valley.' I can mint Robert Kennedy half-dollars for a lot less than thirteen million bucks. Hmm . . ." But the Nobel Prize wasn't the point.

Keeping Robert Heinlein alive a few years longer: was *that* the point? It shouldn't be. Heinlein wouldn't have thought so.

Would the science fiction field really have collapsed without the Menace From Earth? Tradition within the science fiction field would have named Campbell, not Heinlein. But think: was it magazines that had sucked Andrew Minsky into taking advanced physics classes? Or . . . *Double Star, Red Planet,* Anderson's *Tau Zero,* Vance's *Tschai* series. Then the newsstand magazines, then the subscriptions, then (of course) he'd dropped it all to pursue a career. If Proxmire's staff investigated his past (as they must, if he was at all serious), they would find that Andrew Minsky, Ph.D., hadn't read a science fiction magazine in fifteen years.

Proxmire's voice came from the other room. "Of course it would be a major chunk of funding. But wouldn't my old friends be surprised to find me backing a scientific project! How's the coffee coming?"

"Done." Andrew carried the pot in. "I'll do it," he said. "That is, I and my associates will build a time machine. We'll need funding and we'll need active assistance using the Washburn accelerator. We should be ready for a man-rated experiment in three years, I'd think. We won't fail."

He sat. He looked Proxmire in the eye. "Let's keep thinking, though. A Navy officer walks the tilting deck of what would now be an antique Navy ship. An arm circles his throat. He grips the skinny wrist and elbow, bends the wrist downward and throws the intruder into the sea. They train Navy men to fight, you know, and he was young and you are old."

"I keep in shape," Proxmire said coldly. "A medical man who performs autopsies once told me about men and women like me. We run two to five miles a day. We die in our eighties and nineties and hundreds. A fall kills us, or a car accident. Cut into us and you find veins and arteries you could run a toy train through."

He was serious. "I was afraid you were thinking of taking along a blackjack or a trank gun or a Kalashnikov—"

"No."

"I'll say it anyway. Don't hurt him."

Proxmire smiled. "That would be missing the point."

And if that part worked out, Andrew would take his chances with the rest.

He had been reaching for a beer while he thought about revising the time machine paper he'd done with Tipler and Penrose four years ago. Somewhere he'd shifted over into daydreams, and that had sent him off on a weird track indeed.

It was like double vision in his head. The time machine (never built) had put William Proxmire (the ex-Senator!) on the moving deck of the *USS Roper* on a gray midmorning in December, 1933. Andrew never daydreamed this vividly. He slapped his flat belly, and wondered why, and remembered: he was ten pounds heavier in the daydream, because he'd been too busy to run.

So much detail! Maybe he was remembering a sweaty razor-sharp nightmare from last night, the kind in which you know you're doing something bizarrely stupid, but you can't figure out how to stop.

He'd reached for a Henry Weinhard's (Budweiser) from the refrigerator in his kitchen (in the office at Washburn, where the Weinhard's always ran out first) while the project team watched their monitors (while the KCET funding drive whined in his living room.) In his head there was double vision, double memories, double sensations. The world of quantum physics was blurred in spots. But this was his kitchen and he could hear KCET begging for money a room away.

Andrew walked into his living room and found William Proxmire dripping on his yellow rug.

No, wait. That's the other—

The photogenic old man tossed the spray hypo on Andrew's

couch. He stripped off his hooded raincoat, inverted it and dropped it on top. He was trying to smile, but the fear showed through. "Andrew? What I am doing *here?*"

Andrew said, "My head feels like two flavors of cotton. Give me a moment. I'm trying to remember two histories at once."

"I should have had more time. And then it should have been the Washburn accelerator! You said!"

"Yeah, well, I did and I didn't. Welcome to the wonderful world of Schröedinger's Cat. How did it go? You found a young Lieutenant Junior Grade gunnery officer alone on deck—" The raincoat was soaking his cushions. "In the rain—"

"Losing his breakfast overside in the rain. Pulmonary tuberculosis, consumption. Good riddance to an ugly disease."

"You wrestled him to the deck—"

"Heh heh heh. No. I told him I was from the future. I showed him a spray hypo. He'd never seen one. I was dressed as a civilian on a Navy ship. That got his attention. I told him if he was Robert Heinlein I had a cure for his cough."

"'Cure for his cough'?"

"I didn't say it would kill him otherwise. I didn't say it wouldn't, and he didn't ask, but he may have assumed I wouldn't have come for anything trivial. I knew his name. This was Heinlein, not some Wisconsin dairy farmer. He *wanted* to believe I was a time traveller. He *did* believe. I gave him his shot. Andrew, I feel cheated."

"Me too. Get used to it." But it was Andrew who was beginning to smile.

The older man hardly heard; his ears must be still ringing with that long-dead storm. "You know, I would have liked to talk to him. I was supposed to have twenty-two minutes more. I gave him his shot and the whole scene popped like a soap bubble. *Why* did I come back *here?"*

"Because we never got funding for research into time travel."

"Ah . . . hah. There *have* been changes. What changes?"

It wasn't just remembering; it was a matter of selecting pairs of memories that were mutually exclusive, then judging between them. It was maddening . . . but it could be done. Andrew said, "The Washburn accelerator goes with the time machine goes with the funding. My apartment goes with no time machine goes with no funding goes with . . . Bill, let's go outside. It should be dark by now."

Proxmire didn't ask why. He looked badly worried.

The sun had set, but the sky wasn't exactly black. In a line across a smaller, dimmer full Moon, four rectangles blazed like windows into the sun. Andrew sighed with relief. Collapse of the wave function: *this* was reality.

William Proxmire said, "Don't make me guess."

"Solar power satellites. Looking Glass Three through Six."

"What happened to your time machine?"

"Apollo Eleven landed on the Moon on July 20, 1969, just like clockwork. Apollo Thirteen left a month or two early, but something still exploded in the service module, so I guess it wasn't a meteor. They . . . shit."

"Eh?"

"They didn't get back. They died. We murdered them."

"Then?"

Could he put it back? Should he put it back? It was still coming together in his head. "Let's see, NASA tried to cancel Apollo Eighteen, but there was a hell of a write-in campaign—"

"Why? From whom?"

"The spec-fic community went absolutely apeshit. Okay, Bill, I've got it now."

"Well?"

"You were right, the whole science fiction magazine business just faded out in the 'fifties, last remnants of the pulp era. Campbell alone couldn't save it. Then in the sixties the literary crowd rediscovered the idea. There must have been an empty ecological niche and the lit-crits moved in.

"Speculative fiction, spec-fic, the literature of the possible. The *New Yorker* ran spec-fic short stories and critical reviews of novels. They thought *Planet of the Apes* was wonderful, and *Selig's Complaint,* which was Robert Silverberg's study of a telepath. Tom Wolfe started appearing in *Esquire* with his bizarre alien cultures. I can't remember an issue of the *Saturday Evening Post* that didn't have *some* spec-fic in it. Anderson, Vance, MacDonald . . . John D. MacDonald turns out novels set on a ring the size of Earth's orbit.

"The new writers were good enough that some of the early ones couldn't keep up, but a few did it by talking to hard science teachers. Benford and Forward did it in reverse. Jim Benford's a plasma physicist but he writes like he swallowed a college English teacher. Robert Forward wrote a novel called *Neutron Star,* but he built the Forward Mass Detector too."

"Wonderful."

"There's a lot of spec-fic fans in the military. When Apollo Twenty-One burned up during reentry, they raised so much hell that Congress took the manned space program away from NASA and gave it to the Navy."

William Proxmire glared and Andrew Minsky grinned. "Now, you left office in the '60s because of the Cheese Boycott. When you tried to chop the funding for the Shuttle, the spec-fic community took offense. They stopped eating Wisconsin cheese. The San Francisco *Locus* called you the Cheese Man. Most of your supporters must have eaten nothing but their own cheese for about eight months, and then Goldwater chopped the milk price supports. 'Golden Fleece,' he called it. So you were out, and now there's no time machine."

"We could build one," Proxmire said.

Rescue Apollo Thirteen? The possibility had to be considered . . . Andrew remembered the twenty years that followed the Apollo flights. In one set of memories, lost goals, pointlessness and depression, political faddishness leading nowhere. In the other, half a dozen space stations, government and military and civilian; Moonbase and Moonbase Polar; *Life* photographs of the Mars Project half-finished on the lunar plain, sitting on a hemispherical Orion-style shield made from lunar aluminum and fused lunar dust.

I do not commit murder under any circumstances.

"I don't think so, Bill. We don't have the political support. We don't have the incentive. Where would a Nobel Prize *come* from? We can't prove there was ever a time line different from this one. Besides, this isn't just a more interesting world, it's safer too. Admiral Heinlein doesn't let the Soviets build spacecraft."

Proxmire stopped breathing for an instant. Then, "I suppose he wouldn't."

"Nope. He's taking six of their people on the Mars expedition, though. They paid their share of the cost in fusion bombs for propulsion."

Greg Benford called me in March of 1988. He wanted new stories about alternate time tracks for an anthology. I told him that the only sideways-in-time story in my head was totally unsaleable. It's just recreation, daydreaming, goofing off. It's about how William Proxmire uses a time machine and a hypodermic full of sulfa drugs to wipe out the space program.

Greg made me write it.

I called Robert to get dates and other data, and asked if I could use his name. I had so much fun with this story! I made lots of copies and sent them to friends. I sent one to Robert, of course. That was only a few weeks before his death.

And now I'm thinking that sometimes I really luck out. Robert's death feels bad enough, but it would be one notch worse if I didn't know he'd read this story.

Elsewhere you will read of a personal debt: the full proofreading job he did on *The Mote in God's Eye.*

Can you imagine what his life would have been like, if all the would-be writers out there had learned that *Robert Heinlein* could be persuaded to *do* that? He was kind of reluctant to claim credit for the final shaping of *Mote;* but it was his.

Robert Heinlein was the science fiction writer who cracked the mainstream and put the rest of us on the road to respectability and big bucks.

Half the people in the space program, today and for this past half century, were lured in by Robert Heinlein and those who followed his path.

Ideas are the cheapest thing in this business. The idea that creates a best-selling novel isn't worth half the money; it's worth a bottle of scotch or brandy, you name the brand. We all know it; but who taught us?

The ideas in any Robert Heinlein novel have guided other writers through a dozen books. He couldn't use them as fast as they came. The water bed, the linear accelerator or mass driver, muscle-powered wings for low gravity, the "Universe" ship, were all his. (I called them "slowboats.")

He was the man most likely to see his ideas used by others. He liked it; he must have considered it flattering. When Theodore Sturgeon was suffering from writer's block, Robert mailed him a list of something like fifty story ideas. Ted used that list for the rest of his life.

He lived an interesting and involving life. He married one of the more admirable human beings. They made each other rich. Josef Stalin may have influenced more people directly, but in the long run Robert Heinlein may have had a greater effect on the future. He was admired and envied for more than half a century, by the brightest human beings on Earth.

His death wasn't sudden or unexpected. He was not cut off in his prime.

So why were most of the Science Fiction Writers of America acting like we'd been shot?

Well, it just seemed—just this once—Death would make an exception. This was **Heinlein.**

RAH RAH R.A.H.!

Spider Robinson

Spider Robinson was born in the Bronx, New York in 1948. He has a B.A. in English from the State University of New York and began writing professionally in 1972. Many honors have been bestowed on his writing, including Hugo and Nebula awards. His recent novels include Time Pressure and Callahan's Lady. *He collaborated with his wife, Jeanne Robinson, a former dance choreographer and dancer, in writing* Star Dance, *which won triple awards. He has two articles here. The first piece,* Rah, Rah, R.A.H.! *was originally published in* Destinies *over a decade ago. The second one,* Robert, *has been written for this volume.*—Editor.

Concerning "Rah Rah R.A.H.!":
    When Jim Baen left Galaxy, *shortly before I did, it was to become SF editor of Ace Books. Ace promptly became the largest publisher of SF in the world, printing more titles in 1977 than any other house.*
    Suddenly Jim found himself in custody of a great many cheese sandwiches.
    So he built the magazine he had always wanted Galaxy *to be and couldn't afford to make it, and he named it* Destinies. *It was a quarterly paperback bookazine from Ace, a book filled with fiction and speculative fact and artwork and all the little extras that make up a magazine, and it was the most consistently satisfying and thought-provoking periodical that came into my house, not excluding* Omni *and the* Scientific American. *I did review columns for the*

first five issues, dropping out for reasons that in retrospect seem dumb.

So one day shortly after I quit writing reviews for Destinies, *Jim called and offered me a proposition: he would send me a xerox of the newest Robert Heinlein manuscript, months in advance of publication, if I would use the book as a springboard for a full-length essay on the lifework of Heinlein, for* Destinies. *The new book was* Expanded Universe, *which by now you will almost certainly have seen and therefore own; let me tell you, it blew me away.*

The following is what came spilling out of me when I was done reading Expanded Universe—*and when I used it as my Guest of Honor speech at Boskone, the 1980 Boston SF convention, it was received with loud and vociferous applause. Perhaps I overestimated the amount of attention people pay to critics. Perhaps the essay was unnecessary.*

But oooh *it was fun!*

A swam of petulant blind men are gathered around an elephant, searching him inch by inch for something at which to sneer. What they resent is not so much that he towers over them, and can see farther than they can imagine. Nor is it that he has been trying for nearly half a century to warn them of the tigers approaching through the distant grasses downwind. They do resent these things, but what they really, bitterly resent is his damnable contention that they are not blind, *his insistent claim that they can open up their eyes any time they acquire the courage to do so.*

Unforgivable.

How shall we repay our debt to Robert Anson Heinlein?

I am tempted to say that it can't be done. The sheer size of the debt is staggering. He virtually invented modern science fiction, and did not attempt to patent it. He opened up a great many of SF's frontiers, produced the first reliable maps of most of its principal territories, and did not complain when each of those frontiers filled up with hordes of johnny-come-latelies, who the moment they got off the boat began to complain about the climate, the scenery and the employment opportunities. I don't believe there can be more than a handful of science fiction stories published in the last forty years that do not show his influence one way or another. He has written the definitive time-travel stories

("All You Zombies—" and "By His Bootstraps"), the definitive longevity books (*Methuselah's Children* and *Time Enough For Love*), the definitive theocracy novel (*Revolt in 2100*), heroic fantasy/SF novel (*Glory Road*), revolution novel (*The Moon Is a Harsh Mistress*), transplant novel (*I Will Fear No Evil*), alien invasion novel (*The Puppet Masters*), technocracy story ("The Roads Must Roll"), arms race story ("Solution Unsatisfactory"), technodisaster story ("Blowups Happen"), and about a dozen of the finest science fiction juveniles ever published. These last alone have done more for the field than any other dozen books. And perhaps as important, he broke SF out of the pulps, opened up "respectable" and lucrative markets, broached the wall of the ghetto. He continued to work for the good of the entire genre: his most recent book sale was a precedent-setting event, representing the first-ever SFWA Model Contract signing. (The Science Fiction Writers of America has drawn up a hypothetical ideal contract, from the SF writer's point of view—but until *Expanded Universe*— no such contract had ever been signed.) Note that Heinlein did not do this for his own benefit: the moment the contract was signed it was renegotiated *upward.*

You *can't* copyright ideas; you can only copyright specific arrangements of words. If you could copyright ideas, every living SF writer would be paying a substantial royalty to Robert Heinlein.

So would a lot of other people. In his spare time Heinlein invented the waldo and the waterbed (and God knows what else), and he didn't patent them either. (The first waldos were built by Nathan Woodruff at Brookhaven National Laboratories in 1945, three years after Heinlein described them for a few cents a word. As to the waterbed, see *Expanded Universe.*) In addition he helped design the spacesuit as we now know it.

Above all Heinlein is better educated, more widely read and traveled than anyone I have ever heard of, and has consistently shared the Good Parts with us. He has learned prodigiously, and passed on the most interesting things he's learned to us, and in the process passed on some of his love of learning to us. Surely that is a mighty gift. When I was five years old he began to teach me to love learning, and to be skeptical about what I was taught, and he did the same for a great many of us, directly or indirectly.

How then shall we repay him?

Certainly not with dollars. Signet claims 11.5 million Heinlein books in print. Berkley claims 12 million. Del Rey figures are not available, but they have at least a dozen titles. His latest novel fetched a record price. Extend those figures worldwide, and it starts to look as though Heinlein is very well repaid with dollars. But consider at today's prices you could own all forty-two of his books for about a hundred dollars plus sales tax. Robert Heinlein has given me more than a C-note's worth of entertainment, knowledge and challenging skullsweat, more by several orders of magnitude. His books do *not* cost five times the price of Philip Roth's latest drool; hence they are drastically underpriced.

We can't repay him with awards, nor with honors, nor with prestige. He has a shelf-full of Hugos (voted by his readers), the first-ever Grand Master Nebula for Lifetime Contribution to Science Fiction (voted by his fellow writers), he is an *Encyclopaedia Britannica* authority, he is the only man ever to be a World Science Fiction Convention Guest of Honor three times—it's not as though he needs any more flattery.

We can't even thank him by writing to say thanks—we'd only make more work for his remarkable wife Virginia, who handles his correspondence these days. There are, as noted, *millions* of us (possibly hundreds of millions)—a quick thank-you apiece would cause the U.S. Snail to finally and forever collapse—and if they were actually delivered they would make it difficult for Heinlein to get any work done.

I can think of only two things we could do to thank Robert Heinlein.

First, give blood, now and as often as you can spare a half hour and a half pint. It pleases him; blood donors have saved his life on several occasions. (Do you know the *I Will Fear No Evil* story? The plot of that book hinged on a character having a rare blood type; routine [for him] research led Heinlein to discover the National Rare Blood Club; he went out of his way to put a commercial for them in the forematter of the novel. After it was published he suffered a medical emergency, requiring transfusion. Surprise: Heinlein has a rare blood type. His life was saved by Rare Blood Club members. There is a persistent rumor, which I am unable to either verify or disprove, that at least one of those donors had joined because they read the blurb in *I Will Fear No Evil*.)

The second suggestion also has to do with helping to ensure Heinlein's personal survival—surely the sincerest form of flattery. Simply put, we can all do the best we personally can to assure that the country Robert Heinlein lives in is not ruined. I think he would take it kindly if we were all to refrain from abandoning civilization as a failed experiment that requires too much hard work. (I think he'll make out okay even if we don't—but he'd be a lot less comfortable.) I think he would be pleased if we abandoned the silly delusion that there are any passengers on Starship Earth, and took up our responsibilities as crewmen—as he has.

Which occasionally involves giving the Admiral your respectful attention. Even when the old fart's informed opinions conflict with your own ignorant prejudices.

The very size of the debt we all owe Heinlein has a lot to do with the savagery of the recent critical assaults on him. As Jubal Harshaw once noted, gratitude often translates as resentment. SF critics, parasitic on a field which would not exist in anything like its present form or size without Heinlein, feel compelled to bite the hand that feeds them. Constitutionally unable to respect anything insofar as it resembles themselves, some critics are compelled to publicly display disrespect for a talent of which not one of them can claim the tenth part.

And some of us pay them money to do this.

Look, Robert Heinlein is not a god, not even an angel. He is "merely" a good and great man, and a good and great writer, no small achievements. But there seems to be a dark human compulsion to take the best man around, declare him a god, and then scrutinize him like a hawk for the sign of human weakness that will allow us to slay him. Something in us likes to watch the mighty topple, and most especially the good mighty. If someone wrote a book alleging that Mother Teresa once committed a venial sin, it would sell a million copies.

And some of the cracks made about Robert Heinlein have been pretty personal. Though the critics swear that their concern is with criticizing literature, few of them can resist the urge to criticize Heinlein the man.

Alexei Panshin, for instance, in *Heinlein in Dimension,* asserts as a biographical fact, without disclaimer of hearsay, that Heinlein "cannot stand to be disagreed with, even to the point of discarding friendships." I have heard this allegation quoted several times in the twelve years since Panshin committed it to print. Last week I received a review copy of Philip K. Dick's new short story collection, *The Golden Man* (Berkley); I quote from its introduction:

* * *

I consider Heinlein to be my spiritual father, even though our
political ideologies are totally at variance. Several years ago,
when I was ill, Heinlein offered his help, anything he could do,
and we had never met; he would phone me to cheer me up and
see how I was doing. He wanted to buy me an electric typewriter,
God bless him—one of the few true gentlemen in this world. *I
don't agree with any ideas he puts forth in his writing, but that is
neither here nor there.* One time when I owed the IRS a lot of
money and couldn't raise it, Heinlein loaned the money to me.
    . . . he knows I'm a flipped-out freak and still he helped me and
my wife when we were in trouble. That is the best in humanity,
there; that is who and what I love.

> *(italics mine—SR)*

Full disclosure here: Robert Heinlein has given me, personally, an
autograph, a few gracious words, and a couple of hours of
conversation. Directly. But when I was five he taught me, with the
first and weakest of his juveniles, three essential things: to make up
my own mind, always; to think it through *before* doing so; to get
the facts *before* thinking. Perhaps someone else would have taught
me those things sooner or later; that's irrelevant: it was Heinlein
who did it. That is who and what *I* love.

Free speech gives people the right to knock who and what I love;
it also gives me the right to rebut.

Not to "defend." As to the work, there it stands, invulnerable to
noise made about it. As to the man, he once said that "It is
impossible to insult a man who is not unsure of himself." Fleas
can't bite him. Nor is there any need to defend his literary
reputation; people who read what critics tell them to deserve what
they get.

No, I accepted this commission because I'm personally annoyed. I grow weary of hearing someone I love slandered; I have
wasted too many hours at convention parties arguing with loud
nits, seen one too many alleged "reference books" take time out to
criticize Heinlein's alleged political views and literary sins, heard
one too many talentless writers make speeches that take potshots
at the man who made it possible for them to avoid honest work. At
the next convention party I want to be able to simply hand that
loud nit a copy of *Destinies* and go back to having fun.

So let us consider the most common charges made against
Heinlein. I arrange these in order of intelligence, with the most
brainless first.

I. Personal Lapses

(Note: all these are most-brainless, as not one of the critics is in any position to know anything about Heinlein the man. The man they attack is the one they infer from his fiction: a mug's game.)

(1) *"Heinlein is a fascist."* This is the most popular Heinlein shibboleth in fandom, particularly among the young—and, of course, exclusively among the ignorant. I seldom bother to reply, but in this instance I am being paid. Dear sir or madam: kindly go to the library, look up the dictionary definition of fascism. For good measure, read the history of fascism, asking the librarian to help you with any big words. Then read the works of Robert Heinlein, as you have plainly not done yet. If out of forty-two books you can produce one shred of evidence that Heinlein—or any of his protagonists—is a fascist, I'll eat my copy of *Heinlein in Dimension.*

(2) *"Heinlein is a male chauvinist."* This is the second most common charge these days. That's right, Heinlein populates his books with dumb, weak, incompetent women. Like Sister Maggie in "If This Goes On—"; Dr. Mary Lou Martin in "Let There Be Light"; Mary Sperling in *Methuselah's Children;* Grace Cormet in "—We Also Walk Dogs"; Longcourt Phyllis in *Beyond This Horizon;* Cynthia Craig in "The Unpleasant Profession of Jonathan Hoag"; Karen in "Gulf"; Gloria McNye in "Delilah and the Space-Rigger"; Allucquere in *The Puppet Masters;* Hazel and Edith Stone in *The Rolling Stones;* Betty in *The Star Beast;* all the women in *Tunnel in the Sky;* Penny in *Double Star;* Pee Wee and the Mother Thing in *Have Space Suit—Will Travel;* Jill Boardman, Becky Vesant, Patty Paiwonski, Anne, Miriam and Dorcas in *Stranger in a Strange Land;* Star, the Empress of Twenty Universes, in *Glory Road;* Wyoh, Mimi, Sidris and Gospazha Michelle Holmes in *The Moon Is a Harsh Mistress;* Eunice and Joan Eunice in *I Will Fear No Evil;* Ishtar, Tamara, Minerva, Hamadryad, Dora, Helen Mayberry, Llita, Laz, Lor and Maureen Smith in *Time Enough For Love;* and Dejah Thoris, Hilda Corners, Gay Deceiver and Elizabeth Long in *"The Number of the Beast—."**

Brainless cupcakes all, eh? (Virtually every one of them is a world-class expert in at least one demanding and competitive field; the exceptions plainly will be as soon as they grow up. Madame Curie would have enjoyed chatting with any one of them.) Helpless housewives! (Any one of them could take Wonder Woman three falls out of three, and polish off Jirel of Joiry for dessert.)

*An incomplete list, off the top of my head.

I think one could perhaps make an excellent case for Heinlein as a *female* chauvinist. He has repeatedly insisted that women average smarter, more practical and more courageous than men. He consistently underscores their biological and emotional superiority. He married a woman he proudly described to me as "smarter, better educated and more sensible than I am." In his latest book, *Expanded Universe*—the immediate occasion for this article—he suggests without the slightest visible trace of irony that the franchise be taken away from men and given exclusively to women. He consistently created strong, intelligent, capable, independent, sexually aggressive women characters for a quarter of a century *before* it was made a requirement, right down to his supporting casts.

Clearly we are still in the area of delusions which can be cured simply by reading Heinlein while awake.

(3) *"Heinlein is a closet fag."* Now, this one I have only run into twice, but I include it here because of its truly awesome silliness, and because one of its proponents is Thomas Disch, himself an excellent writer. In a speech aptly titled, "The Embarrassments of Science Fiction," reprinted in Peter Nicholls' *Explorations of the Marvelous,* Disch asserts, with the most specious arguments imaginable, that there is an unconscious homosexual theme in *Starship Troopers.* He apparently feels (a) that everyone in the book is an obvious fag (because they all act so macho, and we all know that all macho men are really fags, right? Besides, some of them wear jewelry, as *real* men have never done in all history.); (b) that Heinlein is clearly unaware of this (because he never overtly raises the issue of the sex habits of infantry in a book intended for children and published in 1962), and (c) that (a) and (b), stipulated and taken together, would constitute some kind of successful slap at Heinlein or his book or soldiers . . . or something. Disch's sneers at "swaggering leather boys" (I can find no instance in the book of anyone wearing leather) simply mystify me.

The second proponent of this theory was a young woman at an SF convention party, ill-smelling and as ugly as she could make herself, who insisted that *Time Enough For Love* proved that Heinlein wanted to fuck himself. I urged her to give it a try, and went to another party.

(4) *"Heinlein is right wing."* This is not *always* a semantic confusion similar to the "fascist" babble cited above; occasionally the loud nit in question actually has some idea of what "right wing" means, and is able to stretch the definition to fit a man who

bitterly opposes military conscription, supports consensual sexual fredom and women's ownership of their bellies, delights in unconventional marriage customs, champions massive expenditures for scientific research, suggusts radical experiments in government; and; has written with apparent approval of anarchists, communists, socialists, technocrats, limited-franchise-republicans, emperors and empresses, capitalists, dictators, thieves, whores, charlatans and even career civil servants (Mr. Kiku in *The Star Beast*). If this indeed be conservatism, then Teddy Kennedy is a liberal, and I am Marie of Romania.

And if there *were* anything to the allegation, when exactly was it that the conservative viewpoint was proven unfit for literary consumption? I missed it.

(5) *"Heinlein is an authoritarian."* To be sure, respect for law and order is one of Lazarus Long's most noticeable characteristics. Likewise Jubal Harshaw, Deety Burroughs, Fader McGee, Noisy Rhysling, John Lyle, Jim Marlowe, Wyoming Knott, Manuel Garcia O'Kelly-Davis, Prof de la Paz and Dak Broadbent. In his latest novel, *"The Number of the Beast—,"* Heinlein seems to reveal himself authoritarian to the extent that he suggests a lifeboat can have only one captain at a time. He also suggests that the captain be elected, by unanimous vote.

(6) *"Heinlein is a libertarian."* Horrors, no! How dreadful. Myself, I'm a serf.*

(7) *"Heinlein is an elitist."* Well, now. If by that you mean that he believes some people are of more value to their species than others, I'm inclined to agree—with you and with him. If you mean he believes a learned man's opinion is likely to be worth more than that of an ignoramus, again I'll go along. If by "elitist" you mean that Heinlein believes the strong should rule the weak, I strongly *dis*agree. (Remember frail old Professor de la Paz, and Waldo, and recall that Heinlein himself was declared "permanently and totally disabled" in 1934.) If you mean he believes the wealthy should exploit the poor, I refer you to *The Moon Is a Harsh Mistress* and *I Will Fear No Evil*. If you mean he believes the wise should rule the foolish and the competent rule the incompetent, again I plead guilty to the same offense. *Somebody's* got to drive—should it not be the best driver?

---

*I know it sounds crazy, but I've heard "libertarian" used as a pejorative a few times lately.

How do you *pick* the best driver? Well, Heinlein has given us a multiplicity of interesting and mutually exclusive suggestions; why not examine them?

(8) *"Heinlein is a militarist."* Bearing in mind that he abhors the draft, this is indeed one of his proudest boasts. Can there really be people so naive as to think that their way of life would survive the magic disappearance of their armed forces by as much as a month? Evidently; I meet 'em all over.

(9) *"Heinlein is a patriot."* (Actually, they always say "superpatriot." To them there is no other kind of patriot.) Anyone who sneers at patriotism—and continues to *live* in the society whose supporters he scorns—is a parasite, a fraud, or a fool. Often all three.

Patriotism does not mean that you think your country is perfect, or blameless, or even particularly likeable on balance; nor does it mean that you serve it blindly, go where it tells you to go and kill whom it tells you to kill. It means that you are committed to keeping it alive and making it better, that you will do whatever seems necessary (up to and including dying) to protect it whenever you, personally, perceive a mortal threat to it, military or otherwise. This is something to be ashamed of? I think Heinlein has made it abundantly clear that in any hypothetical showdown between species patriotism and national patriotism the former, for him, would win hands down.

(10) *"Heinlein is an atheist,"* or *"agnostic,"* or *"solipsist,"* or *"closet fundamentalist,"* or *"hedonistic Calvinist,"* or . . . Robert Heinlein has consistently refused to discuss his personal religious beliefs; in one of his stories a character convincingly argues that it is *impossible* to do so meaningfully. Yet everyone is sure they know where he stands. *I* sure don't. The one thing I've *never* heard him called (yet) is a closet Catholic (nor am I suggesting it for a moment), but in my new anthology, *The Best of All Possible Worlds* (Ace Books), you will find a story Heinlein selected as one of his personal all-time favorites, a deeply religious tale by Anatole France (himself generally labeled an agnostic) called "Our Lady's Juggler," which I first heard in Our Lady of Refuge grammar school in the Bronx, so long ago that I'd forgotten it until Heinlein jogged my memory.

In any event his theology is none of anybody's damned business. God knows it's not a valid reason to criticize his fiction.

(11) *"Heinlein is opinionated."* Of course, I can't speak for him, but I suspect he would be willing to accept this compliment. The

people who offer it as an insult are always, of course, as free of opinions themselves as a newborn chicken.

Enough of personal lapses. What are the indictments that have been handed down against Heinlein's *work,* his failures as a science fiction writer? Again, we shall consider the most bone-headed charges first.

II. Literary Lapses

(1) *"Heinlein uses slang."* Sorry. Flat wrong. It is *very* seldom that one of his *characters* uses slang or argot; he in authorial voice never does. What he uses that is *miscalled* "slang" are idiom and colloquialism. I won't argue the (to me self-evident) point that a writer is *supposed* to preserve them—not at this time, anyway. I'll simply note that you can't very well criticize a man's use of a language whose terminology you don't know yourself.

(2) *"Heinlein can't create believable women characters."* There's an easy way to support this claim: simply disbelieve in all Heinlein's female characters, and maintain that all those who believe them are gullible. You'll have a problem, though: several of Heinlein's women bear a striking resemblance to his wife Virginia, you'll have to disbelieve in her, too—which could get you killed if your paths cross. Also, there's a lady I once lived with for a long time, who used to haunt the magazine stores when *I Will Fear No Evil* was being serialized in *Galaxy,* because she could not wait to read the further adventures of the "unbelievable" character with whom she identified so strongly—you'll have to disbelieve in her, too.

Oddly, this complaint comes most often from radical feminists. Examination shows that Heinlein's female characters are almost invariably highly intelligent, educated, competent, practical, re-sourceful, courageous, independent, sexually aggressive and suffi-ciently personally secure to be able to stroke their men's egos as often as their own get stroked. I will—reluctantly—concede that this does *not* sound like the average woman as I have known her, but I am bemused to find myself in the position of trying to convince *feminists* that such women can in fact exist.

I think I know what enrages the radicals: two universal characteristics of Heinlein heroines that I left out of the above list. They are always beautiful and proud of it (regardless of whether they happen to be pretty), and they are often strongly interested in having babies. *None* of them bitterly regrets and resents having been born female—which of course makes them not only traitors to their exploited sex, but unbelievable.

(3) *"Heinlein's male characters are all him."* I understand this notion was first put forward by James Blish in an essay titled, "Heinlein, Son of Heinlein," which I have not seen. But the notion was developed in detail by Panshin. As he sees it, there are three basic male personae Heinlein uses over and over again, the so-called Three-Stage Heinlein Individual. The first and youngest stage is the bright but naive youth; the second is the middle-aged man who knows how the world works; the third is the old man who knows how it works and why it works, knows how it got that way. All three, Panshin asserts, are really Heinlein in the thinnest of disguises. (Sounds like the average intelligent man to me.)

No one ever does explain what, if anything, is *wrong* with this, but the implication seems to be that Heinlein is unable to get into the head of anyone who does not think like him. An interesting theory—if you overlook Dr. Ftaeml, Dr. Mahmoud, Memtok, David McKinnon, Andy Libby, all the characters in "Magic, Inc." and "And He Built a Crooked House," Noisy Rhysling, the couple in "It's Great To Be Back," Lorenzo Smythe, The Man Who Traveled in Elephants, Bill Lermer, Hugh Farnham, Jake Salomon, *all* the extremely aged characters in *Time Enough For Love,* all the extremely young characters in *Tunnel in the Sky* except Rod Walker, and all four protagonists of *"The Number of the Beast—"* (among many others). Major characters all, and none of them fits on the three-stage age/wisdom chart. (Neither, by the way, does *Heinlein*—who was displaying third-stage wisdom and insight in his early thirties.)

If all the male Heinlein characters that *can* be forced into those three pigeonholes are Heinlein in thin disguise, why is it that I have no slightest difficulty in distinguishing (say) Juan Rico from Thorby, or Rufo from Dak Broadbent, or Waldo from Andy Libby, or Jubal Harshaw from Johann Smith? If Heinlein writes in characterizational monotone, why don't I confuse Colonel Dubois, Colonel Baslim and Colonel Manning? Which of the four protagonists of *"The Number of the Beast—"* is the *real* Heinlein, and how do you know?

To be sure, some generalizations can be made of the majority of Heinlein's heroes—he seems fascinated by competence, for example, whereas writers like Pohl and Sheckley seem fascinated by incompetence. Is this a flaw in *any* of these three writers? If habitual use of a certain type of character *is* a literary sin, should we not apply the same standard to Alfred Bester, Kurt Vonnegut,

Phil Dick, Larry Niven, Philip Roth, Raymond Chandler, P.G. Wodehouse, J.P. Donleavy and a thousand others?

(4) *"Heinlein doesn't describe his protagonists physically."* After I have rattled off from memory extensive physical descriptions of Lazarus and Dora and Minerva Long, Scar Gordon, Jubal Harshaw and Eunice Branca, complainers of this type usually add, "unless the mechanics of the story require it." Thus amended, I'll chop it—as evidence of the subtlety of Heinlein's genius. A maximum number of his readers can identify with his characters.

What these types are usually complaining about is the absence of any *poetry* about physical appearance, stuff like, "Questing eyes like dwarf hazelnuts brooded above a strong yet amiable nose, from which depended twin parentheses framing a mouth like a pink Eskimo Pie. Magenta was his weskit, and his hair was the color of mild abstraction on a winter's morning in Antigonish." In Heinlein's brand of fiction, a picture is seldom worth a thousand words—least of all a portrait.

But I have to admit that Alexei Panshin put his finger on the fly in the ointment on p. 128 of *Heinlein in Dimension:* ". . . while the reader doesn't notice the lack of description while he reads, afterwards individual characters aren't likely to stand out in the mind." In other words, if you leave anything to the reader's imagination, you've lost better than half the critics right there. Which may be the best thing to do with them.

(5) *"Heinlein can't plot."* One of my favorite parts of *Heinlein in Dimension* is the section on plot. On p. 153 Panshin argues that Heinlein's earliest works are flawed because "they aren't told crisply. They begin with an end in mind and eventually get there, but the route they take is a wandering one." On the *very next page* Panshin criticizes Heinlein's later work for *not* wandering, for telling him only those details necessary to the story.

> In "Gulf," for instance, Heinlein spends one day in time and 36 pages in enrolling an agent. He then spends six months, skimmed over in another 30-odd pages, in training the agent. Then, just to end the story, he kills his agent off in a job that takes him one day, buzzed over in a mere 4 pages. The gradual loss of control is obvious.

Presumably the significant and interesting parts of Panshin's life come at steady, average speed. Or else he wanted the boring and irrelevant parts of Joe's life thrown in to balance some imaginary set of scales. (Oh, and just to get the record straight, it is clearly stated in "Gulf" that Joe's final mission takes him many days.)

All written criticism I have seen of Heinlein's plotting comes down to this same outraged plaint: that if you sit down and make an outline of the sequence of events in a Heinlein story, it will most likely not come out symmetrical and balanced. Right you are: it won't. It will just *seem* to sort of ramble along, just like life does, and at the end, when you have reached the place where the author wanted you to go, you will look back at your tracks and fail to discern in them any mathematical pattern or regular geometric shape. If you keep looking, though, you'll notice that they got you there in the shortest possible distance, as straightforwardly as the terrain allowed. And that you hurried.

That they cannot be described by any simple equation is a sign of Heinlein's excellence, not his weakness.

(6) *"Heinlein can't write sex scenes."* This one usually kicks off an entertaining hour defining a "good sex scene." Everybody disagrees with everybody on this, but most people I talk to can live with the following four requirements: a "good" sex scene should be believable, consensual (all parties consenting), a natural development of the story rather than a pasted-on attention-getter, and, hopefully, sexually arousing.

In order: Heinlein has never described *any* sexual activity that would cause either Masters or Johnson even mild surprise. In forty-two books I can recall only one scene of even attempted rape (unsuccessful, fatally so) and two depictions of extremely mild spanking. I have found *no* instances of gratuitous sex, tacked on to make a dull story interesting, and I defy anyone to name one.

As to the last point, if you have spent any time at all in a pornshop (and if you haven't, why not? Aren't you at all curious about people?) you'll have noticed that *none* of the clientele is aroused by more than five to ten percent of the available material. Yet it all sells or it wouldn't be there. One man's meat is another man's person. Heinlein's characters may not behave in bed the way you do—so what?

It has been argued by some that "Heinlein suddenly started writing about sex after ignoring it for years . . ." They complain that all of Heinlein's early heroes, at least, are Boy Scouts. Please examine any reasonably complete bibliography of early Heinlein —the one in the back of *Heinlein in Dimension* will do fine. Now: if you exclude from consideration (a) juvenile novels, in which Heinlein *could not* have written a sex scene, any more than any juvenile-novelist could have in the forties and fifties; (b) stories sold to John Campbell, from which Kay Tarrant cut all sex no matter who the author; (c) stories aimed at and sold to "respectable," slick, non-SF markets which were already breaking enough taboos by buying science fiction at all; (d) tales in which no sex subplot was appropriate to the story; and (e) stories for *Boys' Life* whose protagonists were *supposed* to be Boy Scouts; what you are left with as of 1961 is two novels and two short stories, all rife with sex. Don't take *my* word, go look it up. In 1961, with the publication of *Stranger in a Strange Land,* Heinlein became one of the first SF writers to openly discuss sex at any length, and he has continued to do so since. (Note to historians: I know Farmer's "The Lovers" came nine years earlier—but note that the story did not appear in book form until 1961, the same year as *Stranger* and a year after Sturgeon's *Venus Plus X.*) I know vanishingly few septuagenarians whose view of sex is half so liberal and enlightened as Heinlein's—damn few people of *any* age, more's the pity.

(7) *"Heinlein is preachy."* "preachy: inclined to preach." "preach: to expound upon in writing or speech; especially, to urge acceptance of or compliance with (specified religious or moral principles)."

Look: the classic task of fiction is to create a character or characters, give he-she-or-them a problem or problems, and then show his-her-their struggle to find a solution or solutions. If it doesn't do that, comparatively few people will pay cash for the privilege of reading it. (Rail if you will about "archaic rules stifling creative freedom": that's the way readers are wired up, and *we* exist for *their* benefit.) Now: if the solution proposed does not involve a moral principle (extremely difficult to pull off), you have a cookbook, a how-to manual, Spaceship Repair for the Compleat Idiot. If no optimal solution is suggested, if the problem is left unsolved, there are three possibilities: either the writer is propounding the *moral principle* that some problems have no optimal solutions (e.g. "Solution Unsatisfactory" by R.A.H.), or the writer is suggesting that *some*body should find a solution to this dilemma because it beats the hell out of him, or the writer has simply been telling you a series of pointless and depressing anecdotes, speaking at great length without saying anything (e.g. most of modern mainstream litracha). Perhaps this is an enviable skill, for a politician, say, but is it really a requirement of good fiction?

Exclude the above cases and what you have left is a majority of all the fiction ever written, and the overwhelming majority of the good fiction.

But one of the oddities of humans is that while we all want our fiction to propose solutions to moral dilemmas, we do not want to admit it. Our writers are *supposed* to answer the question, "What is moral behavior?"—but they'd better not let us catch them palming that card. (Actually, Orson and I are just good friends.) The pill must be heavily sugar-coated if we are to swallow it. (I am not putting down people. *I'm* a people. That bald apes can be cajoled into moral speculation by any means at all is a miracle, God's blessing on us all. Literature is the antithesis of authoritarianism and of most organized religions—which seek to replace moral speculation with laws—and in that cause we should all be happy to plunge our arms up to the shoulders in sugar.)

And so, when I've finished explaining that "preachy" is a *complimentary* thing to call a writer, the people who made the charge usually backpedal and say that what they *meant* was

(8) *"Heinlein lectures at the expense of his fiction."* Here, at last, we come to something a little more than noise. This, if proved, would seem a genuine and serious literary indictment.

Robert Heinlein himself said in 1950:

> A science fiction writer may have, and often does have, other
> motivations in *addition to* pursuit of profit. He may wish to
> create "art for art's sake," he may want to warn the world
> against a course he feels disastrous (Orwell's *1984*, Huxley's
> *Brave New World*—but please note that each is intensely
> entertaining, and that each made stacks of money), he may wish
> to urge the human race toward a course which he considers
> desirable (Bellamy's *Looking Backward*, Wells' *Men Like Gods*),
> he may wish to instruct, to uplift, or even to dazzle. But the
> science fiction writer—any fiction writer—must keep
> entertainment consciously in mind as his prime purpose . . . or
> he may find himself back dragging that old cotton sack.

> (from "Pandora's Box," reprinted
> in *Expanded Universe*)

The charge is that in his most recent works, Robert Heinlein has subordinated entertainment to preaching, that he has, as Theodore Sturgeon once said of H.G. Wells' later work, "sold his birthright for a pot of message." In evidence the prosecution adduces *I Will Fear No Evil, Time Enough For Love,* the second and third most recent Heinlein novels, and when *"The Number of the Beast—"* becomes generally available, they'll probably add that one too.

Look: nobody wants to be lectured to, right? That is, no one wants to be lectured to by some jerk who doesn't know any more than they do. But do not good people, responsible people, enlightened citizens, *want* to be lectured to by someone who knows more than they do? Have we really been following Heinlein for forty years because he does great card tricks? Only?

Defense is willing to stipulate that, proportionately speaking, all three of People's Exhibits tend to be—*by comparison with early Heinlein*—rather long on talk and short on action (*Time Enough For Love* perhaps least so of the three). Defense wishes to know, however, what if anything is wrong with that, and offers for consideration *Venus Plus X, Triton, Camp Concentration* and *The Thurb Revolution.*

I Will Fear No Evil concerns a man whose brain is transplanted into the body of a healthy and horny woman; to his shock, he learns that the body's original personality, its soul, is still present in his new skull (or perhaps, as Heinlein is careful not to rule out, he has a sustained and complex hallucination to that effect). She teaches him about how to be female, and in the process learns something of what it's like to be male. Is there any conceivable way to handle this theme *without* lots of internal dialogue, lots of sharing of opinions and experiences, and a minimum of fast-paced action? Or is the theme itself somehow illegitimate for SF?

Time Enough For Love concerns the oldest man in the Galaxy (by a wide margin), who has lived *so* long that he no longer longs to live. But his descendants (and by inescapable mathematical logic most of the humans living by that point *are* his descendants) will not let him die, and seek to restore his zest for living by three perfectly reasonable means: they encourage him to talk about the Old Days, they find him something *new* to do, and they smother him with love and respect. Do not all of these involve a lot of conversation? As I mentioned above, this book *has* action aplenty, when Lazarus gets around to reminiscing (and lying); that attempted-rape scene, for instance, is a small masterpiece, almost a textbook course in how to handle a fight scene.

But who says that ideas are not as entertaining as fast-paced action?

"The Number of the Beast—" (I know, on the cover of the book it says *The Number of the Beast,* without quotes or dash; that is the publishers' title. I prefer Heinlein's.) I hesitate to discuss this book as it is unlikely you can have read it by now and I don't want to

spoil any surprises (of which there are many). But I will note that there is more action here than in the last two books put together, and—since all four protagonists are extraordinarily educated people, who love to argue—a whole lot of lively and spirited dialogue. I also note that its basic premise is utterly, delightfully preposterous—and that I do not believe it can be disproved. (Maybe Heinlein and Phil Dick aren't *that* far apart after all.) It held my attention most firmly right up to the last page, and indeed holds it yet.

Let me offer some more bits of evidence.

One: According to a press release which chanced to land on my desk last week, three of Berkley Publishing Company's top ten all-time bestselling SF titles are *Stranger in a Strange Land, Time Enough For Love,* and *I Will Fear No Evil.*

Two: In the six years since it appeared in paperback, *Time Enough For Love* has gone through thirteen printings—a feat it took both *Stranger in a Strange Land* and *The Moon Is a Harsh Mistress* ten years apiece to achieve.

Three: Gregg Press, a highly selective publishing house which brings out quality hardcover editions of what it considers to be the finest in SF, has already printed an edition of *I Will Fear No Evil,* designed to survive a thousand readings. It is one of the youngest books on the Gregg List.

Four: *The Notebooks Of Lazarus Long,* a 62-page excerpt from *Time Enough For Love* comprising absolutely *nothing but opinions,* without a shred of action, narrative or drama, is selling quite briskly in a five-dollar paperback edition, partially hand-lettered by D.F. Vassallo. I know of no parallel to this in all SF (unless you consider Tolkien "SF").

Five: Heinlein's latest novel, *"The Number of the Beast—,"* purchased by editors who, you can assume, knew quite well the dollars-and-cents track record of Heinlein's last few books, fetched an all-time genre-record-breaking half a million dollars.

Plainly the old man has lost his touch, eh? Mobs of customers, outraged at his failure to entertain them, are attempting to drown him in dollars.

What's that? You there in the back row, speak up. You say *you* aren't entertained, and that proves Heinlein isn't entertaining? Say, aren't you the same person I saw trying to convince that guy from the New York *Times* that SF is not juvenile brainless adventure but the literature of ideas? Social relevance and all that?

What that fellow in the back row means is not that ideas and opinions do not belong in a science fiction novel. He means he disagrees with some of Heinlein's opinions. (Even that isn't strictly accurate. From the noise and heat he generates in venting his disagreement, it's obvious that he hates and bitterly resents Heinlein's opinions.)

I know of many cases in which critics have disagreed with, or vilified, or forcefully attacked Robert Heinlein's opinions. A few were even able to accurately identify those opinions.* I know of none who has succeeded in *disproving,* demonstrating to be false, a single one of them. I'm sure it could happen, but I'm still waiting to see it.

Defense's arms are weary from hauling exhibits up to the bench; perhaps this is the point at which Defense should rest.

Instead I will reverse myself, plead guilty with an explanation, and throw myself on the mercy of the court. I declare that I *do* think the sugar-coating on Heinlein's last few books is (comparatively) thin, and not by accident or by failure of craft. I believe there is a good reason *why* the plots of the last three books allow and require their protagonists to preach at length. Moral, spiritual, political and historical lessons which he once would have spent at least a novelette developing are lately fired off at the approximate rate of a half dozen per conversation. That his books do *not* therefore fall apart the way Wells' last books did is only because Heinlein is incapable of writing dull. Over four decades it has become increasingly evident that he is not the "pure entertainment" song and dance man he has always claimed to be, that he has sermons to preach—and the customers keep coming by the carload. Furthermore, with the passing of those four decades, the urgency of his message has grown.

And so now, with his very latest publication, *Expanded Universe,* Heinlein has finally blown his cover altogether. I think that makes *Expanded Universe,* despite a significant number of flaws, the single most important and valuable Heinlein book ever published.

Let me tell you a little about the book. It is built around a previously available but long out of print Heinlein collection, *The Worlds of Robert A. Heinlein,* but it has been expanded by about 160%, with approximately 125,000 words of new material, for a total of about 202,500 words. Some of the new stuff is fiction, although little of it is science fiction (about 17,500 words). But the bulk of the new material, about 84,000 words, is nonfiction. Taken

---

*—As distinct from the opinions of his protagonists.

together it's as close as Heinlein is ever going to get to writing his memoirs, and it forms his ultimate personal statement to date. In ten essays, a polemic, one and a half speeches and extensive forewords and afterwords for most of thirteen stories, Heinlein lets us further inside his head then he ever has before. And hey, you know what? He doesn't resemble Lazarus Long much at all.

For instance, although he is plainly capable of imagining and appreciating it, Heinlein is not himself able to sustain Lazarus' magnificent ingrained indifference to the fate of any society. Unlike Lazarus, Heinlein loves the United States of America. He'll tell you why, quite specifically, in this book. Logical, pragmatic reasons why. He will tell you, for instance, of his travels in the Soviet Union, and what he saw and heard there. If, after you've heard him out, you still don't think that for all its warts (hell, running sores), the United States is the planet's best hope for an enlightened future, there's no sense in us talking further; you'll be wanting to pack. (Hey, have you heard? The current government of the People's Republic of China [half-life unknown] has allowed as how limited freedom of thought will be permitted this year. Provisionally.)* You know, the redneck clowns who chanted "America—love it or leave it!" while they stomped me back in the sixties didn't have a *bad* slogan. The only problem was that they got to define "love of America," and they limited its meaning to "blind worship of America." In addition they limited the definition of America to "the man in the White House."

These mistakes Heinlein certainly does not make. (Relevant quote from *Expanded Universe:* "Brethren and Sistren, have you ever stopped to think that *there has not been one rational decision out of the Oval Office for fifty years?*"—[italics his—SR]). In this book he identifies clearly, vividly and concisely the specific brands of rot that are eating out America's heart. He outlines each of the deadly perils that face the nation, and predicts their consequences. As credentials, he offers a series of fairly specific predictions he made in 1950 for the year 2000, updated in 1965, and adds 1980 updates supporting a claim of a sixty-six percent success rate— enormously higher than that of, say, Jeane Dixon. He pronounces himself dismayed not only by political events of the last few decades, but by the terrifying decay of education and growth of irrationalism in America. (Aside: in my own opinion, one of the best exemplars of this latter trend is Stephen King's current

*At press time, they have given every sign of having changed their minds.—SR.

runaway bestseller *The Stand,* a brilliantly entertaining parable in praise of ignorance, superstition, reliance on dreams, and the sociological insights of feeble-minded old Ned Ludd.)

It is worth noting in this connection that while Heinlein has many scathing things to say about the U.S. in *Expanded Universe,* he has prohibited publication of the book in any other country.* We don't wash family linen with strangers present. I don't know of any other case in which an SF writer deliberately (and drastically) limited his royalties out of patriotism, or for that matter any moral or ethical principle. I applaud.

Friends, one of the best educated and widely traveled men in America has looked into the future, and he is not especially optimistic.

It cannot be said that he despairs. He makes *many* positive, practical suggestions—for real cures rather than Band-Aids. He outlines specifically how to achieve the necessary perspective and insight to form intelligent extrapolations of world events, explains in detail how to get a decent education (by the delightful device of explaining how *not* to get one), badly names the three pillars of wisdom, and reminds us that "Last to come out of Pandora's Box was a gleaming, beautiful thing—eternal Hope."

But the last section of the book is a matched pair of mutually exclusive prophecies, together called "The Happy Days Ahead." The first is a gloomy scenario of doom, the second an optimistic scenario. He says, "I can risk great gloom in the first because I'll play you out with music at the end."

But I have to admit that the happy scenario, *Over the Rainbow,* strikes me as preposterously unlikely.

In fact, the only thing I can imagine that would increase its probability would be the massive widespread reading of *Expanded Universe.*

Which brings me to what I said at the beginning of this essay: if you want to thank Robert A. Heinlein, do what you can to see to it that the country he loves, the culture he loves, the magnificent ideal he loves, is not destroyed. If you have the wit to see that this old man has a genuine handle on the way the world wags, kindly stop complaining that his literary virtues are not classical and go back to doing what you used to do when SF was a ghetto-literature scorned by all the world: force copies of Heinlein on all your

---

*—at presstime I learn that the book can be obtained in Canada. I follow the logic; the two countries are Siamese Twins.

friends. Unlike most teachers, Heinlein has been successfully competing with television for forty years now. Anyone that *he* cannot—convert to rationalism is purely unreachable, and you know, there are a hell of a lot of people on the fence these days.

I do not worship Robert Heinlein. I do not agree with everything he says. There are a number of his opinions concerning which I have serious reservations, and perhaps two with which I flat-out disagree (none of which I have the slightest intention of washing with strangers present). But all of these tend to keep me awake nights, because the only arguments I can assemble to refute him are based on "my thirty years of experience," of a very limited number of Americans and Canadians—and I'm painfully aware of just how poorly that stacks up against his seventy-three years of intensive study of the entire population and the entire history of the planet.

And I repeat: if there is anything that can divert the land of my birth from its current stampede into the Stone Age, it is the widespread dissemination of the thoughts and perceptions that Robert Heinlein has been selling as entertainment since 1939. You can thank him, not by buying his book, but by *loaning out* the copy you buy to as many people as will sit still for it, until it falls apart from overreading. (Be sure and loan *Expanded Universe* only to fellow citizens.) Time is short: it is no accident that his latest novel devotes a good deal of attention to the subject of lifeboat rules. Nor that *Expanded Universe* contains a quick but thorough course in how to survive the aftermath of a nuclear attack. (When Heinlein said in his Guest of Honor speech at MidAmeriCon that "there will be nuclear war on Earth in your lifetime," some people booed, and some were unconvinced. But it chanced that there was a thunderstorm over the hotel next morning—and I woke up three feet in the air, covered with sweat.) Emergencies require emergency measures, so drastic that it will be hard to persuade people of their utter necessity.

If you want to thank Robert Heinlein, open your eyes and look around you—and begin loudly demanding that your neighbors do likewise.

Or—at the very least—please stop loudly insisting that the elephant is merely a kind of inferior snake, or tree, or large barrel of leather, or oversized harpoon, or flexible trombone, or . . .

(When I read the above as my Guest of Honor speech at the New England Science Fiction Association's annual regional convention,

Boskone, I took Heinlein's advice about playing them out with music literally, and closed with a song. I append it here as well. It is the second filksong* I've ever written, and it is set to the tune of Old Man River, *as arranged by Marty Paich on Ray Charles'* Ingredients in a Recipe For Soul. *[If you're not familiar with that arrangement, the scansion will appear to limp at the end.] Guitar chords are provided for would-be filksingers, but* copyright is reserved *for recording or publishing royalties, etc.)*

*A filksong is not a typo, but a generic term for any song or song-parody sung by or for SF fans.

Ol' Man Heinlein
(lyrics by Spider Robinson)

```
D        G7      D              G7
Ol' man Heinlein    That ol' man Heinlein
   D         A7          Bm         E7
He must know somethin'    His heart keeps pumpin'
   A        Asus          A    A+       D
He just keep writin'    And lately writin' 'em long


   D             G7           D        G7
He don't write for critics    Cause that stuff's rotten
   D          A7          Bm      E7
And them that writes it    Is soon forgotten
   A         Asus          A    A+    D
But ol' man Heinlein    keeps speculatin' along

F#m     C#7 F#m    C#7  F#m    C#7   F#m    C#7
You and me  Sit and think  Heads all empty except for drink
F#m       C#7 F#m    C#7  F#m       C#7    Em     A7
Tote that pen Jog that brain  Get a little check in the mail from Baen

D     G7         D      G7
I get bleary      And feel like shirkin'
   D         A7          Bm       E7
I'm tired of writin'      But scared of workin'
   A       Asus          A     A+      D
But ol' man Heinlein      He keeps on rollin' along

Abm     Eb7   Abm     Eb7   Abm      Eb7  Abm  Eb7
You and me   Read his stuff  Never can seem to get enough
Abm     Eb7 Abm       Eb7  Abm      Eb7  Abm  F#m    B7
Turn that page  Dig them chops Hope the old gentleman never stops


   E          A7         E    A7
So raise your glasses    It's only fittin'
   E    B          C#m  F#7
The best SF that was ever written
   E   E+    E6       Am      E     C#m   F#7 B7   E
Is Old Man Heinlein       May he live as long as Lazarus Long!
```

ROBERT

Spider Robinson

The Lone Ranger was hanging by his fingertips from—

(What has this to do with Robert Heinlein? Patience, friend. This may be the last time I will ever write about him for publication, and I intend to ramble.)

—by his fingertips from the edge of the cliff, not a silver bullet to his name, fifty Apache stamping on his knuckles, dozens of hungry wolves waiting at the base of the cliff, a suppurating flesh wound in his shoulder, and worst of all, Tonto was gone, mistakenly believed Kemo Sabe had betrayed him, wasn't even trying to save him, would go around after the Ranger was dead telling everyone what a fink that white guy turned out to be—

—when suddenly Mom remembered she had to do the dishes, and put the comic book down.

I have just described, in toto, my late mother's diabolically sneaky and terribly effective method for teaching her children to read. For my sister, Little Lulu was substituted for the Lone Ranger, but the basic principle was the same. Hook 'em, and then leave 'em alone with the comic book. I *had* to know what happened to the masked man; there were graphics to supply hints, and if a word gave me trouble I could refer back to text already read aloud to me and see if I could find it. By the time I was six,* a

---

*I have stated several times before, in print, that all this happened when I was *five,* because that's what Mom always said. As I was proofreading this piece, my wife proved to me that I must have been six, because my family did not move to Long Island until I was that age. I can only say that if my mother couldn't even manage to get my *name* right (she kept calling me by another first name until I was twenty), it's not too surprising that she fudged a date . . . In any case, it's time to set the record straight. Six, not five.

teacher reported to my mother that I was a freak reading prodigy, ready to tackle books which did *not* have pictures in them. Mom smiled . . .

And one day she handed me a magic talisman. A small card with my name on it. "Take this down to the library next to the candy store," she said, "and tell them to give you a book." I walked to the library (this was back when it was safe for six-year-olds to walk the streets unsupervised on Long Island) and there was taken in hand by a librarian. I do not remember her face or name, and have since been unsuccessful in trying to trace her, but I owe her a large debt of gratitude.

Because she sized me up, told me to wait right there, and came back with a volume entitled *Rocket Ship Galileo*.

The first and arguably the worst of the legendary Heinlein Juveniles (he himself so rated it), it concerned three boys who built a rocket ship in their spare time, with the help of Uncle Don the atomic scientist, and flew it to Luna, where they found die-hard Nazis hoping to put World War II into extra innings, and okay maybe it wasn't Shakespeare but there was no doubt at all in my six-year-old mind that it was what the doctor ordered and why the preacher danced. I devoured it, and pausing only to act out the entire story with my kid sister (she got to be Uncle Don Cargreaves and the Nazis; I played all three boys), I raced back to the library.

The librarian was a bit surprised to see me; it had been only twenty-four hours, and there were a lot of words in that book for a six-year-old. But I recall her smiling when I asked anxiously if she had any more of this. (Librarians are a little like crack dealers when it comes to addicting small children.) She nodded, and brought me *Red Planet*. I was a third of the way through it before I got it home. My sister enjoyed being Willis, the Martian bouncer . . .

Of course, this could only go on for so long. This was 1954: there were only eight Heinlein juveniles in existence, and *Starman Jones* and *The Star Beast* had not yet reached my library. By the second week, I was a strung-out six-year-old junkie facing Panic in Reading Park. The librarian tried me on some other authors— worthy ones, no doubt, but it was like giving aspirin to a cold turkey. She tried Tom Swift, about the only other SF there was for kids, and that helped but not enough. Finally I wore her down: she confessed that there were other Heinlein titles in the building, in the adult section . . . and that a kid who could get his Mom to write a letter to the Library could have his card stamped with a letter "A," *allowing him to take out adult books.* I was back with that letter the next day, because it took me most of the night to get my mother's handwriting and signature down cold, and soon I was facing *half a dozen new Heinleins.*

(Later there would be an enormous flap when my mother, a devout Catholic, idly picked up *The Puppet Masters,* stubbed her eyes on a rather mild sex scene, and wrote to the library assailing them for giving such things to children. She was very bemused when they showed her a letter of authorization in what she had to agree was her own handwriting . . . but that is another, and uglier, story.)

A week later, after twenty minutes of staring at that shelf, trying to make a new Heinlein materialize by sheer will power, I noticed something. *All* the books in that section had a yellow sticker on their spine, depicting a hydrogen atom being impaled by a V-1, just like the Heinlein books did. Perhaps they were in some way similar? I pulled down one at random. It was a Cyril Kornbluth collection . . .

Which is how I became a science fiction reader, which was crucial in my becoming a science fiction writer, from which every single thing in my life that I care a damn about has flowed, so it is fair to say that I owe virtually everything to Robert Anson Heinlein. (And to that anonymous librarian, bless her—and most of all to my mother!)

And the amazing thing is that mine is not even an unusual story. I venture to guess that half the SF readers alive could tell a similar one. He started many of us, at early ages.

I thought I was done with writing about Robert.

I really did. For publication, I mean. I don't think I've written many letters to friends that didn't quote him at least once in some connection or other, and it's impossible to advise a young writer without quoting him. But when I typed the number thirty at the end of the eulogy I contributed for the Heinlein Obit issue of *Locus,* I thought I was finally done with writing about him for print.

Some may have felt I had already gone rather overboard in that direction . . .

In 1980 I wrote, at the request of Jim Baen, the essay "Rah Rah R.A.H.!," which appears elsewhere in this volume. I knew when I wrote it that I was going to make some people mad . . . but I was angry myself. Still, I was relieved when, with some misgivings, I used it as my Guest of Honor speech at the 1980 Boston Science Fiction Convention, and received three separate standing ovations during its delivery and a fourth at its conclusion. It was pleasant to have confirmed what I had hoped: that Heinlein-bashers were loud out of all proportion to their numbers. The piece was duly printed in *New Destinies,* and excerpted for the jacket copy of *Expanded Universe,* and brought in a large amount of fan mail, every piece of it favorable.

Then one night, in the middle of a party, I got a phone call.

I won't say from whom. A Big Name. Someone I admire so much that the simple fact of a phone call from *him*—at this point I'd been in the business less than a decade myself—caused me to begin grinning and stammering almost as much as I would have had it been Robert himself. We chatted for a bit, and finally I asked to what I owed this call. —Well, he said, I wanted to do you a favor.

—Oh?

—Yeah, I heard through the grapevine that you're planning to include that Heinlein piece you wrote in your next story collection.

—That's right.

—Well, listen to your uncle: don't do it . . .

He would not say why not. The best I could get out of him was that certain people would be very pissed off if I did, and it might not be good for my long term career interest. It was all very well, he said, to publish such a thing in a magazine, that could be forgotten a week later, but book form was a very different proposition. And he just wanted to be sure someone was looking out for me, keeping me from stumbling into hot water through youth and inexperience. He hung up. —Who was that? my friends asked. —Oh, nobody, I said, and went back to my party.

I was mystified, baffled, and very unnerved. I mean, I *respected* this man—and still do. And I had no idea what he was talking about. I thought long and hard before deciding to ignore his advice.

And every time since that day that something has gone wrong with my career, every time a story that I was sure was good bounces or a book doesn't get reissued or a Best SF of the Year editor ignores me again, I wonder if I made a mistake in deciding to include "Rah Rah R.A.H.!" in my collection *Time Travelers Strictly Cash*. At the time that book was published, I had won a Nebula Award and been nominated for others; since its publication I have never received another nomination. In my happier hours, I tell myself this is coincidence, chance.

But I don't care either way. I had to write that essay, and will keep it in print for as long as they keep asking. Robert was my first, you see. He took my literary virginity. My first writer, the first adult I ever ran into who wasn't talking down to me, the man who taught me my craft and so much more.

So I've kept on writing about him, or about myself in relation to him, whenever I got an excuse, and I'm glad of another one now. Thank you, Yoji . . .

I once received three full credits in college for turning one person on to RAH. Armed only with a typewriter and a tape recorder, I produced a multimedia essay on his lifework to that point, incorporating eighty pages of text and ninety minutes of taped readings, and submitted it as term paper for an Independent Study project. It was so impassioned and so massively documented with textual references that I actually succeeded in persuading an English professor that the unicorn of Literature might conceivably exist from time to time somewhere in the dark forest of Science Fiction. This may seem a small thing in these times, when universities offer courses in SF and there are such things as SF academics, but in 1967 that woman was the first living human associated with the field of education who had ever conceded in my hearing that SF might occasionally be more than pernicious trash.

In 1975 the Nebula Awards Banquet was held in New York. I cadged a free ticket by agreeing to entertain as a folksinger prior to the awards ceremony. I'd have crashed if I'd had to: Robert Heinlein was being given the first ever Grand Master Nebula. I had been a professional writer for three years, I had never met Robert, and who knew how long he or I would live?

Before the banquet began, I joined the horde of SFWA members loitering in the lobby of the Algonquin, all of us hoping to catch a glimpse of the great man. I overheard several colleagues gleefully anticipating a bloodbath. "Haldeman actually had the nerve to show up," one of them chortled. "Heinlein'll rip his head off and drink out of the hole." Joe Haldeman, it must be explained, had just published his remarkable first novel *The Forever War*. These writers explained to me that since Joe had "stolen" "Heinlein's concept" of powered combat suits, and since his book embodied a certain disrespect for military traditions (grunts were *required* to shout obscene abuse at their officers every day, for example), Heinlein was sure to go for Joe's throat if he saw him. After all, everyone *knew* that Heinlein was a cranky old fascist . . .

Robert arrived, and the room swarmed around him. Jim Baen, who loved him more and better than any other editor he ever worked with, took on the task of making introductions. My companions' eyes lit up as Haldeman appeared, looking apprehensive but determined. Murmurs arose as he moved up in line, and reached the buzz stage as he stepped forward and Baen said, "Mr. Heinlein, I'd like to present Joe Haldeman, author of—"

"—*The Forever War,* of course," Robert said, striding forward and thrusting his hand out. "It is an honor to meet you, sir. That may be the best future war story I've ever read!"

A little while later Joe drifted away, his shoes an inch from the carpet, beaming aimlessly. My companions were quite disappointed . . .

A timeless time later Baen was presenting *me* . . . and Robert did it again. "Oh, you're the fellow who writes the Callahan's Bar stories. I like your stuff . . ."

I remember very little of the rest of that evening.

That's not true. Of unofficial events I recall only that Robert and Ginny were the most striking couple I had ever seen . . . and I have a vague memory of singing for them and the assembled company; I must have sung Jake Thackray's "Ulysses the Dog," because I remember sending Robert the lyrics at his request afterwards.

But I vividly recall the awarding of the Grand Master Nebula itself.

When it was announced, the entire room leaped to their feet as one and applauded for six solid minutes, the longest standing ovation I have ever witnessed. By the time they let him speak, Robert's cheeks were wet. "My brother, Major General Lawrence Heinlein," he said, his voice full with emotion, "once told me that there are only two promotions in life that mean a damn: from buck private to corporal, and from colonel to general officer. I made corporal decades ago . . . but now at long last I know what he meant about the other. Thank you." And we applauded him for another three minutes . . .

In 1976 I met him again, in Kansas City, when he was Guest of Honor at the World Science Fiction Convention. (He was the only person ever to have been a Worldcon GoH *three* times.) I stood on line for an hour in a villainously hot lobby to ask for his autograph. The following anecdote is excerpted from my anthology *The Best of All Possible Worlds:*

> Picture it. I stammer, a brash twenty-seven-year-old in the presence of my hero. He remembers my name. He likes my bar stories. He appreciates the nice reviews I've given him in *Galaxy.* I introduce my wife; he bows and makes small talk with her. I grin like a demented pumpkin and my heart goes thumpa thumpa—
> —then it skips a beat.
> Because he is looking down at the book I have carried a thousand miles for him to autograph. He has just signed umpteen hardcover copies of his newest novel, and now he sees clutched in my fist an extremely battered and tattered old paperback with the cover scotch-taped. It is a collection called *The Unpleasant Profession of Jonathan Hoag* (also called 6 X H). My necktie has come undone somehow, and I am perilously close to babbling.
> "Mr. Heinlein, sir, I fetched this particular book because it contains my single personal all-time favorite story of yours of all time, sir."
> He is used to people gibbering at him; he nods and waits politely.
> "It's called 'The Man Who Traveled in Elephants'—" and his face sags slightly and I panic oh hell what did I say wrong fix it fix it "—I mean, hell, that's just my opinion, who am I—" and then I break off, because whatever he is doing with his face is the opposite of frowning.
> "That," he says slowly, "is my own personal favorite—and no one's ever had a nice word to say for it until now."
> "Sir," I say fervently, "I have read that story ten times in nineteen years, and I have literally never seen that last paragraph when it wasn't blurry. I end up grinning and crying every time."
> Again he . . . almost recoils slightly, as though I've pinched him. "That was my single specific intention. You're the first person who's ever told me that I succeeded."

He signed my crumby paperback with a grand flourish, and I thanked him and floated away, moving my legs occasionally so as not to scare passersby.

I ended up editing *The Best of All Possible Worlds* solely so I would have an excuse to reprint "The Man Who Traveled in Elephants."

A brief word about that anthology, even though it is presently between printings: the concept, invented by Jim Baen, was that I should pick five of my all-time favorite little-known stories and reprint them . . . then go to the authors of those stories and ask each to pick, as companion piece to their own, *their* all-time favorite little-known story by someone else. In this way, we'd all get to share forgotten or overlooked treasures with the world. It worked out so well that I can't believe the damn thing is even temporarily out of print, but the point of relevance here is the story that Robert selected to accompany his:

"Our Lady's Juggler," by Anatole France.

If you don't know it, you'll have to go look up *The Best of All Possible Worlds,* because the only decent translation I've ever been able to find is the one I did myself for the book. For now I'll say only that it is a deeply religious story, which most Catholic school children have force fed to them at an early age. One of the characters is the Virgin Mary. It is also a profoundly moving story—but to have it selected by Robert Heinlein, widely considered one of the great Agnostics, as one of his favorites startled me considerably.

Which leads to another anecdote.

In Ed Regis's recent wonderful book *Great Mambo Chicken and the Transhuman Condition,* there is an entire chapter on the repeated efforts of Keith Henson and the Alcor Foundation to get Robert to agree to be cryogenically frozen after his death, in hopes of eventual resurrection. I was aware of this effort while it was going on: Henson wrote to me, entreating me to help him persuade Robert. I politely declined to argue with Robert on so personal a matter, but I certainly wished Henson luck: if any human I ever knew deserved even an outside chance at living forever, it was Robert Heinlein. And I could not help but wonder why he had turned Henson and the others down. They were willing to waive the usual fee for him. Sure, it was a long shot—but consider the prize! And what did he have to lose?

The day Robert died I was on the phone with Jim Baen, sharing the grief. At some point I brought the subject of cryonics up, and said I wished now I'd had the guts to at least ask Robert why he'd said no.

"I asked him once," Jim admitted . . .

So when I finally met Henson a few months ago, at a party at his home, I was able to tell him that I knew the answer to the mystery that had driven him crazy for so long. He was all ears . . . and then when I told him, he stared off into the far distance with a baffled, frustrated look and was silent for a long time.

"How do I know it wouldn't interfere with rebirth?" is what Robert told Jim . . .

Once Robert mailed me a cheque, out of the blue.

I was flabbergasted. He had met me twice, years before, heard me sing for ten minutes at a banquet, signed an autograph. Period. No other contact between us at that point. I was dead broke and about to miss a rent payment—I still do not see how he could have known that; even my agent and my parents didn't know—and the cheque was for exactly a hundred dollars more than the rent.

Too terrified to cash it, too desperate not to, I wrote at once and said that I did not know how he had divined my need, but I intended to treat the money as a loan at current interest rates. Ginny replied immediately that I was welcome to pay the money back if I wished (". . . without interest; we do not accept interest from friends . . .") but it was not necessary: if I wanted, I could pay the loan *forward* to some other starving colleague some day instead. To this day, the code for one of my bank-machine cards is derived from the date and amount of that loan . . . for there is no chance that I will ever forget them.

I know he did the same thing for Phil Dick, once—Phil wrote of it, saying he disagreed with every opinion Robert ever held, but that, "He knows that, knows I'm a flipped-out freak and still he helped me and my wife when we were in trouble. That is the best in humanity, there; that is who and what I love." Ted Sturgeon also told me several stories of Robert's generosity with money and ideas: among other things, he gave Ted the idea for his classic story, "'And Now the News—'."

Thank you, Robert, wherever you are now . . .

Then there was the time that he called long distance to say Happy Birthday to my daughter, whom he never met.

My family and I were in New York; Jeanne had been invited to dance with Beverly Brown Dancensemble at the Riverside Dance Festival. I wrote to Robert with a technical question about pressure suits, and mentioned that we were all enjoying New York, except that our daughter Luanna (now Terri) was a little scalded at being screwed out of a birthday party since she didn't know another kid in the Apple. Just a whimsical throwaway detail.

On Luanna's seventh birthday (*how did he know the date?*) he called (*how did he get the New York number?*). I started to stutter and fumfaw, and he said, "You and I can talk some other time: put Luanna on." And he spoke with her for over ten minutes. She seemed puzzled at first, to be speaking to an old man she'd never met, but she hung up smiling. She said that he told her "not to worry so much about dates, that I could have *two* birthdays, one when the calendar says, with you and Mom, and one when I get home to my friends. And a lot of other stuff I don't remember." She said that he was funny, but nice. She was clearly puzzled by the importance I seemed to attach to the event, but seemed to grasp that she should be flattered by it, and did her seven-year-old best.

A grand old gentleman.

I remember the time I got my hands on an advance review copy of *Friday.* I noticed that it was dedicated to Ginny and thirty other people, all female first names, several of them known to me to be SF writers, many unfamiliar. There was a Jeanne on the list.

"'ey," I said to my wife. "Heinlein dedicated a book to you!" "Go on," she said, "he met me once for ten seconds on an autograph line when he was Worldcon Guest of Honor; it's got to be some other writer named Jeanne."

The next day a hardcover copy of *Friday* arrived. In addition to the formal autograph in the flyleaf, the dedication page is inscribed, "To Jeanne (and Spider), Robert," and her name is circled.

He had style, he did.

Once I visited my cousin Clare at her office in New York. As I chatted, my eyes kept involuntarily, and inexplicably, sliding sideways to a bookshelf in the corner. I tried politely to keep my gaze on hers, but she caught me at it finally, and sighed, and said, "Go ahead; look." So I let my eyes go where they wanted. Of course! Clare is the children's books editor at Scribner's, successor to the one who worked with Robert. There on her wall were all the Heinlein Juveniles, original editions in alphabetical order, just the way they were in the library when I was six years old: a powerful subconscious gestalt.

"That happens with about half the visitors I get," Clare said.

His fighting spirit never left him, through countless medical crises over forty years—not even at the end, when emphysema racked him so cruelly. I spoke with him by phone not long before the end, when he had been hospitalized for the fourth time in a year: I called to speak with Ginny, but he insisted on coming on the line.

(In passing, I'd like to mention the extent of the debt all of us in SF owe to Virginia Heinlein. For four decades she served as Robert's first reader, copy editor, executive secretary and body-guard, assisting in his blood-donation drives and other projects, and she kept him alive and happy long after medical science had written him off. Science fiction *owes* her.)

Although he had to pause for breath before each word, his voice was strong and confident. I'd heard that reading had become a chore for him; I offered to read onto cassette some excerpts from the novel I was working on, and when he heard it was about a whorehouse he expressed comically keen interest. We both laughed . . . and that night I spent hours talking into a microphone.

I don't know whether he ever played the tapes. I don't really want to know: as long as no one tells me different, I can cherish the awesome possibility that the last book *Robert* ever read was one of *mine* . . .

I guess I'm done writing about him again . . . for another few years, anyway. I will close this with the words I used to end my eulogy for Robert in *Locus:*

I can't believe he isn't going to dance at my funeral after all. I've always said that I wanted to live forever or die trying . . . but now that I know there isn't going to be a new Heinlein novel out every couple of years, I'm a little less enthusiastic.

But I keep remembering the closing line from *"The Number of the Beast—,"* when Zeb Carter says they've finally seen the last of The Beast (who, of course, is Heinlein himself):

"Friend Zebadiah," asks Sir Isaac Newton the dragon, ". . . are you *sure?"*

No. No, Sir Isaac, I can't say that I am. It would be just like the Old Man to come back from the dead . . . and win another Hugo. Wouldn't it?

Vancouver, British Columbia
7 January 1991

HEINLEIN

Robert Silverberg

Born in New York City and educated at Columbia University, Robert Silverberg published his first book Revolt on Alpha C *in 1955. He is the winner of numerous honors, including several Hugo and Nebula awards. Author of over a hundred books, his novels include* The Book of Skulls, Dying Inside, Lord Valentine's Castle *and* Tower of Glass. *He edited the* New Dimensions *series of anthologies from 1971 to 1980. With his wife Karen Haber, he currently edits* Universe, *an anthology of original science fiction.*

The word that comes to mind for him is *essential*. As a writer—eloquent, impassioned, technically innovative—he reshaped science fiction in a way that defined it for every writer who followed him. As a thinker—bold, optimistic, pragmatic—he set forth a pattern of belief that guided the whole generation of youngsters that grew up to bring the modern technological world into being. As a man—civilized, charming, resilient in the face of difficulty—he was a model of moral strength and a powerful pillar of support for many who may not even have been aware of his quiet benefactions.

The writing first. He was the most significant science fiction writer since H.G. Wells. I don't necessarily mean the *best* science fiction writer: that's too nebulous a term, because one could argue that so-and-so was a superior prose stylist and that so-and-so was unequalled in the dexterity of his plotting and that so-and-so had deeper insight into human character, and so forth. But the three so-and-sos I have in mind, each of whom was able to outdo

Heinlein in some aspect of his craft, would, I think, instantly agree with me that Heinlein was one of his masters, was in fact the writer who had done the most to determine his attitude toward the writing of science fiction. Without him, I suspect, most of the classics of modern science fiction would never have been written.

Wells invented the basic form a century ago. Propose a plausible but startling thesis (invaders come to Earth from Mars; traveling backward and forward through time is possible; a clever scientist can reshape animals into a semblance of human form) to begin with. Assemble a cast of sympathetic and clearly depicted characters and drop them into the midst of the crisis. Develop the implications of the thesis by showing the characters struggling with the ongoing crisis. Tell what happens in clear, precise, and unmelodramatic prose. And provide a resolution to the basic story problem that grows convincingly out of the fundamental nature of the situation, the people involved in it, and the way the universe works as best we can understand it.

Within the space of about fifteen years Wells systematically invented nearly all the fundamental science fiction themes that the rest of us have been exploring ever since, and set them forth in novels so well told that they have retained great popularity among readers everywhere. His example is a towering one: how odd, then, that within a generation science fiction should have become, at least in the United States, the dreary, debased thing that it did.

What happened was that it went in two directions, neither of them good. One school of writers—its apostle was Hugo Gernsback, the founder of the first American science fiction magazine—produced interminable droning lectures instead of readable stories, retelling the basic Wellsian themes in leaden prose. Bald bespectacled scientists delivered endless yards of arid narrative, festooned with footnotes. The other school—which grew out of the late nineteenth century dime-novel tradition— went in for wild, breathless tales of action and adventure, also using the basic Wellsian canon of plot situations but populating them with mad scientists, beautiful young female journalists, jut-jawed heroes, and other caricatures. Neither kind of writing could hope to appeal to more than the most specialized kind of audience: studious, emotionally retarded men on the one hand, and callow, emotionally undeveloped boys on the other.

In 1937 the leading science fiction writer of the period, 27-year-old John W. Campbell, Jr., was given the editorship of the leading science fiction magazine of the time, *Astounding Stories.* Campbell at once proclaimed a revolution. Out with the mad scientists and the lovely imperiled lady journalists; out with the footnotes, too. He wanted writers who knew how to tell a story adults could read without gagging and who believed also that a story should be *about* something. What he wanted, in effect, was science fiction with Wellsian intellectual intensity and with the kind of appealing straightforward prose that any non–science fiction writer—the contributors to *The Saturday Evening Post,* say—would be expected by his audience to provide.

A number of new writers came forward to meet Campbell's new requirements, and their names are hallowed ones in our community: Isaac Asimov, Theodore Sturgeon, A.E. van Vogt, L. Sprague de Camp, Lester del Rey. But of that whole horde of brilliant beginners, the one who made the greatest impact was the 32-year-old Robert A. Heinlein.

There was so *much* of him, for one thing. His debut came with a short story, "Life-Line," in the August 1939 issue. Then came another short in November and a third in January 1940—and that one, the remarkable mood-piece "Requiem," immediately signified a writer of major importance. A month later there was the two-part serial " 'If This Goes On—' " and three months after that the novelet "The Roads Must Roll" and then the novellas "Coventry" and "Blowups Happen"; and Heinlein was only gathering force, for 1941 brought the novels *Sixth Column* and *Methuselah's Children,* the short novel "By His Bootstraps" (under a barely concealed pseudonym), the astonishing innovative novelet "Universe," and several others, with more to come in 1942 before the exigencies of World War II turned his attention temporarily in other directions.

But it wasn't by volume alone that Heinlein seized command of science fiction. His belief that a story had to make sense, and the irresistible vitality of his storytelling, delighted the readership of *Astounding,* who called for more and even more of his material. John Campbell had found the writer who best embodied his own ideals of science fiction. In one flabbergasting two-year outpouring of material for a single magazine Heinlein had completely reconstructed the nature of science fiction, just as in the field of general modern fiction Ernest Hemingway, in the 1920s, had redefined the modern novel. No one who has written fiction since 1927 or so can fail to take into account Hemingway's theory and practice without seeming archaic or impossibly naive; no one since 1941 has written first-rate science fiction without a comprehension of the theoretical and practical example set by Heinlein.

The nature of his accomplishment was manifold. His underlying conceptual structures were strikingly intelligent, rooted in an engineer's appreciation of the way things really work. His narrative method was brisk, efficient, and lucid. His stories were stocked with recognizable human beings rather than the stereotypes of the mad-scientist era. And—his main achievement—he did away with the lengthy footnotes of the Gernsback school and the clumsy, apologetic expository inserts of the pulp-magazine hacks and found an entirely new way to communicate the essence of the unfamiliar worlds in which his characters had to operate. Instead of pausing to explain, he simply thrust character and reader alike into those worlds and *let communication happen through experience.* He didn't need to tell us how his future societies worked or what their gadgets did. We saw the gadgets functioning; we saw the societies operating at their normal daily levels. And we figured things out as we went along, because Heinlein had left us no choice.

So he transformed everything in science fiction. The readers loved his work, and so did his fellow writers. The transformation became permanent and irreversible: Heinlein's technical standards became the norms by which editors, critics, and writers defined the excellent in science fiction.

As for Heinlein the thinker—

Others in this volume, I suspect, will deal with his position as an inspirational philosopher at the dawn of the age of space. Suffice it here for me to say that he provided a vision of the future that seemed attainable and worth attaining, and that others set about the job of attaining it *specifically because they had had Heinlein's vision to guide them.*

Not that he was infallible. The film *Destination Moon,* which he conceived, demonstrates that. Its 1949 image of a single-stage spaceship built by a private group of entrepreneurs and hastily fired off to the moon ahead of schedule, without any sort of preliminary testing because sheriffs waving cease-and-desist orders are closing in, is preposterously far from the realities of the actual event of twenty years later. So too are the details of the flight, with its frantic mid-course corrections desperately worked out with scratchpad calculations, and the frenzied climactic attempt to shed weight in order to make the homeward liftoff.

(Somewhat more melodramatically handled in the movie than in Heinlein's own story version—probably because other writers were called in to give the film more of a Hollywood flair.)

That Heinlein's imagination fell short of the subsequent Apollo Eleven realities is worth noting not only because it shows us the limitations of even the keenest-eyed of seers but also because it illuminates just how much of the first moon flight Heinlein was able to get *right*, twenty years before the fact. He failed to foresee the multistage rocket, the vast national effort that the launch would require, the immense technological support system that would be necessary, and, most strikingly, the extraordinary live telecasts of the moon mission itself. But what he did capture was the fundamental essence of the enterprise: the importance of going to the moon, the *look* of the floodlit and gantried spaceship as it makes ready for takeoff, the feel of the voyage itself. We smile at the simplistic aspects of Heinlein's story; we shiver with awe when we consider how powerfully and well he visualized and communicated to us the underlying realities of the enterprise.

And as for Heinlein the man—

I wish I had spent more time with him. We met perhaps a dozen times over twenty-five years: not nearly enough, but for much of the time we lived on opposite coasts, and after I became his near neighbor, only seventy miles away, his weakening health and increasing reclusiveness made it difficult for me to see him. We exchanged letters and phone calls; I regret that there was little more than that.

He was a delightful human being, courtly, dignified, with an unexpected sly sense of humor. I met him first, so far as I can recall, at the 1961 World Science Fiction Convention in Seattle, where he was Guest of Honor. He amazed everyone there by holding an open-house party in his suite and inviting the entire convention to attend. That would be unthinkable today, when five or six thousand people go to such conventions. The attendance in 1961 was only about two hundred, but it was still a remarkable gesture: Heinlein in his bathrobe, graciously greeting every goggle-eyed fan (and a few goggle-eyed writers) who filed into the room. We struck up a correspondence after that convention. I remember telling him that I had already published seven million words of fiction—I was only 26, but very prolific—to which he replied, "There aren't that many words in the language. You must have sold several of them more than once." And went on to tell me how Isaac Asimov's wife had complained that Isaac worked so hard that all she saw of him was the back of his neck: "Isaac stopped just long enough to point out that they had two children," Heinlein commented. "Then he resumed dirtying paper at his usual smoking-bearing speed. (Come to think of it, you don't have any children, do you?)"

On the other hand, when he asked me in 1962 if I was planning to install a bomb shelter in my newly purchased house and I said no, that I'd rather be atomized swiftly than live in post-nuclear America, a long, chilly silence ensued. The soon-to-be author of *Farnham's Freehold* wasn't going to look kindly on someone who was willing to admit that there were circumstances under which he'd just as soon not survive. But later he forgave me, and never a harsh word passed between us again—not even when I reprinted his story "The Year of the Jackpot" in one of my anthologies and failed to notice that the printer had left out the all-important last three pages. He was the soul of courtesy as he gently called the horrifying omission to my attention.

A great writer, an extraordinary man, a figure of high nobility: there was no one else remotely like him in our field. Within the science fiction world there were many who disagreed with him about many things, but there was no one who did not respect him, and there were a good many, myself included, who came close to revering him. It has been hard to grow accustomed to his absence: he has left an immense empty place behind. But his books are still here, and always will be. For those of us who knew him, however slightly, there are warm inextinguishable memories. And even those to whom his very name is unknown feel his presence daily, for he was one of the molders of the world in which we live.

THANK YOU

Harry Turtledove

Harry Turtledove was born in 1949 in Los Angeles. He started at Caltech but dropped out and ended up earning a Ph.D. in Byzantine history at UCLA. He has taught at UCLA, Cal State Fullerton and Cal State L.A. His historical training has provided the background for six books in the Empire of Videssos, a fantasy analog of the Byzantine Empire. His novels include The Misplaced Legion, An Emperor for the Legion, The Legion of Videssos, *and* Swords of the Legion.

I never met Robert A. Heinlein. In one way, I regret that very much. In another, I find that it matters very little: while I never saw the man in the flesh, I learned to know him and to admire him through the words he set down on paper.

As I write this, I am forty-one. I am one of the legion who, in our younger days, met science fiction for the first time through his juveniles. Those books encouraged me to find others, and I soon found out how much the field as a whole owed to Heinlein, and how different—and how much less—it would have been had he decided to work elsewhere.

Heinlein's stories and books entertain, yes, but they do much more than that. They encourage their readers to think, encourage them to look at the so-called laws of nature and so-called laws of society in a new way, encourage them to wonder how things might be if those laws were a little different—or a lot different. They encourage freedom. In the world in which we live, freedom, sadly, needs all the help it can get. Heinlein gives it that help—and in abundance.

None of that, however, is what I aim to talk about here. Literally millions owe Robert A. Heinlein the debt of many hours pleasantly spent. My own debt is a great deal larger and more specific. Without a few of Heinlein's words, I very much doubt that I should have attained whatever success I have earned as a science fiction and fantasy writer.

Like so many others, I started trying to write when I was very young. I have the proverbial half-million words in the trunk: words no one but I will ever read, because they aren't worth reading. In the later 1970s, as I learned my craft, I began to sell a couple of pieces: a novelet here, a sword-and-sorcery novel there.

Trouble was, not only was I selling occasionally, I was also writing occasionally. Sometimes weeks would go by between chapters of that novel; months would lie between the end of one project and the start of another. If I had trouble with a story, I'd just quit in the middle. I was somebody who sometimes wrote. I wasn't a writer yet.

I should have been, too, because I had time on my hands. In 1978 and 1979 I taught Byzantine history at UCLA while the professor under whom I'd studied held a guest appointment at the University of Athens. On his return, I was out of a job. I was also engaged at the time. The combination is not one which delights a prospective father-in-law.

I had an idea for a large writing project, what turned out to be the four books of the Videssos Cycle (had I known at the outset *how* large the project would end up, I never would have had the nerve to tackle it). Before I started work, I took out my copy of the January 1974 issue of *Analog* and reread, for the umpty-umpth time, Heinlein's guest editorial there, "Channel Markers." Among other things, Heinlein offers in the editorial what he calls "Five Rules for Success in Writing." They are the best—and simplest— (utterly characteristic of Heinlein to do both at once) writing rules I have ever found. For those who have not been fortunate enough to encounter this editorial, I repeat them here:

First: You must *write.*

Second: You must *finish* what you write.

Third: You must refrain from rewriting except to editorial order.

Fourth: You must place it on the market.

Fifth: You must *keep* it on the market until sold.

I can't pay Robert A. Heinlein back for the favor he gave me through those rules. If one of my readers takes them as seriously as I did, I'll have paid some of that favor forward instead. I think Heinlein would have preferred it that way, anyhow.

As I said, I'd read "Channel Markers" many times before. It had encouraged me to keep in the mail those pieces I managed to produce, and thus was partly responsible for the few sales I'd already made. Now, reading it again, I told myself I would seriously apply Heinlein's first and most important rule: you must *write*. I resolved to write for an hour a day, every day, until the story I had in mind was through.

At first it seemed easy. Not only was I fueled by the initial burst of enthusiasm a new tale brings, I was also single, otherwise unemployed, and living by myself. Day after day, I faithfully put in my hour. Sometimes, being a procrastinator by nature, I put it off till the dead of night, but that didn't much matter: I was often up in the wee smalls in those days.

Then, about a month after I started my daily regimen (which was, of course, putting no bread on the table), I landed a tech-writing job, largely on the basis of my handful of previous publications. That took up a big chunk of my day, and a big chunk of my energy. I thought hard about setting the novel aside, but I kept going. If you are going to be a writer, I told myself, you must *write*.

I kept writing. The four Videssos books took three and a half years to finish. I did very little other writing during that time, but did manage to turn out and sell a couple of short stories along the way. By keeping other stories I'd previously written in the mail (You must *keep* it on the market until sold), I made a couple of other sales.

Meanwhile, I developed a backlog of ideas I hadn't been able to work on because I was busy with the tetralogy. Once it was finally done, I started in on them, one after another. I've been at it ever since. Since 1979, the only things that have kept me from putting in my daily hour are being too ill to write, going out of town, and having a birth or death in my family. The most important single attribute for a writer, maybe even including talent, is stubbornness.

Along with helping me acquire the discipline any writer needs, my work on the four Videssos books also gave me far more control over my craft than I had had before. The stories I wrote began to sell more and more regularly. That was just as well, too, for in

1984 my wife Laura gave birth to our first child. The extra money came in handy.

Even after the Videssos books were complete, they took a long time to find a home. Finally, though, in April 1985, almost two years after I finished the series, I got a late-night phone call from Judy-Lynn del Rey, telling me her husband Lester had decided to buy it. To say I was delighted is an understatement, as you can well imagine.

Not too long after that, I took my courage in both hands and wrote Robert A. Heinlein a fan letter. I began it quite simply—I said "Thank you," which is how this essay got its title. That's just what I did: I thanked him for (then) close to twenty-five years of reading pleasure, and I also thanked him for "Channel Markers" and explained how I had taken its five rules as my working principles. Then I thanked him again.

I didn't particularly expect a reply. I knew Heinlein was both busy as a writer and far from young—and also that, if he answered all the fan mail he got, he wouldn't have the time to be busy as a writer. I didn't worry about it. He'd already told me so much; I just wanted to tell him a little, to let him know someone out there had been listening.

But one day a week or two later, Laura called me at my nine-to-five job. "The mail just came," she said. Her voice sounded a little funny. I wondered why, until a moment later she added, "You have a letter here from Robert A. Heinlein."

I gulped too, then managed to say, "Read it to me."

She did. It was a short, friendly, typewritten note. Below his signature, Heinlein had added in his own hand, "Congratulations on your success with fiction!" I walked on air for the rest of the day. I read the little letter ten or twelve times when I got home. I have it still. It's one of the proudest souvenirs from the writing business I ever got.

Since that day, I've kept writing. I'm getting to the point where I can think about making freelance writing my full-time job somewhere in the next few years. It's what I want to do; it's what I'm working toward. It beats the hell out of driving the freeway five days a week. As Heinlein says, "Do you know of any other occupation in which a man can be his own boss, with no capital investment, no employees to worry about, no payroll to meet, no hours to keep, no need to meet the public other than when and where it suits him, dress how he pleases . . . ?" It sounds good to me.

If it sounds good to you, too, you have to remember one other phrase Heinlein made popular: TANSTAAFL (there ain't no such thing as a free lunch). To live the life a freelance writer lives, you have to follow the rules a freelance writer follows: "every one of them, without fail—and keep on following them, for year after year after year." If you can do it, writing is one of the best sorts of work in the world. But it *is* work, and woe betide him who forgets it.

Maybe someone who reads this volume will find through it and on account of it more of the remarkable work of a remarkable man. I hope so. And maybe, just maybe, someone who reads this little essay, someone who has been talking about writing but never quite found the time (or rather, made the time) in which to do it, or someone who has been writing but hesitated to submit his work to the critical judgment of an editor, will see Heinlein's rules here and borrow courage from them, as I did. And maybe, just maybe, I'll help in some small way with the start of someone's writing career, as Heinlein did in a big way with mine.

He was right again, I find. Paying a favor forward is better than paying it back, because you spread it around instead of confining it between two people. Too often, and with too much reason, we think of trouble spreading. Any glance at the front page of a newspaper will tell you that it does. We'd all be better off if the good stuff got around more.

I'm doing my best. So did Robert A. Heinlein—and what a best it was! So should you.

WHO WAS ROBERT HEINLEIN?

Jack Williamson

Jack Williamson was born in 1908. When he was a small child, his family migrated to New Mexico in what may have been the last covered wagon in U.S. history. Jack Williamson sold his first story to Hugo Gernsback's Amazing Stories *in 1928 at the age of twenty. Jack was a member of the Mañana Literary Society, which met Saturday nights in the home of Robert A. Heinlein in the early 1940s; the other members included Anthony Boucher, Henry Kuttner, C. L. Moore, L. Ron Hubbard, Leigh Brackett and a youngster named Ray Bradbury. Except his time out for his service with the Army Air Force in World War II and more recently as a college English professor, he has dedicated his life to science fiction. The best known of his novels is possibly* The Humanoids. *He has been honored with the Grand Master Award of the Science Fiction Writers of America.*

This book is one answer to that question, but hardly a complete one. His work has been surveyed in revealing detail, but I have seen no life that does justice to the complex, intensely private self I sometimes glimpsed behind the public image.

He was a good friend, a writer I admired, a man I loved. I met him first in 1940, only a year or so after his first story was published. I got to know him best at the informal meetings of what he called the Mañana Literary Society, the Saturday-night gatherings of a few science-fictioneers in his Laurel Canyon home. Cleve Cartmill was often there, Tony Boucher and Phyllis, Mick and Annette McComas. Others now and then.

Following my analyst to Beverly Hills from the Menninger clinic in Topeka, I had come from a pretty solitary life in New Mexico, where I knew no other writers. I had a great deal to learn, and the whole group was enormously exciting to me, Heinlein most of all.

He and Leslyn, his first wife, were citizens of a new world that dazzled me. He was just learning his craft, absorbed with its problems and delighted with his own growing mastery of it—yet always modest about his work; he used to joke about filing the serial numbers off old ideas and never spoke of Art. I enjoyed him vastly. Specifics are hard to recall fifty years after, but I envied his mind, his background, his irreverent wit, his social skills, his bubbling ideas, his gift for original turns of speech.

The Society was never anything formal. We simply spent the evenings drinking a little cheap dry sherry and talking of science fiction and everything else—in those early days you could still read all the stories that everybody wrote. We were all of us friends, joined by a sense that we had rounded the wagons for refuge from a world that still ignored or scorned us. Leslyn was a warmly welcoming hostess.

Pearl Harbor brought those gatherings to a sudden end. I remember the shock of the radio news on that Sunday morning. I called Bob to tell him. We were never again together very much. I returned to New Mexico and became an Army weatherman. Though Bob had a disability retirement, he was soon doing aviation research at the Philadelphia Navy Yard.

I stopped to see him there on my way to the Southwest Pacific in 1945. He showed me through his laboratory, introduced me to other members of the staff, which included Virginia Gerstenfeld, a red-haired athletic fellow worker, and gave a party for me, inviting Sprague de Camp and L. Ron Hubbard and Isaac Asimov—Isaac remembered the affair for his autobiography and says I took the group out to dinner, something I had forgotten. He adds that Hubbard was the star of the evening with his dramatic tales of hush-hush adventure on a destroyer in the North Pacific.

After the war, when the captured German V2s were being tested at White Sands, Harry Stine invited Heinlein and me to watch the firing of the last one. He and Ginny were married by then. After the event they came through Portales to visit Blanche and me. I remember Blanche saying that she had been prepared to dislike him, after what she had heard about him, and confessed that she found him charming.

We were guests of theirs later, at their homes in Colorado

Springs and later in the California redwoods, but those meeting were too rare. I was saddened by his old man's walk and look when I saw him at the Kansas City convention in 1976, where he was guest of honor, but Ginny cheered me later, when she took us to see him in his hospital room on the morning after the surgery that rejuvenated him so remarkably. A very sudden change. In bed, with a bandage around his head, he greeted us with a strong voice and a vigorous handshake—and went on, of course, to write more best-selling novels.

That was the Heinlein I knew, the brightest star of the little group that John Campbell gathered to make the half-dozen years beginning in 1938 the "Golden Age of Science Fiction." He and Campbell, more than any others, made the genre what it is. His high rank in the field was recognized as early as 1941, when he was guest of honor at the Denver World Convention. After the war, his short stories carried science fiction out of the pulp ghetto into such slicks as the *Saturday Evening Post*. His great series of Scribner's juveniles introduced a new generation to science fiction.

By the end of the 1950s, however, another and more controversial Heinlein had begun to emerge. *Starship Troopers,* written though not published as a juvenile, was criticized by some as militaristic or elitist or worse because it seemed to glorify a soldier and called undemocratic because it made citizenship a privilege that must be earned.

Stranger in a Strange Land was begun as something that might have been another juvenile, the story of a human child brought up by the Martians and ignorant of Earth and human culture. Abandoned in the middle and picked up again with a more complex aim, the book became a wide-ranging satire on conventional religion and human society in general, and finally the vehicle for an inquiry into free love and mysticism. A kind of cult bible across college campuses in the 1960s, it became Heinlein's first best-seller.

Though both books won awards, they alienated some of his older readers; I myself felt I liked his earlier works better. Charles Brown, the editor-publisher of *Locus,* confirms my own impression that his later works appealed to an entirely different audience. For my own part, I've always felt that the juveniles will probably last as his most enduring work. After *The Moon Is a Harsh Mistress* the only books I enjoyed to the end were such novels as *Friday,* where his earlier patterns of character and action were dominant.

In fact, of course, there was only one Heinlein. The author of "Life-Line" also wrote *The Number of the Beast*. He was simply more complex than most of us suspected, and driven by a passion for privacy, as witness that high fence around his home in the redwoods.

I always wanted to know him better. Growing up in Kansas City, Missouri, most of a century ago, he must have inherited pretty much the same set of inhibitions that I was acquiring in rural New Mexico. They were no handicap to either of us in writing for the pulps, but I think much of his later work was shaped by his revolt against them. He told me once that he had stopped writing for *Analog* because Campbell allowed no adult treatment of sex.

Trying to understand him, I suppose his training at Annapolis and his five years as a Navy officer must have given him the social persona that he used to shield his private self, and perhaps the philosophy that shaped his work, but that is only my own speculation. I'm sure he never encouraged any Boswell, but he is surely worthy of a more complete biography than I have seen. I hope his diligent and fair-minded Boswell does appear while good sources are still available.

I want to know who he really was.

FAREWELL TO THE MASTER*

Yoji Kondo and Charles Sheffield

Born in Japan, Yoji Kondo has lived in the U.S.A. since 1960 and is now an American citizen. He holds his Ph.D. in astronomy and astrophysics from the University of Pennsylvania, and has been with NASA since 1965. At the time of the Apollo missions to the moon, he was head of the Astrophysics Laboratory at the Johnson Space Center. He currently serves as director of the International Ultraviolet Explorer satellite observatory at Goddard Space Flight Center. He has taught as an adjunct professor at the University of Oklahoma, the University of Houston, the University of Pennsylvania, and George Mason University.

Dr. Kondo served as president of the IAU (International Astronomical Union) Commission on "Astronomy from Space," and is currently president of the IAU Commission on "Close Binary Stars." A recipient of the NASA Medal for Exceptional Scientific Achievement, he has published over 130 papers in refereed scientific journals, and has edited eight books in astronomy and astrophysics. He holds a black-belt in judo and aikido, and his favorite pastimes include teaching and practicing martial arts. —Charles Sheffield

We sincerely wish that this article could have been delayed well into the next century. Robert Heinlein once predicted that by the twenty-first century either the so-called civilization of ours or he would be gone from this planet. He was too great and gentle a soul to want the first option; *he* departed from us instead. It is up to the rest of us to make sure that the still-impending doomsday does not happen.

*The title of this article is, of course, a reference to Harry Bates's famous story "Farewell to the Master," which was the basis for one of science fiction's best known movies, *The Day the Earth Stood Still.*

Robert Anson Heinlein was a multi-dimensional, many-faceted man; a great writer, thinker, and visionary. We were both privileged to know him personally. We felt honored to be included in the "Heinlein list" given in *The Number of the Beast,* and one of us (YK) has an alter-ego in *The Cat Who Walks Through Walls.* However, perhaps no one except his wife Ginny understood and appreciated all his many sides. We saw only one or two aspects of the man, and mostly in a context little to do with science fiction. In terms of his long life and long science fiction career, our acquaintance was also relatively recent (since 1979), but we were very impressed by what we saw. What follows is our personal and perhaps biased view.

In our minds there is no doubt at all that Heinlein was and is *the* Grand Master of science fiction. What science fiction is today, including its general acceptance within society, came largely through his efforts.

More than anyone else, he gave the field broad readership and *credibility.* He had the mind of a poet, engineer, and scientist, and that combination made it possible for him to create stories of a realistic future which were personally engrossing and technologically fascinating. He had an excellent relationship with working scientists, characterized by mutual respect and appreciation, and since he spoke the language of science, and liked to talk to and listen to scientists, it should be no surprise to find that his stories are always firmly rooted in today's science, and offer rational projections for the science of tomorrow.

His books enthralled millions of readers throughout the world, and inspired them to aim high—including aiming for the stars. Without the enthusiasm for space exploration engendered by Heinlein and others who followed the trail that he blazed, the coming of the space age might have been delayed substantially. It is certain that a number of our professional colleagues would have followed different career paths, had they not in their youth been stimulated by the science fiction of space exploration.

Heinlein is read first for the simple joy of exciting stories. The scientific and technological background, with an art that conceals art, is so skillfully introduced that its arrival is seldom noticed. This, perhaps, is the reason that Heinlein is not usually the name that comes first to mind when people talk about "hard science fiction" writers. However, the hard science is always there. For example, the orbit descriptions given in his early novels could be written only by someone who understood celestial mechanics.

And one of Heinlein's lasting legacies is the introduction of the term "free fall." No one else has ever produced a term that describes the physical condition so psychologically precisely and yet so accurately. The common alternative, "weightlessness," is misleading, since people tend (wrongly) to identify weight with mass, and body mass is unchanged during free fall.

The impressions of exciting stories and cleverly-presented science come early. When we re-read Heinlein, we find increasingly that there is much more. His stories are filled with thought-provoking views on the nature of human beings. Since his perspectives are often in conflict with the conventional wisdom of both "liberals" and "conservatives," it is not surprising that Heinlein has been regarded by his critics as both a reactionary and a radical.

His protagonists espouse philosophies fundamental to the continuation of the human species—survive, and thrive—but at the same time his heroes and heroines are always compassionate. Heinlein would never admit as hero a person who was a bully, or truly evil, or apathetic, or mediocre. His love for personal strength of character, combined with societies permitting maximum freedom and independence of the individual, often leads him to be identified with libertarianism. We feel that an attempt to fit him into any sort of *ism* does the man an injustice. He found his fellow humans a constant source of compassion and amusement, and he accepted them as *humans,* not plaster saints or devils. He did not pretend them to be what they are not, although the fashion among ideologues of all sorts tends to take the opposite viewpoint.

The first time we each met Heinlein was in Washington, D.C., in July 1979. He had been testifying to a Joint Session of the Congressional Committees on Aging and on Science and Technology, and we were invited to join him and his wife (separately—we did not at the time know each other) for lunch and for dinner. Our mutual agent, Eleanor Wood, arranged this for CS, and Heinlein arranged it with YK whom he had corresponded and spoken with through the introduction of his brother, retired general Lawrence Heinlein. We had enjoyed Heinlein's fiction for many years, but did not have a clear idea what the man himself would be like. It quickly turned out that the last subject that he wanted to talk about was science fiction, although when one of us (YK) mentioned that he had been spoiled by reading only Heinlein books lately, Heinlein quickly recommended the names of several authors and their books. All the books he recommended were good reading—but not so easy to obtain. It was necessary to wander as far north as Montreal to find all of them.

After some discussion of the aging process, which he had studied far more than we had (he joked that at his age it was a necessity), the talk turned to the manned and unmanned space programs of the world. It was clear that he already knew a surprising (surprising to us then; not now) amount about it. He quizzed one of us (CS) politely but in great detail on the past, present, and probable future of remote sensing of the Earth from space, and put his finger on the key problems that might arise if the U.S. program should be moved to commercial operation. (It was; they did arise, and they have not yet been solved!)

Soon after our first meetings with Heinlein, we were pleased to receive an invitation to join him and Ginny in Annapolis for his 50th class reunion at the Naval Academy. There, amid a group of aging captains and admirals, the conversation concerned itself not at all with science fiction. It was on the nature and function of the modern navy. Heinlein's own naval career had been cut short when he was invalided out in the early 1930s, defined as "totally and permanently disabled" with tuberculosis. However, his interest in naval matters was undiminished. It was fascinating to hear him, long before the Falklands War in 1982, expressing his misgivings about the vulnerability of conventional battleships, even equipped with the most modern defenses, to airborne missiles. He gave very precise reasons for his concern. We had the feeling that a couple of his old naval colleagues didn't care for the direction of his argument, but they could not refute it. Heinlein had, as an old bearded Navy colleague said with a twinkle in his eye at the 55th Reunion of his Academy class, "the annoying habit of knowing the facts."

That same Annapolis party offered a glimpse of another side of Heinlein's character. He told us that American culture did not allow men to cry, and that since crying is good for the soul, he had to teach himself how to weep. YK pointed out that in Japan, a man is permitted to cry in certain special circumstances; one might cry, for example, at the death of one's mother, or a general might cry at the news of the death of a worthy adversary. Someone present said "That's gallant!", and Heinlein seemed to agree.

It was at the same 55th reunion that Heinlein proved that neither disease nor major brain surgery had affected his mental abilities. He gave a party, and as each new arrival came in he would introduce the newcomer to everyone in the room, by name—and he continued to do this, without error, until there were at least thirty people present. We should point out that these were not people he previously knew; many were guests of other Academy graduates, whom he was meeting for the first time.

Heinlein was also a regular participant at the Citizen's Advisory Council on National Space Policy. He said little, compared with some of the others present, but what he did say carried great weight. More than almost anyone, Heinlein had the property of *gravitas,* which made everyone who came into contact with him take him seriously. And with good reason. He knew a lot, he had thought about what he knew, and he was endlessly inventive.

We found in our subsequent conversations with him that he was at home with all sorts of subjects, and liked to discuss them either in person or over the phone. The topics ranged from contemporary problems of physics and astronomy, to Zen and the classic (2,500 years old) book on strategy by Sung-tsu. He understood the essence, if not always the technical details, of each subject. He was willing to study those details, if necessary, even when they were tedious. However, his intuition and intellect generally took him quickly to the heart of problems, unhampered by superficial or "authoritative" versions that were not logically self-consistent.

In the world of action, Heinlein was a fencing champion and a master marksman while he was a cadet at the Naval Academy. He also took the "rough-and-tumble" hand-to-hand combat course, which combined the essence of several martial arts. He preferred realistic fighting to sports. To him, fighting was a serious business, to be taken seriously. A student of martial arts can tell that the fighting scenes in Heinlein books are written by an author who really knew how a fight must be won. With the recommendation of YK, Robert Heinlein was accorded the honorary rank of a black-belt in aikido on his eightieth birthday, for his embodiment of the spirit and his exceptional understanding of the principles of the martial arts.

Robert Anson Heinlein died two months before his 81st birthday, which would have fallen on July 7th, 1988. His remains were cremated and his ashes strewn at sea with full military honors. It was a fitting farewell to the grand master who was also a gallant warrior.